Meet Me at Midnight

Jacqueline Navin

JOVE BOOKS, NEW YORK

MEET ME AT MIDNIGHT

A Jove Book / published by arrangement with
the author

PRINTING HISTORY
Jove edition / May 2001

The Penguin Putnam Inc. World Wide Web site address is
http://www.penguinputnam.com

ISBN: 0-515-13054-0

A JOVE BOOK®
Jove Books are published by The Berkley Publishing Group,
a division of Penguin Putnam Inc.,
375 Hudson Street, New York, New York 10014.
JOVE and the "J" design
are trademarks belonging to Penguin Putnam Inc.

PRINTED IN THE UNITED STATES OF AMERICA

10 9 8 7 6 5 4 3 2 1

Prologue

IN MARIA BENEFITO'S house of pleasure, there was a large bedroom on the third floor. Three twelve-foot-high windows lent a spectacular view to where the canal fed into the sea. These were framed with velvet draperies of deep purple dripping with gilded fringe meant to warm the cold, pink-veined Italian marble of the walls and floors. Upon the carved tester bed lay a boy of sixteen. He was awake, his dark-lashed green eyes fixed on the gamboling nymphs painted on the ceiling. His hands were folded behind his head, fingers buried in a thick mass of loose curls that showed myriad shades from dark-blond to brown in this early-morning light.

His body was well into the changes of burgeoning masculinity. The bare torso, showing above the silk coverlet wound about his narrow hips, revealed only vestiges of bony boyishness. An abundance of muscle that came from his love of the outdoors and his newfound hobby of boxing gave him the appearance of being older. A fine, soft dusting of hair had sprung up in the indentation in the center of his breast, on his limbs, under his arms and at his groin, and lightly on the backs of his broadening hands. More proudly, the stuff had begun to grow unevenly on his upper lip and chin. At least twice a week he reverently took a razor to it and shaved it clean.

Corinne, an energetic blond whose services had been thrust upon him last evening, stirred beside him, then slept on. She was young—only three years his senior—and pretty. Not at all like some of the jaded tarts to whom he had been subjected. Before she had retired to her well-earned rest, her experienced hands brought him physical release. He would not call it pleasure. The whole exercise was still too terrifying to be that.

It was his father who had insisted he be "entertained" by the pretty courtesan. The Marquis de Marquay's idea of a perfect evening was to deliver his son into the hands of an expensive Cyprian and adjourn to explore the finer points of his own debauchery. These father-son outings to the exclusive whorehouses of each city they visited were never divulged in the boy's frequent letters to his mother back in the French countryside. When writing to the Marquese, the boy told her he was having many adventures. Which wasn't a lie, strictly speaking. Later, he would learn to deceive as adroitly as Lucifer, but for now he was still caught in a war over his innocence, and that particular bastion had not yet been breached.

There was much he did not mention in those letters. She might have guessed his misery, knowing her husband as she did, but her responses were cheerful and full of affection. This made him miss home desperately, which surprised him. He had never thought to long for the place that had seemed to him exhaustively boring. He had been anxious, as any boy would be, to break out and see the world. This he had indeed done—his father's world. For seven months they had traveled together, ostensibly for him to learn the family business. All he had learned was that an untrained boy from the provinces with no formal education outside of his childhood tutor, a sense of humor his father didn't appreciate, and a failing to stomach large amounts of liquor were considered resounding failures among the circles in which they presently moved. He was weary and homesick and disillusioned, for the tenuous bond between himself and his father seemed to strain with every day.

The door to the chamber opened and the Marquis entered, startling the boy. Tall, still handsome—although not for much longer after his life of dissipation would have done with him—and arrogant beyond measure, Marquay was a bold, hard man. There was no sentiment about him, nor esteem for anything outside possessing talent in the realm of financial dealings and classic masculine vices, both of which he boasted a fine repertoire.

He took three steps inside the chamber and stopped. "Corinne, wake up."

The stylish courtesan rose naked from the bed without a bit of modesty. Sleepily, she made her way to the door and shut it behind her without ever opening her eyes.

The boy sat up. He felt even more defenseless than usual. His father's clothed form towered above him while the remnants of his youthful shyness had him clutching the bedsheet over his lap. Embarrassment stole up his neck to ignite tiny fires in the tips of his ears. Although young, his mind was quick, and it grasped on the certainty that his father wanted him to feel every bit the awkwardness of his situation.

"Raphael," he said, and the boy cringed at his name spoken low. Like a threat. "Get your breeches on, boy. We must talk about you going home."

His heart leaped, spun, soared for an instant with so much joy it made him dizzy. "Home? When?"

"Now. This morning. I am going on to Milan. You will return to France." He paused, his eyes darting to his son, then sliding away. "To your mother."

"Sir!" Raphael's heart skidded to a stop. He was being dismissed. He was being sent home in disgrace. "What—why?"

Marquay's color rose as he crossed his arms over his

chest. Raphael had seen that hue before—often, in fact. And just as frequently, as now, he had no idea what he had done to deserve it. He drew back onto the sinfully soft pillows that abounded in the bed. Just last night he had felt like a sheik among such luxury. Today, he felt like an insect caught in the sights of a hungry lizard.

"There is something you must know, something . . ." Marquay rubbed his palm across his mouth to wipe away the moisture collecting on his upper lip. "I tried to ignore the doubts, go on as if it didn't matter. Not that I could ever fully accept you, doubting as I did that you were mine. Your mother . . . damn her. There was no way to know if she lied when she shouted her confession at me in the heat of argument or all the other times she denied it. It was only that once, mind, that she said it, and she was madder than an Irish banshee at the time. I shouldn't give it credence. But I can't seem to stop *thinking* about it." Again, his gaze touched the boy, and again he looked away, as if he couldn't bear what he saw. "I tried to look for signs of resemblance, as if that would answer the question. I spot them at times, then I question myself. You have your mother's coloring, but is that my jaw? My nose? It's no good." He gave one, quick shake of his head.

Raphael began to tremble because although he didn't understand completely what his father was saying, a terrible gnawing feeling began to work at the edge of his awareness. Something catastrophic was brewing in these words, like gathering thunderheads collecting into a vicious storm. He said, his voice barely a whisper, "Sir, I am sure if I have done anything to displease you, I can explain—"

"It's no secret you've been a disappointment to me. You seem to have none of me in you with regards to temperament. In that regard, I can believe you are no relation, and that is where I am inclined to rest. These months together have only strengthened that certainty, and then last night, with that Cyprian . . . why, you seemed almost *reluctant*. And I thought, 'That is it, the sign. How much more different could two men be?' And I realized you cannot be my son."

Raphael didn't react. He had always sensed his father's dislike. Even before Marquay had abandoned his wife and son nine years ago, driven away by the vicious miasma of violence and spite into which his marriage had descended, Raphael had known there was nothing that bonded them in any semblance of the sentiment most sons and fathers felt. But this . . . to think all along the man he had tried so hard to please, hated and worshiped and thought of as father was not that at all!

A sleek stab of pain cut from his liver to his gullet. Raphael's mouth worked, his lips dry and tight as he strove to recover. "Sir, I can explain my actions. She was so . . . enthusiastic and I hardly knew her. I have not much experience—"

He cut off. Marquay had turned away. The Marquis placed a velour pouch on the hand-painted bureau and headed for the door. There he paused. "There is money to hire a coach. I shall never know if she did welcome another man to her bed, and if that man sired you. Therefore, I shall not disown you. Your position as my heir will remain unchanged. I have no other issue, after all. However," he added, swallowing hard and setting his teeth edge to edge, "I will not continue our private farce any longer. The plain truth is I cannot stand the sight of you. You will go away from me. And you will stay away from me."

Raphael was horrified to find his eyes were stinging. "Sir—"

But what was there to say? The words stuck in his throat, thick and unwieldy and tight with emotion he was afraid to express.

Marquay finally looked at him, cold, contemptuous eyes raking like demon's claws. "It is not a regular occurrence that a boy your age is informed of the likelihood of his being a bastard. Do surprise me for once, Raphael, and take it with a liberal dose of dignity. It would give me great relief to avoid an unpleasant scene." He pulled the door open and left.

In the wake of this inauspicious farewell, Raphael Giscard, Viscount de Fontvilliers, sat in the opulent Venetian whorehouse and wept. Then he dried his eyes, dressed, and took up the pouch his father—his father?—had left. Weighing it in his hand, he looked out over the canal and thought.

Bastard?

So many things occurred to him, flashes of memories, comments he never understood, the awareness always with him that there was something wrong with him and that it kept him from being loved. It all fell into place as neatly as a patched quilt.

Bastard.

He decided three things then and there.

The first was that it would be the last time he cried.

The second was that the tender, soulful, provincial boy who had trailed foolishly behind a man who could never look at him without abhorrence had to die. With a conscious exertion of will, Raphael killed him. Smothered him, pushing him way down deep inside, so that he would never be able to find his way to the surface again.

The third was that in this world, where there were only masters and fools, he would never be anyone's fool again.

It was quite another person who arrived home to the crumbling chateau in Amiens. His English mother, Violetta Aubry Giscard, Marquese de Marquay, often sat and stared at him, sometimes commenting on how much he had changed.

"It is simply that I am growing older, Mother," he would reply. But she wasn't deceived. Her eyes would narrow and she'd continue to stare, but he wasn't ready to confront her yet. He waited as the raw wounds crusted over. One evening, as they sat in the dim light of the salon, he told her, with no preamble, what Marquay had said.

She grew still, was silent, her eyes slightly rounded and glazed for a moment before her lids lowered, veiling her secrets. "What he told you was a lie, Raphael," she asserted in a quavering voice.

He remained calm. After all, the man who had grown from the wounded, lost boy no longer had feelings to feed an angry heart. "Then why did he despise me so?"

She bit her lips together and her brow creased. He could almost hear her thoughts, scrabbling for purchase as the debris of her deception began to slide away from her. "I did tell him something once, just to make him angry. We were fighting and he had taken up with some wretched Italian Contessa." She looked to her son, panicked appeal in her face. "I just wanted to hurt him, as he had hurt me so many times. I made up some story about . . . about an under gardener and myself. I knew it would make him wild with jealousy. I never dreamed he would hold on to it, let it come between you."

Three words, spoken hard and in biting tones, came from Raphael. "Was it true?"

Her mouth twitched, turning down in an ugly way. He didn't need to hear her affirmation, but she burst forth with a torrent of explanations. He refused to hear them. Phrases like ". . . lonely, I needed to feel loved . . ." and ". . . had other women and I wanted to show him . . ." only swirled on the edge of his consciousness.

Bastard, then.

She claimed that a reconciliation with Marquay ended the affair quickly. She'd always assumed he'd been Marquay's son. In fact, she promised with vehemence, she was sure of it. And the other man was dead of fever long since, so what did it matter?

When Raphael had had enough, he rose and told her he would be leaving. He had made arrangements to go to England to live with his maternal grandmother, his only surviving grandparent. He wanted to go to university there.

Violetta's reaction was predictably distressed. Her marriage choice, made in direct violation of her parent's will, had been seen as a defection by her family, and never forgiven. The rift had not mended even when the Marquay union, so rapturous in the beginning, fell into misery. Even then, Violetta often complained, the miserly heart of the old woman could not soften to ease a daughter's suffering. Raphael considered that his mother was apt to make such sweeping and dramatic statements and wondered if his grandmother were truly hateful. He had met her only a handful of times, and knew her to be as harsh, as critical, as uncompromising an old bird that ever was, but she was the only family he had left who hadn't betrayed him.

Upon arriving in London, he was received by the Countess of Wentword as she sat in her chaise in the gaudy, overdecorated withdrawing room. She favored excess in everything but emotion. One bejeweled hand resting on the carved armrest, the other holding up a lorgnette encrusted with a dazzling selection of diamonds, she inspected him imperiously. Although seeming outwardly unmoved by his sudden presence, he sensed an excitement within her, a delight at having her only grandchild within her grasp.

Under this intense regard, he didn't so much as shift a finger. The same steady stare she leveled at him, he sent right back her way. At last she pronounced, "Very well. You will go to university. I insist on Oxford. I could never abide Cambridge men."

It suited him to comply. He took a degree in philosophy from Trinity College. By the time his matriculation ended, his masters were glad to see him go. They had long since grown tired of him arguing circles around them, quoting the great logisticians and cleverly manipulating the most insignificant argument. Moreover, his vices were legend, and the administration's efforts to contain his destructiveness had been exhausting. They bid him farewell with happy smiles.

Raphael entered society with the parcel of cronies and hangers-on he had collected at university. He was an instant sensation. The women found him intriguing and attractive, the men hung on his wry, often cruel, wit.

He languished at White's—winning mostly, but unconcerned when he lost. He bedded whom he wished without ever allowing sentiment to enter into it. When he had to, he attended the social duties in the ballrooms and drawing rooms of his grandmother's friends. This was never done generously, for he kept the grudging respect and gratitude he felt for the old woman a closely guarded secret.

Over the years his mother wrote to him. He replied, short polite missives that gave nothing but the barest details of his present existence. She visited from time to time. He was never rude when she came, although he hardly allowed her infrequent visits to impede his normal routines.

As for the man the world thought of as his father, he was true to his word and did not disinherit him. The lands that were attached to his title of Viscount passed to Raphael upon the gaining of his majority, and he managed them with finesse. The income from these fed the extravagancies of his infamous lifestyle.

Their paths crossed from time to time. The disappointment and hurt he had felt as a callow youth had been carefully nursed into loathing. This rage increased with every chance encounter until every biting word exchanged between them throbbed with antipathy. It always felt good to flay the man with his unerring wit. It kept all the rest at a distance.

However, there was an acute irony to the situation that did not escape Raphael. Marquay may not have sired him, but he certainly had created him. After years of honing the icy steel of his heart, two men could hardly be found to be more similar.

Chapter One

The home of the Earl of Suffolk, Mayfair, London
March 5, 1816

SUFFOLK, RAPHAEL NOTED, did not suffer any pangs of conscience at showing his wealth. This was the most prestigious ball of the season, and there had been no stinting on extravagance to be sure that every one of the illustrious guests knew it. The flora crowding every surface, the gilt columns, the leaded prisms dripping from gas-lit lusters and huge mirrors multiplying hundreds of beeswax candles into millions were all calculated to leave one breathless.

Raphael was breathless, all right, but not from the duke's lavish decor.

Wing-shaped brows forked over his long, finely pointed nose. His wry, elegant mouth whitened with tension as jade-colored eyes slitted back and forth over the crowd of dancers on the parquet floor. His stare looked critical, even derisive, but it was not directed at the whirling couples. They were merely a splash of watercolors bleeding into one another. His sights were turned inward, where agitated demons stirred.

"I say, Fontvilliers, you're going to crush the glass."

He blinked, and looked down at the delicate flute in his hand. It was filled with a much too fine champagne to appease his palette this night. His fingers were wrapped around it as if it were an ale mug—white-knuckled. The tracery of tendons bulged to betray his tension.

Darting a glance to his side, he found Richard Evens, Lord Martinvale, wearing a frown of concern. The man's face usually manifested the most somber appearance of the four friends. Fontvilliers, Martinvale, Atvers, and Strathford—known as the Bane of the Ton. A title, it must be noted, they relished.

Immediately Raphael relaxed his body and donned a droll smile. "My thanks for the reminder. Lady Suffolk would hardly care for my bleeding all over her fine carpets. Not to mention the desecration of valuable Baccarat." Tossing the contents of the crystal flute to the back of his throat as if it were cheap gin, he placed it on a tray shouldered by a passing servant. Surveying the room, he inhaled deeply. "Now, let's get me out of my poor humors. What amusements are about tonight?"

On his other side, Lord Charles Atvers, whose youthful face, slight frame, and modest height made him look to be all of twelve years of age, gave one of his high-pitched sniggers and pointed to the fourth member of their group, who was just now making his way across the dance floor.

Appearing distinctly perturbed, Colin Strathford, Marquis of Strathford, was nearly as tall as Raphael, but with darker hair and an almost swarthy complexion. He had a certain degree of charm when he wished to display it. At other times his wit had a sharper edge, and there was something of a subtle, one-sided rivalry between himself and Fontvilliers, who was the acknowledged leader of the group.

"Good God, that woman is a trial," he growled as he drew up to his three bosom bows. "I can barely abide her company."

Martinvale was astonished. "You make complaint of the woman who is to be your wife?"

Folding his arms across his chest, Strathford shrugged. "What does one thing have to do with the other?"

"Do you not think it wise to wed someone for whom you have a measure of affection?"

Atvers bleated shrilly, and Strathford scowled while wedging his arms tighter across his chest.

Raphael cocked a brow at his friend. "Really, Martinvale, you sometimes amaze me with your naïveté. For a rake and a scoundrel of the first rank—which is how my grandmother refers to the lot of us, I am proud to report— you have some discordantly romantic ideas. Affection, you say? What has that dubious trait have to do with any of this monstrous mating ritual we are witnessing?"

He swept his long, elegant hand toward the members of polite society crowded into the ballroom. "This is the marriage market you see laid before you. A bartering of goods, and by that I mean wives for money. Alliances struck between families and fortunes advanced because the bottom line of it all is not *affection*, you pitiful dolt, but *how much.*"

Strathford, always ready to challenge, replied, "Are you saying you do not believe in love, Fontvilliers?"

"Love?" Raphael nearly choked. "What you see is lust, my friend, and nothing more. The man, the mighty hunter, lusts after the enticements cast by the alluring female. Their papas lust after their dowries. *Love* is only a term to make the whole matter more palatable."

"Love is not for men such as we are, I quite agree," said Strathford, "but to say it does not exist—you are wrong. "

Snatching a fresh glass of champagne from the tray proffered by a waiter, Raphael sipped and rolled the sweet liquid around on his tongue. The action distracted him from the growing knot of sour tension in his chest.

Love.

It did not exist. He of all people knew well the destructive nature of that obsession people mistakenly named

love. They called it that to excuse it, then composed plat-
itudes and odes to exalt it, but it wasn't lofty. It was erotic
appetite, it was craving, yes, but it was possession most of
all. It was primitive and clawing and he wanted no parts
of it.

Love. No such thing.

Lord, he was in a foul mood tonight. It was probably
the sniping he had endured from his grandmother at dinner. She always stayed with him during the season, and
she had this night, as was often her wont, treated him to
her usual diatribe on the sorry state of his character. She
likened him to other unsavory fellows she had known and
despised in her time. Marquay's name was mentioned.
Raphael hated that; hated even to be reminded of the man's
existence. It always left him raw.

And now these idiots were talking about love, for God's
sake!

"Then you are a fool," Raphael pronounced, careful to
keep his voice even.

Atvers giggled.

"Fontvilliers," Martinvale interrupted. "I wouldn't have
thought you could shock me so thoroughly, but indeed you
have."

Pressing his hand against his chest, Raphael executed a
small bow. "I regret I offend you, my tender friend. The
truth is ugly. In a room supposedly full of *love*"—the word
dripped with sarcasm—"I see nothing to impress me."

Martinvale jerked his head to a couple just coming off
the dance floor. "See there. Julia Brodie and Sir Simon
Blake. She's not an heiress, not even from a terribly impressive family, but quite the delight of the *beau monde*
this season. Blake, now he's a decent fellow, likable, intelligent. I submit them in evidence to challenge your theory, Fontvilliers. Their *grande passion* is the talk of the
ton."

Glancing at the couple under consideration, Raphael saw
they were smiling at each other. He thought they looked
like brainless idiots with those dunce-like expressions on

their faces. "An infatuation, nothing more. It will fade as soon as his finger is bound with gold, as such things invariably do."

"It is assumed they will become engaged before the season is out," Strathford practically crowed. He had a penchant for goading him. Sometimes Raphael doubted that there was true friendship between them. "It shall be the perfect end to a whirlwind *romance*. They are, to prove you wrong my jaded friend, *in love*."

Raphael narrowed his eyes. The female had her back to him, but he could see the face of the fool, this *Simple* Simon. He seemed the type to wallow in such fatuity. Thin and tall. The type women had been sighing over since Byron made it fashionable for men to be wan and sullen. He did appear to be quite taken with the girl.

Raphael wanted to laugh, but he couldn't seem to. "He is so randy for her," he purred as he lifted his glass to his lips, "he is ready to split his pantaloons."

Atvers exploded with piercing laughter.

"But what if it *is* love," Strathford pressed. "The real and lasting kind that wise men through the ages have exalted? Then, you would be wrong, my friend."

"That is an oxymoron, Strathford. No wise man exalts the concept of love. And Pascal—who was, by the by, extremely wise—tells us nothing is lasting. *Our reason is always deceived by fickle shadows,* says he."

"Oh!" Atvers ejaculated. "He is calling in the philosophers now! Beware!"

But Strathford was not put off. "I wager it *is* love, and that you, Fontvilliers, are wrong."

Turning his head slowly, Raphael's jade eyes flickered over his friend's saturnine face. "A wager against love? Strathford, you do the impossible; you intrigue me. How do you propose to set the wager to the test?"

"I could apply my considerable talents to seducing the chit. If I can break them apart, then it obviously was not 'true love.' "

Raphael's smile was as warm as a barracuda's. "But if

you are wagering against your success, how can I know you will apply it *enthusiastically*?"

"Are you suggesting I would cheat?"

"Strathford, you forget I know you too well. Scruples are not among your best character traits."

"You could spread a rumor," Atvers shot in eagerly. "Raise questions about her virtue. Blake may put her aside."

"That has merit," Raphael considered. "But anyone can confuse and obfuscate with lies. *I* offer a counter challenge. *I* shall test the girl's devotion." His top lip curled tighter, derisive and amused at the same time. "I say I shall have her gazing at me with her round, limpid eyes, her little rosebud mouth all agape. In no time, my friends, she will be completely oblivious to her dear Simple Simon. So much for love."

"The devil you say!" Martinvale ran a nervous hand through his hair. "You suggest to ruin the girl over a wager. Fontvilliers, this is—"

"Not at all. She need not be ruined. Only the four of us will know. I will provide proof to you three that her affections are no longer directed toward Simple Simon, naturally, but this business need not extend beyond us."

Strathford declared, "I say it is worth five thousand to find out which one of us is in the right. By Ascot. It must be done by opening day."

"Agreed." Raphael said it without hesitation. A hot, pinching flood of satisfaction spread through him, like warm honey in his veins. It slaked something in him, and he felt instantly calmer and as pleased with himself as a well-fed cat.

His gaze settled again on the couple, this time concentrating on the girl. What was her name? Julia something.

She turned as Simon folded her hand in the crook of his arm. They headed directly toward Raphael, then veered off to exit the ballroom out one of the sets of French doors leading to the terrace.

Unusual coloring, he noted. Among the throng of pale and powdered lovelies, she stood out. Her auburn hair, straight as a pike, was sleek and gleaming in the candle-light. Pulled back in a simple chignon, it was elegant next to the bouncing cap of sausage curls into which the other women's locks were set. Strong chin, rather long nose, high, sharp cheekbones framed out her finely boned face. Her brow and lashes were much darker than her hair, providing a startling setting for eyes that seemed, from this distance, rather pale. They might prove hazel, he thought. Her mouth was wide and lush with full lips, the top one slightly overlapping the lower. They looked bee stung, or roughly kissed.

He was startled out of his inspection by a curious stirring in his loins. That mouth . . .

Atvers's whine cut into his thoughts. "How do you propose to do it, Fontvilliers?"

"Gentleman, attend." He ran the tip of his tongue over his lips, which had suddenly gone dry, and cast about for some more champagne. "There is one thing which is every woman's weakness. That is their vanity. " He flagged down a passing servant.

"Then you will flatter her?"

He coughed a scornful laugh as he exchanged his emptied one with a full flute. "Not at all."

Strathford looked at him askance. "Then . . . you will admire her good works."

"You have missed the point, my bosom friends. I shall not *do* anything. Women are accustomed to being pursued, and adept at refusing advances they do not desire. Therefore, how to seduce a woman who does not wish to be seduced . . . is to do nothing."

"What—?"

"I shall explain." He smiled and placed his glass on a nearby table. Reaching inside his jacket, he pulled out a pair of snow-white gloves. "Each woman must take pride in her measure against the feminine ideal. Women have a need to regard themselves as doing good for others." He paused as he pulled the soft kid over his long fingers. "This tendency, combined with their natural propensity to meddle, results in one thing which all woman find irresistible. That is what I propose to offer to Miss . . . er. Miss?"

"Brodie."

"Exactly."

He looked at each one of them in turn. Atvers looked like a salivating dog, Martinvale was pale, and Strathford smug. And all three were utterly confused.

In contrast, he was delighted. The demons were loosing their hold already. And the champagne, he decided, was excellent. He took up his glass and sipped leisurely.

"What is it?" Atvers demanded excitedly.

"Intrigue," Raphael supplied, and set off across the dance floor.

J ULIA BRODIE WAS acutely aware of Simon's hand at the small of her back as he led her out onto the terrace. Low and soft, his voice came from close behind her, almost at her ear. "I have been waiting all night for a chance to be alone with you."

Bowing her head to hide her flush of pleasure, she fought a smile. Three times during their courtship, Simon had kissed her. Light airy kisses that brought a pleasant glow. When tonight he had suggested that they take the air, she suspected he might steal a fourth.

She hoped so. It had been foremost in her mind even as she had made her toilette and donned the pale green watered silk trimmed with froths of embroidered lace, thinking all the while, *Will Simon kiss me tonight?*

And now . . . now he would.

"There you are!" someone called.

Julia's head jerked up as she straightened, aware only now how she had been leaning in toward Simon's tall, slender form. Her sister, Laura, headed straight for them. Switching her gaze to Simon, Julia saw his frown. He *had* been planning to kiss her!

"I . . . I shall find us some punch," Simon offered stiffly, pulling himself into an almost military stance. His light brown hair gleamed in the gaslight, slick with macassar oil. His good looks appeared pinched. Without another word he headed back inside to fight the crowds pressing around the refreshment tables.

Laura never spared him a glance as she drew up to her sister and grasped her arm. "Did you see how handsome the Marquess of Strathford looks tonight? He was standing with a group of men, and he far outshone the other three."

Rolling her eyes heavenward, Julia replied dryly, "Yes, Laura. Indeed, he is hard to miss. When I saw him, he was dancing with Lucy Glencoe, the woman everyone knows he is going to ask to be his wife before the season is out."

"Oh, Julia, it's just not fair! He doesn't even notice me."

The words were so plaintive, but Julia knew she could not relent. "Laura, so many other fine gentlemen are here. My goodness, just look around you. It is the event of the season. I'll not have you moping about."

"I cannot help myself. He is so . . ."

Julia couldn't keep herself from smiling. "Yes, I know. Handsome."

Laura pouted prettily. "Well, he is."

"Poor Laura." She reached out for her sister's hand. She did feel badly for her, but not too much. Laura would find someone, someone to truly love her, just as Julia had. Simon was a dashing, sought-after baronet. They had fallen in love quickly. It would just take Laura a bit longer.

They were in London, after all, at the heart of the season, being invited to all the most fashionable parties, moving within the circles of the most elite aristocracy. It was all like a dream, an incredible, fabulous dream come true. Here they were, two commoners with nothing to boast of in their lineage but a determined mother and hardworking father, dancing at midnight in the Duke of Suffolk's mansion.

Why her sister insisted on mooning over someone unattainable, Julia would never understand. But it was so like Laura, who loved the dramatic. The more maudlin, the better.

Laura's grip on Julia's hand tightened. "Here comes that wretched Lucy." Her scowl instantly transformed into a bright, artificial smile. "Hello, Lucy!"

Lucy Glencoe curled her lips just barely. "Hello, Julia. Laura." Not stopping, she continued on her way to a group of the more elitist debutantes who would not deign to socialize with a pair of banker's daughters.

Laura's dark eyes shot darts of resentment to the girl's stiff back. "I hate her. And not just because she is set to marry Strathford. She is the worst snob. She is jealous of you."

Julia was startled. "Why? What could she envy me?"

"Julia, really, do not be so obtuse. People are always talking about you, and with nothing but good to say."

She flushed with pleasure she was too embarrassed to show. "I hardly believe anyone cares that much."

"They do. You are the reason we received vouchers to Almack's. Lady Jersey *adores* you, she's always saying how sweet and nice you are." Julia blanched inwardly at the insipid description as Laura continued to gush. "Everyone thinks you very clever—but not too clever, of course."

Of course not, Julia thought miserably. What a high crime that would have been.

Laura sighed. "Oh, don't look at me like that, I do not mind. I have plenty to be jealous of in a sister such as you, but the curse of it is—" She paused. "I like you, too."

"And I you," Julia countered with a rush of affection, "which is why I want you to stop pining for Colin Strathford. He is taken, the same as if he were already married."

With a toss of her carefully constructed pile of gleaming blond curls, Laura sighed. "Very well. At least I will go have a look to see if I like anyone. But I shall warn you, if I don't find someone who strikes my fancy, I fear I shall weep the whole ride home."

Julia raised her brows doubtfully. "Oh, and when you spot someone who you think makes a fine beau, determine whether or not he has a wife and children before falling head over heels. I find being introduced before losing your heart is quite handy at avoiding these pitfalls."

If they had been at home, Laura would have given her a push, or pulled her hair. As it was, she scrunched up her face in an exaggerated *moue*, then flounced away in a swirl of yellow taffeta. Julia laughed softly and shook her head. Impetuous Laura. Ah, well, she thought, wrapping her arms around her bare shoulders, life was never dull with Laura's quandaries, most of which, thankfully, existed only in her imagination—

A dark shape loomed in the corner of Julia's eye, startling her an instant before something very large and very solid brushed forcibly against her side. As she was knocked backward, her skirts tangled about her ankles. She felt herself falling. Her hands shot out to clutch two handfuls of fine wool.

Strong fingers grasped her upper arms, keeping her from spilling ignominiously onto the polished flagstones. In a smooth motion, she was thrust forward again, coming to rest against a hard, unyielding body.

Her cheek brushed against the downy softness of a white lawn shirt, and she could detect the aroma of spice mingled with a hint of soap. A titillating masculine scent which she thought, in a dazed, rather befuddled blur of awareness, was most incredibly pleasant.

With her balance restored, she raised her head. At such close range, she found herself staring into twin points of vivid green. They seemed to be as disconcerted as she.

"Sir?" she breathed.

"Mademoiselle?" he answered in a low, equally soft tone.

Neither one of them moved. Her limbs were beset by a strange lassitude. Her head felt light. They were immodestly close. As close as she and Simon had been when he kissed her.

Her mind registered the shocking impropriety of their proximity, but she seemed at a loss to be able to think of what to do about it. She was aware he was very tall. His body was hard against hers. She was cognizant of every inch of it, and every inch of her own softer, more pliant form crushed up against it.

It was he who recovered first. He swore softly, unintelligibly, and shoved her from him. Her limbs returned to her control, although she was still trembling enough to set her teeth chattering.

Seeking to gain her composure, she looked away from those startling eyes and directed her attention to brushing out the creases in her mint-colored silk skirts. "I do say," she said, "this is quite strange . . . I . . ." She didn't know how to finish the sentence. The knot in her stomach radiated strange, distracting waves of tension along her limbs, and her words got lost among the disconcerting sensations.

"I must beg your pardon." His voice was smooth, cultured, and deeply resonant. "I was not looking where I was going. Terribly rude of me, but then," he added with a self-deprecating cough, "that is something for which I seem to have a special gift."

She raised her eyes. There was enough distance between them now to see his entire face. It was a strong face, and it made an immediate, and powerful, impression. Transfixed, she could only murmur, "You are forgiven."

"It . . . it was inexcusable for me to touch you that way. I . . ." One broad-palmed hand came up to rake a forelock off his brow. He didn't wear pomade, so the gloved fingers dug a smooth path. His hair softly fell back into exactly the same place. "I only hope no one saw." His gaze flickered toward the house. "I would hate for my clumsiness to reflect badly on you."

"I am sure it will come to nothing."

He smiled. It seemed a sad smile. "You are kind. Thank you for that. Tonight, in your prayers . . . . No. Just know it does my heart good to find a soul such as yourself. I needed to know there was at least one such as you in the world. You arrived just in time, you see, to save me from utter dejection on the matter. Thus, you have my gratitude as well as my apology. Good evening, mademoiselle."

Abruptly he turned on his heel and walked away. His long stride took him to the far corner of the terrace where he stood alone against the stone baluster and braced his hands on the sandstone surface. As she watched, he slowly bowed his head so that the silver moonlight bathed the back of his hair, his stooped shoulders, the bent contour of his prostrate form. Perfect chiaroscuro, she mused, studying the play of light and shadow before her as intently as she would a masterpiece.

What a strange man. She wondered what had him so wretched? Surely not their little mishap. His distress was far more profound than to have been merely that.

What was it he had said—that swift, self-effacing remark about rudeness? And needing to know there was someone like her—what did he mean?

She was not an impulsive girl. Far, far from it. Julia Elizabeth Brodie had mastered self-discipline at an early age. Her mother had inundated her with the precise code of etiquette required of a lady. Julia was perfectly prepared for a society fraught with exacting strictures on the behavior of its members, most especially its female members. Therefore, there was no doubt in her mind that she should turn away, forget the mysterious stranger whose destiny had briefly—and literally—brushed against hers for a moment.

She should retreat toward the house, where the pools of light spilled through the French doors, and wait for Simon to return.

And yet . . . Taking three steps in his direction, she stopped herself. It was obvious he desired solitude and her attention would be likely to embarrass him further. She should respect his need for a private moment

But she couldn't just leave him like that.

She closed the distance before she realized she had even made up her mind.

Chapter Two

IF THE MAN heard her coming, he didn't react. He stayed bent over, as if in prayer.

Julia raised her hand to pluck at his sleeve, but hesitated. The tumult of being in his arms moments ago was fresh in her memory, so that the thought of even this innocent contact gave her pause. She asked softly, "Sir, are you unwell?"

He raised his head and looked at her with those eyes filled both with accusation and appeal. She swallowed. Her voice was smaller when next she spoke. "May I get you anything?"

Offering a rough laugh, he replied, "I am afraid I have been given enough for one evening."

"I do not understand. What have you been given?"

"Justice."

She blinked, then frowned.

"I beg your pardon." He shook his head as if to clear it. "Here you are showing kindness and I am being cryptic. Quite unconscionable of me."

"No. I am intruding. I will take myself away posthaste. It is just that you appeared to be . . . not yourself."

His smile warmed, more genuine now. "Miss, you do

not even know my name. How is it you know this is not myself?"

How did she? It was an odd thing to say, now that she thought about it. "I-I suppose I don't know. It was only my impression."

Indeed, he made a strong one. It was hard to look away, as she found earlier when her reason had told her not to draw near. As if some voice, some alert, cautious voice, was warning her of . . . well, of danger.

He was not so much handsome as arresting, with features that reminded her of the busts of long-ago statesmen she had seen while in Rome. The high forehead with the stubborn lock of hair spilling down upon it, the strong nose, the cleft in the long chin all begged to be studied. His eyes remained locked with hers, unwavering, heavy-lidded. They seemed fathomless; a doorway to places shrouded in secrets. His lips were sensuously curled, yet with a cruel twist that left one guessing whether or not they were mocking the viewer, the world, or merely himself.

What was it about this man that made him so remarkable? His hair had no fabulous luster, his form was not especially elegant. He was, in fact, a bit more rugged than the dandies of fashion favored. Than Simon, for example. Broader shoulders, but still lean. He was imposing, not ingratiating. Commanding, not pretty.

"Miss?"

"Sir!" Pressing her fingers to her temple, she smiled apologetically to cover her embarrassment. Lord, she had been nearly lost in contemplation of his appearance!

"I was saying you should go back to your friends." His gaze lifted above her head, and she detected a measure of canniness in him as he surveyed the others on the terrace. "You do not wish to be seen with a man like me." His eyes settled on her once again, and softened. "And yet, selfish fiend that I am, I thank you for coming. Your compassion has lifted some of my burden."

A man like me? "But I did nothing," she answered.

"You did, you know. You didn't even realize it." Angling his head slightly to one side, he stared at her. Studied her, really. She felt caught by that gaze, as if he were divining her entire nature. The warning voice started up again, but she was as powerless to act on it as she had been before. What could it be he saw in her to look at her like that?

"You are an innocent. So genuine." He reached out a hand. For a dizzying moment, she thought he would touch her. Her breath locked in her throat and the sound of her own heartbeat beat a thunderous tatoo in her ears. She dreaded it. And yet she didn't.

He seemed to catch himself just before the long, tapered fingers brushed her skin. He dropped his hand to his side. "You see, I am not to be trusted. I am tempted and, too weak to resist, I comply. Run, child."

Puzzled, paralyzed, she said, "Sir, you are deeply troubled. Is there nothing I can do to help you?"

A tiny smile trembled at the corners of his mouth. When he spoke, his voice had softened. " 'When virtue and modesty enlighten her, a beautiful woman is brighter than the stars of heaven.' "

A familiar feeling stole over her, hot and exciting like a flush. It was what always happened when she stole moments in the duke's library, surrounded by the books she read in clandestine rapture. It happened when she browsed the Renaissance art her father had shown her when she had accompanied him on a business excursion to Italy. Why it would happen now, with this man, she didn't understand. But she said, "That is so lovely. Is it Mr. Shakespeare?"

"Ankhenaton. An Egyptian pharaoh. And you are wrong, mademoiselle. It is you who are lovely." He stopped, then smiled, giving her a chiding look. "You make me forget myself again. You must go. I cannot repay your generosity by further risking your reputation. However, your aid this night to a stranger in need is gratefully acknowledged.

Please know you have made a difference to me and my difficulties."

She opened her mouth to speak, but he held up a single finger to stop her. His smile faded and he grew insistent. "Please trust me, although I am the fiercest liar you will ever meet. For your own sake, and the sake of my conscience, leave now."

Bewildered by the swift and confusing progression of their conversation, she stood bemused for a moment when a hand clasped her waist from behind. The moment before she was jerked backward, she saw his gaze harden. She only had time to think it a frightening sight, then she was whirled about.

Simon's face was nearly unrecognizable, stiffly disapproving with his blue eyes appearing flat in his handsome face. "Julia," he said sternly. "We must go inside now."

A faint resentment glimmered. The man with the green eyes was telling her to leave; Simon was telling her to leave. She did not like either of these men ordering her about. And she did not *wish* to go.

Which she didn't quite understand.

The rebellious bubble that frothed to her throat she quashed as effectively as she had any others that had threatened over the years. With a lift of her chin she said, "Yes, of course." She cast a look at the man with the green eyes, opening her mouth to bid him farewell.

The haunted expression had returned. He gave her another sad smile and one swift shake of his head to warn her off. She said nothing.

Simon, less subtle, pulled her away almost painfully. "Come," he repeated, and it sounded like a command. Her resentment flared a bit brighter as he stalked back to the ballroom with her on his arm.

"Simon—"

"Come," he repeated sharply, leading her out of the ballroom and into the connecting parlor.

He found her a seat, which she sank into gratefully, for her knees did not feel at all trustworthy. He stood with his back against the wall, the shallow rise and fall of his chest and the stern set of his jaw a harbinger of his great irritation. She had never seen him angry before.

Her own displeasure, however, was no less. "Would you kindly tell me what that scene was about?"

"Julia," he began. His voice sounded strangled. "How could you speak to that man?"

"That man? Do you know him?"

"He is the Viscount de Fontvilliers."

"He is French?" Yes, there had been the slightest trace of an accent, not even enough to give him away. She remembered now that he had called her mademoiselle. Just the recollection of that rasping voice, and the way his hands had held her so tight, so close, sent a fresh ripple of jagged, pleasant pricking along her spine.

"He is half French," Simon said. "His mother was a Wentword. Why his grandmother, the contess, tolerates him, I'll never understand. He does nothing but disgrace her." Some of his vexation receded. "I suppose you had no way of knowing all of this. A delicately nurtured lady such as yourself has not been exposed to the raw sort of gossip that surrounds him."

So, he was a scoundrel, was he? But he was a scoundrel with a conscience that pained.

Simon continued, "Nevertheless, it was a monstrous mistake to associate with him. I do not want you to do it again."

Julia started. She stood.

By the year's end this man would be her husband. It was something they both understood perfectly. But he was not her husband yet. "I do not think it is appropriate for you to inform me with whom I am permitted to associate."

Simon's jaw dropped. He looked rather odd, standing there gaping like that.

Her heart pounded madly and she realized that even as she grappled with fear, there was a pleasant feeling as well. "I understand he may have an unsavory reputation, but now that we are acquainted, even if it was by way of unconventional means, I shall not cut him if we meet again."

She had spoken with dignity and authority, a far cry from the quivering mess she felt inside. Now she waited, wondering what Simon would do. In an instant, her ruined future flashed through her mind.

It took a long time for him to respond, by which time she had frightened herself half to death. When he did, it was simply to say, "I am disappointed in you, Julia."

The patronizing comment brought a fresh flood of irritation, washing her fears clean. "I must go find Laura," she said. Pushing her way through the people clustered in the labyrinthine rooms of the mansion, her flustered state must have been in evidence, for she drew some stares of vague curiosity.

Laura was coming off the dance floor, her face flushed, with a broad, brilliant smile upon it. Blessed with fashionable coloring and a slim figure with enough curves to win her jealous glances from less well-endowed girls, she looked radiant enough to rival the season's loveliest debutantes. She caught Julia's eye and waved.

Then she turned as her dance partner bowed low over her hand. Julia stared. The dark head, the long, elegant form . . .

The Marquess of Strathford had just finished waltzing with her sister.

"I am most grateful for the honor, Miss Brodie," Julia heard him murmur. Laura dipped into a shallow curtsy while continuing to smile adoringly up at him. Julia blanched at her sister's obvious display of feeling.

The marquess straightened, his eyes catching Julia's. There was a glint in the brown depths, as if he found something amusing. Touching his forelock, he was gone.

As soon as he was out of earshot—at least, she hoped he was out of earshot—Laura began to gush, "Oh, Julia! He danced with me! *He danced with me!* I thought I would expire on the spot. We floated . . . it was magic." She ended with a huge and dramatic sigh.

It gave Julia a chance to interrupt. "Laura, please. Where is Mother? I think I am ready to go home."

"Oh, I want to stay, Julia. How could I leave now? I am in heaven, I tell you."

"All the more reason to make a graceful exit now, before you make a fool of yourself. The gossips will have a feast with you mooning about." It was a waspish thing to say, and quite unlike her. Julia regretted it the moment it was out.

"You are cross. Why?" Laura gave her sister a crafty look. "Where is Simon?"

Julia avoided her sister's eye, knowing she couldn't hide the truth. "We quarreled," she admitted tersely

"Oh, how dreadful for you. Anyway, Julia, I simply must tell you what happened. I was standing on the edge of the dance floor—"

"Later, please. I know I . . . am a bit out of sorts. I wish to hear every detail when we are home, truly I do. But it is late. Everyone will start leaving soon, anyway."

"Oh, very well. He cannot dance with me again in any event." She paused. "For whom are you looking?"

Julia started, appalled at her own indelicate behavior. While talking to Laura, her eyes had been scanning the faces of the crowd, searching for a certain troubled countenance with a sensual mouth and aquiline profile. And she had been worried about Laura's tactlessness! "I was not looking for anyone—only the duke or duchess so that we may take our leave." She forced a bright smile. "Are you ready?"

They went in search of their mother, locating her in the ladies' retiring room, pleading a headache. Julia knew it was a ploy to distance herself from the pressures of the unforgiving matrons of the *ton*. Desdemona Brodie and her children were accepted into their company under the auspices of the Duchess of Cravensmoor. However, the sweet-hearted older woman had not felt up to coming tonight, and Desdemona had been on her own against the starched snobbery of London society. Not an unmanageable situation, Julia supposed, for her mother was imposing enough herself, but harrowing enough that Desdemona had wished to duck into the lounge for a bit of a reprieve.

Rising off the chaise, Desdemona smoothed her iron-gray hair and agreed readily to an early departure. They had their wraps fetched, and a footman ran down the queue of vehicles lined by the curb to have their carriage brought up.

On the marble steps outside the house, Laura lingered to breathe in the cool night air. "Oh, it is a glorious night, isn't it?"

Their mother walked briskly to the street as the carriage was brought to a stop. "Stop dawdling, girls."

As she was about to enter the carriage, Julia felt a tug on her arm. Her first thought was that it was Simon. Then a crazy, dizzying idea grabbed her and she whirled, half expecting to see Fontvilliers.

An old beggar smiled a gap-toothed grin at her. His grizzled face was as wrinkled as a dried apple, and his long, unkempt hair hung in limp gray strands all the way to his shabby collar. "Spare a ha'penny, Yer Majesty?" he crowed. "I'm to see the king, ya know. Got ta git me fine ladies some flowers."

Laura, who was standing just behind Julia, drew back in horror. "He's mad!"

"He's drunk," Mother declared in disgust, ushering the near-hysteric Laura past the intruder and safely into the carriage. Reaching for Julia, she said, "Come quickly."

Julia found it difficult to move. The man was so gaunt. His clothes hung on him as though there were nothing but bones rattling about underneath.

"Julia!"

"Can you give him nothing?" she asked as she turned away.

Her mother's hand on her arm was tight as she nearly

shoved her daughter inside the Cravensmoor carriage. "Don't waste your pity on him, and not a farthing, either."

"Someone should call the constable to come drive him off," Laura said with a shudder as she nestled into the luxuriant upholstery.

Julia glanced out the window as she settled across from the other women. The old man was still standing there, shambling about, looking for a benefactor.

Just then four men appeared on the steps of the mansion. One of them was the Viscount de Fontvilliers.

Laura gave a small cry. "Mother, there he is! The Marquess of Strathford. Up there, see! With those others."

She leaned forward to get a better look at the marquess, but Julia's eyes never strayed from the broader, taller form as Fontvilliers trotted down the steps and waved to his driver farther up the queue.

The old man shambled up to Fontvilliers. He said something to him, probably his claim of having an imminent audience with the king and needing to festoon his womenfolk with flowers. Fontvilliers responded by throwing his head back and letting out a rich, deep laugh. Digging in his pocket, he drew out a coin and tossed it to the man as he and his friends set off to meet their carriage.

Julia let out her breath in a rush as their own conveyance lurched forward. She hadn't realized she had been holding it in.

She caught one last glance of the old man as he opened his hand and looked at his boon. Then he fisted it again and held it up, whooping in delight. "Thank ye, me fine gent!" he roared and performed a spry jig.

It must have been a great amount of money, Julia thought.

⌒⌐

"YOU OWE ME a new pair of shoes," Strathford groused. "The chit trod all over my poor feet."

"Done and done," Raphael replied magnanimously. The carriage dipped into a pothole, jostling the four of them soundly. Martinvale cursed, but the smile stayed affixed to Fontvilliers's lips.

"You are in too fine a mood," Strathford observed. "It frightens me."

"I do not deny it."

Martinvale muttered, "Ah, so persecuting innocents cheers you, does it?"

"I refuse to be bullied out of my fine spirits, so cease your complaining. You remind me of *Grandmère*."

Atvers laughed. "She hates it when you call her that, you know."

Raphael's tone was as smooth as whiskey. "Yes, I know."

"What about the girl? What did she say, what did she do?"

"The girl is . . . interesting. And surprisingly attractive. More so than I had thought at first. Quite superior, actually. I believe she will do quite well for this little adventure."

Martinvale shielded his eyes and shook his head.

Strathford laid his head back against the plush upholstery. "And I am stuck with her ninny of a sister. I will be lucky to escape this folly without being maimed."

Atvers cackled, "See if Fontvilliers will purchase you a new set of feet!"

"I cannot believe you are doing this thing," Martinvale said. "It is too far, even for you, Fontvilliers."

"It may be you have lost your taste for sport." Raphael's chuckle held a bit of a bite. "But I would guess we have not even yet begun to plumb the depths of our depravity."

"You *are* enjoying yourself," Martinvale accused.

Ah, yes, he was. The girl had surprised him. Delightful, with fascinatingly mobile features and eyes that had turned out to be topaz—the first of their kind he had ever seen. Direct, intelligent, not at all silly or missish as one would expect from a girl who considered herself in love.

It was a shame to hurt her, but he couldn't dwell on it. He had a wager to win, and something to prove.

Martinvale was muttering something about depravity. Atvers leaned forward, his face full of anticipation. "What do you do next?"

"I shall arrange to meet her—seemingly by chance, of course. And we shall discover some of the many subjects we have in common."

"And they are?" Strathford drawled.

"I have no idea." He sighed, as if explaining himself had suddenly become tedious. "I hardly expect she will share my interests. Not many women of her ilk enjoy a buxom bed-partner, fine whiskey, and a high-stakes hand of twenty-one. That is where your task becomes important, Strathford."

"Me? What do I have to do with it?"

"Why do you think I insisted you dance with her sister? The girl shall become a valuable source of information."

"You cannot mean that I am to pay her court? She is a simpleton!"

"You will call on Laura tomorrow. During the course of your conversation, mention Julia. If I miss my mark, it won't take too much prodding to get that one to talk."

"I cannot call on her. My family is betrothing me to Lucy Glencoe."

Raphael examined his thumbnail. "Are you afraid I will win if you help me?"

No one dared breathe for a space. Strathford, too, hesitated. "I have plans tomorrow."

"Plans." It was more a challenge than a question.

"I plan to be sleeping in after a night spent between the thighs of a plump, delicious whore at Madam Delvina's"

"Don't be ridiculous." Raphael sounded bored. "You are not going to Delvina's."

"Where are we going?" Atvers sounded like an excited child.

"To number 13 Bond Street."

"Gentleman Jackson's rooms?"

"Boxing!" Strathford huffed. "At this hour? The devil you say."

"I am in the mood for a more violent sport tonight. And," he added, bestowing a glacial smile on Strathford, "*you* are going to be my sparring partner."

Chapter Three

THE DOOR TO the study burst open and Julia whirled, slipping the book she had been reading behind her back. One of her younger sisters, Leah, a pretty girl with glossy chestnut hair and large brown eyes, stood in the doorway, her bow shaped mouth agape. She was sixteen years old, three years younger than Julia. Laura was between them at eighteen. Behind Leah came Hope, twelve, and Marie, eight.

"You will never guess who is here!" Leah announced.

"Then I shall not bother to try."

"The Marquess of Strathford."

Julia dropped the book. It landed behind her feet with a plop. She had learned the marquess was one of Fontvilliers's elite bosom bows. The four friends were found everywhere together.

"Is he alone?" she asked.

"Yes, of course. He came to see Laura! She's upstairs getting ready. Mother has him in the parlor, with her grace." She paused, hiking a fist on her flat hip. "And what are you doing in here, anyway? You know Mother doesn't like it when you go through the duke's books."

"The duke doesn't mind," she defended. The Duke and Duchess of Cravensmore had no quarrel with the Brodie children making use of anything in their house. Mr. and

Mrs. Brodie, however, were quite a different matter. The five girls were carefully instructed to stay mainly in their prettily appointed bedchambers, making appearances only at luncheon and tea. These they were to take in silence. If they were directly spoken to, they were permitted to speak, but only with the most minimal responses so as not to monopolize attention.

And most especially, Mother had forbidden Julia the use of the duke's library, despite the fact that the jovial man heartily encouraged her interest. It was Mother's viewpoint that the proper upbringing of a lady should not include the sorts of dangerous notions with which books could fill a girl's head.

Just her luck, Leah was the biggest tattletale of the family.

"I was just dusting."

Leah dived for the floor, snatching the book from behind Julia before she could react. "Give that to me," Julia demanded.

"What is this? What are *pa-her-a-ohs*? Does Mother know you're reading this?"

"Leah, please give me back my book—I mean, the duke's book."

Leah shrugged and held out the volume. Julia took it back and ran her hand reverently over the leather binding. "It's *pharaohs*."

"Oh, who cares. Are you coming to see the marquess? I want to hear what he says. I know ways to find out what is going on so that no one will know." She stopped, her eyes widening as she realized what she had just said. Slyly, her crafty little gaze flickered meaningfully to the book Julia held in her hands. "You won't tell, will you?"

"Dear heaven, my sister is an extortionist." But she was only too pleased to agree to the implied terms.

"Miss Julia," Betty, a parlor maid, said, sticking her head in the doorway. "Mr. Simon requests you receive him."

"Is the marquess still here?" Leah demanded.

Betty replied politely, "I believe the marquess has secured permission to escort Miss Laura to the park."

"Mother let her go with him to the park!" Leah exclaimed just as Simon came in. He paused, disconcerted as the younger Brodie girl sped out of the room. The maid gave a curtsy and followed. Julia stood very stiffly, holding the book on pharaohs over her breast. "Hello, Simon."

He executed a stiff bow. "Julia." Frowning, he asked, "Who is at the park?"

"If you must know, the Marquess of Strathford called on Laura this morning. Mother allowed them to go upon the strut."

He paused at her cool reply. "Forgive me for my presumption. I didn't come here . . . I came to . . . You see, I was thinking . . . that . . . I-I owe you an apology."

"Apology?" She was stunned. "I thought you would be still angry."

He smiled. "Yes, well, I admit these kind of things don't come easy to me. I'm not saying you were right, either," he amended, holding his hand up to ward off any show of gratitude for his magnanimous repentance, "because I still believe Fontvilliers and his minions—one of which is parading this very minute with your sister, I might add— are the worst sort. But I will admit to overreacting when you had no way of knowing how derelict the man is. Had you known, I am certain you would not have acted as rashly as you did."

For an apology, it sounded an awful lot like a dressing down. However, Julia was too grateful to have the little tempest blown over to make comment. "I accept," she said.

"Accept? Oh, yes, right." He smiled again and took a step forward. Julia skittered out of his reach.

"My little sister has divulged her ability to eavesdrop without detection," she imparted tactfully. "We were just discussing this dubious talent when you arrived."

"Leah? Why, the little fox."

"May I offer you tea?"

"Fine. We could take it in here."

"Excellent. I love being near these old tomes. I'll call Betty." She went to ring the bell to summon the servant. When she returned, Simon was scratching his head.

"What did you mean, you want to be near old tombs?"

"Tomes," she corrected, laughing. "Books."

"Oh. Books. Yes, well"—he looked askance at the crowded shelves about him—"there certainly seem to be a lot of them. Wretched dust collectors. I'm glad not to be in the parlor with your mother and the duchess, though. I wasn't quite up to making light conversations with ladies today." He gave her a look that was almost chiding. "I did not sleep very well last night, you know."

"How unfortunate," she said instead of the apology she should have tendered. It was decidedly uncomfortable not to utter those two words—*I'm sorry*—even though she had done nothing wrong.

The tea arrived. As Betty was setting it up, Simon said, "I tell you, I am displeased that Strathford has taken a liking to your sister. Those four scoundrels—the Bane of the Ton, as they are known—are nothing but trouble, and your family would do well to shun them, one and all."

"What exactly have Fontvilliers and his friends done wrong?" she asked, seating herself on one of the old, beaten leather chairs and reaching for the teapot.

"It is not what they do, Julia." The patronizing tone of his voice embarrassed her, especially with Betty present. "It is who they are. I know you are hopelessly unknowing of these kinds of things, and rightly so, but there is such thing as evil in this world, and men like Fontvilliers are rotten with it."

Evil? As she poured Simon's cup and dropped three sugars into it, she remembered how Fontvilliers had tossed the mad beggar a coin. Had it been a guinea? A shilling?

"It is in all they do," Simon continued, sitting back in his chair. He held out his hand for his cup. She passed it to him. "Fontvilliers is dedicated to dissipation, Julia. If he continues on his present course, no person in good standing will even acknowledge him."

Julia bowed her head over her own cup, her gaze lost in the steam curling off the surface of the amber brew.

She heard his heavy sigh. "I'm sorry. I'm lecturing again. I would like to make it up to you." His tone was softer, almost penitent. "Do you think you would enjoy an outing? I was thinking we might go to the Royal Academy of Arts."

Julia looked up, surprised.

Simon smiled, a warm and loving look, and she felt a huge welling of affection for him. "The Italian collection is visiting!" she exclaimed. "How did you know I loved Renaissance art?"

"Do you?" He laid his cup on the table and rose. "I didn't know it, actually." Holding his hand out to her, he drew her to her feet. "I suppose this is one of those instances when a man has a second sense when it comes to the woman he . . . holds in high esteem." He touched her face.

He started to bend his head toward hers when she remembered. "Leah," she whispered. "She could be watching."

He hesitated, as if weighing the repercussions if he indulged himself. With a visible effort, he pulled away. Straightening, he jerked down his morning coat and cleared his throat. "Quite right. Ah, perhaps we should join the ladies in the parlor after all. A game of whist might be enjoyable to while away these afternoon hours." He crooked his arm at her. "Shall we?"

Her whole body was trembling. She felt relieved he hadn't kissed her and told herself it was the uncertainty of being spied upon that was the reason. But she was . . . disturbed somehow.

These torrid thoughts brought a pall over her restless spirits as she sat through a rubber, then another. There was a disturbing notion as the afternoon wore on that something had changed—and she had the oddest notion that it was her.

RAPHAEL STOOD WITH his shoulder against the wall, arms folded over his chest as he stared at the entrance to the museum. Taking out his watch fob, he checked the time. A couple drifted by, the man lifting his quizzing glass at Raphael. Raphael razed him with a glare of his own, satisfied when the man's stare fell away.

They were late, he groused silently. He detested being kept waiting.

He was already in a foul enough mood. Glancing over his shoulder at the painted marquee touting the Florentine Masters exhibit now being featured, he felt his muscles tighten. Italy. Why the devil did the art have to be from Italy?

A carriage with the Cravensmore crest pulled up, and he straightened. Turning, he strode across the courtyard, paid his fee, and entered the Royal Academy of Arts. It was easy to merge with the crowd ambling into the first chamber.

He pretended to browse, taking his time. This allowed the others to catch up. Finally he heard Strathford's voice call out his name in a tone that sounded satisfactorily surprised. He wiped any sign of expression from his face and turned.

Strathford was the lone male among the three women— Laura, Julia, and the Duchess of Cravensmore, who was acting as chaperone. Simon Blake was gone, of course. A last-minute message from his solicitor—a not particularly scrupulous fellow who had a fondness for certain entertainment Raphael happened to know of—had been handy in getting that distraction out of the way. Clever how Raphael had taken the other man's idea and used it for his purpose, first having Strathford insist he and Laura go along, and then having the poor fool called away. Sometimes, he found his own resourcefulness quite astonishing.

He was determined not to waste time in getting close to Julia Brodie

She was standing with her arm linked through the duchess's. Her topaz eyes were wide and startled in recognition. The beauty of them hit him in a strange way, like a well-aimed left jab straight in the gut.

He did not in any way acknowledge her. Pulling his gaze away, he addressed his friend. "Strathford. What a delight."

"Really? But I believe I had mentioned I was escorting the younger Miss Brodie to the Academy."

"Ah. I now recall you did." They had thought it best to get this established right from the first. Raphael had sensed Julia was too bright to believe blindly in such a flagrant coincidence. Best to admit to some of it, rather than have her suspect to just what extent he had gone to arrange this meeting. "I suppose that is what gave me the idea, though I didn't realize it at the time. Strange how those things work."

Strathford pretended to remember his manners and presented him to the women.

The only indulgence he allowed himself when introduced to Julia was to crinkle his eyes slightly in the corners and twitch up one corner of his mouth. Their previous meeting was a secret shared between just the two of them—the first of many such confidences he planned.

She colored slightly, a becoming blush high on her prominent cheekbones. He held her gaze for a fraction of a moment too long before turning to her sister, and then the duchess. Bending low over the latter's frail hand, he brushed the back of it with his lips. Raising his head, he smiled into the wrinkle-shrouded face. "Raphael Giscard, Viscount de Fontvilliers, Your Grace. At your service."

The old eyes sparked and she smiled. "A pleasure, certainly, young buck."

Straightening, he said to Strathford, "My dear friend, how have you managed to surround yourself with so much beauty? It is enviable."

The blond twittered. Out of the corner of his eye, he saw Julia glance down at her folded hands, betraying her nervousness. The urge to move ahead pressed, making him tense. With uncharacteristic impatience, he thought, *Come now, Strathford, invite me along, quickly.*

On cue, Strathford said, "I suppose you could join us if you wish."

Raphael smiled as if the idea hadn't occurred to him. Bending his head to the duchess, he asked, "Would that be acceptable to you, Your Grace?" His eyes were trained on the old woman, but every nerve in him was aware of the dismay of her auburn-haired companion.

If it were possible for such a wizened face to blush, the duchess's certainly did. Raphael crooked his elbow at her. "We're going to look at some pictures," she said rather inanely, slipping her bony fingers into the fold of his arm.

"It's going to be wonderful," Julia reassured her. There was an edge of anticipation in her voice. "I cannot believe it. The Italian collection, Your Grace."

The duchess appeared perplexed. "No, I don't know the direction. Ask *him*."

Julia looked over and patted the woman's hand fondly. Raphael maneuvered himself between her and the duchess, offering his free arm. "Miss Brodie, would you do me the honor?"

A ripple of confusion fluttered over her. He was being unforgivably forward, he knew. So did she. Her eyes cast away, as if seeking an unseen person for the answer of what to do with this conundrum. But her sister was already swept off by Strathford in a swirl of blue skirts and bouncing blond curls.

He willed her to accept.

"Of course," Julia murmured at last. Her gloved hand rested lightly on his arm. He was acutely aware of that tiniest of pressures as they headed to the first wall of paintings.

The duchess squinted as she gazed around her. "Burlington's old place, you know. Used to come here as a girl." Her face grew a bit wistful. "Ah, yes. Fine days they were."

"It's a museum now," Julia said rather loudly. "No one has used this as a residence for years. Burlington is gone."

"The champagne is gone?" the duchess queried, confused. "Are they serving champagne? No, I can't have any of the stuff. Puts me to sleep."

Julia soothed her. "We are here to see the exhibit, Your Grace. Come. This way."

When Raphael realized the old creature couldn't hear, he almost laughed out loud. Oh, indeed the fates were with him! Firstly, Miss Julia Brodie proved a woman of immense attraction—more so today with her pale copper hair set fully aflame by the sunlight and that spectacular complexion glowing with vitality. Now their "chaperone" appeared a deaf, possibly even delusional, elderly matron whom he had charmed as easily as if she had been a sixteen-year-old fresh out of the nursery.

He led them to the first painting, entitled *Primavera*. "Do you like Botticelli, Your Grace?" he inquired solicitously.

The duchess wrinkled her nose. "I do not care for Italian cuisine, no."

"Ah," Raphael said, nodding sagely. "Far too fond of the tomato, I say."

"Them and the Frenchies are too fond of the garlic as well," she answered with a definitive nod. "And always putting cream in everything. It ails my liver too much."

He shot Julia a baleful look and chuckled. "Quite right. No doubt the solid English fare you are used to sits best with your constitution."

"Who the devil are those people?" the duchess wanted to know, squinting at the masterpiece.

"Venus," Julia answered, pointing to the figure in the center. "See how she presides over the rest? And there is Spring, spreading her bounty. And Flora pursued by the ugly blue Zephr." Her excitement caught as she recognized another figure. "There is Venus's lover, Mars, paying not a bit of attention to her! And the Graces, dancing together in a circle." She stepped closer, studying two of the three sisters who were depicted regarding each other with a solemn, secret look. "Botticelli's faces are incomparably lovely. See the tranquility and the mystery that he captures. One wonders what silent pact they seal in that sisterly glance."

Raphael could think of a reason, a rather sordid reason, and one Miss Julia Brodie would not have known for two woman to be staring into each other's eyes like that. A sour, distant part of his brain silently snickered. It attempted to coax him back to comfortable cynicism even while another part marveled at Miss Brodie's brilliant eyes as she studied the painting, that sumptuous mouth half-caught in a smile.

She sighed and mused wistfully, "And they are all dancing barefoot in an orange grove." That threatened smile burst fully upon her face, brilliant for a moment before she looked at him and her features froze. Like an ice block laid in the path of the sun, the pleasure melted into self-consciousness, ending in her clearing her throat as she veiled those extraordinary eyes with sooty lashes and glanced away.

Her discomfiture was immensely attractive. "How charming your analysis," he said. "Do you not agree, Your Grace?"

The duchess was once again bewildered. She peered more closely at the painting. "I don't see a chalice."

Smoothly he bent over to get closer to her ear. "If you like, you could take a bit of ease over on that chaise while we dawdlers linger." He led the duchess to a seat, sending Strathford a meaningful glance that had him taking Laura the other way in a smooth reversal of direction.

Leaving him alone with Julia.

After depositing the duchess on a cushioned divan, he returned to Julia's side, taking up their tour once again. She walked stiffly, but there was a leashed excitement in her as they strode along. "And what do you think of the Florentine artists, Miss Brodie?" he inquired politely.

"Their work is magnificent, of course."

He smiled wickedly. She sounded so prim. He said, "You are very knowledgeable about art. I am quite impressed." They moved to the next row of paintings and paused.

"I traveled with my father once to Italy."

He sidled closer. "Admit it, you know more than a tourist's penny's worth about Italian art. You are a woman of keen insights, Miss Brodie."

Predictably, she did what all ladies of good breeding did when a bold man gave a compliment; she changed the subject. "You were very kind to the duchess."

"She is a dear woman. Besides, charming innocents is chief among my vices, according to the gossips. That is requisite before I corrupt them, I suppose. Surely you've heard that about me by now."

As they paused before a Donatello sculpture, her glance betrayed a canniness no woman of her ilk should possess. "What an odd thing to say."

He shrugged. "I do not deny my nature, Miss Brodie. Nor am I ignorant of the fact that I'm not the sort of man of whom your Sir Simon would approve."

She looked away, as much as an admission as he needed. He went on, "I daresay, he was not pleased to find you in my company that evening. You should listen to him, Miss Brodie. From all reports, Simon Blake is a good man."

She tilted her head at him, as if she were considering him. He had to admit, it was a pretty effect. He felt his pulse jump. "But the duchess does not object to you," she said, "does she?"

"The Duchess of Cravensmore is a tender-hearted soul who would pardon Satan himself." He smiled then. After an uncertain pause, she did as well.

A flash of her lying beneath him, locking her gaze with his, her luscious lips parted just as they were right now, came upon him all at once, hitting him hard enough to hitch his breath in his throat.

He turned quickly away, focusing on the painting in front of them. It was a disturbing representation of a massive eagle hovering over a chained man. Prometheus bound, with the bird eating the victim's liver every day only to have the organ regenerate each night—the mythical hero's punishment for stealing fire from the gods.

Julia shivered and turned away from the dramatic scene. "I'm afraid I don't like that one."

Raphael stared at it for a moment longer, eyes narrowing as tension filled him. He had seen this painting before, in Italy. He had been young, then, and immune to the tragedy of the painting. Not so now.

Abruptly he said, "Let us move on." He placed his hand on the small of her back, feeling her spine stiffen under his palm. She didn't rebuke him, however. He swirled his fingertips in the slightest of caresses just above the rise of her derriere, finding he was not quite able to hold himself back from doing so. Steering her toward another painting, he paused. "Now this one I like very much."

It was Correggio's *Jupiter and Io.* Disguised as a roiling cloud that eloquently signified the darkness of passion, the Olympian enveloped the naked maiden. The vague impression of a man's profile bent to kiss her upturned face was barely discernable in the folds of the cloud. The painting was incredibly erotic.

"Yes," she said softly. "It is quite . . . breathtaking, isn't it?"

She appeared to be torn between her appreciation of the painting and her embarrassment. Eventually, the latter won out and they moved on. He caught a whiff of her scent as she passed him. He followed like a keen-nosed hound, a smoky curl of pleasure coiling in the pit of his stomach.

She wasn't immune, either. Although she tried to appear studiously interested in the art, she was obviously self-conscious. In her stiff movements he read that she was as aware of him as he was of her.

Leaning his shoulder against the wall, he regarded her with a lazy smile. "Miss Brodie, I think you are a fraud."

She started. "I beg your pardon?"

"A fraud, mademoiselle. I say you are not at all what you seem." He paused, purposefully provocative, as he pushed off the wall and moved to her side. "Although you tend to be rather reluctant to share your opinions, your mind is bristling with intriguing reactions to the art. You are not at all reserved, though you try to be. Oh, don't worry. I doubt anyone else but a fellow rogue like myself would know the signs. Parents school their daughters not to exhibit any interests that go beyond silk ribbons and tatting—I understand this. No doubt you've been taught it unseemly to converse on intellectual topics. It seems a shame, when you obviously have more to offer."

"You can see so much, can you?" she said, a sharp edge to her voice.

Her golden eyes blazed. Oh, enchanting!

She went on. "You are quite astute for a man whose reputation has it that he rarely pays attention to much beyond cards and . . ." She paused. "Other male interests." Turning her head away with a smart jerk, she tacked on an indignant, "And I hardly find it complimentary to hear myself referred to as a 'fellow rogue,' as you say."

"I've offended you."

"Not at all." Those three words were as clipped and sharp as an indignant schoolmistress. Oh, she was in a snit all right, and it suited her deliciously.

"I cannot help it, you see." He shrugged, slipping behind her to a proximity just short of proper. "I know it is considered rude, but there are two reasons why this is beyond my control. One is myself. It is just my nature to speak my mind. It can seem rude at times, although some find it refreshing. At least, they tell me that. Do they flatter me, do you think?"

She turned her head, startled at his nearness. He smiled at her. She didn't move away, which surprised him. "What is the second reason?" she asked.

"You, of course." He inclined his head so that his lips were mere inches from her ear. "You intrigue me too much."

Oh, it was true. She *did* intrigue him. He felt the reaction of her nearness hum all along his nerve endings, a powerfully pleasant sensation.

She finally stepped away. "You are far too bold. And your tongue too deft. If you think me flattered, you are mistaken."

"I am merely being honest. I've just told you how it makes for trouble—honesty, that is."

She was trying not to smile. "You *are* incorrigible, aren't you? The talk of your being something of a rogue has proven quite accurate, I can see."

"But you shall make up your own mind, shall you not?" he challenged.

She considered him for a moment. There was a shrewdness in her eyes that he hadn't noticed before.

But, if he was not mistaken, she was having fun. As was he. He *liked* engaging this woman, he realized. He hadn't thought to enjoy her this much.

"Your conversation is rather ridiculous, monsieur le viscount. I'm afraid I am still unsure whether I've been insulted or not."

"I assure you, you have been most profoundly complimented. I find you interesting. I like interesting, Miss Brodie. It is only men who are not confident of their intellectual abilities who prefer women to pretend not to have any themselves." He smiled gently, bestowing a smoldering look upon her, ripe with innuendo. "I am not unconfident of my abilities."

She walked to the next display case, her posture erect. The betraying smile that teased her lips wouldn't be quelled. He knew she wasn't really displeased. She mused, "Yet by your own admission, you are not a man of convention."

"True, mademoiselle." He lapsed into silence as they contemplated some exquisite pieces of enamelled terracotta. "If I may," he said after a moment, "propose an arrangement of sorts. If we are friends—or do I presume? We *are* friends, are we not, Miss Brodie?"

She was a bit taken aback at his presumption. He *was* moving rather quickly, but the thrill of the game had him. "I-I suppose," she stammered.

Oh, really, this was too easy.

"As friends, then, may I propose that your modesty be curbed when in my company? I do enjoy your gifts." He had to exert an effort to keep his eyes from dipping to her breasts. "And would lament not having the benefit of your eager and insightful mind."

Staring at him, she was apparently amazed at what he had said. More than that, there passed over her exceedingly pretty features a thinly veiled excitement. He had tapped into something there. He felt it with the preternatural instinct of a predator.

It was time to retreat, let his words take root, yet her look so entranced him, he took a step forward and touched her chin with a crooked forefinger. "Do not blush. It makes you far too pretty."

She went rigid. Without meeting his eyes, she took a step backward.

He had erred. He had rushed her. Damnation! Why had he moved so fast?

His mind raced to recover.

"Miss Brodie, my forwardness is inexcusable. You see, this is why there is wisdom in listening to those who would warn you against me." He moved away and executed a stiff bow. "I shall take my leave of Her Grace and trouble you no more."

Her expression didn't thaw, but she said, "Do not quit the place with so poor a spirit. Let us . . . let us catch up to my sister and the marquess. They are probably looking for us in any event and will wonder if you leave suddenly."

Raphael nodded after a pause. "Thank you, Miss Brodie. I believe the solution you propose is just the thing."

He chided himself soundly as they wound their way among the display cases to join Strathford and Laura. It wasn't like him to be sloppy, not when there was a wager at stake. More than the money, it was the pride involved. And he had trifled with it because he had become too eager.

Eager for that mouth, the feel of her against him. Beneath him.

Soon enough, he counseled silently. Soon enough she would be his, caught as tightly as a rabbit in the jaws of a snare.

Soon enough.

Chapter Four

"Dɪᴅ ʏᴏᴜ ᴍᴀᴋᴇ arrangements to see Laura again?" Raphael asked as he relaxed with a brandy in his study.

"I did. But it is getting damned expensive. Which reminds me, you have not yet reimbursed me for the museum fees."

Raphael fished out a wad of pound notes and peeled off a few. "That should cover it," he said absently, tossing them at his friend.

Strathford didn't bother to tell him it was too much. Then again, it was likely that Raphael already knew this. This show of magnanimous generosity was his way of gloating.

"Why are you so put out, Strathford? Is your overconfidence slipping?"

"Not at all," Strathford countered fiercely. "Julia Brodie is, according to her sister, *absolutely* consumed with affection for Simon Blake. And take my word for it—it is useless to attempt to make love to a woman whose heart lay in another's hands." His snarl lapsed into sulleness. "Even so, it annoys me that it is myself with whom you are pitted against in this wager, and yet I am conscripted to lend aid."

"Of course you must. It would not be a fair chance without the playing field being evened out. The drawback of my nefarious past is offset by the information you bring in through that nitwitted sister of hers. You wouldn't want it said you had failed to compete fairly for the boon."

"Your reputation is fast on the mend with her, I tell you. Your fawning over that shriveled old hag was quite convincing. That, I'll admit, I found rather disgusting."

"The duchess? Why, I thought her charming."

"She was daft! And she couldn't hear a thing."

Raphael chuckled. "What better qualifications should a man bent on seduction require from a chaperone? But, it is not merely her incompetence that pleases me about the ancient darling. I admit, I find her amusing. I am rather fond of old people, you know."

"Does that affection extend to your dear grandmother? I thought the two of you had a distinctly *un*-fond relationship."

Raphael's voice tightened. "Sometimes I find you most annoying, Strathford."

The other man squirmed uneasily in his seat under the weight of Raphael's glare. "What is next?" Strathford asked to divert him.

"The theater. You shall suggest it. Simon and Julia will accompany you and Laura. Properly chaperoned, of course. There is a particular play I wish Miss Brodie to see." Pushing six tickets across the table, he leaned back and reached inside his coat for a crisp cigar, imported from America.

Strathford's brows raised when he saw the title of the play. "You are moving swiftly, aren't you?"

Raphael lifted a candle, pausing as he pressed the tip of the cigar to the flame. Puffing until the end glowed, he replaced the candle and let his head fall onto the high back of the leather chair. "She must have no time to think her way out of this in between assaults. Yet these assaults must be gentle, evocative, even as they are relentless." He drew thoughtfully on the cigar. "For a strong woman, a woman of Julia Brodie's character, one cannot bully her into compliance. One simply steps over the line of decorum and invites her to follow. She must take that fateful step on her own. Or at least she must think it was on her own."

"It is certainly not that easy," Strathford scoffed.

"Easy? I do not say it is easy. It is simple, however. Entice. That is the key."

"All right, I admit I am curious. How do you intend to entice her, then?"

He smiled a wolfish smile up at the ceiling. "My good man, it has already been done."

"FONTVILLIERS!"

"Raphael paused in the center hallway of his town house. He swung around with insolent slowness to face his grandmother descending the stairs.

"Where are you going?" the Countess of Wentword demanded. "I sent a message that I wished to speak with you. Didn't you receive it? I have matters I need to discuss with you."

Weighing his options, he decided it was best to get the interview over with. "Très bien, Grandmère," he said with a bow, hiding his pique.

"If you wish to speak French, I suggest you go back to France. We speak English in this house."

"But this is my house."

"Do not get pert with me. I am your elder."

Just to annoy her, he replied, "Certainement."

She glared at him, but said nothing as they sat on the matching settees placed across from each other.

She was a large woman dressed plainly and in dark colors. The effect was to make her exterior an apt reflection of her austere personality. She wore spectacles on the bridge of her nose and they magnified her eyes so that she always seemed to be staring intently at a person. This most found disconcerting. Raphael didn't. He reclined in his chair and didn't move a muscle.

"You count yourself very clever, don't you?" she said.

"Your penchant for sarcasm never flattered you. You would do well to curb it as it makes your resemblance to your father positively alarming."

Stroking his jaw with long fingers, he said sharply, "What is it you wished to speak to me about? I have tickets for the theater tonight."

"Debauchery." The word was thrown out like a challenge. "I wish to know whether you have filled your belly with it enough to have done with it."

"Was that all? The answer is no, I am not done yet." He made to rise.

"Sit down, you ungrateful cur!" She stopped and reigned in her temper with an effort. "I took you in when there was nowhere else for you to go. You are my grandson, you are my only family. But"—she paused, settling back in her chair—"I don't like you. I abhor your behavior and am ashamed of your reputation. It is time you thought of your position, your responsibilities. Marriage, to put a sharp edge on it. Marriage, Raphael."

He relaxed back in his seat. "Really, Grandmother, must we do this tonight? Have we not established my stand on the matter?" He stood up and went to the window. "I believe I've been excruciatingly clear."

"I fail to appreciate your aversion, Raphael. Take a bride, wed and bed her, and get on with planting a child in her belly. It shouldn't be too difficult. From the rumors, you've had half the women in London."

"You flatter me."

Narrowing her eyes, she raised her index finger and pointed at him. "You are tragically infatuated with your own carnal nature. When I think of the waste . . . It is not the point before us. Your character is rotten, that is accepted. However, you still have a duty."

"But marriage, as you know, is nothing but a torment. And wives can be so tedious, *Grandmère*." He pretended to shudder as he continued. "I hear some desire conversation and companionship, for God's sake. I cannot abide such an encumbrance."

Her voice dropped to dead seriousness. "If you do nothing about it, I will arrange it myself. Let me find the girl. You need do little. You owe me that much."

With a flick of his wrist, he waved her off and strode to the door. "James, please bring my redingote." Turning back to his grandmother, Raphael said, "The burden of respectability bores me. If you go about fetching up wives for me, you shall only bring embarrassment to yourself, for I assure you I will refuse."

"*You* are a wretch," she said with disgust. "I am quite annoyed with you."

"We're stuck with each other, aren't we, dear Gram? Pathetic." James returned with the expensive redingote. Raphael threw it about his shoulders with a flourish. "Now if that is all, I shall be on my way."

The old witch had plenty more to say, and Raphael knew it, but he didn't give her a chance. He departed, snatching up his hat and rushing headlong into the welcome abyss of the night.

———◦———

THE PLAY AT Covent Gardens, for which Colin Strathford had produced six very difficult to obtain tickets—care of Fontvilliers—was *Romeo and Juliet*. Shakespeare was back in fashion, and the theater was packed full. Desdemona and Francis Brodie presided over their two older daughters and their escorts. Julia and Simon, having quite recovered from their quarrel, looked content. Laura, in her usual display of enthusiasm, was delighted to be in the company of the marquess, and yet he, whose idea it had been, didn't seem to be enjoying himself at all.

"I do say"—Simon leaned over the armrest of his chair in the first box to speak close to Julia's ear—"I find my dislike of Strathford's presence may ruin my evening. But my pique disappears when I see the excitement on your face."

Julia cast a glance at the marquess, sitting with his typical ennui next to Laura, as that one diligently scanned the seats below with her opera glasses for prominent faces. "His attitude borders on insulting. Why did he propose tonight's outing if it doesn't please him?"

"Why do men like Strathford and his ilk do anything?"

"Perhaps we have overlooked the attractions of my sister's company."

His gloved hand closed over hers. "Indeed. Laura's sparkle tonight would charm anyone."

"Shh. The play is starting."

Julia was transfixed from the moment the opening lines were spoken. This particular play was not her favorite of the bard's. She had always thought Romeo a bit of a cad and the story too tragic to be truly enjoyed. But she liked the nurse and the reckless, brash Mercucio. Most of all, she admired Juliet's strength, her determination, her willingness to rebel against the confines of her family and challenge the fates for a chance at happiness.

The actress was brilliant in the part, and the scene at the masked ball, when the lovers meet and steal a clandestine kiss, was magical. By the end of the first act Julia was feeling unaccountably emotional.

"There, there," Simon said solicitously, fishing in his waistcoat pocket for a handkerchief.

"It is just that their words were so moving, and knowing what happens . . ." She took the embroidered linen and dabbed it to her eyes, sniffing gently.

He was dismayed. "This is not like you."

He was right, of course. It was deplorable manners to allow herself to be overcome in this way. She cast a wary glance at her mother, happy to see Desdemona had noticed nothing.

"Silly girl," Simon muttered, making it sound like an endearment. "Let us go for some refreshments."

She nodded, resolving to cease this immediately. Simon deserved better than to be humiliated by a weepy-eyed female in front of good society.

RAPHAEL LIFTED HIS opera glasses, watching as the Brodie party rose and exited the box, which was situated opposite the theater from his.

"Shall we fetch a drink?" he asked, rising. "We have that bit of business to attend to."

His companion for the evening, Lady Catherine Drummond, gave him a catlike smile and rose, taking his arm. Raphael had been acquainted with Catherine for a long time. Beautiful, quick-witted, with excellent manners, she was one of the less notorious members of the *demi-monde*. This made her the perfect choice for his accomplice.

As for Catherine's compliance, they had struck an agreeable business arrangement. Her requirements were stiff, but he didn't mind paying for the best. Regarding Catherine's concerns about her carefully tended reputation, Raphael had confidently assured her of Julia's sterling character. No matter how titillating the lies he told, Julia would never utter a single word out of confidence. The whole endeavor was just too enticing for the woman to refuse.

As they came down the curved staircase into the lobby, he spotted his prey. She was clinging to Simon's arm in a way that made him angry just to look at. He strode forward, practically pulling Catherine in his wake.

Catherine squealed and reached both gloved hands toward Blake, hurrying forward. "Simon! My goodness, it *is* you."

The look of astonishment on Blake's face was amusing, as was his controlled politeness. Raphael enjoyed every moment of the man's discomfiture. Sir Simon Blake had never met Catherine Drummond, to be sure, but he was too busy trying to feign a pleasant greeting to realize it.

"How *are* you?" Catherine gushed. "Lud, how long

has it been?" As arranged, the buxom blond stepped so as to direct Simon's attention away from Julia.

Raphael moved.

"Miss Brodie," he whispered, slipping his fingers around hers and tugging her around.

She turned, and her puzzled look gave way to surprise. A delicate halfsmile played on her lips as she stared at him.

And he her. She looked beautiful. Her eyes were bright, her hair swept loosely back from her face in a most flattering arrangement. Her dress was of fine crepe, draping over her long figure in loose, butter-colored folds. Strings of pearls looped through the short capped sleeves and interwove with a tasteful touch of lace at the scooped neckline.

He found his throat a tad dry. "It is excellent to see you again. Forgive my forwardness."

"Not at all, monsieur le viscount. It is always a delight."

"I simply had to know if you were enjoying the play," he said, swiveling just right to cut her off from Simon and Catherine. "What do you think of Romeo and Juliet's foolish infatuation?"

"They are indeed charming, but I find them both too impulsive."

"Then you disapprove of them?"

"Not at all. Despite their frivolity, I cannot help myself but be caught up in their tragic fate."

"Ah, so you are sentimental."

She laughed. "I suppose everyone is when it comes to ill-fated lovers."

"Yes." He paused, pinning her with a meaningful stare. "The allure of forbidden love is quite potent."

She laughed. "It seems you are a sentimentalist, too."

"Mind, you mustn't let anyone know my secret. It would play monstrous havoc with my reputation."

Her eyes sparkled, that topaz gaze was as brilliant and mysterious as that of a cat. "Which you seem to find to be both a burden and a matter of some pride, depending on your mood."

The observation was quite astute. He must remember she was no simple miss to be led this way and that with a bit of flattery.

Dropping his tone to a more confidential level, he murmured, "You are a woman of deep feelings, mademoiselle, and most incredible intuition. Perhaps that is what draws me to you."

"You have a habit of speaking with shocking intimacy, monsieur le viscount," she said without any coyness. "I am not sure that it is quite proper."

"Of course it is not proper. The things I do rarely are. For example, as soon as I spotted you in the box across from mine, I found myself having the most curious experience. I was sitting in my seat, attempting to attend to the play, and found myself, upon a certain line or clever turn of the plot, wondering what you thought of it. I rather wanted you seated beside me so that I had but to lean over"—he let his eyes lower to her lips—"to ask you your opinion. I was quite certain it would be illuminating. How I envied Sir Simon the enjoyment of hearing your insightful comments."

It wasn't a lie, that he'd thought of her often during the first act, wishing she were seated beside him instead of across the theater. She was a woman who kept much of her self held back, and damn his perverse soul, he couldn't help but be intrigued by that. In the rigid strictures of her world, she could no more discuss Shakespeare than don trousers and ride down Picadilly.

Why should it make him angry? he wondered. Why did it give him such delight to coax that timid mind to the fore? Was it simply because it was forbidden? He had never been adept at resisting temptation.

"I am afraid I would disappoint you," she said at last. "You give me far too much credit"

"I've embarrassed you. I am sorry, Miss Brodie. Let us talk of the mundane things, safe things." He stopped, looked about in a semblance of alarm. "Good God, do you see Lady Catherine?"

"Lady Catherine?" Turning slightly to peer at the other woman who was still speaking to Simon, she said, "I hadn't realized she was with you."

"Is she still talking with Blake? Ah, yes, there she is."

He studied the critical appraisal Julia gave to the other woman and fought a smile. She hadn't been concerned with the woman at all when Simple Simon was speaking with her, but her interest was definitely piqued now. That pleased him.

"Why, monsieur le viscount, you do take your duties as chaperone quite seriously."

"Yes. Yes, I must. Lady Catherine is a friend."

"Oh," she murmured.

"You misunderstand. I escort her as a favor. She is my responsibility tonight. It is the least I can do."

She looked back to him, puzzled.

He inclined his head apologetically. "I am being rather mysterious, aren't I? I am sorry. But you will allow that it would be deplorable for me to speak out of turn regarding another's unfortunate situation."

The bell rang, signaling the end of the intermission.

Julia started, looking as if she had just been shaken awake from a daydream. "I suppose I should be getting back to my seat." She hesitated, clearly reluctant. Raphael's spirits surged and he wavered, too, for a moment, wondering if he dared push further.

A sudden wish that he wasn't trapped by this infernal wager hit him. If not for the damnable strategy he had laid out for himself, he'd linger, even barge in on their box—Lord knew he was adept at getting his way when he set his mind to it. But, blast and bloody hell, he had to pace himself for that ultimate boon.

No, not the money, but the lovely Miss Julia Brodie herself.

Having learned his lesson from his misstep at the museum, he forced himself not to linger. As he was about to say good night, a man stepped up to them and declared in a loud voice, "Fontvilliers, I say!"

He knew who it was even before he turned his head to glower at the intruder. "Atvers," he said in a flat tone, "what an unwelcome sight."

The small man's eyes gleamed. They were fastened directly on Julia. "Whom do we have here?" he purred, running his tongue salaciously over his lips.

"What are you doing here?" Raphael countered, not caring if he drew stares. He wished he could smack the leer off that boyish face. The swell of swift, blinding anger didn't strike him as unreasonable, and yet he'd be hard-pressed to explain it.

"I merely wanted to be introduced to the lady. You cannot fault me for that, can you?" Again he paused and perused Julia's fashionable form. "You look exquisite tonight, Miss Brodie."

Raphael fought the impulse to lay hands on the man. He didn't like the way Atvers was leering at her, as if she were to be inspected. A hot flush of protectiveness broke him out in a sweat as he willed the man to evaporate.

As if she picked up on his displeasure, Julia's own response was reserved, wary, like a cat with hackles at full mast. She addressed Atvers with stiff formality. "I am afraid I do not know you, sir."

"Charles Atvers, at your service." He swept his short body into a bow and erupted with one of his unpleasant giggles. "An old school chum of our friend here."

Raphael stepped forward, shouldering the shorter man out of the way. It wasn't a smooth move, but he didn't care. "Come, Miss Brodie, let me return you to your party."

"Good to meet you, Miss Brodie," Atvers piped up, standing on his tiptoes to get a last glance at Julia from over Raphael's wide shoulder.

"Pardon him," Raphael said through his teeth as he pulled her away. What had possessed Atvers to take such a bold action? A mistake he would regret, Raphael promised himself.

"I see them over there," Julia said, pointing to where Blake was standing with an older couple. They must be Julia's parents. Briefly Raphael thought of ingratiating himself with them. From all reports, they were rapacious society addicts, and his pedigree practically assured him a warm reception. But Simple Simon was definitely not impressed with his superior status. The man sensed the rivalry that was brewing between them. And he wasn't stupid, either. Yes, Blake posed a certain threat Raphael didn't intend to underestimate.

Raphael executed a slight bow and said, "It is always my greatest pleasure to see you again. It would be improper to tell you how much. Enjoy your evening."

It was important to leave abruptly. And to have the last word.

It would make her think about him.

But when he was back in his box, it was his own thoughts caught up with the spirited woman he had just left. He stood at the rail, looking across the theater, waiting for Julia to take her seat. He saw her enter her box. Simon was behind her, speaking with the older gentleman who must be Francis Brodie, Julia's father.

"That went well," Catherine said, turning her brilliant smile at him. Her eyes angled up at him coyly, and she said, "Now that I've done my part, what do you say the two of us slip out and retire to my boudoir?"

Raphael held up a finger to stay her as he watched the opposite box.

He saw Julia as she moved to the chair, saw her stop, look down at the tufted cushion. She picked up the rose he had arranged to be left for her, staring at the slender stalk, the perfect white petals.

He grinned.

Simon came up behind her just then, noticing the flower in her hand. Raphael saw her say something, lifting her shoulders before taking her seat. She was pretending not to know from whom the gift had come. But she knew.

Another secret, just between the two of them. Simon was moving further outside the delicate circle of shared intimacy which Raphael was carefully constructing. The thought thrilled him.

Simon turned back to resume his conversation, apparently no longer curious about the rose. Julia swirled the rose in her hand, bringing it up to her nose and touching the silky petals to her cheek. Just then, she looked up and across the theater, straight at Raphael, as if she had suddenly become aware of him watching her.

He nodded, a half-smile playing on his lips. Funny. He couldn't seem to breathe.

Perhaps it was excitement, merely. It was going so damnably well.

Julia glanced away as the curtain opened for Act Two.

"Raphael?" Catherine prompted, her tone taut with impatience.

"What?" He finally turned to her. "Your boudoir, you say? Tempting offer, Catherine, mightily tempting." He raised her hand to his lips and brushed a kiss along her knuckles. "But we must stay through the second act. After that, I am afraid I'll have to send you home in my chaise. I'll hire a cabriolet for myself, as I've got an appointment at White's to keep tonight."

Lady Catherine didn't hide her disappointment, but she was too dignified to make any pout or protest, for which he was grateful. He wanted to concentrate on the people in the box opposite his. He studied Julia, rather than the stage, observing how her father touched her shoulder, and she leaned forward for him to whisper something in her ear that had her laughing. He wondered what the joke was, wondered what a father would say to an adult child that would cause her to laugh like that.

Watching them was like looking at a painting of an idealized landscape—some perfect, pretty world he himself had never known. And she . . . she was as exotic as a brightly plumed bird from the Spanish colonies in America. She lived a life he couldn't fathom, but she fascinated him, drew him. He found himself calculating the time and place for their next meeting.

He was very anxious to see her again.

Chapter Five

JULIA STEPPED INTO the small walled garden, a carefully tended patch that stretched from the back of the Cravensmore town house all the way to the mews. Rows of carefully clipped hedges and artfully arranged shrubs were laid out in a formal design among which was scattered blossoming plants to add color. In the center was a columned gazebo built in neoclassical design as a shelter for the ladies to take in the air and the lush foliage without being exposed to the damaging sun. It was here she found Laura.

Advancing, Julia saw her sister was writing. She quickly whisked whatever it was into the folds of her skirts when she noticed Julia's approach. "Hello, Julia," she said with false brightness. Laura was always wretched at deception.

Julia had a good idea what it was that had kept her sister so busy she had almost allowed her to sneak up on her. "Mother wishes to see you. She's in the yellow drawing room."

"All right." She rose rather clumsily, trying desperately to keep the handful of papers hidden.

Julia held out her hand and said, "I can take those, if you want, so Mother doesn't see them. Oh, don't look innocent, Laura. What are they, your love letters to the marquess?"

In a blink Laura's expression shifted from sweet to defensive. "You'd better not tell. Oh, Julia, if you do I shall positively hate you!"

"You are not meaning to send those to him, are you?" At Laura's expression, Julia groaned. "Do you not recall the shameful behavior of Lady Caroline Lamb and how she pursued Lord Byron?"

"Oh, of course you would think of nothing but the scandal of it all. Well, maybe I don't care so much what people think!"

"You would do well to mind your reputation," Julia countered tightly.

"But what of my heart, Julia? I cannot help myself! Colin is the most distinguished of men. . . . Oh, never mind. You can't understand. No one understands."

"What are you saying, Laura? Of course I understand. I have Simon."

"Simon," Laura scoffed with a stamp of her petite foot. "Forgive me, Julia, but you are hardly an expert on passion just because you and Simon have an *understanding*. I mean, you had a strange man send you a rose at the theater the other night, for goodness' sake, and he didn't think anything of it."

"I told him I didn't know who sent it, and that most likely it was left in error," Julia said lamely. Indeed, Simon had been remarkably uninterested in the trinket and had accepted her explanation without question. As for the lie . . . well, she didn't know for certain that Fontvilliers had arranged to have it placed on her seat. "Simon and I understand each other, that is all."

"How can you be so *sensible* about it all? I mean, you never get weepy when you miss him, you don't write poems to him—"

"Is that what you were doing? Writing poems? Oh, Laura, really, I can't believe you'd bother with such foolishness."

"Foolishness, is it? What would you know of it? Lord, Julia, when did you become such a prig?"

The accusation brought Julia up short with an indignant gasp.

Laura was not finished. "How can you say you're in love? You are not lost or confused or sick to your stomach or restless. You're . . . you're perfect! Perfectly calm, perfectly poised. How can you be so . . . blasted . . . perfect?" Whirling she spread her arms wide, throwing her head back in a dramatic pose. "Love is insanity, it is totally losing yourself to desire—"

"Stop it!" Julia shouted all of the sudden, startling both her sister and herself. Her heart had risen and was now most painfully lodged in her throat, where it beat a rapid flutter like a bird trapped there. She felt she was choking.

She *had* felt a taste of madness, hadn't she? Was it that weak, dizzy feeling she got when a saturnine face came into focus from across the theater or that sensuously curved mouth quirked up in that particular fashion that made the Marquis de Fontvilliers look every bit the rake and scoundrel he was purported to be?

But that was not *love*. It was merely the allure of a mysterious man. She was a sensible woman—everyone said so. Love was not madness—it was the quiet, contented feeling she felt in Simon's company. It was calm, uncomplicated, gentle affection that lasted a lifetime and beyond into eternity.

She knew exactly what love was. What she didn't know was why she was trembling. She struggled to sound calm. "Go inside now and see Mother. And if she spies those poems, she'll forget your age and give you a thrashing over her knee."

Laura paused, cornered. Finally she bit her lips and gazed down at the sheets. "Will you take them for me? Promise you won't look at them!"

Julia sighed, folding her arms over her chest. She was still very cross with Laura. However, she relented. "I give my word."

Laura thrust them into Julia's hand. "I always know I can trust you to keep your word."

When she was gone, Julia didn't move for the longest time.

Everyone knew how trustworthy Julia Brodie was. Honorable, dependable, sensible Julia.

Dull, predictable, agreeable Julia.

She shook off the thought. What foolishness was this—listening to Laura!

Taking the kitchen entrance, she crept up the back stairs and went to the bedchamber next to her own to place the poems under her sister's pillow. She was just leaving when a maid entered.

"There you are, miss. This just came for you in the post." She held out a letter. Julia took it, examining the wax imprint. It was not one she recognized.

Flipping it over, Julia saw her name was printed on it. She didn't recognize the handwriting either. It was bold and angular and not very neat. A man's writing, but not Simon's.

Opening it, she read:

> *I keep thinking of that silly play. Do you know how many times I have seen it performed and never thought twice of it? And yet I cannot seem to put it from my mind, as if layers of meaning within the wretched thing are just now opened to me.*
>
> *I may burn this, I may send it. If the latter, I will forgive you totally should you toss it into the fire yourself. If only my character were as strong. Yet, perhaps I have furnished you with a smile. I shall hope so, in any event. I am yours, now and always,*
> > *Raphael Giscard, Viscount de Fontvilliers.*

"Miss?"

Clutching the paper to her breast, she looked up at the servant. "Yes? What?"

Beth appeared puzzled. "Will there be a reply?"

"No, thank you—wait. Yes. I . . ." What was she thinking? She squelched the impulse to dash off a note. Taking a steadying breath, she said, "No, Beth, thank you. There is no reply at this time."

Hurrying to her room, she slipped the letter into a rosewood secretary by the window.

He had wondered if she'd burn it. Perhaps she should. She wouldn't.

She took it out and read it six times before Debra, the ladies' maid she shared with her sisters, came in that evening to dress her hair. The skilled woman was just twisting it artfully into a pile of coils on her head when Julia's mother entered the room.

Coming up from behind, she rested her hands on her daughter's shoulders and smiled at her in the mirror. "Are you wearing the blue satin tonight? I remember when you had it on last. The Feltons' musicale, I think. Simon couldn't keep his eyes off you."

Had he? She didn't recall. Instead, she had a vivid recollection of the pale yellow crepe she wore to Covent Garden and the way a pair of glinting green eyes had swept appreciatively over her body. It had made her . . . oh, Lord, it made no sense, but it had made her *hot* as if his gaze were fire.

She wasn't fooled by Fontvilliers. He looked at her like he wanted to devour her, he took far too many liberties. He was a rake, through and through. But he was an appealing one, a man who somehow knew things about her. How did he know she kept her true thoughts hidden, guessing so adroitly that she longed to converse on topics with more substance than the latest fashions? What he had said at the museum, about mamas keeping daughters sheltered from knowledge, limiting them to the world of stitches and ribbons and the latest rage of the *ton*—those words had brushed the most tender spots deep in her soul. He was flagrantly impudent, shocking in the extreme, too bold by half, but he was also irresistible and she couldn't deny she was quite beside herself with a very improper interest in the dashing viscount.

"Julia, are you listening to me?"

Realizing her mother had been talking, she brushed away the troublesome thoughts like cobwebs cloying to her hair. "Yes. The blue satin dress, you said. I . . . I always thought it rather drab."

"But if Simon likes it, you should wear it. Debra, air the blue satin, will you? And if you would step outside for a moment, you can see to Laura now. The marquess is escorting her to a dinner party. You can finish with Julia later."

Desdemona went to the bed and sat on the edge. Hers was a flat figure, sharp and full of angles. Her face was the same. Not a beauty, not even handsome, she could look imperious enough to set her children's knees to quaking.

Desdemona said, "Laura was upset today. She said you disapprove of the Marquess of Strathford for her. Your father and I do not agree. Need I remind you that he is a fine catch? He may lack Simon's affability, but he does possess a title, and a fortune." She pretended to pick fussily at the chenille counterpane. "I would hate to think you jealous, Julia."

"I am not jealous. It is just . . ." Sighing, she tried to put her misgivings into words. "Don't you think it odd that the Marquess has developed this interest in Laura when all accounts have it that his parents wish him to marry Lucy Glencoe? She has pined for him for weeks now, and he never had any time for her before. Now suddenly he is the ideal suitor, and yet he cannot seem to manage any show of enthusiasm for the very outings he himself has suggested. I find it very odd, and I am afraid for Laura to get caught up with him. He has a wretched reputation."

"Perhaps he finally noticed your sister's charms. They are, in my estimation, far superior to the Glencoe girl."

Julia knew it was hopeless to argue with her mother. "Undoubtedly you are right. And yet, I cannot help but worry if he is good for her."

Her mother smiled indulgently. "You are spoiled by your own tremendoous good fortune. Simon may be a mere baronet, but he is popular with the *ton*. He shall make you a suitable husband."

She didn't mean to allow her irritation to creep into her voice. "Ours is a match of *affection*."

Her mother's stare grew frosty. "Indeed. Affection is desirable in a marriage as long as the man is *suitable*. You know that I have been determined that you and your sisters should each make excellent marriages. I'll even admit I schemed a little, although I never hurt anyone over it. And where has all my plotting landed us? Only in a fashionable town house and my daughter the toast of the *beau monde*. Did I not promise you it would all happen, that we could one day be part of it—the *bon ton*? The world of nobility and wealth and elegant people. We did it."

"Yes, you did, Mother," Julia said without much enthusiasm.

Desdemona laughed and angled her head to one side, appearing girlish in her unabashed delight. Her eyes twinkled, softening her for a moment. "When you turned sixteen, I told myself there was time. Then seventeen and then eighteen, and I began to despair."

Her mother stood. "But it all happened, just as I knew it would, and just in time. Your father's friendship with the duke, his wonderful business proposal that turned out a fortune for the bank's trustees, it all came to pass, and not a moment too soon. Thank God, for you, Julia, you are my jewel." She cupped Julia's face in her hands. "You know how much your father and I are depending on you, and your sisters look up to you. This season is merely the first of many in which the Brodies shall take a prominent place in society."

There were legions of things Julia wanted to say. They were all suddenly crowding in her throat, choking her, burning her. *Mother, I'm not at all sure about all of this. Mother, I think I'm unhappy and I don't know why. Mother, please don't depend on me, I'm not strong. I'm not strong.*

But all she said was, "Yes, Mother."

"Good. I am pleased that is settled." Desdemona gave

her a reassuring smile. "I had better see to my own toilette, or I shall be disgracing you in front of your young man." She left with an airy laugh.

Julia sat for a moment, then stood and went to the wardrobe where the selected dress hung. Had Simon admired it? She hadn't noticed. The blue satin was lovely, a pale robin's egg shade of blue trimmed in ecru lace. A stunning dress, expertly crafted. It just . . . It wasn't . . .

Without having the slightest knowledge why, Julia collapsed on the bed in a heap of uncontrollable sobs.

IT WAS DAYS later, and Raphael found himself roaming the shops of Bond Street. He had been restless of late, bored with everything and everyone. When he got like this, as he did from time to time when the demons roused to test their claws, he usually closed himself in his study and brooded over a bottle of fine port. Today, however, the walls of his town house wouldn't hold him.

He had thought a diversion the thing, and took himself out of the house in hopes of a reprieve. He wasn't a dandy by any stretch of the imagination, but he did have a healthy appreciation for a finely tailored coat and high-quality leather boots, so he thought that perhaps a browse along the fashionable storefronts would cure what ailed him. But it was worse being out here, with people looking at him, greeting him, trying to make conversation. He felt like growling at them all. He didn't need to. They had only to take one look at his face, and they backed off with murmured regards.

He remembered Julia at the play, twirling the rose he had given her in his hand, cocking her head to one side as her father whispered something, some private jest, in her ear. Why did that bother him so? And Simon, looking on fondly, as if he belonged.

Damn it all, he had felt a surge of something raw and deadly within him, and he knew it was the beautiful simplicity of that scene. No dramas being acted out, no dark secrets spewing out of their putrid hiding places to poison everything in their path, no one glaring or sniping or pleading or brooding. Just the plain and uncomplicated exchange of a casual comment, enjoyed and then forgotten.

Christ, he was being a sapskull, simpering about such a stupid thing as that!

He tried the booksellers, but nothing caught his interest. For the first time, he came out of there without a parcel tucked under his arm. Next he tried his tailor, but none of the sketches shown him garnered any interest, and the stupid man kept gossiping in the most annoying manner.

Back out on the street, he prowled along, his thoughts turned inward. He was growing impatient with this inexplicable affliction.

And then he saw a particular face, and he felt his heart stutter in his chest. The vague, all-over tension that had gripped him found at last its focus. He didn't stop to plan what exactly he should do about this unexpected fortune, didn't even think that in this precise game he played, he couldn't afford to be impulsive. He just stepped off the pavement into the street and headed directly toward Julia Brodie.

She was with a child, a pretty girl with dark corkscrew curls streaming down her back, who was saying, "May we go to the confectioner's shop, please, Julia?" as they waited to cross the street. He knew that Julia was the eldest of several girls. This must be one of her sisters.

She bent down to look into the solemn brown eyes of the girl who seemed to be about eight years of age. "You know Mother said no sweets."

Amused, Raphael watched the child nod glumly.

"And you must always mind Mother."

An even less enthusiastic nod followed.

Julia hesitated. "Well . . ." She sighed. "We do have a wait before we are to meet back at the carriage. And Mother need not know, necessarily. . . ."

"An excellent solution," Raphael said, stepping forward to make his presence known.

Julia froze, then looked up at him, staring up from her kneeling position in front of the child.

He was standing tall against the cloud-bedecked sky, his dark hair combed loosely back from that high patrician brow. Dressed in dark trousers and a morning coat, he looked lean and elegant and uncompromisingly rakish. The way he smiled, as if there were a conspiracy already going between them, made her heart dip.

He tipped his hat, bowing slightly. "Good morning, Miss Brodie," he said. "What an unanticipated delight."

A sharp blossom of pleasure bled into her limbs. To her embarrassment, she found she was still bent like a limp marionette over her little sister. Straightening sharply, she tried very hard to appear calm. "Monsieur le viscount. Indeed, it is a surprise."

His smile deepened as his eyes flickered to Marie. "I do not believe I've had the honor of making the acquaintance of your young friend here."

"My sister," she said. "This is my youngest sister, Marie Brodie."

"She's a lovely child," he said, holding out a gloved hand. "Your servant, Miss Marie Brodie. I am Raphael Giscard, Viscount de Fontvilliers." His eyes flickered to Julia's momentarily. "My friends call me Raphael."

With impeccable manners, Marie touched his fingers and bobbed a quick curtsy. "Pleased to meet you."

"Am I correct in assuming you two are in the process of deciding the merits of obedience versus indulgence? To whit—whether or not to yield to temptation and visit the confectioners?"

Julia explained quickly. "Our mother will be here shortly, and we are to take tea with a friend, and she so dislikes our appetites to be spoiled."

"Spoiled? Why, how can having what you want spoil anything?"

"Indeed," Julia said dryly, quite recovered now from her

shock. "It does not surprise me to hear you say so. I am of the understanding self-denial is not an affliction of yours."

"I should say not," he countered, acting horrified at the suggestion. "I rather favor gratification. It is so much more rewarding." His bold stare made her overly warm, and just when she thought she would burst into flames, he deflected it to the child. "Do you not agree, Miss Marie, that we should please ourselves—at least sometimes?"

"Spoken like a true scoundrel," Julia interjected, but it sounded gentle and almost teasing. That surprised her. She wasn't flirting with him—was she?

His grin was eloquently mischievous, and utterly charming. "Indeed, mademoiselle, I never deny how deserved my reputation is. Yet, I stand firm on my opinion that a dip into self-indulgence is in order. As it happens, my grandmother—who is a countess and well-acquainted with the merits of moderation—is monstrous fond of her bonbons. In point of fact, if I accompanied you to the shop, and purchased a few delights to tempt her, I might just brighten up her day. See, you would actually be doing a poor old woman a favor."

Glancing down at Marie, Julia saw she was spellbound, her little bow mouth gaping open in awe and a definite modicum of adulation.

He kept his head inclined, as if he continued to address the child, but his green gaze lifted impishly to Julia. "And that being so, you would be doing me no small kindness to accompany me and act as my adviser on the best confections."

Julia crossed her arms and bit the insides of her cheeks. She really shouldn't allow him to cajole her so well. "You are appealing to a child, monsieur le viscount. That is hardly fair. And surely you have better things to occupy you today."

"Not at all. Today was shaping up as a humdrum sort of day. No scandals about, no gossip in the works—the worst sort of days for scoundrels such as myself."

She could not keep up a serious mien under the assault of clever teases.

Marie whirled to her sister. "Oh, please, Julia, say yes."

Raphael bent forward and said, in a tone throbbing with amusement, "Yes, Julia. Please say yes."

She found it hard to look away from his eyes. Some unnamable sensation crept along her nerves, pooling in tingling puddles in her palms and the pit of her belly. He really was impossible and took no pains to hide it, either. And just as thoroughly impossible to resist.

She answered, "Well, perhaps for a minute or two, then we really must be going."

Marie clapped her hands and they set off.

Raphael kept up a stream of questions that had Marie talking animatedly about her family. He managed in short shrift to elicit the facts that there were five Brodie sisters and she was the youngest, that Julia was her favorite and Leah her least favorite, and Laura was merely to be tolerated while Hope was quite lovely but often too pensive to be much fun. And Mother was strict and Father worked hard and the Duke and Duchess of Cravensmore were wonderful fun and Marie loved them very much.

Julia liked the way Raphael seemed to listen raptly to the little girl's happy chatter. He had a talent for making one feel as if she were the most singularly fascinating person in the world. She remembered how he had been at the museum with the duchess, treating her with tender deference.

He made Julia feel that way, too, as if she were the only person on Earth with which he wanted to converse.

At the confectioners Raphael pronounced to the shopkeeper, "Sir, we have a little expert here who is to sample your wares. If you would kindly assist her, she is to have whatever pleases her."

A moment later, as Marie surveyed an array of licorice and sugared nuts and various chocolate confections, Raphael's hand closed over Julia's and he pulled her behind a tall shelf of stacked boxes ready to be stuffed with sweets and tied with the shop's trademark magenta ribbon.

"Monsieur le viscount—"

Her protest was cut off. "It is good to see you, Julia."

His eyes blazed, holding a kind of greed that made her heart flip queerly. It was as near a caress as she could imagine without the benefit of touch.

Somewhat weakly, she said, "I have not given you permission to call me by my given name."

His brows shot up. "Indeed, did I address you informally? I suppose I must have. I've thought of you so often these past days, and always as Julia."

The hot crawl of pleasure over her skin pricked gooseflesh along its path "I daresay you've had other things to occupy your thoughts."

He shook his head slowly. "No. Nothing as pleasant or as vexing as you."

Darting an anxious look over at her sister, she mused, "You do have a way of charming women. Of all ages."

He laughed and followed her gaze. "It's in the art of temptation."

"Ah," she said, nodding, then chuckled and shook her head. "You really are shameless, aren't you? You admit it, and don't think for a moment I don't know that you use all the same tactics with me."

"Indeed, I am at a loss, Miss Brodie . . . but I called you Julia once and it feels much more appropriate, at least in private, than the formalities that are in order. Will you indulge me?"

"I dare not," she said truthfully.

"And yet you seem like a woman who enjoys a dare."

She did delight in the challenge of him. If nothing else, he made her pulse hum in the most marvelous manner. Every sense seemed to come alive in his presence. "Very well, you may address me informally, but in private only. It would be quite unseemly otherwise."

"Agreed." He grinned. "And you must call me Raphael."

"Monsieur, you are—"

"It is only fair," he interjected. "And a man in my position never gets to hear his given name. It is my title, always, even among my family and friends. Let it be different between us. We'll tell no one."

"I know I'll regret this later, but . . ."

He snatched her gloved hands in his, injecting heat up into her arms. "Thank you, Julia." His green eyes bathed her in warmth.

"You are welcome." She bit her bottom lip and smiled. "Raphael." It was a name that suited him, incurring subconscious associations with the legendary and mystical archangel, the vibrant genius of the Renaissance painter. Raphael was a perfect name for him.

She said, "I should check on Marie. She will stuff herself until she is ill if I don't stop her."

"Let her enjoy herself. Childhood contains so few pleasures."

He was serious, she realized, and reacted with surprise. "Have you found that to be true?"

"Indeed," he said vaguely.

She angled her head. "I have often wondered about your past. What kind of child you were. You so often seem unhappy."

"I am always in the best spirits when with you," he countered, but his smile seemed strained.

She wasn't fooled in the least. "Was it that you were lonely?" she inquired.

The heightened awareness he always felt in her presence changed. His chest grew tight, and he found himself clenching his jaw. A vision came to him, of himself as a youth, rolling a red ball in a hallway. Slouched against the one wall, feet splayed before him, he threw the ball to the opposite wall. Bounce and catch. Bounce and catch.

And then he remembered a door opening. There was no wallpaper on these walls. The whitewash was thin on the scarred surface. The servant's wing?

Bounce and catch.

Memory unfolded. It was his father who appeared at the door, his face red—that particular shade Raphael came to be used to seeing on Marquay's classic features when he looked at his . . . son—and mouth twisted in anger.

What are you doing, you little bastard?

He had heard the word, but it hadn't meant much more than an angry insult at the time.

Bounce and catch.

Clotilde had come up to lounge behind him, her overblown charms on display. She was wearing a thin chemise that barely came to her fleshy white thighs. Raphael looked at her, his eyes darting to the large brownish circles of her nipples visible through the thin cotton. Her hair was mussed, her lips swollen and red. Marquay was tying his cravat, his movements sharp and angry as he glared down at his son.

Raphael had known Mama cried over his father's coming here. Why did he do it so often, so openly, when it made Violetta miserable and caused so many terrible fights? He hated his father.

He loved his father. And that was much worse.

Bounce and catch.

As to his father's question, the boy hadn't known why he'd come. He still didn't know now as a man as it came back to him. What a confusing mess it had all been.

Soon after, his father had left the chateau for good. Voluptuous Clotilde had gone with him, been his mistress for a while before he cast her off. Raphael had seen her once, very many years later, drunk, her wasted beauty nearly obliterated by life's inclemency.

"Yes, I suppose I was lonely," he managed to say without it sounding as pitiful as it might.

"That is a sadness that never seems to abate," she said, almost as if she knew something of it. "Families can sometimes . . . disappoint."

His eyes narrowed. The demons were waking, pricking the tender parts inside him, but he could still focus on this interesting tidbit she offered. "I would not have guessed your family was afflicted with any failings."

"Would you not?" She looked away, carefully blank-faced.

He swallowed, crushing the awakening beasts into submission. He had a purpose with this woman, and cursed her for enticing him off task. It was not *his* emotions that were supposed to be moved.

"How is Lady Catherine?" she asked. The studied modulation of her voice, the fact that she chose *this* topic to change the direction of the conversation, told him everything. A diabolical grin nearly claimed him.

He suppressed it and settled back into the game. "How good of you to ask. She is troubled. I am beside myself with worry for her."

"It is good of you to be so solicitous."

"I do it for my friend, the lady's brother, whose family is sick over what is happening. They are good people, and I . . . Well, of all people, I should bear some of the responsibility."

"Why do you take the blame?"

"Because of who I am. My reputation is well earned, Julia. I have not lived a good life. If another makes the same mistakes I myself have made, how can I not feel it my duty to intervene?"

She blinked. He'd surprised her with that. It was good, he had to admit. He hadn't even known that was how he would approach it.

It felt good to be back in control.

Her face, so open and readable, so lovely, was turned up at him. He went on. "I sometimes feel I have much to make up for. Helping Catherine . . . it is a penance of sorts. Only I am not doing very well at it."

"You do not sound very much like the scoundrel you pride yourself in being, monsieur le viscount—" She stopped, then smiled. "I mean, Raphael."

"Thank you," he said in deference to her remembering to use his name, and added, "Perhaps I am different. Perhaps that night at the Suffolk ball, the kindness of a woman who didn't even know me gave me something to believe in."

Raphael watched her tautly, wondering how much of this she would believe. It was going far, he knew, even for him, and yet part of it was true. There *was* something different about him since meeting her. He—who had never had to expend one whit of effort to coax a woman into his bed—knew what it was like to want a woman to mind-numbing distraction.

Her body—yes. That extraordinary lithe form taunted him. Her lively mind held so severely in check was a challenge, as well. He wanted to awaken her. He wanted to command her, dominate her, shatter that infuriating veneer of calm and decorum—unnerve her, strip away her defenses. Good God, he wanted to free her, even if it would destroy her.

He wanted to possess her. Never before had he wanted something this completely.

She was looking at him with her pale eyes glittering invitingly. The elegant brows swept one delicate arch over each. Christ! He wanted to kiss her so badly. . . .

A cautionary voice told him to halt. It was wrong—too soon. She'd flee and he'd lose ground. Yet he leaned toward her, lowering his head. Her lashes drifted downward. She stayed exactly where she was. Waiting for him.

Marie exclaimed. "Julia? Raphael! Where are you? I see Mother outside. She is looking for us."

Julia stiffened, frozen in his arms for just one moment. He was going to lose her, lose this chance. So Raphael did something that shocked the both of them.

He touched his tongue to the soft, pliant lips that hovered just out of reach of his own. Swiftly, delicately, he ran it along the upper contour, indulging in this slightest of tastes. Just a lick, nothing more.

Marie's tone grew serious. "She looks cross. Oh, dear."

Julia's eyes flew up to his, locking gazes for one . . . two . . . three heartbeats. Then she stepped back, her face a mask of confusion. Like a mouse dashing through the claws of a clumsy cat, she dashed out from behind the rows of boxes.

Pausing a moment to smooth her skirts, she walked out from behind the shelves with a breezy stride. "Come then, sweetheart," he heard her say to the child, "we must hurry. Do not worry, I will explain everything to her."

Raphael found he was shaking. That amazed him, and yet it didn't exactly surprise him. Ignoring the ache in his loins, he came around the stacked boxes.

Julia looked over her shoulder at him, almost as if she were afraid of him.

As well she should be, he thought, feeling a rush of frustration. Just as quickly as it came upon him, though, it dissipated. He didn't want her to fear him. He wanted . . .

Oh, yes, he still wanted.

Julia fussed with her sister's tiny coat before they exited the shop. "Remember your manners, Marie, and thank monsieur le viscount."

"Thank you so much," the pretty child said and bobbed a curtsy. She scrambled to the door.

Julia paused, staring at him. Her mouth opened. It closed. She frowned and looked away, seeming to be confused.

"Good day, Miss Brodie," he said, rescuing her from her discomfiture even while he wondered at the impulse that was so unlike him.

"Yes." She swallowed, composing herself quickly. "Yes. Good day," she said, and left.

Through the large window, he saw her reunion with her mother. The woman did certainly appear to be displeased with her daughters once she took in the direction from which they had come and ascertained their transgression. She swept them unceremoniously along the street and out of view.

"Sir? Would you like me to wrap these up for your grandmother?" The young clerk smiled, all eagerness to please. "I have the little girl's selections here."

"Sweets for *Grandmere*?" Raphael's laughter was jarring and incongruous with his present mood. He cut it off abruptly.

Leaving money on the counter, he exited the shop and headed toward his carriage.

Chapter Six

JULIA WAS RESTLESS as she and Simon strolled through the Cravensmore's private garden. Simon was attentive, trying to cajole her into a better mood. However, his efforts only seemed to drive her spirits lower.

He was a wonderful man, she thought, catching him for a moment in profile. Heavy brows and a sharp nose were saved from being too severe by the contrasting sensitivity of his mouth. His cheekbones were high with slight hollows underneath, an effect that made him look arrogant at times. But then, one had only to note his kind, expressive eyes and that illusion was shattered.

Glancing away, she couldn't bear to look at him anymore. He was so perfect and she . . . Good God, what would happen if anyone had seen her with Raphael at the confectioners? He had *licked* her mouth, for heaven's sake, and what had she done? Had she protested, had she fled? Had she flailed him with a single word of indignation she should, by rights, have felt?

But she hadn't felt indignant, or insulted. She had felt exhilarating excitement that had had her quaking and utterly lost.

Simon was so right about Fontvilliers. He was a dangerous man. Simon must never know what almost happened. And it must never, never happen again.

"Julia?"

Starting, she pressed her hand to her forehead. It was damp with perspiration. "I-I'm so sorry, Simon. What were you saying?"

He looked at her with concern. "Tell me what I can do to help you out of your doldrums."

She wanted to cry. Never had she felt so wicked. "Oh, Simon. I am so sorry."

"Is it something serious that has upset you?" With one step he was closer. His was a pleasant smell, a comforting smell, in the same way the library smelled of leather and tobacco when she sneaked in to converse with the duke without her mother knowing.

His hands were on her shoulders. Unable to resist, she swayed toward him and lay her head on his chest.

He didn't embrace her the way she wanted him to. She hated herself for the vision that intruded on her brain, of another crisp shirt, another masculine chest—wider, more muscular, exuding a frightening degree of heat.

She shouldn't be comparing Simon to Raphael. A woman would be mad to be having these thoughts. Simon Blake was one of the most eligible, sought-after men of the *ton*. And Raphael was merely a flash of lightning—brilliant and beautiful but deadly when it strikes too close.

Hitching in a bracing breath, she threw her head back and stared into Simon's startled eyes. Then she closed hers and kissed him.

She kissed him hard, pressing her closed lips painfully against his. Shocked, he didn't move. Pulling away, she raised her eyes with a dawning sense of dread. What had made her act so rashly—she had disgraced herself!

But he wasn't looking at her with condemnation. His eyes were soft. Yes, there was desire there, the same desire she had seen in Raphael's—no! She mustn't think of him!

"Julia," he whispered. He pulled her to him, and kissed

her, this time softly, moving his mouth over hers while his hands clutched her shoulders tightly. She gave herself up to that kiss, wanting desperately for it to fill her with Simon, to burn away all betraying thoughts of another.

The sound of Leah's giggles broke them apart with a flood of humiliation.

A T THE MARTINVALE ball, Raphael made a great show of escorting Lady Catherine about. He glimpsed Julia, catching her eye on him more than once, but made no overture to speak to her.

She must think him penitent for what had almost happened at the confectioner's. He was, in his way, but not for the reasons one would think. He had betrayed himself, and he'd not forgive it easily. Himself *or* her.

Giving Julia a wide berth would whet her interest, quicken her curiosity. Catching her eyes on him from time to time, he saw he was correct. It was small consolation for the bitter frustration that had his nerves on edge.

By midnight he had had enough of the little subterfuge. He sent Catherine home in his carriage, putting up with a show of seductive pouting when he again declined her invitation to accompany her, and joined his friends in the private salon.

He had no sooner poured himself a drink and was seated when Martinvale said, "I believe we need to talk. I have a proposition."

The tall, rangy man moved around the room restlessly. Raphael, reclining on a leather divan with a snifter of brandy cradled in his palm, following the fellow with his eyes. Across from him Strathford was toying lazily with a Sevres dish, twirling it on his fingers like a top.

"By all means," Raphael purred, smiling at his friend's worried face. He had a fair idea what troubled him.

"I can no longer abide this wretched exercise. I am pleading with you to call off the wager. I have had occasion to speak with Miss Brodie—" At the sharp look Raphael gave him, Martinvale rushed to add, "Miss *Laura* Brodie. And I must say I am more against this wretched business than ever. She is a delightful girl, an innocent. To ruin her and her sister over a small matter of opinion—it's appalling."

"Then do not bother yourself with it," Raphael said, sipping his brandy. Rolling it around on his tongue, he savored the sweet smokiness of the fine liquor, taking great pains not to demonstrate the least bit of the agitation gnawing at his gut.

This damnable wager . . . it was like a stone around his neck. He'd have liked to take Martinvale's direction and nullify the entire affair. If not for this ridiculous challenge, he'd . . . what? Who the devil was he fooling? He'd be bored stiff. But much more calm of mind, that was for certain.

Strathford snorted. "Yes, my friend. Rest easy. Fontvilliers is not having very much luck with her, in any event." His eyes lifted from the precarious angle of the china dish to clash with Raphael's. "Blake is as present as ever."

Raphael looked at him. "Well, we are not wagering on Simple Simon's fidelity, are we? It is the lady who will choose. And I assure you, Strathford, she will choose me."

Martinvale began to pace in earnest. "I do not understand how she could be vulnerable to your rather obvious efforts. She has a name as a most sensible girl, and surely she's heard of your reputation by now."

"There is a Jewish proverb that says, 'Truth is the safest lie.' Therefore I do not deny my past, but rather use it to advantage. I reach down inside myself and find some dank, mysterious bit, something of an emotional nature. It is catnip to women. They cannot resist it. I dust it off and toss it out, like a morsel to tempt her. I build the fantasy of a rake on the brink of reform. Women want desperately to believe in the ultimate triumph of goodness."

Was that what he was doing? He wanted to believe it

was, that he was in control of the jerking path this seduction had taken.

Of course it was his plan. He just hadn't put it into
words before, that was all. He had been going on instinct,
and one does not always know exactly where instinct
leads.

Strathford put the valuable piece of china down with
a clatter and sat up, leaning his elbows on his knees as
he peered at Raphael closely. "I don't believe you. It is
not all games. Not anymore. I saw you with her. You want
her."

Raphael tensed. As he had done on many occasions,
he wondered if Strathford were truly a friend. "It is not
a crime." Raphael made an effort to sip his brandy as ca-
sually as he had before. "But I never neglect the greater
goal. The time will come, my good fellow, when she will
indeed be mine. Until then, I demonstrate restraint." He
squinted at the amber liquid in his glass and murmured,
"*Admirable* restraint."

Martinvale nearly lunged at him. "If it is true and you
do have affection for the girl, then call this off, Fontvilliers."

"Affection!" He stood, horrified. "Martinvale, your
brain has gone to pudding, I swear. Who said anything
about affection? For Christ's sake!" He whirled, raising
his finger and narrowing his eyes, truly angry now. "And
if you have no stomach for this sport, if you've lost your
nerve, then bow out now. But you had better not reveal
our purpose. I would consider it the most ultimate of be-
trayals."

Martinvale shifted from one foot to the other, not meeting Raphael's eye.

Raphael growled, "You've thought of telling her,
haven't you? Well, my friend, we have many years together of good companionship, but I will promise you as
sure as you breathe that should Miss Brodie receive one
inkling of what we are about, you will be ruined most
thoroughly. No hostess will receive you, no gentleman

will do business with you. I will design a vengeance far beyond anything you imagined I would be capable of."

Martinvale looked away, defeated.

They were interrupted by the arrival of Atvers. "Sorry, mates," he said, striding his jaunty stride and affecting the slang of cockney hired cabriolet drivers that was the infatuation with many young men of fashion. "My mother had some deb she wanted—"

He cut off as Raphael grabbed the man by his coat, shoving him up against the wall. His feet actually dangled off the floor.

"Do not ever, *ever* speak to Julia Brodie again. Not at the theater, not at a ball, not even if she trips over your broken, bleeding body in the gutter. Do you understand me?"

For once, the man was speechless. His eyes bulged out, his jaw slack. He could only bob his head.

Raphael released him as suddenly as he had attacked. Taking a moment to straighten his coat, he took a deep breath, let it out, and said, "I'm done, gentlemen. Good night." And then he stalked out the door, leaving the three stunned men in his wake.

EVEN MORE STUNNED were the various members of the *ton* in the park the following day when the Viscount de Fontvilliers was seen along the riding lanes. No one could say they had ever spied him engaging in this particular society ritual. It was known Fontvilliers detested anything to do with *haute society*. Therefore he did not frequent Rotten Row or promenade along the Serpentine, where the sole—and to his mind ridiculous—object of the sport to see and be seen.

He couldn't give a good goddamn about the dull passions of these stuffed shirts, which was why he brought a book with him so as to discourage unwanted discourse. As he lounged by the Serpentine, he glanced up from the pages, idly taking in the shocked faces as his peers passed him by. He disregarded them as unimportant. There was only one face he was looking for. He had it on good authority that Julia Brodie enjoyed a morning turn in the park.

The thought of seeing her again was making concentrating on Spinoza terribly difficult. He persevered with a vengeance, unwilling to admit his distraction.

The struggle didn't last long, for he caught sight of her before too long. It was her hair that alerted him from a ways off—that dark shade of auburn. It seemed to catch fire in the daylight, a blend of dark gold and aged copper.

As he had selected a rather prominent spot, he directed his attention back to his book and acted surprised when he heard a feminine voice speak his name. Looking up as if reluctant to part from the open pages in front of him, he found she had pulled up in the open cabriolet. The duchess was by her side.

He broke into a smile that wasn't at all forced.

"Monsieur le viscount," Julia said, her pleasure obvious. She had no guile in her, this one. He supposed she'd forgiven him for his outrageous . . . *lick* the last time they met.

Turning to the old woman, Julia said, "You remember the viscount, Your Grace."

"Indeed, I shall not dismount. Talk to him from here," the duchess answered, astonished at the request. To Raphael, she smiled and said, "Good to see you again, young man."

"Your servant, madam," Raphael said loudly. "I must say you look especially fine this morning."

She must have heard correctly, for she seemed pleased. It was clear Julia appreciated his kindness to the old woman. It surprised him that it would matter so much to her. It was such a small thing, to give the charming old creature a few moments of acknowledgment.

He closed his book and stood, coming to cock his

elbow on the door of the conveyance. "Enjoying this mild weather, are you?"

Julia held his eye. "Indeed we are. And you? It seems you are reading."

He had closed the book and folded it under his arm. "To pass the time while I wait for you."

His honesty was, of course, dismissed with a laugh. "You must think me daft if you think I am so easily flattered," she scolded. The look she gave him was meant to be chastising, but he found it unwittingly sultry. She had no idea how sexy she was, he thought. Imagine what else lay untapped within those enticing depths.

She was saying, "It must be an engrossing book. Tell me, what are you reading?"

"What?" Christ! "Oh, Spinoza." Good. His voice sounded fine. He had to glance at the spine, however, to remember the title. "Ah . . . *The Foundations of a Moral Life*."

She laughed. "I see you are serious about your personal reformation."

"I have an interest in the anatomy of reason."

"Is that because you have a dearth of reason, or a surplus?"

"My goodness, Miss Brodie, you are in a sparring mood today."

"I don't know the term," she said with a pretty frown.

"A boxing term. It means light combat between two opponents."

"Ah, well, one must keep one's wits sharp." The toss of her head was something he wouldn't expect of her. It was a tad coquettish. "Especially around such an infamous scoundrel as the Viscount de Fontvilliers."

He leaned in, drawn by that feminine gesture with the primitive attraction of any male of a species on the scent of a mate. Her color was high, as was his pulse, and the very air between them thickened, obscuring all of those unimportant beings out there in the world. Just she and him. It happened every time they were together. She was so damnably sensual—and completely unaware of it, which made it all the more potent. And he wanted her with a palpable ache.

"A scoundrel? I daresay, Julia, you tempt me to show you just how much of one I can be."

It didn't frighten her that he said it, but she glanced apprehensively at the duchess, whose patience was clearly being tried at the prolonged delay. Thank God the old woman could follow none of this unconventional discourse.

Damn. Damn! He was getting tired of waiting, and damned uncomfortable, too. His loins felt as if they'd be cast in lead.

Just a little while longer.

"We should be off now." Julia's voice held the regret they shared. "Enjoy your reading."

"I shall." Regarding the book for a moment, he impulsively held it out to her. "Unless you would like to peruse the pages."

"Is there a message within you believe me in need of?" She took the book and eyed it with amused speculation. "With regard to leading a moral life?"

"I am of the opinion that all lives can be enhanced by a thorough reading of the major philosophers. Yet, come to think of it, it has done nothing to put me on the path of greater wisdom." His look was mischievous. "Sometimes, meeting someone unexpectedly, say on a terrace one evening, can have a more profound impact on one's personal salvation than several hundred years of dead thinkers."

"You are a man of surprising sentiments." Pressing the book against her chest, she wrapped her arms around it, as if protecting it. "And unsuspected talents. You have other interests besides those of the typical rogue."

"It is my gift, alas, to ever defy categorization. Enjoy the volume, Miss Brodie."

"Thank you, monsieur le viscount. I believe I shall."

The duchess waved goodbye, and they set off down the lane. It really was a bright morning. The dance of water on the Serpentine seemed to Raphael to suddenly be most charming.

He left the park in an excellent spirit, so much so that many commented on it. Most decided it boded nothing good. They reasoned that if a man like Fontvilliers were up in humors, it certainly meant he was involved in some sort of iniquity. They would, of course, in this instance be quite correct.

Chapter Seven

RAPHAEL WOKE, SURGING up into a sitting position with a gasp. The fine linen bedclothes were in a tangle about his legs. His hair was damp, stuck in clumps to his forehead, and his heart raced as he battled to regain his breath.

The dream again. He rubbed his eyes with the heels of his hands. Grabbing the watch he had carelessly tossed on his bedside table, he saw it was just past three in the morning. Fumbling, he found the tinderbox and lit the candelabra. His hand shook. Swinging his legs over the side of the bed, he hung his head and raked both hands through his hair.

The same nightmare. Over and over through the years, ever since he had sailed for England, it had reoccurred. Some details varied, but he was always on a ship, very like the one upon which he had crossed the Channel. He would stand at the rail. In fact, he had done so often during the crossing. In his dream he was compelled for some reason to lean out and peer into the heaving gray waters. It was as if he were looking for something, but he never knew what. Farther and farther he leaned until he lost his balance and fell. The sea always sort of parted for him, like a welcoming embrace that was so sexual in its metaphor that it had always given him the chills. He hit water—felt its cold. Then the darkness and the panic, and he would awaken abruptly, clammy and sweating.

This night the dream had been different, however. He had seen, finally, what had garnered his fatal interest in the silky depths of the water. A sinuous movement of fin, a sparkle of iridescent scale, a glimpse of gently floating hair. A woman. A mermaid.

He leaned out for her, reached for her, and this time, as he fell, he strained forward, eager to meet the sea and discover the mysteries of the woman enrobed in its depths.

When he was submerged, he felt her hands on him. The darkness yielded enough to see her. Auburn hair, golden eyes, a bare-breasted siren with a fin thrusting powerfully where her legs should be, and she smiled at him, held her arms out for him.

It was Julia.

He found he could breathe somehow, and he wasn't afraid any longer. He kicked and a tiny whirlpool caught the two of them up in a swirl, and then she was kissing him. Her hair twined around them. Impudent, tip-tilted breasts pressed against his chest. He felt himself harden, felt her brush against his swollen sex, inviting him to mate. It seemed to him a puzzle just how mer-people did such a thing, but in the dream it was perfectly understood that they would make love. She disengaged herself, beckoning him to come with her as she floated backward, away, into the darkness. And then it swallowed her, and he found he could no longer breathe. He was drowning, like he had done in all of those hundreds of dreams before, waking with a gasp of burning breath to fill his lungs full of precious air.

Julia. It was Julia who had called him into the sea.

Coming to his feet, he padded barefoot to the window to fling open the shutters. The air cooled him immediately. But he was still trembling.

No sense in overthinking this thing, he cautioned himself. It had been a long time since he had bedded a woman, much longer than was his usual habit. That was all that was wrong with him. That was why his desire was flaring so drastically out of control.

For Julia Brodie, no less. Who was she, anyway? A fairly plain miss, actually, compared to the fabulous beauties he had known, had made love to, had forgotten. Of course, her golden eyes were extraordinary. He liked her hair, as well. He had never seen hair quite like that. Deep, rich, glossy, like mahogany. Not so plain, then, but not a woman to make him burn this way. It didn't make sense. Except, of course, his coincidental bout of celibacy of late. It was the only explanation.

What to do? He would bed her, in time. His body stirred, hardened just at the thought. Yes, he would bed her, and when he did, he would give her no quarter, no gentleness, no allowance for virginal modesty. He knew exactly how he would take her.

But when would that be? Tomorrow? Next week? Next month? Good God, he was going mad.

A courtesan was out of the question. He had never cared for bought women, even of the highest quality. The few times he had stooped to purchasing sex, he had found his interest disintegrate when the idea occurred to him, as he inevitably did, that this particular whore may have serviced his father. Of course, he knew that even such a proliferate debaucher as Marquay couldn't have had every woman in Europe. Still, it had made Raphael seek other, more exclusive arrangements.

The problem was, he had grown bored with mistresses. He had come to consider them no better than the whores. Oh, certainly, some modicum of affection entered into it. The women he took to his bed were always as eager for the sex as was he. He liked that. And they were experienced without being jaded. He needed that.

But they were so ordinary. After a while, they all were just so very unsatisfactorily *ordinary*.

What to do about the condition in which he now found himself?

There was Lady Catherine. He would wager that if he

showed up on her doorstep right now, she'd send any present occupant of her boudoir out into the cold night bare-assed and sputtering without a second thought in order to have Raphael.

His mind recoiled from the thought. He didn't want Catherine.

But his body was in agony. And Catherine was so convenient.

She didn't live far.

Turning away from the window, he went to the basin and had a quick bath. He winced at the chill water, but reasoned the colder, the better.

It only took a few moments to dress and slip out the door.

J ULIA WAS SHOCKED when her mother put an arm about her and pulled her up close to her side while they were at the Earl and Countess of Brunly's soiree. Desdemona was rarely affectionate. Smiling, the older woman said, "Are you having a good time tonight?"

"Of course, Mother. It is a lovely evening," she replied.

It wasn't, though. It was deadly boring, but her present malaise was no fault of the host and hostess, who were well known for their elite private parties. The guest list was exclusive, the food excellent, and the conversation always lively and full of wit.

She might as well admit it—she was restless because *he* was not here, and not likely to be. It was impossible a man like Raphael would be invited. Even if he were, it was well into the evening, and *no one* came late to one of the Brunlys' functions.

Still, she kept craning her neck to see over the heads of the guests, watching for a head taller than the rest with a shock of blond-streaked hair spilling rakishly onto a high brow.

Desdemona gave her daughter a squeeze and a smile. "I want you to have fun tonight. It is going to be a very special night." Her gaze shifted and she exclaimed in a voice that was uncharacteristically shrill, "Here is Simon with our drinks."

He looked especially fine this evening. She wasn't certain why, but his eyes seemed to contain a bit more intensity, and there was this secretive little smile on his lips ever since he had arrived at the house to accompany them to the party.

"Madam," he said, handing Desdemona her punch. To Julia, he said, "There is a full moon tonight, and the air is exceptionally mild. Would you care to take a turn in the gardens?"

Before Julia could respond, her mother rushed, "Oh, do, Julia. The Brunly gardens are absolutely fabulous. You must see them."

Casting her mother a puzzled look, she took Simon's arm and allowed him to lead her to the terrace. The night was indeed lovely, with a soft breeze thick with earthy dampness and the sweet scent of spring in its prime. Simon commented on it as they strode down the path lighted with torches stuck into the softened ground, and she murmured her agreement. Then he did something completely unlike him. He pulled her into a small alcove enclosed on three sides by tall hedges.

He laughed. "Do you think anyone saw us?"

She felt her body go rigid, felt her temper stir a bit. "Simon, what are you doing?"

"I thought we would want a bit of privacy for this." He took in a quick bracing breath. "The night is perfect, and you look so beautiful. Everything is right, Julia. I've spoken to your father and he's given his consent. Your parents are as excited about this as I am, and as I hope you will be, too."

To her astonishment, he knelt down on one knee. Taking her hand in his, he gazed up at her. His blue eyes were just in the path of the moonlight. They almost glowed. She was struck by his masculine beauty, by the sleek fashionableness of him.

He said, "I would be deeply honored if you, Julia Brodie, would consent to do me the honor of becoming my wife."

RAPHAEL ARRIVED AT the Brunlys' with his grandmother in tow. She was not pleased at all to be tardy. In tandem to his own black mood, the result was a combustible argument during the entire ride in the carriage.

He hadn't wanted to come, but his grandmother had insisted, something she rarely did. He supposed it was why he eventually agreed to bring her. He'd never admit it to anyone, but the old girl was about the only one on this earth who could get him to do something he didn't want to. It wasn't her disapproval that moved him but the simple fact that one had to make certain sacrifices for the sake of relation. The Countess usually didn't require much from him, so he acquiesced once in a while. But only occasionally, and never cheerfully.

Imagine, therefore, his wicked delight to find that the Brodies were also in attendance. It completely reversed his simmering rage. He spotted the sister and the mother. Where was Julia? Some place close. Yes. Now he could feel it. The air was charged, and he smiled secretively to himself.

The night was going to be more enjoyable than he had anticipated.

"Fontvilliers, I had no idea you would be here," Martinvale said, coming up to greet him.

Raphael was too busy scanning the faces around him to even glance at the man. "Is Julia here tonight?"

"She is with Simon, so you are out of luck."

"Nonsense. Luck is what you make of a situation." Stroking his chin, Raphael considered his options

It was excellent good fortune that delivered her into his hands tonight. Too bad Catherine was not here. He might launch into a "confession" he had cooked up, orchestrate a bit of a crisis with Catherine playing a plumb part. But the wretched woman was not likely to be participating any longer.

The impulse to go to her bed had been a disaster. She had received him ready enough, but even after several stiff whiskeys and a good deal of imagining on his part, her charms still seemed overblown, her seductive innuendoes monstrously infantile. He had been determined, however, to give his body release, if not satisfaction, but holding her in his arms, stripping off her stockings and untying his own cravat, he had realized that was not possible.

He had dressed and went to the door, all without a word of explanation. Pausing, he had looked back to see her with her golden hair atumble, her unbound breasts quivering with rage, her eyes wide and dark as pools of pitch. She was a gorgeous woman, and he had to wonder what was wrong with him.

He had apologized, which was unlike him, tried to explain, which he never did. He felt quite bad about the entire matter. She, however, sat silently as he assured her it was nothing to do with her, watching him with a bitter, knowing look.

If only she hadn't said, "There is another woman. It is *her*, isn't it?" He had been livid. It was all he could do not to tell her she was wrong, that the problem was not something so peurile as an infatuation with another, but that he simply didn't desire her and that she wasn't as charming as she thought herself.

Enough of his reason remained, however, for him to realize she was only speaking the truth. He left without a word, but his temper stayed tight.

All right. He accepted it. Julia Brodie was in his blood, like an infection, like a drug. The only cure was to take her as soon as possible.

And here he found himself at the same party.

His grandmother came to his side, touching his arm lightly. The look on her face was stiff. "I'm not well, Fontvilliers," she said. "I wish you to take me home." Her cunning must be slipping, he thought, for as soon as she spoke, her gaze slipped past him and she appeared decidedly anxious. "Immediately, please. I will not tolerate dawdling."

Still caught up in his plans, he cast an absent glance over to follow hers. Merely a group of men conversing—

Raphael's heart skidded to a stop.

The pressure of his grandmother's hand on his arm tightened. Her voice came to him as if from a great distance. "Let us go, Raphael. We can slip out unnoticed."

He shook her off.

Marquay looked much changed since the last time he had seen him. Older. His face was puffier, his jowls sagging in the way typical of those dedicated to dissolute living as they age under the burdens of their misuses. His eyes, once intense and brown, seemed smaller, faded, and sunken under thick brows that were knitted together as he caught sight of Raphael. He stopped in midsentence and stared back.

Raphael remained frozen. His mind refused to work. He could only fasten on that arrogant face while his pulse slammed into his temples like a dull ax.

Marquay started over. For one foolish moment, Raphael thought of spinning on his heels and fleeing. He suddenly felt overwhelmed, stifled, like he were becoming smaller somehow. Younger.

He glanced to his grandmother, who stood rigidly erect, anticipation etched in every line of her face. He couldn't stand the compassion he saw on that severe face, and he turned away, squaring his shoulders as the Marquis approached.

Marquay first regarded his mother-in-law. No words were spoken, not even for the sake of civility. The animosity between them throbbed for a moment before he turned to Raphael.

"Fontvilliers," Marquay said in a smooth, cultured voice, "I am only speaking to you because it would be noted by the wags if I did not. And since you would be unlikely to make the effort, as is proper, then I must, if only to avoid speculation." His smile was not warm, nor combative. Just bland, as if he were only marginally interested in making conversation.

Raphael's tone was measured, guarded. "How magnanimous of you. A dubious pleasure, sir. Do not expect me to be grateful."

The countess drew in a hissing breath. "Not here, Fontvilliers!"

"Not at all. I expect nothing from you, boy."

He heard his grandmother's skirts rustle as she hurried away. Martinvale hovered far enough away for them to conduct their conversation in private, and so Raphael indulged himself in a tone sharp with bitterness, a sign that the beasts were waking. "It has occurred to me from time to time that a word from you, and I would be disclaimed. I would end up with nothing and publicly named a bastard. I've often asked myself why you haven't done it."

Marquay's voice was less smooth. His eyes never left Raphael. "Because I cannot be *sure*," he barked, a bitter sound. "That will teach you to trust a woman. I wonder at your propensity to cling to their skirts. Imagine dancing in attendance to your grandmother at your age, and her being mother to that viper who is responsible for all of this in the first place."

"You are giving me advice?" Raphael's response came from somewhere even before he knew what he was going to say. "As far as I could ever tell, the only thing you thought any woman was good for was to knock them on their backs and give them a good plowing."

With a thin smile, his father replied, "Isn't it yours, as well? Or are you unmanned in the bedroom as well? I always had serious doubts about you, boy, after you failed so miserably in the man's world I tried to show you."

Raphael seethed inside, but outwardly, he remained calm. "I have no troubles with women, in any room, I assure you. Fortunately for me, I seem to be rather adept at attracting them, and it is so much cheaper than having to shell out a handful of coins for every little favor." Marquay's eyes flared wide. Raphael purred, "Perhaps it is because I do not share your fundamental loathing of their sex."

He had scored a hit. His father scowled. "First you scold

me for loving too many women, now accuse me of hating them."

"Fucking women is not loving them."

"Is that what you learned at Oxford? What philosopher espoused that particular wisdom?"

Somewhere in the back of his numbed brain, he thought it odd that his father would know he had studied the philosophies at university. Why would he have bothered to learn such a thing? However, he was not about to allow Marquay the offensive. "It is a simple logic. Allow me to explain. You see, what one desires but cannot have, one fears. What one fears, one must master. What one cannot master, one must destroy. Isn't that why you and Mother ripped each other to shreds every day in our cozy little chateau in the Loire Valley?"

Flustered, Marquay waved a hand in an attempt at disgust. "You are as worthless as you ever were, boy. A man my age takes some comfort in knowing that in this time of monumental change in the world, some things remain the same." He left without a farewell.

In his wake, Raphael found himself trembling and grateful that his grandmother had gone. It was like being caught with one's trousers down—the less witnesses the better.

Martinvale stepped up and grabbed a handful of Raphael's coat, pulling him over to a door. "I am getting us out of here," Martinvale said. It was not often Raphael allowed another to take control. This time, he did not argue.

They entered the hall, running into a throng of people. The sound of applause burst upon them suddenly. Raphael started. "What the devil is that?" Looking up, he stopped in his tracks. "Martinvale," he murmured, staring at the couple on the stairs.

It was Simon Blake. By his side was Julia Brodie.

Simon held a glass of champagne. People in the crowd were raising their own glasses and shouting, "Here, here!"

Julia smiled. Was she truly so lovely as to make a man's knees week just to look upon her? He recalled that when he first saw her that night at the Suffolk mansion, he hadn't been particularly moved. And yet now, with the embers still glowing of the biting rage his father had stirred, he had to hold himself back from rushing up the steps and snatching her away from Simon's side.

Blake was speaking. "And to the Brunlys', I would like to extend my thanks. Let us all raise our glasses in appreciation for their having consented to allow Miss Brodie and myself to make the announcement at their home, in front of this illustrious company."

Another chorus rang out. Raphael frowned, puzzled. He took a step toward the couple. Martinvale pulled him back.

"Can't you see what is happening? They have announced their engagement."

"What? That is nonsense." Raphael felt as if a blow had connected to his chest. His head reeled. "Utter nonsense."

Simon turned to Julia and a look passed between them. Several people rushed them as they descended the risers together, and a flurry of exclamations rippled through the room.

"Raphael," Martinvale said softy in his friend's ear, "let it go. See how happy they are. I'm begging you, don't destroy that. Let the wager go, or choose another to prove yourself. Leave Julia Brodie be."

She did look happy. Perfectly happy, with the handsome baronet on her arm. And him all smiles. Triumphant. He thought she was his.

But he would not take her away from Raphael. Julia Brodie was *his*, Goddamn it. He needed her!

He needed her—to win the wager.

"No," Raphael growled.

"It is too late. They are already promised."

"It is not too late," he shot back, a bit too loudly. "I have until Ascot."

A few people turned to look. Raphael cleared his throat and pretended to adjust his sleeve. "I have until Ascot," he repeated in a lower tone only Martinvale could hear. "But I will have her under me, screaming her devotion to me and only me long before then, my friend."

Chapter Eight

THE NOTE READ: *I must see you immediately. Come to the park today at noon with Strathford.*

It was not signed, but Julia knew it was from Raphael.

She also knew she should tear it into a hundred pieces and throw it into the fire.

She was betrothed. She belonged to Simon—it was official, and she had no business engaging in this "friendship" which was completely inappropriate, and which Simon would certainly disapprove.

She placed the note with the other, in the drawer in the secretary desk in her bedroom.

At luncheon she ate sparingly. Her mother remarked on the high flush of excitement in Julia's cheeks, but supplied her own reason. "We're all so thrilled about the engagement, dear," she murmured confidentially, patting Julia's hand.

Looking down at the emerald and diamond betrothal ring Simon had given her, Julia continued to brood.

When the Marquess of Strathford arrived, Julia hung back in the doorway of the parlor, still caught in indecision, while Laura slipped on a spencer. Julia eyed him speculatively, in his smartly cut coat, crisp trousers, and polished boots. He was very much the rake, he even carried himself with an air of arrogance that grated on her. He was, however, discrete. There was no sign he knew of the letter his friend had sent to her, or that he was expecting her to accompany himself and Laura on the strut except that his gaze lingered on her a bit too long when he bade his farewells. Then again, it might only have been her imagination.

Torn with indecision, she watched the two of them until they were all the way to the curb. Laura was so happy, so unabashed about it, and in contrast, Julia felt miserable. She couldn't do it. Every bit of sense in her told her to stay exactly where she was, but she simply couldn't tolerate the idea of disappointing him—or herself? She fetched her shawl and hurried out just as the footman was pulling away the step from the side of the carriage. "Do you mind if I come along?" she asked breathlessly.

Strathford smiled and welcomed her in, sealing her certainty that she was making a terrible mistake. And yet, she climbed in next to her frowning sister, who did nothing to hide her pique at Julia's intrusion, and settled her tension-stiffened back against the squabs.

Laura's spirits recovered quickly, and thank goodness for it. Her chatter filled the time in the carriage, leaving Julia to her own thoughts as they pulled into the park. They paraded by the Serpentine, then turned into another lane.

"I thought we would visit the ducks," Strathford said as they drew to a stop. "The fowl in this park have absurdly human personalities. I think it will amuse."

They found a bench well back from the trampled mud at the water's edge. Julia sat and stared at the wild geese without really seeing them. She would have a reckoning with her own wickedness for having come, but for now she pushed those thoughts aside and wondered why Raphael had sent for her.

She had no explanation for the primitive thrill she felt whenever she was with him, the vague restlessness when she was not. Sometimes it worked to tell herself she was merely happy to see a scoundrel making peace with his errant ways, the same as any humane, caring person would be. Even she found this a bit thin, however, and the comfort it gave her never lasted long.

A gentle tap on her shoulder startled her. Strathford leaned over to whisper in her ear. "He's over by the birch trees, waiting for you."

She swallowed hard and nodded. Strathford backed away quickly, resuming his casual stance behind Laura, who was laughing at a pair of geese aggressively charging at their fellows. Squawking most terribly, they ran headlong, beaks open in a way that seemed to Julia to be more nasty than funny. Laura noticed nothing as Julia slipped away.

Raphael was reclining against a white-barked trunk, feet crossed, hands tucked up under his arms, looking in the opposite direction. He didn't seem to hear her approach.

Pausing, Julia tried to settle the sudden grip of emotion that seized her by the throat at the sight of him. She'd have known him anywhere. No one had shoulders that broad, nor quite that air of insouciance in the languid positioning of his body.

She said his name, and he turned. His streaked hair was tousled by the wind, spilling over that noble brow in a way that made her wince with the need to smooth it down.

Pushing off the tree trunk, he stood before her. "Thank you for coming."

She had decided in the carriage that a straightforward approach was best. "You said in your note you needed to see me."

"Yes." He took a step closer. His eyes were vivid green. They burned into hers, as brilliant as the emerald Simon had given her.

Blanching at the disloyal thought, she said, "Are you in trouble?"

He moved closer still. She had the most absurd sensation of being stalked. There was an air about him today of recklessness. And danger. Deadly danger for a woman who had promised her troth to another.

She was uncomfortable with his proximity, but forced

herself to meet his gaze with a willful lift of her chin. "Worried about me?" he asked. "Why does that please me so?"

Lowering her eyes, she said, "Please, if you will just tell me what the matter of concern is. I should not linger alone with you. I have risked enough already."

"Very well." She fancied she could feel the brush of his breath against her temple. He wasn't that close, surely. She didn't dare look to find out. "I am in need of you as a friend, Julia. You see, trouble has found me, despite my best efforts to make a better show of my life, and I find myself somewhat at a loss. What would the wags say to that, do you think? The infamous Fontvilliers a doddering mess."

She did glance up then and, yes, he was very, very close. Intrigued, she urged, "Raphael, please tell me what has happened."

"I will. But I must have your assurance that you will keep it in the strictest confidence. Not even Simon can know."

"Of course. Not a word will I speak of this, I swear it."

Closing his eyes for a moment, he inhaled deeply. "You remember the Lady Catherine Drummond?" Opening his eyes, he saw her nod and continued, "I was trying to help out a friend by escorting her about, taking her mind off the disgraceful gentleman to whom she had formed a most unfortunate association. If you will forgive a bit of vanity on my part, even we rakes have a code of honor. The man with whom she had become enamored has none. Catherine's family were monstrously worried that she would compromise herself. I have known the family for years and offered my services."

"It was very kind of you to care enough to become involved." She hoped to sound aloof, approving. Instead, she feared he could hear the relief in her voice at finding his role with the woman whom she had frequently spied as his companion was not one of an amorous nature.

"Oh, no, sweet lady." He shook his head woefully. "It was wretchedly inadequate. You see, I thought I *was* helping. Then, the lady confided that she had transferred her feelings to me."

In a careful tone, she asked, "And you did not return her feelings?"

"No. Dear God, I wish I could. By not doing so, I destroyed her."

"You cannot take responsibility for your lack of feeling. She must understand that."

He feigned regret as he continued. "She does not. That night at the Suffolk ball, there was a terrible scene in the carriage on the way. Catherine threatened to go back to her former admirer, to offer him her innocence. She was hurt and she wanted to punish me. I didn't take her seriously. I left her alone until both our tempers settled. But later I began to worry. She had gone missing, you see, and I wondered if she was capable of going through with her threat. I went looking for her. When I found her, it was too late. She had made good on her threat, you see. I had failed her."

"Oh, no." Julia pressed her hands over her mouth.

"I told you that night that justice had been served, and it had."

Raphael stole a sideways glance to gauge the effect of his words. They seemed to have her in a very satisfying state of distress. He was doing an admirable job of delivering his story convincingly, but it was a chore to keep his mind on the task and his hands off her. She looked so lovely, and he was so hot for her it was boiling his brain.

"You blame yourself?" she asked, looking at him with such compassion in her eyes, he almost felt a pang of guilt. What a shame to despoil that tender trust.

"But how can I *not* feel responsible? Don't you see the wretched irony? I was helpless to prevent someone I cared about from descending into the very depravity in which I once reveled." He gave her a soft smile. "That was what I was thinking when I went to the terrace. I was so caught in my thoughts, I didn't see you. I almost knocked you over."

"You were quite beside yourself that night, but that was some time ago. I am at a loss to understand why those events vex you so acutely now."

"Ah, there are consequences to every evil deed. Even

though I resumed my duties toward Catherine after that night, I could not undo my error. I left her alone that one time when she most needed me, and that failure sealed a dreadful mistake that can never be undone. You see, Julia, Catherine is with child."

She covered her mouth. Her eyes blazed, rounded orbs of golden fire.

"I am going to marry her," he continued, trying to control his rising excitement. She was so open, so guileless, and she believed him completely. God, all he had to do was reach out for her, pluck her like a ripe rose, and she would deny him nothing.

"But do you love her?" she demanded with surprising vigor.

"The issue of love is of no consequence." He watched her closely. Something made him say, "You still believe in that, don't you? Love? Ah, you poor little thing. It is a fool's game. A lie, a cheat, a pretty tale with as much substance as Father Christmas or Queen Mab of the Faeries."

"Surely you do not mean that," she said, taken aback.

"I do," he answered truthfully. "Indeed I know it most profoundly. And do not look at me so. It is I who pity you, for your inevitable disillusionment is one I would not wish upon a bitter enemy."

She shook her head as if to clear her confusion. "But, Raphael, this situation is far worse than lack of affection between yourself and Lady Catherine. To raise another man's child as your own, have him inherit before your own sons—" She broke off, her eyes speaking volumes.

Yes. To raise another man's child as one's own. It was . . . what? Not done? Intolerable? Marquay would agree, no doubt. Darkly, he said, "Most men would be repelled at the idea."

She seemed at a loss, then did something that shocked him. She took his hand. Twining her gloved fingers in his, she looked up at him, clear golden eyes staring straight into his. An extraordinary thought occurred to him. What would it be like to have her look at him like that—for real?

The exhilaration he had felt just seconds ago emptied out of his body.

This wasn't real. It was all lies, or at least most of it was. His self-loathing, that was not completely falsified. He had a healthy reservoir of contempt for himself from which to draw upon, and had ruthlessly made use of it. But what if . . . what if he looked back into those eyes and knew they were really seeing *him*?

The anguish in her face left him feeling strange all of a sudden, as if worms were slithering in the pit of his belly. It was an unfamiliar sensation, this tinge of remorse, this vague dissatisfaction.

He crushed it and closed the gap between them.

Her eyes widened, alarm registering on her features. She dropped his hand.

He spoke softly, treading with care. Because if he didn't kiss her soon, he was going to implode. "I needed to tell you. It seemed the most important thing left for me to do once the decision was made, to have you understand." Stripping off his glove, he raised a naked hand to her cheek. One stroke, and her eyes drifted shut. "I wonder why it was so vital. Sometimes when I'm with you, I don't understand myself."

A slight frown drew the delicate arches of her brow down, and she shook her head as if warning him not to breach the thin line of propriety they had thus far managed to avoid crossing. He smiled, knowing she was now ruled by her senses, and those were in his command.

Forget that everything she believed him to be was a lie. Forget the bitterness in acknowledging that. She was here, in his arms, at last—at last. That was all that mattered.

Leaning forward, he brushed his lips lightly against her smooth forehead. His nose filled with her scent. It had driven him nearly mad, the need to drink in the sensual, evocative blend of subtle spice and jasmine.

"You have become very important to me, Julia." He slipped his hand about her waist and drew her closer. His breath caught as this caused her weight to shift and her breasts brushed up against his chest. "Our friendship . . . it is more. To me, you are so much more." She made a token effort to resist. He tightened his hold. "No. Let me say it. Just this once, then I'll never speak of it again."

Her rigidity melted and her body turned supple, pliant, easily pressed along the length of his. His hand slid up her back, to the nape of her neck to cradle it as he tipped her head back to gaze into her face.

She made no further move to pull away. Seeming dazed, she merely stared back at him with a blend of anxiety and anticipation.

He was almost dizzy with excitement. "My feeling for you is not simple. Nor is it permissible. But . . ." He blinked, trying to focus. He forgot what he was to say. That cat-eyed gaze had him spellbound. That mouth beckoned, draining him of thought. The soft contour of her breasts pressed tightly up against his chest emptied him of purpose.

"I cannot think!" she protested.

Think? Who could think? "No, no. You must not try to think."

That damnable detached voice in the back of his head started in on him, warning that it would be far more effective if he left her now, and just recompense as well. Yes, leave her wanting, aching, as he had been these days past. Let her suffer as she'd made him suffer. If he pulled back before his lips touched hers, it would decimate her.

It was exactly the right reasoning, except he simply couldn't resist. No man could.

He kissed her.

~~~~~

THE MOMENT BEFORE his lips closed over hers, Julia felt a wild burst of panic flower in her chest. If he had hesitated but a moment, if his mouth had not come up against hers right then, she might have found the means to flee.

Or perhaps not. Why would she flee when it was the last

thing she wanted to do? Every inch of her body strained forward, seeking to know what Raphael Giscard's kiss would be like.

He wasn't gentle. His was a kiss of passion, tinged with something desperate and demanding. From the first moment of contact, her breath was completely gone. Shimmers coursed through her in a pulse timed to the beat of her heart. The last vestiges of rationality fled.

Slanting his mouth, he moved his lips against hers in a play of touch that left her gasping and sent her headlong on a tide of heady sensation.

Simon had never kissed her like this.

Then his tongue touched her bottom lip, and he opened his mouth. The shock of what he was doing gave her pause. It was so very exciting, she didn't think a moment of stopping him. Yielding, she was immediately subject to his ravenous tongue, touching, tasting, exploring the inside of her mouth. He groaned softly, tightening his hold on her waist, pulling her so that her hips slammed up against the strong sinew of his thighs.

Simon would never do a thing like this.

His tongue plunged deep, entangled itself with hers, stroking with some primitive rhythm that tightened the tips of her breasts into aching peaks. Her knees went weak and she clung to him for support. The sound of their breathing was labored, loud; his mouth consumed her. She made a small sound, a kind of whimper and curled her fists tightly around his shoulders.

Simon's kisses had never reduced her to this.

Simon. My God, what was she doing? She fought for breath as she twisted away. "Please, stop. We must stop."

His chest rose and fell, timed with her own rapid breathing, and his face was like a thundercloud, only inches from hers. He didn't release her. "A man of honor would, wouldn't he? The fool would offer a pretty apology and let you slip through his fingers. I am not a fool."

She tried to turn away, but he held her face in his large hands, not letting her go. He seemed to know that if she could escape that green gaze, she would have a chance. "Nor are you a gentleman," she accused.

She felt the pressure of his fingers increase reflexively. His whole body seemed to blanche for a moment, and then he was once again his arrogant, mocking self. "Damn right, I am not a gentleman. I don't care about you, or your reputation, or your promise to Simon or all the dictates of this idiotic society in which we live. I only care about myself, what *I* want. Do you hear what I am telling you?"

"You are frightening me—"

"Oh, you are right to be frightened."

"Let me go. This is wrong, this is madness. You are to marry Catherine, and I am promised to Simon."

"You belong to me in a way you will never belong to him." His hips thrust suggestively, and the ridge of hardness rested with startling heat against her abdomen. His breath fanned over her face. "Did you think I should hide my desire for you? Look at me, Julia. That's right, right into my eyes. What is it you see, I wonder? A figment of your imagination, a conjuring of what you would have me be, or the real man—flawed and imperfect? I want you to know the truth for once. I am showing you exactly what I am."

She opened her mouth to reply, but nothing came out in the fraction of a moment before his mouth sealed over hers once again. He bent her back over his arms, arching her so that her breasts jutted out against her chest, making her feel exposed and at his mercy. Then his mouth left hers and traced a fiery path down the column of her neck, leaving her whimpering as snakes of pleasure slithered over her flesh, making her skin exquisitely sensitive. His hands moved up from her waist. Slowly, with a frustratingly feathery touch, he trailed his fingers across her rib cage, then cupped a heaving breast in each palm and lay his cheek in the valley in between.

She ground her teeth together in agony of indecision. Her brain was screaming for her to *run!* but her limbs refused to obey.

"I do not play gentle, Julia." His thumb grazed her aching

peak, ripping a sob from her as pleasure jolted through her. She splayed her hands against his chest, intending to push him away but found herself gripping his hard shoulders. Searing heat ripped through her, emptying her of the will to resist.

"And I don't play nice." He flicked his tongue into the crevice between her breasts.

"Please," she whispered brokenly. "Don't do this to me. We are in public, for God's sake. What have I done to you that you would humiliate me like this?"

Jerking up his head, his eyes caught fire in the slanting sunlight that fell over the planes of his face. He broke off, releasing her and turning away. The back of his hand came up to his mouth as he squeezed his eyes closed. She could see his profile, that classic silhouette as she pulled in great gulps of air.

"I cannot do it," he rasped.

She wrapped her arms around herself. Her teeth were clattering, she was trembling so violently. Her lips felt sore, bruised. Her soul felt the same. She was hot, burning inside as if she would be incinerated on the spot and nothing would be left of her but a scorch mark on the tender shoots of spring grass.

What had he done to her?

When he spoke again, his voice was harsher, louder, sharper. "Get out of here," he ordered. "This is why you do not dally with men outside the bounds of what is proper—" He broke off, shaking his head. His hands raked through his hair in violent strokes. "No, God, it is not you. It is I who am at fault. My pride, my vanity . . ."

He struggled visibly. She only watched, caught in a trance as the sensations his kiss had evoked died out and her mind slowly returned to normal functioning.

"This can never happen again. Never." His vehemence frightened her. His eyes blazed, his jaw worked. He wouldn't look at her.

For a long moment the only sound was the rough saw of each rapid breath as he inhaled, exhaled. When he finally turned to her, his expression was fierce, and full of bitterness. "This is the last time we can see each other. We both have our lives to return to, people that need us, depend on us. This is the last time we can speak. I cannot trust myself any longer." He paused, glaring at her. "Say something, damn it all."

Say something? Her heart was screaming an incoherent wail, her mind was numb. What should she say?

She opened her mouth. To her utter horror, she felt the hot sting of tears in her eyes. "I can't . . ." *What?* Can't leave? Can't stay?

Even she didn't know.

He scowled. "Do you not see how useless it is? Our worlds are too different. I am not at all what you need. I never could be. It would be disaster. Now"—he paused, drawing himself up to his full height—"tell me goodbye."

A sudden sob welled up in her throat, catching with a sound like a wounded kitten. She never said a word.

He walked away, leaving her quite alone. More alone than she had ever been in her life, it felt.

She had to pull herself together. She had to understand what was happening to her. Staying right where she was, she focused on getting her head to clear and think of what to do next.

It was a full fifteen minutes later and all she could come up with was to return to Laura.

Chapter Nine

"MY FAMILY IS growing annoyed," Strathford complained in Raphael's study a few nights later. They had gathered here in anticipation of going out later on, probably to Whites, but it was unlikely now. Two bottles of whiskey were down already and a third was well under way, and all of them were the worse for it.

Strathford's mood had worsened with each emptied glass. "My mother is set on Lucy for me and is increasingly impatient with my dallying with the Brodie girl."

"Then drop her," Raphael replied blithely. "I no longer need you."

Atvers hooted, then piped down immediately upon receiving a dark look from Raphael. The insipid twit knew he was on thin ice. Raphael wondered why he tolerated him. He'd never really liked him.

"That sure of yourself, are you?" Strathford goaded. "Ascot is barely a month off, Fontvilliers." He stood and filled his glass, emptied it, and filled it again.

Raphael watched him carefully. Strathford's veneer of civility was thinning as he drank more and more. "I know exactly when opening day is. I no longer need you close to Laura Brodie. Drop her."

"Thank God," Martinvale muttered, taking a long draught.

Strathford turned his frown onto the other man. "What do you care on the matter? You don't have your rod stiff for her yourself, do you?"

"My God, Strathford, you're disgusting!" Martinvale declared.

"Not that I'd blame you. I admit, she's a pretty thing. The other day, her hair struck me as particularly attractive when it caught the sunlight a certain way. It is the palest shade of blond." His smile was lopsided.

Martinvale peered at him over the rim of his glass. "You were out and about in the daytime, were you? I always assumed you slept the afternoons away, emerging at twilight. Like a vampire."

Undisturbed, Strathford went on, "I was given to a sudden fantasy of it unbound, around her naked body. I confess I did a good deal of imagining that day, while Fontvilliers was trying his best to get his hands up her sister's skirts."

Raphael willed himself to stay cold and unaffected by the reference to the day in the park when he had met Julia. He had pressed his advantage and won an unanticipated boon. That kiss . . . it was . . . ah, it was a magnificent moment. A glorious fulfillment of everything he had anticipated. The carnal temptations had been difficult to resist. What had happened afterward—that crazy, snarling attack of insanity that had him blathering like some dough-headed idiot, he didn't understand. He wasn't sure he wanted to. It had been disturbing.

"You are not thinking of bedding her!" Martinvale exclaimed.

"Why not? Am I not good enough for her?" The edge to Strathford's voice cut away the pretense of casual amusement.

Atvers snickered, drowning the sound in his cup.

Raphael regarded the lot of them with impatience. "Leave off seeing Miss Brodie, Strathford. And stop acting like your fraternal instincts have been insulted, Martinvale. The girl is not your concern."

Strathford put his glass down slowly and turned his bleary eyes toward his host. "Nor is she yours, Fontvilliers, and I resent your high-handedness. I am not indebted to obey you, like some medieval peasant." He advanced, almost threateningly, and drew his lips back in a sneer. "I tell you, I cannot wait to see you brought down. So high, so mighty, and so arrogant—the inimitable Viscount de Fontvilliers shall finally be shown for the blowhard he is."

There was short, intense silence. Raphael broke it with his insulting drawl. "So you have something to prove, do you? I had wondered at your motivations for offering the wager."

"Damned right. When you fail, I'll make certain everyone knows. You will be the laughingstock of the *ton*, Raphael. Maybe that will teach you a bit of humility, which is a dose of medicine you are, in my estimation, sorely in need of."

"Wretched plan, as I aim to win. And you, old friend, have just declared yourself no friend at all. I suspected all along that this was war."

"I am sick of your friendship. You have Martinvale and Atvers—that simpleton!—fawning and tripping over themselves in admiration for you. You preside over them like some despotic ruler with your delusions of superiority. You are not better than the rest of us, Fontvilliers, and I'll be damned if I'll scrape and bow before you."

Strathford started to prowl as he continued. "Not three weeks ago, Julia Brodie accepted Blake's proposal. She did so, despite your clever little manipulations, Fontvilliers, because she understands the fundamental difference between our sort and hers. In short, my good man, she is too good for you. She inhabits a world we can only stand outside of and peer into, like starving urchins with their noses pressed up against the poulterer's shop window."

That particular image struck Raphael hard.

It was exactly like that. Longing, knowing he was unworthy. Deep, clawing wanting.

Reaching for his coat, the marquess continued as he shrugged it sloppily onto his shoulders. "We can declaim it, deride, ridicule, and pretend to denounce it, but it changes nothing," Strathford snarled. "It is a fact, Fontvilliers, that you are no better than the rest of us. There are women in this world men like us cannot touch. I learned that a long time ago. It is time you, too, must learn."

For Raphael, these words were like a swarm of wasps, stinging a thousand places, filling his head with an infernal buzz.

Strathford shouted, words slightly slurred, "I hereby declare I am no longer the minion of the Viscount de Fontvilliers!" He grinned and shot a look over his shoulder. "And I'll have the chit, Martinvale. I may have to marry Lucy, but I'll get my piece of pretty Miss Laura." He paused, then smiled. "You can wager on it if you like."

"Why don't you leave before Fontvilliers kills you," Martinvale said. "Or I do."

Executing a wavering bow, Strathford stomped out.

Atvers laughed and Raphael tried unsuccessfully to quirk up a corner of his mouth.

She's too good for you.

Raphael's throat was too dry. Damn, he felt wretched.

He was tired of this waiting, that was all. His body needed release.

She inhabits a world we can only peer into, like starving urchins.

"Another drink?" Martinvale offered.

Raphael held out his glass. His eye caught his friend's careful glance as he poured the amber liquid nearly to the top.

Martinvale said, "Strathford is wrong. You don't need to prove anything."

Shaking his head, Raphael countered, "Oh, but he is not wrong. I've always known it, Martinvale. She *is* too good for me."

"I am surprised to hear you say that. I was sometimes under the impression that you hated her."

Startled, Raphael asked, "Why?"

"She deserves a good life, Fontvilliers. She deserves to be happy. She's never done anything to you, or to anyone else to merit what you have in store for her."

A sharp, sour feeling tightened his throat. Raphael curled his lip and defended himself sharply. "She is happy. I am making her very happy. She enjoys our encounters. What, did you think I was assaulting her, forcing my odious attentions on her?"

Martinvale blinked, somewhat surprised at the vehemence of Raphael's response. "I have no doubt of the effectiveness of your charming methods. But you are using her. It is cruel, Raphael. You can't be unmoved by what will happen to her once you have your way." When he got no response, he demanded in a passionate voice, "Don't you feel the slightest bit of guilt? My God, Fontvilliers, are you human?"

"Human enough to want an exciting woman just the same as any man." His brows drew down in a pronounced V. "Why should it not be me to have her? What reason on earth can you give me to step aside for Blake? What gives him the right and not me?"

"Because he loves her," Martinvale countered. "And she loves him."

That cut. It sliced a swatch of pain right through the center of him, quick and clean and throbbing so much that it left Raphael breathless for a moment. And he sneered all the harder because of it. "Love?" He almost choked on the word. "How can she love him when she wants *me*?" Forcing himself to calm, he added, "But that is what we are here to establish—this myth known as *love*."

"She wants you?" Martinvale shook his head. "How can she want you? Have you forgotten that all you've done is trick her? When have you ever spoken anything close to truth to her? The man she finds interesting—is any of him remotely genuine?" His voice sharpened and he had the audacity to look angry. "Want you? She doesn't know the first thing about you, man." He strode for the door, pausing only long enough to retrieve his hat.

Leaving Raphael with Atvers, who for once stayed wisely silent.

Raphael rose, poured himself another drink, then sat down again, but he didn't take a drop.

Martinvale might be correct. Raphael would admit that. Hadn't he himself felt it, when he had her in his arms—that regret that she wasn't truly looking at *him*? And that stupid impulse he had allowed to twist him in knots to show her something of himself, the ugliness, the greed inside him. Would she still want him then? Christ, he had almost frightened her off and ruined everything.

And guilt? What kind of man could look into those golden eyes and lie and not feel guilt? He didn't know if he should be relieved or ashamed that that man was not him.

But he could no more stop this than he could a charging bull. It was part of what Strathford had said. He, Raphael Giscard, Viscount de Fontvilliers, would prove himself immune to the injustice that separated his sordid life from the charmed existences of those God favored. But part of it was that he had to prove himself a man fully in control of his own destiny—inviolate, invulnerable, dependent on no one, not even the stirrings of his own appetites. His father's painstaking tutoring had driven home the importance of being impervious to any other human being.

Even someone like Julia Brodie.

And as for the original wager—the ridiculous notion of love—if the blasted thing did exist, even in the imaginations of poor deluded souls, then he would triumph over that as well.

Eᴀᴄʜ ᴅᴀʏ Jᴜʟɪᴀ kept an eye on the salver in the center hall used for posts. She was very careful about it. She would walk by and glance down oh-so-casually, searching for her name written in large scrawled letters that bespoke of an impatient man, an undisciplined man. Not Simon's much more pleasing neat, blocked letters.

It was Raphael for whom she yearned. She simply waited and waited until one day there it was, among the other correspondence addressed to Papa and Mother and the duke and duchess, written in his hand which she had memorized from reading over and over his other two letters.

Snatching it up, she ducked into the cloak room and ripped open the seal. There were only three words, but they brought her to her knees.

It read: *Come to me.*

After the shock, after the first sweep of tidal thrills, there was blistering fury. It came, hot and swift, to set Julia's blood to boiling.

How dare he summon her like a common trollop. *How dare he!*

He had gone too far, even for him. A scoundrel he might be, but even the lowest of that kind knew his place. She was a gently-bred miss, a member of the *ton* by grace if not by breeding, and *an engaged woman.* It was unthinkable to ask her to venture out alone to call upon a man!

How typical of the infamous Fontvilliers, how unfeeling and insensitive to the delicate observance of manners of the respectable world. *He* didn't observe them, being a rake of the first class. Could he really expect her not to?

Folding the letter, she slipped it inside her bodice.

He had been pursuing her all along and she . . . she had been so flattered, so filled with excitement that she had allowed each infraction to notch her forward. To this.

Come to me. It didn't even seem insane to think of going—that was the madness of it all. A part of her was exhilarated by it. She had allowed him to bring her to the

point where she could rationalize the most outrageous behavior because it was what she wanted to do.

Oh, yes, it was what she wanted. What could she have
been thinking to have allowed it to go this far?

That was the problem. She hadn't been thinking, not
since the moment she—literally!—fell into his arms.

Taking out his note, she read it again. In her mind's eye
a vision of him flashed—heavy-lidded eyes, arrogant nose,
the sensually curved mouth. A thick rope of desire twisted
deep inside her stomach.

She pressed her hand over her breast and closed her
eyes, determined to stay resolved.

⁓

I T WAS ONE-THIRTY in the morning before Raphael admitted Julia wasn't coming.

He was alone in the house. His grandmother was gone
for a fortnight, up in Yorkshire with friends. That left the
house depressingly silent as the mantel clock mocked him
with each passing minute.

The toll of half past the hour brought him surging up
out of his chair and raking both hands through his hair. He
paced a tight circle, paused, thinking desperately as to what
had gone wrong.

Clearly, he had miscalculated.

A short laugh escaped him, a huff of self-deprecation.
Serves him right, he thought. Maybe she'd prove as stal-
wart as she needed to be. And maybe he wasn't as irresistible as he thought.

But he couldn't let it lie. Lord help him, he couldn't
walk away from her even if he wanted to. She held everything in the palm of her hand, and so he must hold her in
the palm of his. It was as set in his mind as his intention
to keep breathing, and as vital.

What to do, what to do?

He admonished himself, realizing he was forgetting his
own lessons. Patience—titillate, intrigue. Don't push. Step

over the line, and beckon, and she'd come of her own volition.

Yes. So he would wait.

But not with patience. He'd long since run out. Meanwhile, he'd give her something to remind her that she was not out of his thoughts for a moment.

―――――――

JULIA THANKED GOD no one was about when Mary came into the study with the note and the rose. Julia sometimes sneaked off to read, but it was a common known secret among the servants just where they could find her on most occasions.

On this one, she was having very little success concentrating on the book in her hand. The sound of Mary's arrival brought her with a start out of the thoughts that had put themselves between her mind and the words printed on the page.

"This came for you, Miss," Mary said, bringing Julia the gifts while smiling happily for her mistress.

Mary assumed they were from Simon. But Julia knew the minute she saw the rose identical to the one he sent at the theater. And the note, in that bold, impatient script.

"Thank you," she managed calmly, taking the items.

"It's a lovely rose, miss," Mary said, then left her alone.

Julia tore open the letter. It read, *I shall wait again tonight.*

Her hands started to tremble.

Resolving to write him a smart reprimand, she dashed to the duke's desk and picked up the quill from the well. From the top drawers, she drew out a clean sheet of paper.

She gave up on the idea as soon as she set the pen to the paper. She simply could not summon the right words. She took up the book again, but it was no use.

After tea and a rest, she was still as agitated as ever, but managed to dress and ready herself for the night's obligation. A soiree with Simon.

When had she started to think of her outings with Simon as obligation?

———

RAPHAEL PACED. IT was only half past ten, but he didn't really expect her to come. Bloody hell, what was happening—how could he have misjudged so badly?

His mind contrived any number of ideas to rectify the situation, and summarily rejected every one of them. He wrote three separate notes to be delivered on the morrow, tearing each one up as soon as it was written.

No, he had to trust his instincts. If he pursued her, he'd send her fleeing, maybe for good. Let her take her time. She'd come to him eventually.

But what if she didn't?

Could he let her go? He should. Lose graciously, concede the wager, leave off thinking of her and put her out of his mind. His blood.

He didn't think he could do it, though. In fact, he knew he'd never manage it.

———

WHEN THE LETTER came on the third day, Julia was expecting it. She had dreaded it all day . . . and looked forward to it. Despite the tremor of delight that came with its delivery, she had already made up her mind that this was impossible. She couldn't have these things being delivered every day—someone was bound to take note eventually. Raphael had to stop. She had to make him.

Did she dare go to him, as he commanded? If not, how else could she speak with him? She was hardly in a position to hire a carriage on her own and travel in broad daylight to his residence. She would have to do it. Oh, Lord, it made her insides mush just to imagine it.

Unfolding the note, she felt her pulse jump. One word, scrawled with all the arrogance in the world. *Tonight.*

Oh, he was so sure of himself, was he? Yes—she would go to him, but with a mind to putting this business—and him—out of her life for good. A sick, wrenching feeling pressed into her chest, but she threw her chin out and told herself to stop being such a ninny.

She went into the parlor with her mother and sisters. They were looking at sketches for new dresses. The mood was high, and as soon as she entered, Marie flew at her, waving a picture drawn on a card.

"Isn't this lovely, Julia? Mama says I can have it made up for your wedding. But I have to have blue, because she says you are going to have yellow."

Julia tried to smile. "Yellow?"

Desdemona was frowning at a dress design. "Oh, something bright and pretty."

"A soft, creamy shade better suits my coloring."

She sighed, as if greatly put upon, and looked up. "Will you never trust me? I know what suits you best, Julia. I am your mother." She paused, then added, "What is wrong with you? You looked peaked."

Julia pressed her hands to her cheeks. "Do I? I-I suppose I'm not feeling very well."

"Go lie down, then. We have a ball to attend tonight."

With her throat alarmingly tight, Julia fled into seclusion, fearing the pricking at her eyes heralded an outbreak of tears. As soon as she entered her room, she took out Raphael's note and put it in the escritoire with the others.

Tonight. Yes. Tonight was the night for goodbyes.

Chapter Ten

THE FRONT DOOR to the Raphael's Mayfair residence was opened by a footman in a powdered wig. Before Julia could speak, he said. "The countess is in the country for the weekend."

Swallowing against the lump of panic lodged in her throat, Julia said, "I would like to see the viscount, if he is at home. Tell him Miss Brodie wishes to speak with him."

He didn't reflect any shock as he said, "Very good, Miss Brodie. This way, please." The servant turned and led Julia inside the house. She hesitated, taking in a shaking breath to brace her nerves, and entered.

The smooth manner of the servant was disturbing. It made Julia think that the appearance of women clamoring an audience with his master at odd hours of the night was not uncommon. Shame flashed hot, taking turns with the giddy rush of excitement as she entered the marble-floored hall, passed through it, and headed to a parlor just off the base of the grand staircase.

The town house was magnificent, but it lacked the warming touches a woman might have added. If she were in a different frame of mind, she might have been impressed with the fine statuary placed about, the boldly hued paintings of dramatic scenes from history, myth, and Bible. She paused at one such painting, a startling depiction of Judith bending over a sleeping Holofernese, his hair held fast in her hands, her blade at the ready. Julia had always admired the courageous Jewess who, when her people were on the brink of surrender after enduring a terrible siege, sneaked into the enemy camp and seduced its ruthless leader with sex and wine. While he slumbered afterward, she cut off his head and took it back to her fortress in a basket to display in the dawn's light and send her tormentors to heel.

What a strange painting for Raphael to possess, she mused, passing it to keep up with the butler. He arrived at a door, rapped, and then opened it. "Master, there is a young lady here to see you." The door swung the rest of the way, the servant stepped aside, and Julia found herself standing alone, facing a very surprised Viscount de Fontvilliers.

They simply stared at each other for a moment. Then Julia took a step in the room.

Raphael rose out of the overstuffed chair in which he had been seated. His coat was off, his sleeves rolled up to bare his muscular forearms all the way to his elbows. The rumpled shirt he wore was opened in the front in a deep vee, revealing a glimpse of darkly hued skin lightly sprinkled with hair. Without benefit of a waistcoat, the loose material billowed from his wide shoulders to be snagged at the narrow waistband of his trousers.

She had never seen a man's arms bared like that. And the powerful cording in his neck drew her eye against her will. It took some effort to appear unaffected by his state of dishabille. She feared she wasn't very successful.

"My God. You came," he said, his voice husky.

She swallowed against the painful dryness of her throat. She heard the door behind her click shut softly.

A half smile played on his lips. "How did you get away?"

She was glad her voice sounded strong. "I begged a headache and they went to the ball without me. I hired a carriage from home. It was little trouble, really."

He didn't move, not for the longest time. She, too, stood frozen, her hands grasping her reticule as tightly as if a band of thieves faced her.

Then he said, "And what of Simon, Julia?"

He looked so calm, staring at her with those clear, pale green eyes that seemed to catch the firelight.

It was with some effort she found her voice. "You misunderstand. I have come to talk to you. There are things that must be said between us. I fear we have gone too far in our . . . our . . . friendship." Goodness, this was a wretched time for her wits to desert her. "I must make you understand that we must . . ." Her throat convulsed. She swallowed, steadied herself, and finished, "Stop speaking. You must be reasonable about this."

His brows twitched together. "I am listening."

All the words she had carefully rehearsed seemed to desert her. "It is all dreadfully wrong. I am to marry Simon and this—"

"No, you're not," he interrupted.

She was astonished. "I-I most certainly am. I love Simon. I'm going to marry . . ." The words died out as she realized that she didn't believe them. She turned away, disconcerted, unable to bear the knowing look he wore.

He said, "You don't love Simon."

"I do." It was more like a plea than a statement.

"You are here with me."

"I came to talk, to tell you why I can no longer . . . You wouldn't stop sending the letters, and I had no choice. I—" She broke off, for his hand came up to the base of her neck, the warm palm resting on the curve just above her shoulders. She hadn't heard him move up behind her. She closed her eyes. "Please do not touch me."

"I am not going to marry Catherine."

She whirled on him. "What? Why?"

"There was no child. I am free, Julia." His sensuous mouth curled. "Are you pleased?"

She paused, hating to admit it. Pleased? How inadequate

a word to describe the numbing flush of relief that swept through her.

He reached for her and she moved away. "It doesn't change anything. I am betrothed to Simon, and I *am* going to marry him."

"You ache so badly, then, for the life he will provide you?" He crossed his arm over his chest and peered at her down his long, aquiline nose. "Simon offers you endless day, months and years filled with tea parties and cotillions and balls and musicales. Every season fraught with social jockeying and boring gossip and long, long speeches by insufferable bores who will adore you. They will capture and hold you with their adoration, and you will sit prettily and speak little because it is what everyone expects of you. You are so good at providing what they want, and soon it will be your greatest accomplishment."

He had moved forward, step by step until he had backed her up against the wall. His head lowered so that his mouth was just next to her ear, his breath tickling the small hairs at the back of her neck. "And you will grow terrified as the years stretch on, afraid they will discover it isn't really you they admire at all, but a fantasy you've woven for them, a role you play like an actress on a stage. Afraid they'll see all the parts of you that burn with rebellion against their safe, silly world. Ah, but take heart. After a time, those rebel feelings shall cease to exist, and you will *be* one of them truly. Everything within you will shrivel and die—"

She cried out wordlessly, waving an arm wildly to shut him up. Tears had sprung, scalding rivulets down her cheeks to spill onto her heaving chest.

"Why does it upset you?" he asked, grasping her shoulders. "You came to tell me that this is the future you choose, isn't that right?"

He turned her and she looked up at him. Oh, God, he was so beautiful to her. A sudden wrenching inside reminded her just how vulnerable she was to that masculine beauty. Those hard planes and angles of his face, they told her of a hard life. She burned to know what had forged this man who hated the world and yet, in his eyes she saw such sadness it was like looking into a great masterpiece and letting the work fill you with emotion.

"I don't want to marry Simon," she blurted. She hadn't known she was going to say that, or say anything at all. When she heard the words come out, she wondered if they were true. They felt true.

"I no longer love him. I did once. I-I wish I still did!" Dismayed, she felt like mists were parting in her mind, and she could see more clearly those things which until now only taunted her with vague hints of their existence. "I've changed. No. Maybe not changed. Maybe I'm finally realizing that I'm not what I thought. I'm not what I'm supposed to be. I don't want to be safe and reliable and everybody's darling anymore." She pressed her fingers to her temples. "There's something wrong with me. I don't want what other girls want. I thought I did."

"You were told you did." His smile was slow, comforting. His hands cradled her face, thumbs wiping away the wetness on her cheeks. "You are not meant for their petty world." He studied her for a moment. "You are afraid of me."

"No," she denied, humiliated that he could see it.

"Yes, you are. Well, you are a sensible girl to be afraid. *None but a fool or madman would dispute the authority of experience.*"

She looked at him.

"The philosopher, Hume," he clarified, then continued, "I've treated you very badly." He released her. "There. You are free. Free to go if you wish." His face was unreadable, unreachable.

She stood alone, feeling bereft without the comforting bite of his fingers into her flesh.

Where would she go? Her world had just been destroyed with his keen little assessment of her future. "I don't want to go."

"Poor girl. Look at you. You are miserable."

"You are, too," she said. "Is that why you sent for me?"

"You know why I sent for you." His eyes were penetrating flames of green fire, burning into her. "You know what manner of man I am. You know what I want."

"I did not come to . . . for that."

"Then why did you come, Julia? To tell me that you love Simon? But you don't. To tell me to leave you alone, to part ways with amicable understanding? That is not what you want, either, is it? So, tell me, why have you come?"

She understood now that she had misled herself. She had pretended she didn't want that which she burned for. "I don't know why," she stammered. "I'm not certain of anything anymore."

"Yes, you are," he told her calmly. "You simply do not wish to accept it."

He was right. She was in love with him.

That was why she was here.

With unerring instincts, he sensed her weakness and stepped in to close the small gap between them. She felt his hands slide around her waist.

His eyes stayed locked on hers. "You know I want you."

She nodded.

"You want me as well. And *that* is why you are here, Julia."

He had her in his arms now, his large, strong body pressed up against hers. Like a taper touched to a well-soaked wick, the contact was incendiary. She went up in flames right there in his arms, even before he bent his head to kiss her.

He kissed her hard, full of passion, demanding she yield. She did—with everything in her, she let herself be taken into his kiss and gave it all back to him.

His hands tangled in her hair, ripping out pins as he grabbed a handful of the rich tresses and held her fast. He smelled wonderful. The heady scent of soap and salty perspiration and man filled her head, feeding her hunger for him.

This terrible, urgent desire that flamed in every part of her turned her legs to aspic, so she had to cling to him, braced against the lean power of his body. She was desperately afraid he would stop, that he would be the one to remember that this was wrong and leave her, as he had done in the park, with the terrible emptiness that had ground away at her until she was a raw bundle of nerves. Therefore, she grasped him tightly, as tightly as she could and opened her mouth to the thrust of his encroaching tongue.

The boldness of his penetration didn't shock her. Rather, she reveled in it letting him tutor her in this intimate way of kissing. He delved deep, mimicking a rhythm that awoke primitive sensations in the pit of her stomach, and then retreated, running lightly along the edge of her teeth before mating with her again. She groaned, stroking the angular planes of his cheek with trembling fingers.

His hands were everywhere, wildly touching where he wanted, sending crackling sensations along her limbs like shooting sparks. She arched into his palm when he slid it up over her breast, sighing with pleasure at the soft brush of his thumb against her sensitive peak. It wasn't enough. Her nipple ached for more and he tantalized it mercilessly with tiny circular caresses until she grabbed fistfuls of his shirt in frustration. She wanted to snatch his teasing hand and bring it to where she needed him to be. And then he touched her *there* and she felt the flood rise within her, a frightening tide of need.

She was utterly gone, abandoned to the fire of him. His kiss had drugged her senseless, his touch robbed her of will. Artfully, he plied her with his fingers, with his clever mouth and brazen tongue until she was spinning out of control.

More than desire, she wanted to belong to him, for him to take her, to seal her fate and rescue her from everything ordinary that had nearly swallowed her whole.

"I am not a gentleman," he rasped, breaking away to

run his tongue along the line of her jaw. "We must be very clear about that." He shifted to play with soft little love bites leading back to her ear and she could feel the hardness of his arousal against her hip. She shocked herself with wondering what it would look like, feel like when inside her.

"Yes." She pressed her palm against the hard-muscled chest exposed by his gaping shirt. "I don't want you to be." The most fascinating swirl of feathery hair growing there was soft and springy. It felt so interesting against the inflamed sensitivity of her fingertips.

"We are no longer playing at innocent flirtation, Julia," he managed to say as she slipped her hands up to his shoulders and across his broad back. The sight of him responding to her questing touch thrilled her.

His voice grew hoarse. "We are beyond that, you and I. You understand?"

She nodded. He was warning her, asking her if she wanted to stop. And all she could do was wonder what came next. He stepped away, and for a moment she thought he had changed his mind, that he *was* going to end this insane temptation right now.

Folding his hand over hers, he said, "Come with me, then. I'll not take you on the carpet like some strumpet off the streets. I want to make love to you in bed. In *my* bed."

Leading her up the stairs, Raphael half expected her to come to her senses and flee through the front door. He didn't know what he would do, then. He'd have to chase her down, do his utmost to bring her back. Beg her if he had to.

Please, God, don't let her bolt.

It didn't occur to him how odd it was for him to be praying. He was not a man who had a great deal of faith in the Almighty.

On the first-floor landing he turned toward the double doors that led to the master's suite. He pulled Julia behind him, stepped inside the open doors with her. He had barely shut them before he was on her, pressing her up against the paneling and covering her mouth with his. His body was ready to explode with frustration, his sex hard, aching, ready.

"You are so lovely. So lovely," he muttered. He couldn't get enough of her, melding with her mouth, twining his tongue with hers, wandering to taste the salty smoothness of her skin. Impatiently he tugged at the neckline of her dress, wanting more flesh.

The most amazing thing of it was that she was just as ravenous. She kissed him in return, threw her head back to invite him to sample the luscious length of her neck, grasped him tighter. At his savage wrestling with her garments as he tried to undress her, she only made impatient sounds, as if she, too, were desperate to be rid of the barriers and give herself to his greedy hands.

He had to get a hold of himself. There would be no rending of her clothes; he could hardly send her home in such a state. Ah, God, but he felt as if he'd waited an eternity for her.

He bent her back, sweeping her knees out from under her with one arm while the other braced her back and caught her up in his hold. He cradled her to him, kissing her as he carried her across the room to lay her on the bed.

He pulled away a bit, wanting to see her. Her eyes were glazed, her lips swollen and roughened to a deep pink from the assault of his mouth. The thrill of that sensual look made him want to chuckle like a demon with a saint in his sights. Running a hand along the side of her neck, he slowly examined the contour of her shoulder, down her arm, took her hand in his and raised it to his lips. Twining his fingers with hers, he leaned over her, drawing her arms over her head.

He paused a moment. Giving her a steady look, he said, "Be very sure."

She tried a smile, a half-hearted effort that wilted before it was full born. "Everything I've been taught tells me this is wrong, but my heart . . . Raphael, in my heart . . ."

He froze. What was she saying? Did she fancy herself in love with him?

Of course she did. He was an idiot not to have realized it. A woman like Julia Brodie did not give herself to a man without love. She *must* love him, or thought she did, in any case.

He released her hands. He was a bit stunned, and suddenly not all that certain what he was doing.

He had won the wager. That had been his purpose. He could quit now. He *should* quit now, and save her this.

But she didn't seem to want to be saved.

Gazing up at him, she placed her hands on his cheeks and smiled. "I have no doubts, Raphael. I feel more sure of myself than I've ever been. There is something inside of me that comes alive when I'm with you. It is like I *am* someone else. Someone I like much better than my ordinary self."

He was caught in the sights of that trusting gaze, and suddenly nothing would do but matching honesty. "Yes. Yes, I know. I feel exactly the same way."

That eased him, admitting that much. The matter was out in the open. He smiled, running a finger along her jaw and thinking how very fortunate he was.

Leaning back on his elbow, his eyes wandered the elegant curve of her neck down to where her chest rose and fell in rapid breaths. Hooking a finger inside the neckline of her dress, he said, "We must get rid of this. Sit up."

She complied, reaching around to fumble with the row of buttons at the back. He brushed her hands aside. "I am fairly adept at undressing a lady," he told her. "I am, after all, a renowned scoundrel." He made short work of the fasteners and slipped his hands into the sides of her dress, pulling her down upon him. His fingers came around inside the material to cup her breasts.

Hissing in a sharp gasp, she arched her back against

him. His teeth sunk into the curve where her shoulder met her neck, raking lightly over the sensitive skin. When his thumbs traced the circle of each nipple outside the filmy batiste of her chemise, he felt her response. She squirmed in his grasp, soft cries of pleasure whispering into his ear to jolt his own excitement to unfathomable heights. He licked the curve of her ear and savored the sound of her reaction each time his palms abraded the hardened peaks.

He worked the dress off, then sat up to strip off his shirt. She stared at him, her gaze touched his unclothed body with an intensity he'd never experienced in any of his former lovers. Or perhaps, it hadn't affected him like this. He felt hot, as if the touch of her gaze was fire and he was being bathed in it.

It was only a matter of time before she noticed he was doing the same thing to her. The chemise was merely a scrap of diaphanous cloth clinging to her curves, revealing everything from the aroused tips of her breast to the softly shaded mystery between her thighs. Overcome by self-consciousness, she brought her hands up to cover herself.

"No," he growled, yanking her hands to her side. "Hide nothing from me. I want to see all of you."

Her teeth caught her lower lip, and he kissed her until she forgot to be afraid. He slid his hands up under the short garment and skimmed the silken flesh of her upper thighs. The power of wanting her was on him again, stealing his self-control. He needed to feel her heat, to test her moist welcome for him. For no other man but him. His fingers threaded through the soft thatch of curls and found what he sought.

She half rose, her eyes round and fastened on his. Her hand shot to his wrist and tried to shove it away.

"Shhh, love," he said, marveling at his own need to soothe her. His body was screaming for release, and he was not a man who practiced a great deal of self-restraint. "Let me make you feel good."

His answer was a throaty sound as he began to stroke her. She froze for a moment, then relaxed, releasing her hold. He smiled, triumphant, but it wasn't a cruel gloating. It was something quite different, quite novel. As unbearable as his own state of excitement was, he wanted nothing more than her pleasure. He knew how to give women release in this method, but had always used the technique in conjunction with the sex act itself. Now, he thought of how it would be to watch her undistracted by his own experience.

"Relax. Yes, that is it," he whispered. He traced his tongue along the seam of her lips. "Open for me, Julia. Part your legs, just a little bit to let me inside."

Hesitantly she slid her knees apart.

"More," he commanded, and she did so with a whimper of resignation. A surge of power seized him. He watched her face as his fingers lengthened the maddening rhythm of his strokes. Her mouth was swollen from his kisses, her eyes brilliant. High spots of color stained her cheekbones. All around her, her gleaming skein of auburn hair was spread wildly across the pillow.

His other hand yanked the neck of her chemise down to expose her breasts. "Say my name," he demanded.

She shook her head and sobbed. "Raphael, please."

"Yes, beg me to take you."

"Raphael, yes. Take me."

His eyes raked over the satiny flesh exposed to his view. The beautiful breasts, small but high and well formed with lovely nipples longing for his touch. Long, long legs and gently curved hips. A willowy waist with flat abdomen and jutting hipbones. "I knew you would be beautiful," he said before bending to each breast to suckle roughly. She responded with passionate cries, her hips moving against his hand as the crescendo built. And when she came, it was sudden, swift, and violent.

He grinned, licking lazily at her breasts. Timing his caressing hand to subside into a soothing motion, he watched her ride out the last of it with a sublime satisfaction.

Now. He could wait no longer. He tugged at the buttons of his trousers while she lay stunned. His eyes were locked fast on the rapid rise and fall of her breasts, their peaks tight and glistening from the wetness of his mouth. Christ, he could barely get his trousers undone. When he had stripped them off, he knelt over her and pulled her knees apart.

His body felt as if he were being roasted alive, but the fire was centered on his turgid shaft and the throbbing need to be inside her. He reached down to grasp her bottom, thrusting her hips upward to make his entry easier.

Slipping inside her welcoming moistness, his breath tore out of his chest in a grinding curse that was both triumph and surrender. Slick, sensual heat. All around him. The feeling was exquisite, but it didn't satisfy him for long. Julia lay under him, her eyes limpid gold as if they were true mirrors that could reflect his true self back to him. He could not bear to wait one moment longer. He selfishly filled her, no longer in control.

He felt her recoil in his arms, saw her grimace as his member encountered the barrier of her innocence. Ruthlessly he pushed through, smothering her cry, taking it into himself and wishing he could absorb the pain as well. He tried to wait, tried to give her time to become used to the feel of him, but his blood raged molten fire in his veins and he had to move. He realized he was whispering things to her, apologies and words he never intended to say, but he could hardly care to stop himself, for his body was racked with incredibly intense sensations with his every thrust.

Again and again, he entered her and she began to move under him, wrapping her legs around his hips when he showed her. His pleasure mounted until he exploded in a sudden rush. Jerking against her, he buried himself deep within that tight sheath, stifling an involuntary growl against the soft skin of her neck as his pleasure peaked in a brilliant flash of delirious fulfillment.

Panting and bathed in sweat, he remained braced over

her. Gradually his body cooled. His pulse calmed. His breathing slowed. He rolled to his side, taking her with him. The warm lassitude that was the aftermath of pleasure lingered, filling him with contentment and a strange, unprecedented sense of peace.

She clung to him. He kissed her lazily with a sudden swell of tenderness for her. Raising himself up on his elbow, he peered down into her face, studying it for a moment. She was lovely, truly lovely. He felt a surge of something foreign, a possessiveness that whispered, *"Mine."*

He didn't like the slight frown that creased her brow, however. "What is it, *chérie?*" he murmured, brushing his cheek along hers.

She blinked, staring past him at the ceiling. "Now I really am different." And she burst into tears.

"Shhh." He settled beside her, gathering her close. She wrapped her arms about his neck and pressed her face into his chest. "Don't cry. You will give a man cause to doubt himself. You were supposed to have enjoyed that."

"I did," came her muffled answer. "That makes it worse. What kind of woman does that make me?"

"A rather fortunate one," he countered with a lopsided smile.

Her fist pounded once against his shoulder. "Raphael, it is fine for you to be so blithe about it all. You are used to this sort of thing. But, my God, I cannot believe that I've become *that* sort of woman everyone whispers about."

"Well, if it is so, how do you like it?"

That stopped her. She lifted her wet face to stare at him.

"You are worried about being ruined?" he continued. "Ruined for what? For that life you don't want?"

She closed her eyes and sighed. "You have all the answers, don't you, Raphael? You even make it sound simple."

"It *is* simple, darling. You will see." He nibbled the soft cushion of her bottom lip. "You are too used to all those clucking matrons making everything so complex." He laughed, hitching up his voice. "Don't talk to that one, curtsy to that one, stick out your pinkie, don't use that fork for that course, call this one, 'Your Grace,' don't even acknowledge that one exists."

Despite herself, she laughed. "But you are used to minding no one."

"As should you. Do not listen to those fools."

"I should listen to you, then?" she asked with a skeptical smile.

"No, not even me. Are you not paying attention? You must heed to no one. And so," he added with a mischievous smirk, "you are not crying any longer." With the pad of his thumb he traced a wet path along her cheek where a tear had traversed and said softly, "And you were not crying for yourself, after all, but for the loss of the Julia everyone wanted you to be. But it wasn't a loss at all, was it? That Julia never really existed. Poor lamb."

Julia watched his face, that arrogant saturnine face so gentle now as he gazed at her with almost tenderness, and felt a swell of emotion lift inside her breast. She loved him. She loved him so utterly, so completely that she had broken every rule. How could she have thought otherwise, or doubted for a moment that he meant everything to her?

And he? What did he feel—if anything—beyond desire? Could he ever love her? Was Raphael Giscard a man who could love anyone?

"No more worry. Rest," he said, reclining as he pressed her head against his shoulder. She skimmed her hand over his chest and settled down, curling into him.

Strange how perfect a fit she was up against his side. How snug, how right, how content she felt just so.

"We'll have no more questions," he instructed. "And no self-recriminations."

"You told me I wasn't to listen to you," she reminded him.

He sighed in feigned exasperation. "I forgot how quick your mind is. You would remind me of that wayward statement. Already I regret it."

Her fingers swirled idly in his chest hair. "Is there anything else you regret?"

Regrets? Oh, there were many things he regretted. He only said, "My dear, I am a rake and a scoundrel. By my very nature, I have no regrets."

Another lie to add to the fold. He was growing weary of them.

Chapter Eleven

RAPHAEL DOZED.

Julia rose out of the bed and donned her chemise. In her bare feet, she padded to the hearth. A fire had been laid but not lit. She took a taper and touched it first to one of the candles, then set the wood alight.

There was a comfortable chair next to the fireplace. Pulling a blanket off the bed, she wrapped herself up in it, curled up, and stared into the growing flames until the blaze was good and strong.

She felt a marvelous sense of happiness and strangeness mingled together. What she had done was irreparable. One could never take one's innocence back. Instead of the rush of panic and guilt she had felt in those first moments after their lovemaking, she now knew a delicate peace.

It had been nothing at all what she had expected. When he had touched her, inflamed her every nerve, it had been so intense she had thought she might expire. At the same time there was something incredibly intimate that they had shared in those moments, a closeness she hadn't expected. She had always thought of *that* act as one in which a woman succumbs to a man's urges. But it had gone beyond that. A surrender, yes, but not to another. More to one's self. And even that was insufficient to describe it.

"What are you doing all the way over there?" Raphael said.

She smiled at the scratchy, groggy sound of his voice. She found it incredibly sexy. "You were sleeping." She stretched slowly and looked over her shoulder at him. "And I was cold."

"If it is warmth you need, you should have stayed right here." He propped himself up on an elbow and squinted at her, utterly uncaring of his nakedness or the wild state of his hair. Never had he looked so reckless. He looked marvelous. "You are not crying again, are you?"

Coming to her feet, she dropped the blanket and climbed in bed beside him. "I was thinking."

"About?"

She lifted a shoulder nonchalantly. "Thoughts. Private thoughts."

Skimming his fingertips up her arm, he asked. "Tell me about these private thoughts."

"I cannot. They are *private.*"

"I don't want there to be secrets between us." He picked up her hand and began to do shocking things to her fingertips with his tongue. "You see, I am afraid you have decided this was a monstrous misstep and I will lose you all too soon."

"Well, I haven't decided that." It was hard to get the words out. His teeth nipped gently, his eyes watching her all the while, and she had no breath. "Would you so hate to lose me?"

He ignored her question, busying himself with the fascinating way her chemise gaped open enough at the neck to afford him a generous view of what lay underneath.

She pushed his hands away, blushing furiously. "I thought you wished to talk."

"You refused to tell me your private thoughts, so what else am I to do to amuse myself?" His eyes danced as they glided in a silky perusal of her body. She warmed at the desire she saw in his eyes.

She chuckled. "I would say you were incorrigible, but you would only take it as a compliment."

He rolled onto his back, arms folded behind his head, giving her his most disarming smile. "True. Is that what you were thinking over there by the fire? Have you realized yet what a dreadfully wicked man I am?"

She cocked her head at him. "Are you?"

He grinned. "My dear, I promise you I am just getting started."

Just those words sent tremors of sheer delight through her. Then he reached for her and she went to him eagerly.

"I MUST GO."

"Hmmm."

Julia clutched the sheet to her bosom. "I must get home, Raphael."

He shifted so he could look up at her. She was sitting on the edge of the bed where he still lay in languid contentment. "Stay."

"I will be missed. I may have been already."

"Ah, but you good girls are quite a spot of trouble. All right." With a sigh he sat up and scrubbed his eyes with the heel of his hands. "Did you instruct your carriage to wait or do you need mine brought round?"

"Oh, Lord. I did ask Freddie to wait. How long has it been?"

"Hours." He twisted his head to peer at the clock on the mantel. "Christ." He shot to his feet. "It is nearly midnight. My fellows will be here. They were to go to Almack's—some obligation Martinvale couldn't get out of—and then we were to meet here to go on to White's."

They dressed quickly and in silence, but before they left the room, he snatched her to him for a thorough kiss. "God, I'd like to linger all night. No time, though. Quickly, then, follow me."

They crept out of the room and down the main stairs.

Peering outside, Raphael said, "Your man is still there. Out by the street. Here, put on your cloak."

Behind them, the sound of a closing door made them jump. A footman stepped forward, having just come out of the library. "Sir, Mr. Atvers has arrived. I've served him a brandy and asked him to wait."

"Fine, Smith. Thank you."

The servant retreated. Julia remained stiff. Leaning down to look into her face, Raphael said, "It's all right. Smith is discrete."

"I am sure," she answered almost bitterly. "He has much practice."

He hurried her to the front door and opened it. "Did you think I led a celibate life, darling? How do you think I earned my wretched reputation?"

Looking away, she said, "Then perhaps draw on your great experience and tell me what we say to each other now."

"Why, we say *adieu*. It is as simple as that. Now run along."

She flew to the coach and shouted up to the snoozing driver as she climbed in, a bit of a sting in her chest. *Now run along?* It was hardly the farewell she would have wished from the man who was her lover.

Her heart leaped up and lodged in her chest. *Her lover.* Raphael was her lover.

⸻

E*verything is different.*

Julia stared out at the lawn, sprinkled with blossoming tulips imported from Holland, her mind far removed from the cozy drawing room. The duke was reading. Or dozing, really. The open book on his lap and his spectacles perched on his nose were just for show. He was betrayed by soft sawing sounds.

Father was on a short business excursion until tomorrow. The duchess was chatting with Mother, her gnarled hands swiftly working her crocheting. Desdemona listened as she squinted critically at a list in front of her. She had been laboring over the wedding guests for a full two weeks.

Her sisters were around her, as they had been countless times before, and yet nothing was the same.

Everything, *everything* was different.

It had been over a week and she had heard nothing from Raphael. A week. It made her wonder if she had mistook him, if he truly were the cad he was purported to be. Her worries increased when it had occurred to her that there could be consequences to their having made love, but her courses had started this morning and the dread had subsided. No permanent effects, then.

Except, of course, that everything was different.

Laura was to go to Vauxhall tonight—properly chaperoned, of course—with Colin Strathford, and she was a bundle of giddy anticipation. It was the first time her parents were allowing her to go out in the evening with the marquess without one of them in attendance as chaperone. The duchess had been set to accompany them, but a last-minute indisposition sent her to her bed. To Laura's surprise, Mother had not asked her to cancel the engagement, saying that Vauxhall was considered a public place and quite respectable. Why, the Prince Regent himself frequented the place.

Poised on the arm of a chair to better peer through the draperies, she watched for his carriage, intermittently fluffing at the ecru lace frothing at her bosom, and adjusting her curls. The sound of raised voices caught her attention. Curious, she went into the withdrawing room to see what was the matter.

Julia was inside, and Mother and Father. "What is it, what has happened?" Laura asked as she entered.

Her mother didn't look at her. All of her enraged attention was focused on her eldest daughter. Julia stood facing her mother with something like—impossible!—defiance in her eyes.

Julia said, "It is not merely misgivings, Mother, or nervousness. Simon and I have spoken and he understands that my acceptance of his offer of marriage was given under the wrong circumstances."

"How can that be? You yourself have often boasted of the affection you share."

"It is an affection that has not endured."

Another first occurred. Desdemona seemed to be at a loss for words. She appealed mutely to her husband.

Francis Brodie cleared his throat. "This is quite irregular, you know. We feel we are entitled to some explanation."

Finding her voice, Desdemona declared, "It will bring horrid scandal! Tell her, Francis."

"Quite right." Francis nodded. "Scandal is . . . well, it's bad."

Julia looked directly at him. "Simon is a good man, and he deserves a wife that can love him. I am no longer capable of that and it would be wrong to cheat him just to keep up appearances."

Softening, their father said, "What has Simon said, Julia?"

"He . . . he was disappointed, of course." Julia faltered, belying the calmness of her words. Laura could well imagine the depth of Simon's reaction. The man was devoted to Julia, but for all his fine manners and dashing good looks, he had a temper. "He refused to accept my decision. He shares your view that I am merely frightened and it will pass. He has asked me to wait, think upon the matter, although I assured him this would only prolong our inevitable parting. However, I have reluctantly agreed not to announce the breaking of our engagement for a fortnight."

Her mother let out a small cry of relief and shut her eyes. Julia continued, "I felt I owed it to him to respect his wish. But I am quite certain I will not change my mind."

Opening her mouth, Desdemona was about to speak

when her husband laid a staying hand upon her arm. With as much authority as Laura had ever seen her father exert over his wife, he said, "Perhaps we can continue this later, when we've all had an opportunity to think it through. Come, Mona." The hand he had used to restrain her now began to soothe. "Why don't we go upstairs and you can lie down. News like this takes time to digest."

To Laura's shock, her mother complied. Tight-lipped and stiff, she allowed herself to be led out of the room, leaving Julia and Laura in silence. Looking at her older sister, Laura thought Julia looked very frail and small all of a sudden.

"Oh, Laura," Julia said softly.

Laura made a move to come to her sister's side, but Betty came in just then and said, "The marquess is here for you now, Miss Laura."

"Tell him I will be with him directly, Betty."

"Miss Laura is coming right now." Julia looked at her sister and smiled. "Go on. There is no sense in ruining your evening. This will all be here when you return."

"I wish I could stay with you tonight," she said honestly.

"That is sweet, even if it is a fib. You have your handsome marquess taking you to Vauxhall. It is a wonderful outing, and I shall not forgive you if you allow my little troubles to spoil it. Go on, now, and have fun."

Laura obeyed, disturbed as she entered the front parlor where the marquess waited. But once she was in the room and Colin turned toward her—his handsome face showing his pleasure at her arrival—she forgot about Julia's troubles.

Immediately she was aware of a subtle difference in him. Always before, he had been rather detached with her, even seeming to be bored on occasion. Sometimes she had feared he hadn't liked her very much despite the fact that he kept inviting her to outings, but tonight he looked at her quite differently. There was a heat in his dark gaze, a sort of anticipation that stirred a fluttering tremor in her breast.

"Shall we go?" he said. "Let me have your wrap fetched and we can be on our way. I have been looking forward to tonight."

They climbed in his carriage and rode the short distance to Vauxhall. Colin paid the fee and they entered the gate. The pathways of the pleasure gardens were crowded. Colin steered her through them with little difficulty, taking her first to the tumbling platform where costumed acrobats frolicked upon a small stage. They munched roasted chestnuts as they watched. Laura had never heard him laugh before, but he enjoyed himself at the spectacle, and she found her own spirits soaring. Next they headed to the topiary, then down the well-lit avenues where Laura ogled the ostentatious headdresses of the women and Colin exchanged brief greetings with those he knew.

She should by rights be having the time of her life, but she kept thinking of Julia, and feeling guilty that she hadn't canceled her plans. Whatever trouble was brewing, she should be by her sister's side. They always shared everything. In fact it was surprising that Julia hadn't already confided her decision to break off her engagement to Simon. That bothered Laura most of all. Something was wrong.

Colin said, "You seem troubled, Laura."

Her heart gave a queer leap at his familiar address. "I received some rather disturbing news just before you arrived."

"Would it help to talk it over?"

He really was being wonderfully attentive tonight. His warm smile, the solicitous hand holding hers was all she had dreamed of for so long.

Under the power of his affectionate smile, she could scarcely think. "Well, it is to do with Julia. You see, I just found out that she and Simon shall cancel their engagement soon. She wants to do it immediately, but Simon insists she think it over. It is so strange. I don't know why she is doing this."

He took the news harder than she would have thought. He fell into a brooding silence. He seemed very angry—a state he denied when she asked him about it in a tentative voice.

He was obviously lying, stalking along beside her with clenched fists and muttering on about wasted time and five thousand pounds. She didn't dare ask him what he was talking about, and let the matter drop for fear of testing his black mood into a full-fledged temper.

She reconciled herself to having a miserable evening when he suddenly took her arm rather roughly and pulled her into the shadows.

"What are you doing?" she demanded.

"Don't be afraid," he replied smoothly. "This is all part of the experience. Everyone does it at Vauxhall. It is expected. Surely, you knew that."

She pulled back. "I am afraid of the dark."

He folded his arms, his voice tinged with impatience. "I am here to protect you, silly girl."

"I am not silly." Her chin jerked upward.

He took a step toward her. "Oh, yes, you are. You are a foolish piece to be so upset over a mere moonlight stroll."

She hesitated only a moment, then relaxed and allowed him to lead her deeper into the darkness.

"Here is a bench," he said. "Sit with me."

Laura's mind raced, darting over ways to extricate herself from the situation. At her hesitation Colin sighed. "She was correct. By damn, she was."

"Who?" Laura asked, startled.

"Lucy Glencoe. We spoke quite frankly recently. I told her, you see, that my affections were otherwise engaged. When she demanded to know to whom, I had to admit it was you. It was then she said you were . . . well, she called you a ninny and said you were hopelessly naïve. And to think I defended you,"

Her spine straightened like a bolt. "She what? That jealous snipe!"

"But you are indeed such an ingenue, Laura."

"I am not!" She flounced down on the marble bench.

Colin moved behind her, straddling the stone toward her. She didn't move, staring straight ahead until his hand came to cup her chin and turned it so she faced him. She kept her body taut.

In the little bit of moonlight that filtered through the leaves, she could see his face. It was hard, intent. "So, Laura, are you what Lucy accused you of, or will you let me kiss you?"

He was going to kiss her! She had been wanting him to for the longest time. She didn't answer him but let her eyelids drift shut and waited for him.

He slipped the hand that had held her face to the back of her neck and lowered his head. His kiss was a bit rough, she thought. As she recoiled, she recalled Lucy Glencoe's insult. No. She would not act the ninny.

Tentatively she twisted her torso toward him and placed her hands on his shoulders. Colin emitted a gutteral noise, and the pressure on her nape increased. He opened his mouth. She followed. His tongue plunged between her parted lips.

It was a shocking encroachment she wasn't prepared for. Her whole body reacted, stiffening with tension. He backed off, his hands cradling her face as his eyes swept over every feature. "You are so innocent. I forget how much."

Then he was gentle. Softly his mouth came over hers, and she felt her guard drifting down. Pleasure welled up inside as the silky-smooth skin of his lips glided over hers.

His tongue came into play again, this time more deftly. She cried out with a soft, sweet sound at the tremors his invasion caused, like tiny darts of lightening in her veins.

Oh, this was pleasant. It was *wonderful*, she thought. He pulled her up tighter, and she didn't resist.

Then she felt his hand close over her breast, and she went stock-still.

His fingers stroked her through her gown. Forbidden pleasure hit her, and she began to struggle.

"No," he grunted, ducking his head to press hot kisses

along the side of her neck. "Don't be shy, Laura. It is what everyone does."

"No, it can't be." Her hands on his wrists stalled, however, for she was unsure.

"Don't behave like a silly miss. Everyone pretends not to, but you know as well as I that even Lady Jersey has had her share of lovers. The prince has his consorts received at court. It is what all of *haute société* does. Underneath the posturing and preaching, we all accept it."

It was true that even the most exalted scions of the *bon ton* had been known to have affairs. These were whispered about and generally acknowledged, eventually accepted even when illegitimate children resulted.

Her hand weakened. She let him squeeze her bosom. His breathing was jagged and fast. Hers was, too, but from fear. The pleasure she had experienced at first was gone. Unprepared for these intimacies, she could think only that she wanted him to stop. She wanted to leave this place. She wanted to go home.

But she didn't want him to think her a ninny.

His mouth closed over hers. He murmured her name. She liked that, at least, and the pretty compliments he muttered harshly, about her hair and her skin and her eyes. Grabbing her hand, he shoved it down to the hard ridge rising inside his trousers.

She squeaked and snatched her hand back. He dragged her hand again to his crotch, opening her palm to lay it against the rigid heat. "Oh, Laura, please, I'm so hard for you. I didn't realize how much I wanted you. Come now." He rose and swung his leg over the bench, jerking her to her feet. "Come, deeper into the grove over there."

She froze. His fingers were wrapped like a steel vise around her wrist, and he was pulling her into the shadows. Her mind screamed, but she refused to allow a sound to come forth. She wouldn't disgrace herself by giving him something to laugh about with Lucy Glencoe. But to allow him to do this—she knew she mustn't. She didn't even want to!

If she screamed, she thought, her entire reputation would be demolished.

A solitary figure stepped in front of them. Colin started, releasing his hold on Laura. She pulled away, glad to be free, and thought of running. But the shadowed form of the man who had surprised them blocked the way out. Instinctively she sidled back to Colin, shrinking behind him. Rubbing the skin of her wrist where he had gripped her too tightly, she tried to peer at the face of the intruder over his shoulder.

"There you are!" the shadow said in a jovial voice. "I thought I saw the two of you duck off the path. I was calling to you like a madman. Did you not hear me? Well, I was some ways away, I will admit. With the press of the crowds, it was not easy to get over here quickly."

The voice was familiar, but Laura couldn't place it until Strathford said in a murderous tone, "Martinvale."

"At your service. And you, Miss Brodie, it is lovely to see you again. How are you this fine evening? Well, I trust?"

"Quite," she managed, though her voice was shaky. A great sense of relief flooded through her.

"Excellent. I cannot believe my luck to have run into you." There was an awkward pause while the three of them stared at one another. It occurred to Laura in a flash of shame that Martinvale knew exactly what it was he had interrupted. And he seemed determined to remain right where he was so that it would not resume.

"Well, this is good luck all around," Martinvale went on. "I was just about to visit the Indian dancers. Have you seen them yet, Miss Brodie? Oh, you simply must. It is an apparition as if from a dream. Come, I'll show you the way. Are you coming along, Strathford?"

"Momentarily," came the gruff reply.

Somewhat dazed, Laura allowed Martinvale to take her hand and lead her away from Colin. She glanced over her shoulder at him, wondering if he was angry with her. He looked ready to chew raw iron.

She wondered if she had missed her chance with him.

THAT TUESDAY JULIA was supposed to take Leah shopping, but the girl had a tendency to dawdle, and Julia's patience was not what it usually was. Deciding it would teach Leah a lesson in manners, she left without her. She was sorry within a block of the house. Being alone didn't suit her today.

Her first stop was at the milliners to pick up Mother's new hat. That done, she headed to the lending library. The duke didn't fancy the novels she favored, so it was always a good idea to keep a few of the newest ones on hand.

Climbing back into the carriage with her selections, she gasped in shock at what she found inside. Looking as smug as you please, Raphael reclined on the cushions.

Putting a finger to his lips, his eyes danced. "Come in," he said softly. "And please do not make a fuss. I've gone through a great deal of trouble to be discrete."

Chapter Twelve

JULIA WAS STUNNED, but she saw the wisdom in doing what Raphael suggested. She climbed in and took the seat opposite from his. He regarded her with thinly concealed delight. Her insides stirred in little tremors at the glow in his eyes, but she remained outwardly cool.

"How disappointing," he drawled, "that you choose that seat when there is just enough room by me for you to squeeze in tightly. Ah, but I suppose you are angry with me." Rapping on the ceiling of the carriage to signal the driver to go, he then hauled himself to his feet and insinuated himself beside her. "I have missed you too much to care."

"Sometimes I wonder what you do care about." His hand skated up her arm, tracing a light pattern. She shivered at the tremors of excitement this stirred. "Please don't do that."

"You *are* angry. Not that I blame you. I am a beast. That is no doubt how you see it. But I was trying to think of you." At her distinctly unladylike snort, he said, "It is true. I tried to stay away. And you cannot argue it would have been best if I had. But I couldn't stand it any longer, weak-willed worm that I am." His mouth came to her ear, his tone lowering to a whisper. "I am always a miserable failure when I try to be noble."

"Was that what you were doing, being noble?" She stayed rigid, staring straight ahead, trying desperately to hold on to her anger. But she was melting under the warm sensations his touch and the warm brush of his breath summoned within her. "Perhaps the reason you fail so dreadfully is because you do it so infrequently," she managed, closing her eyes against the violent rush of pleasure when his lips brushed against the curve of her ear.

His throaty chuckle washed over her. Her mouth went dry. "No doubt I'd improve with practice," he said, amused. "But then I ask myself why make the effort, when this is so much more rewarding."

She smacked his hands. Undaunted, he tipped her head back. Glancing up at him, she saw his smile fade as he grew serious. "I went nearly mad thinking about you," he said.

"I wonder if that's true."

"You know I am a liar, and I'll admit it. But I am not lying about this. I've missed you horribly."

Left on her own, as she had been these past weeks, she doubted everything she had ever believed about him. "I think I am the one who is mad, to let you do this. I wonder why I do?"

"Because we are of a kind. Two misfits—you and I," he murmured as his gaze wandered over her face, touching on every feature. "And yet, as I recall—and I do recall it, often and in great detail—we fit quite well together."

He kissed her, sealing her mouth over his. She didn't bother to fight the swell of reaction that rose up within her, letting him take command of her mouth until they were both breathless.

"Is that a sign that you forgive me?" he asked softly.

"I have no right to make any demands on you," she said. "You owe me nothing. We promised each other nothing."

"Yet you want to, don't you?"

She flinched. "I don't *want* to want anything from you. It hurts too much when you disappoint me. These weeks after . . . after what happened, I was convinced you had your sport, and were done with me."

His eyes darkened. Stroking her cheek, he said, "I am sorry. I truly am."

And Raphael realized that he was, novel experience that it was.

Strange things happened when he was with her. They were happening now. Desire near crippled him and stirring of another sort, a softer, more tender sort, eddied disturbingly from the nether regions of what he supposed was the general indication of his heart.

The passion he understood. Even now, he fought the hunger roiling in his gut, though his self-mastery did not extend to preventing him from raking his gaze down the length of her body. "I could take you right now. I want to. Christ, I want to so much I can't believe I'm not doing it. I burn for you, Julia. When can I see you again?"

"No." She tried to sit up but he wouldn't let her. "It is impossible. We cannot indulge in some cheap, vulgar affair." She stared at him, eyes blazing. "Did it ever occur to you, or do you simply not care, that there could be *consequences* to what we did?"

He froze. "Good God, Julia, are you—"

"No. I didn't mean that I was, just that it could happen, and neither one of us thought the least about it."

Bemused, he said, "True, I never considered it. The women I've been with usually took precautions, but of course you would not know what to do."

She blushed and looked away.

Grabbing her chin, he pulled her face back to look at him. "Leave it up to me to keep you safe from *consequences*. There are measures a man can take to prevent conception. It was stupid of me not to have thought of it before. It was simply that I was . . . well, I was quite swept away."

"It is not only that, Raphael. We cannot simply carry on."

"Why not? I want you. And you want me. We have both found the struggle to be honorable not only fruitless, but damned unrewarding. Now tell me, what are your family's plans tomorrow evening?"

She shrugged, unsure of what he was getting at. "A private party." Her eyes widened. "Don't you dare make a scene in public!"

"Nonsense, that is not my style. Everyone is going?"

"Except the children, Hope and Marie."

"Good. Beg off at the last minute, and that should leave you effectively alone in the house. Await me in your room. I shall come to you."

"No! My God, Raphael, how could you suggest such an outrageous thing? I most certainly will not!"

"Shh." He laid a finger against her mouth and grinned. "There is nothing to worry about. I am possessed of all manner of disreputable skills, remember? Sneaking into a woman's bedroom is hardly a challenge."

"I hate it when you talk like that." She jerked her face away. "I hate to think of how *common* all of this is for you."

"Not common, darling. Oh, no. Quite extraordinary, I assure you. As for my wicked ways, is it not standing us in good stead?" He lowered his head to peer out the window. "This is your street. Tomorrow night, then. I will come right after they leave."

"Do not dare, Raphael. I swear, I shall not be there."

"Let us not dissemble. You don't even realize the many ways you tell me, even when your words say otherwise, that you crave me as much as I crave you."

"Even if that is true, that has nothing to do with this insanity you propose. I absolutely forbid it!"

He touched his finger to her nose, as one might do a child, and that really got the sparks flying from those glittering golden eyes. "Pray do not be angry with me," he cajoled softly. "I made a mistake in neglecting you for so long. I thought it best to try to put the incident aside, for your sake and my own as well. However, you are a difficult woman to put aside. I was wrong to try, for I have hurt you more by intending to hurt you less."

He was pleased to see the ghost of a smile twist her mouth. "Are you apologizing?"

He frowned. "Of course not. A Giscard never admits to any wrongdoing. It is a family rule." The conveyance pulled to a stop. "Here you are at home. Now, go ahead and get inside. I'll sneak out when the driver pulls around to the mews. I paid him well to keep our secret."

She opened the carriage door, then paused, looking over her shoulder at him. "I never had a secret before I met you. Now I have many."

He ran his knuckle along her jawline affectionately. "A woman *should* have secrets."

"And a man?"

"A man?" He thought of a flippant retort worthy of the leading member of the Bane of the Ton, but it dried up in his throat before he could get it out. Gathering up her books, he pressed them into her hands. "Go on now," he said instead and gave her a gentle kiss farewell.

JULIA HAD NO intention of doing as he had said. She tried to banish all thought of Raphael, but dread gnawed at her as she wondered if he would indeed dare slip into the house as he had threatened. Her anger at him at such a bold threat warred with the thought that he hadn't forgotten her as she had feared. It was for her sake he had tried to stay away. But he couldn't keep himself from temptation. *She* was his temptation. And he was hers.

To keep her mind in order, she concentrated on her bath, choosing a hair dressing, her careful toilette, her selection of jewelry—each thing in its turn as she readied for the Whitby Ball.

Simon had already arrived by the time she joined her

family. He was having a drink with her father and the duke as she entered the room. She returned his frosty politeness with a vague greeting of her own under the anxious eye of her mother. As they entered the carriage, he was polite, making idle conversation on the drive and flawless in his attendance once they arrived at the party. No one outside of the family would ever suspect the strain between them.

Julia could hardly blame him for his coolness. She knew she had hurt him terribly when she had told him she wanted to end their engagement. His self-respect prevented him from supplicating himself, but he stubbornly held on to his view that her misgivings would abate and she would eventually come to see the wisdom of their marrying. The result was that he appeared insufferably superior, a posture she found annoying. It kept away some of the guilt in which she by rights should be drowning in.

Tonight, though, she was not troubled with too much pity for his supposedly broken heart, for she had come to suspect it was more his pride that was wounded by her defection than any tender feelings. Besides, her willpower had run out and she was besieged by thoughts of Raphael.

She wasn't sure she could trust him not to come to the ball, even though he had said he wouldn't. She looked for him, fighting disappointment with the shreds of good sense that still remained in her head when he didn't show. He was true to his word, and thank God for it. At least he was not after a public disaster.

What did he want? Did he think she would consent to a clandestine relationship? He hadn't promised her marriage, or even love. This situation between them—it could not continue. If it did, she knew exactly what that would make her in the eyes of the world—and she wasn't fool enough to think a man and a woman could keep flawless discretion for long in these sorts of matters.

She became aware her mother watched every move she and Simon made. Only someone close to Desdemona, someone sensitive to her mood as Julia was would pick up on the tightly checked anxiety she barely betrayed while continuing the public pretense that all was well and telling everyone who asked the wedding plans were coming along just fine.

They made it an early night, overriding Leah and Laura's protests, arriving home by eleven. Julia's farewell to Simon was nothing more than a half smile, a nearly inaudible, "Good night," and a deep, deep chill.

In her room, she found the maid hadn't been in yet, so Julia lit the lamp with the candle she had brought up with her. Sitting at her dressing table, she began to pull the pins from her hair. Debra arrived and helped her out of her dress. As the maid was shared between Julia, Laura, and Leah when the younger girl was on occasion invited places, Julia told her to go to the others, that she would brush out her own hair tonight. She wanted to be alone.

The clock in the corner tolled half past the hour. Julia stretched. She was tired, although much later bedtimes were her habit since the season began. It was unusual to return from a large crush like a ball before three or four in the morning.

Tension had drained her. Standing, she grabbed her book from a nearby table and turned toward the bed. Then she froze.

From the other side of the room, Raphael walked toward her. Sauntered, actually, as brazen as you please with a lopsided grin and triumph in his eyes as he swept off his black wool cloak with a flourish.

"Oh, my God!" she cried softly.

"I told you I would come. It was thoughtless of you to keep me waiting so long."

"How did you get in? How did you even know which room was mine?" She paused half a heartbeat, then held up her hand. "No. Don't tell me. I think I really don't want to know."

He chuckled, advancing mercilessly. Desire smoldered in his eyes. Her blood thrummed excitedly in her veins. The feeling was like being caught on the edge of a cliff, threatened with the danger of a deadly drop and yet experiencing the most breathtaking vistas imaginable. Being with Raphael was like walking that fine line between ecstasy and disaster. And she had learned that—given this—it was best not to look down.

"I suggest you keep your voice down," he said softly. "Unless your family is used to hearing you talk to yourself in loud, urgent tones."

Her glare was murderous, but she lowered her voice. "I cannot believe your gall."

"Gall? Why I told you outright what I planned—"

"And I told you not to dare to do it!"

"Well, it's done." He spread out his hands. "I am here. Aren't you at least a bit happy to see me?"

"I should call the footmen."

"Excellent idea," he mocked. Damn him for the way his eyes danced. And damn him for having robbed her of any way out of this, and knowing it, too. "I'm certain you can explain all of this to your parents. They seem quite liberal in their—"

"You know, you really are quite annoying when you are gloating."

"I confess I am wounded. I went through all this trouble, and the only thing you wish to do is have a row? I think not." He took her in his strong arms and kissed her roughly.

As quick as it was done, it was finished. He walked away and sat on the edge of the bed. For all his insouciance, he might have been in any drawing room or salon. She wondered if there were any place Raphael wasn't utterly at ease. He drew up one leg, resting its ankle on the other's knee and cocked his head. "So. How was your evening?"

"I want you to leave."

"Of course." He rose and headed for the door. "Although I am surprised you don't mind me being seen."

"You are not amusing, you know. Sit back down."

"Back there?" he asked innocently. "On the bed?"

"Oooh!" She whirled, wrapping her arms about herself. She heard him come up behind her. She didn't fight it when he wrapped his arms about her. "Please," she whispered. "I . . . am afraid."

He buried his nose in the hair behind her ear. His voice lost all of its bluster. It was gentle, and ringing with sincerity. "I swear no one will know. Julia," he said, turning her in his arms until she faced him. "I would never let anything happen to you. I just want to be with you. What would you have me do? Pine alone when we both want each other? As I recall, you were quite put out with me when I tried that. I know this is complete madness, even for me but believe me when I tell you I cannot help myself. It is as simple as that."

Her indignation was melting. The soft light of his eyes seemed to speak to her of a very un-rakish desperation for her to relent, take him into her arms and give him what he wanted—yes, she'd admit it was what they both wanted. "Raphael, you are the most outrageous man."

He took her hands in his and kissed each finger, his eyes locked on hers. "I might hope for something more romantic like 'exciting' or 'delightful' or 'intrepid.'" He turned her hands, kissed her palms.

"Since when do you care about romance?" she asked in a breathless voice. The soft brush of his lips left eddies of pleasure in her hands.

"Since I met you," he replied, pulling on her wrists to bring her to him. His mouth claimed hers, and this time, she wrapped her arms about his neck and kissed him back.

For Raphael, the kiss felt like taking a clean breath after almost drowning. He drank from her mouth the sweet taste of her and let it intoxicate him, warm his blood, fill his senses. She felt so wonderful in his arms. How he'd missed her. He'd not had enough of her, not by far, and these days away had been astonishingly impossible.

He could speak none of this. It was surprising that he felt it, but the need to tell her, lay these feeling bare, was so novel it shook him. Or was that this kiss, this long, liquid kiss that melded them together, seamless and complete?

Joy bubbled up from somewhere inside his being, and

he chuckled, then laughed. She smiled, sharing his delirious pleasure. God, how was it she knew? They kissed quickly in between the laughter as he maneuvered to the edge of the bed. Then he lay her down on her back, and stretched out over her.

He wasn't laughing any longer. When he kissed her now, it was with raw need.

Christ—the door! With a growl, he pushed off the bed and went to lock it. When he headed back to the bed, pulling off his cravat, she was still on her back, propped up on her elbows and watching him with eyes of honey gold.

"Take off your clothes." He whipped the neck cloth off. Sitting back beside her on the bed, he pulled her up and examined her night rail. "Where the devil are the buttons on this thing? Ah, hell, do you like it?"

"What?"

"This dress, this damned nightdress—is it one of your favorites?"

"No, not especially, why—?"

He grabbed the neckline and rent the garment all the way to the waist. The sound of buttons scattering over the floor was crisp and startling. She cried, shocked, and snatched at the parted fabric. He knocked her hands away. Cocking an eyebrow at her undergarment, he rubbed his chin and said, "Your shift looks worn."

She gave him a glare. "Raphael, don't you dare!"

He ripped that, too, pushed her back on the bed, and caught her hands at her sides, holding them there so that his eyes could wander without hindrance. "I love looking at you." Then he kissed her and she mewed softly. He took that as a surrender, an assumption born out when he released her hands and she grasped his shoulders and kissed him back.

He broke away and rose, working swiftly to take his own garments off. "I want to feel your skin against mine," he said, tossing his clothing helter-skelter onto the floor. He sat and pulled at his Hessians. "Damn these boots—

there we are. No. Don't you move. Stay just like that. Don't cover yourself."

Julia felt her skin tingle under the sensual perusal. It made her want to move in the most shocking way. It made her ache. She reached her hands for him. He pushed them aside to let his hot gaze touch her, unhindered and she felt the rush of wetness seep onto her thighs.

"You are making me nervous," she pleaded.

"By looking? If that makes you skittish, what will you do when I touch?"

That sent a ragged thrill right through the heart of her. "Raphael, you are too bold with your words. You are embarrassing me."

At last finished undressing, he braced himself over her. She arched, her fevered flesh seeking contact with his. "A fault of mine, I admit," he murmured, lowered his head to nuzzle her. "However, I was hoping you would like it under these circumstances. It can invigorate the bed sport." He came down on her, full-length, and she moaned at the hardness of him, the heat and the wonderful, masculine feel of supple flesh over steely muscle.

She slipped her arms around his neck, pulling him closer. "Then I shall try it. Kiss me."

He did, melting the last of her tension.

Pulling away, he laughed. "God, I missed you." Lifting a glossy strand of auburn tresses, he mused, "I love the color of your hair. Like copper, only a bit darker. Do you know when the light hits it, it looks like satin?" Liftingh it to his nose, he sampled the scent. "It smells of you."

She smiled and threaded all ten of her fingers in his thick hair. "And yours is so soft. It's the only thing about you that is, I think."

His mood changed. "Come. Show me how much you've missed me." Pulling her hips up against his, he angled his erection inside the folds of her thighs. His voice was low and rough at her ear. "You are ready for me. So hot. I think I have waited long enough."

Powerful arms held her tight as he repositioned himself and penetrated her in one shocking thrust. The feel of him inside her, stretching and hot and slick combined with the sound of primitive pleasure erupting from his throat ignited glorious sensations.

"Christ, Julia. You feel incredible."

He leaned back on his knees, holding her narrow hips in his capable hands and thrust. Glancing down, she could see them, entwined, the contrast of their skin tones, his darker to her fair complexion.

She marveled at his masculine beauty. His arms grasped her firmly, guiding her upward, causing the muscles in his shoulders and chest to bunch. Their flexing movement was like quicksilver, fluid and graceful. He moaned her name and arched into her, harder. The cords on his neck stood out, his hair, damp and wild, clung to that patrician brow she had so often admired and his nostrils flared making him seem feral in those moments just before she spilled over into fulfillment.

Raphael came down with his hands on either side of her head and pulled himself out of her, grinding his hips against her abdomen as the spasms of pleasure took him over. When they subsided, he lowered himself onto his elbows and turned his face into her hair, murmuring something she didn't quite catch.

He had kept his seed from her. This, she surmised, was to protect her from *consequences*. As promised.

Reaching out from his spot in the bed, he grabbed the soft linen from the commode and tenderly administered to their slick bodies before curling himself around her.

She wondered why it couldn't always be like this. It was inexplicable, the safe, secure feeling she found here in his arms. Like a haven. Yet, it truly was the most dangerous place to be. There were other consequences beyond conception, ones he couldn't prevent. Consequences to her heart.

Not for the first time, she wondered what would happen to her when his passion eventually cooled. She would

never have back the innocence she had so freely given.
Nor did she want it so. She would savor these moments
for all of her life.

Other women had married successfully without being
chaste. One heard of actresses or dancers or women who
had been mistresses of other men before they met their
husbands. These matches were often very contented. Therefore, contrary to what she had been taught, some men
didn't mind a wife's having had other experiences. Perhaps they even enjoyed a worldlier partner.

So, she knew her life wouldn't be over when Raphael
left her. Not in that way, at least.

And he would leave. He was a scoundrel, a rake, the.
Bane of the Ton, and he had never been, nor would ever
be, held by any woman. While she couldn't imagine herself with any other, it was a sentiment she was certain
troubled him not in the least.

The sounds of her parents coming upstairs roused them.
Carefully, Julia wrapped her dressing gown around her and
crept to the door to check the lock. She heard Leah call
out a weary good night to the others. One by one, their
doors clicked shut after murmured *adieus* until all was
quiet again.

She laid her head on the cool panel of the door. "My
mother is angry with me, or else she would have checked
in on me."

"Mothers can be tiresome."

"Sometimes." She returned to her bed. Crawling in, she
sat back on her heels and peered at him. "You sound as
if you speak from experience. Is your mother very tiresome?"

"Not anymore."

She gasped. "Oh, Raphael, I am sorry."

"Why? Did you think I meant she is dead? She is alive,
I assure you. I just don't see her."

"That's a shame. Family is one's touchstone. At least
you are close to your grandmother."

His snort dripped with derision as he rose and pulled

on his trousers. "Honestly, I don't know why people say such stupid things." He reached for his shirt. "Family is nothing but a bother."

"I am sorry I brought it up. You have only to say you do not wish to speak about the matter." She was irritated at his unjust attack. "I didn't mean any offense. I hardly see why I am being treated to this fit of pique. I don't feel I deserve it at all."

He stopped, strangely pleased by the scolding tone in her voice. Tossing his shirt back onto the rug, he pulled her down on the bed again. "You are becoming quite a termagant, you know. That was an impressive outburst. Not the first of the evening, either. I always liked your spirit."

She was still cross. "Don't patronize me!"

"Now, add an epithet. 'Don't patronize me, you logger head' is much better. Try it."

"I will not. Get off me."

"Get the *devil* off me.' Or, if you prefer, 'Get the *bloody hell* off me,' which is even better to my mind."

She couldn't help it. She giggled. "You are an addlepated idiot."

"Hmm. It could use improvement, but it is a start."

They laughed, then they kissed. He removed his trousers again and they made love, this time slowly. It gave him a chance to show off some of his skill. She didn't say it in so many words, but he was left with the clear impression that she was indeed favorably impressed with some of the maneuvers.

⌐⌐⌐

IT WAS A long time later. They were talking softly from opposite sides of the same pillow. "I loved Italy," she was telling him. "The Amalfi coast, Capri. Oh, I thought it was glorious. The romance of Venice, the grandeur of the Florentine art, and *Roma*. Rome was spectacular."

He frowned and idly pinched at the bedsheet. "Italy holds bad memories for me."

"When were you there?"

"When I was young. My . . . my father took me. We had a parting of the ways there. Of sorts."

She seemed to miss the heaviness that dragged at his words. "Is France the home you love, then?" she asked. "Once Father brought me to Paris, but it was only for a few days. I saw very little."

"It is overrated. Society rules the city, just as they do here. Trite and boring, the lot of them."

"Were you raised in the country, then?"

"A town in the Loire Valley. No doubt you would deem it very picturesque. I thought it dreadfully provincial."

"Perhaps you will show it to me one day."

He paused, as did she. It was the first reference either of them had made to doing anything apart from making love together. It hinted at a future. "I am never going back there," he said flatly, and when he saw the dullness come into her eyes, he added, for no good reason he could think of, "I'd rather take you to Prague. Now, that's a romantic city."

She lowered her gaze, but he saw the glimmer of pleasure return. It was a novel experience, this woman's hurt or happiness meaning something to him. As was this, what they were doing—lingering in a woman's bed and talking of all things! His body was spent, yet he didn't wish to leave.

The unformed certainty that he should examine this occurrence asserted itself, but he just pushed it away. He was far too content for the onerous chore of self-examination. He never liked what he found, in any event.

Rolling his head on the pillow, he peered at the thin and watery gray sky framed in the window. "Dawn," he said. "So soon."

"No. It is not yet dawn, is it?" Propping herself on an elbow, she squinted over his shoulder. "It must be the full moon. We probably hadn't noticed it, or maybe it was behind a cloud."

He grinned and turned back to her. " 'Look, love, what envious streaks do lace the severing clouds in yonder east; Night's candles are burnt out and jocund day stands tiptoe on the misty mountaintops.' "

Gratified by her expression of astonishment, he laughed. "What exactly amazes you," he inquired imperiously, "that I am literate or that—"

"The wicked Raphael Giscard, the wild and unprincipled rake and scourge of the *ton* quoting love poetry from *Romeo and Juliet*!"

"I'm a disgrace to scoundrels everywhere." He kissed her before rising.

All manner of thoughts raced through his head, gazing at her now with her gleaming mass of hair all tousled and her sultry mouth softly parted. And her eyes, brilliant amber gems, looking up at him like a wounded doe. So appealing. He swallowed. It was hard to turn away.

Chapter Thirteen

THE FOLLOWING NIGHT, Raphael watched Julia across the dance floor at Almack's as she stifled a yawn behind a gloved fist. The gesture, a sign of her fatigue, made him smile.

He was tired as well. Last night had been anything but restful. Indeed, it had left him quite rest*ive*, and impatient to see her again.

The genteel and exclusive gatherings at Almack's, typified by wretched catering and tepid dances and the most staunchly boring members of the elite, were a thing he normally detested. Yet, once again, he shocked one and all by his presence and his polite and altogether agreeable behavior.

He was forsworn to it. His grandmother, before agreeing to secure the coveted voucher, had wrung from him his most sacred oath not to disgrace her. He didn't anticipate any trouble in fulfilling his promise until he saw a man sidle up to Julia. She turned to him and smiled, and Raphael's heart stopped. It was infuriating! What the devil was Simple Simon doing sniffing about? Julia had told him to bugger off, hadn't she?

His keen eyes detected no overt affection pass between them as Julia accepted the punch glass he offered. Then he noted her smile was stiff and that she immediately turned to her sister, taking up their conversation without pausing to even thank Blake.

So, the couple was not cozy, but still he didn't like it. It was torture having to stand apart and watch that polished dandy dance attendance upon her. What had Strathford said that time—outside looking in like starving urchins with one's nose pressed against the poulterer's window?

His former friend had named it soundly enough to land a solid punch to his gut, and Raphael hadn't quite gotten his wind back. Julia seemed particularly unreachable tonight, and not just because of the presence of Simon. Dressed in a cream and apricot dress of empire design, elbow-length gloves and her hair drawn up in a simple twist, she appeared as regal as Diana. As she lifted the punch to her lips and sipped, her eyes lifted and scanned the crowd.

He stepped back reflexively, suddenly feeling woefully out of his element—out of place and not at all scornful of the crowd packed into the room. An interloper, a trespasser. One of the dispossessed watching with watering mouth what he could never have.

He brushed shoulders with someone by accident. When the man turned to confront who it was with whom he had collided, his narrow face drained of color and his beady little eyes widened with shock, and fear. Raphael blazed a glare back until he rushed off.

The sniveling fop. Contempt broke him free of his momentary discomfort. What was he thinking. He was as good—no, *better*—than any of the pedigrees here. He refused to be intimidated by these ... prancing ... powdered ... *ponces*. Recklessly he set off toward the orchestra. It was time to come out of the shadows. He was the Viscount de Fontvilliers, and his blood was bluer than anyone's here. As far as they knew.

And he had every right to dance with Julia Brodie.

However, if he were going to expend the effort, he was going to make it worth his while.

WHEN THE BAND struck up the waltz, Julia was surprised. The reigning matriarchs of Almack's generally frowned on the new dance. It was allowed, but it was rare. A quick glance at them as they huddled in their acclaimed circle overseeing the proceedings through their quizzing glasses, told her that they had not approved this one. She frowned, puzzled. Then how—?

"Miss Brodie, may I have this dance?"

Her world spun for a dizzying moment. She looked up and—yes—it was *him*.

Raphael pointed a toe and executed a smart bow. His eyes danced and he said, "I can't imagine this one is taken."

Of course, it was he who had put the unscheduled dance on the program, he knew it could not possibly be spoken for. Rather numbly, she placed her hand in his, unmindful of Laura gawking or Simon scowling. Raphael took her to the dance floor and slipped his fingers tightly about her waist, pulling her in a tad too close.

She didn't protest. To her surprise, he led masterfully, and she followed without missing a step while she fought with memories from last night. The feel of his hand, the scent of his soap brought a barrage of erotic memory until she thought she'd burst into a pillar of fire on the spot. Neither of them spoke. She wondered if it were obvious, considering how he was looking at her, if anyone else felt the heat coming off him and the sensual promise in those gorgeous eyes that had her locked in their depths.

She felt acutely conspicuous, as if anyone looking at them might guess what they had done only hours ago. A burning flush stole over her, and her confidence faltered. Glancing self-consciously, she saw that people indeed seemed to be watching her. Was it her imagination? "Why are they staring?" she asked Raphael quietly.

Raphael's eyes slid to take in the crowd. "Christ," he muttered. She felt his grip at her waist tighten until it hurt. "Our dance is over," he said through a clenched jaw.

He brought her back to the edge of the dance floor and left her there without another word. Breathless and confused, she stared after his retreating back, wondering what was happening.

Already, a sense of dread was warming the pit of her belly.

A burst of giggles drew her attention, and she looked to find Lucy Glencoe and two of her friends clustered not far away. They were peering at her while exchanging furtive comments behind their fans. When she caught their eye, the girls ducked and erupted in a fresh chorus of derisive snickers.

Dazed, she looked around her. Everyone seemed to be stealing glances her way. And she became aware of a strange buzz. She wasn't certain if it were in her head or if it were indeed the hiss of whispers under the music.

A hand on her wrist jerked her about. Laura was beside her, her eyes as wide as saucers. "That . . . the Viscount de Fontvilliers . . . he's the one they . . ."

A coldness began to grow within her. Julia's vision narrowed to the single focal point of her sister's stricken face.

Laura's voice hitched, "They are saying terrible things, that you and he . . . that there have been indiscretions. Oh, heavens, Julia—what is happening? Why would they make such things up?"

"Tell me," Julia commanded woodenly. "Tell me what they are saying?"

"The rumor is that you and he are *lovers!* That you were discovered, and that there is proof."

All feeling drained out of her.

Simon arrived, anger radiating from him on scalding sheets of heat. She looked at him, saw his pale face, his tense jaw, and understood.

He knew. Everyone knew.

"We are leaving," he said curtly, and propelled her toward the door.

"S O, YOU WON," Strathford said tightly, coming up beside Raphael to stare at Julia being hustled out on
Simon's arm.

Raphael snapped his head around. "What in Christ are
you doing here?"

"I was Laura's escort. You remember her, the delicious
blond you forced upon me? I have to say, I'm finding her
company much more delightful these days. I only hope I'll
be as lucky as you were with her sister. I am optimistic.
They share the same hot blood, after all."

Raphael's hands fisted and a choking dose of self-
disgust lodged in his throat. Good God, he'd been just like
Strathford, and not too long ago. "Get the hell away from
me."

He didn't want to think about the blasted wager, he
didn't give a damn about it. The whole place was buzzing
with the scandal. Somehow, someone had learned of his
and Julia's indiscretions. There was no telling what her
family would do—what Julia would do when faced with
utter ruin.

He had teased her about ruination. And here it was. Not
funny at all. Raphael's gut twisted. He was surprised to
feel guilt. This damned new function of his brain—this
conscience which had suddenly developed. Something
more, though, caught his heart in its grip, pressuring it until
every beat was laborious. It was fear. He could lose her.
He *would* lose her.

Strathford said. "I'm not pleased to concede, but a wager
must be honored, regardless of the fact that I still think
you are wrong. You seduced a girl, nothing more. But I
shall pay out. There is only one last thing I'm wondering,
and that is why did you wait so long to tell?"

He bared his teeth and pressed his face in close to his
former friend. "Because I wasn't done with her, damn you!"

The answer shut Strathford up and sent him away. It
also gave Raphael an explanation for his own sense of

bone-deep loss. After all, he knew the affair with Julia had to end some time. It was just . . . well . . . just that . . .

He wasn't done with her.

L AURA SLIPPED AMONG the potted plants, wishing she could disappear. Simon had taken Julia home, leaving her to face the awful talk and the stares. She was not stepping foot out *there*. She would just hide until they all left. How she would get home after that didn't bear consideration.

Colin Strathford parted the fronds and scowled at her. "What the devil are you doing hiding in there? Get out at once!"

She shied farther into her hidey hole. He hated her, too. She could hear it in his voice, impatient and sharp.

He barked, "Imagine what everyone will say if they see you in there like that. Come on out and I'll take you home."

Tentatively she withdrew. Colin's look was not at all comforting as she came to his side. "I am out five thousand," he said, "and in a hell of a mood, so don't give me a fuss."

She didn't understand what he meant. Five thousand? Five thousand what? He was true to his word, however. He managed to exit the building with as little attention as possible. They were no sooner in his carriage than she burst out in tears.

"Oh, for God's sake!" he groaned. Wrapping his arms about her, she thought he was going to comfort her until he jerked her head painfully back and slashed his mouth over hers.

She was caught between horror at his attack and wanting him, in a way. If he had been more gentle, if he had exhibited any semblance of caring, she would have easily been swept into the dizzying kiss. Even so, being held so tightly in his arms felt good until he pushed her down onto the seat.

She gasped to feel his hands on the bare skin that swelled over her neckline. Too confused to act, she lay immobile while he pressed kisses along her neck. She should let him, she thought. Having given it a great deal of thought, she had decided that she wasn't going to be a ninny. Julia had done it, too—dear God, could that be true?

Julia had, and look what had happened to her.

His mouth lowered to her breasts, devouring her tender flesh. A tendril of sensation began a sultry curl in her stomach, clenching with anticipation. Surely, he did not mean to . . .

She bolted upright when his mouth seared a sensitive peak.

"No!" she cried, pushing him away.

"Don't be a child," he urged roughly. Raising his head, he caught her earlobe between strong, white teeth. His thumb rubbed the aching nub he had just abandoned and she froze, caught in the exquisite sensations. In her ear his breath rasped, making her shiver. "This is the way it is with men and women. God, you've made me want you, Laura."

Fear battled excitement as his hands raised her skirts. She gasped when the cool air hit the exposed skin of her thighs above her garters.

She whimpered, caught in indecision. His touch was exciting, but there was something wrong. He was too hungry. He was frightening her. "Stop. Please. Colin, please."

He broke away to stare angrily into her eyes, and she regretted her hesitation. She wanted to apologize for denying him. She wanted to tell him to go ahead, but for some strange reason she didn't. She couldn't give him what he wanted. She couldn't.

With a muffled curse, he shoved himself away from her. "Blast, woman, you look like a frightened child." Adjusting his trousers with vicious tugs, he sat back with an explosion of breath and stared rigidly ahead, adding, "You *are* a child, damn it all, although you tempt a man with wiles you wield as expertly as any trained courtesan."

Through the haze of her assaulted senses, she heard what he said and the thought registered that she should be insulted. But something was breaking inside her, and she didn't seem to have the energy to respond.

He looked back over at her, his gaze dripping venom. "No need to be afraid. I'm not a rapist, although you deserve it for teasing me."

"I didn't mean to."

"No, of course not. God, you innocents are a plague. I should know better. Damn it, I *do* know better. Men like myself and women like you are never a good mix. But you got to me, *me* who never troubles with a woman who doesn't know exactly what I want. Damn you silly virgins. I thought I'd learned my lesson on that score. Once bitten, they say . . ." He threw himself against the other corner and turned to the window. "It's Fontvilliers's fault—he put me up to it in the first place. Damn him, and damn my own cursed pride!" His laugh was harsh as he shook his head in amazement. "Trust him to get the sister who broke the rules. And I—what do I get? I'm a damned sight poorer and my balls ache like the devil."

She stopped listening, sitting very still as he ranted. She knew now that Colin never wanted her. It was why he had been so testy at first—why he had always been so insistent on Julia coming along with them, asking about her all the time. He had only used her to help Fontvilliers get to her sister. And her naïve cooperation had helped bring it about.

She thought of what she herself had almost done. For him. For this horrid, loathsome man she had fancied herself in love with.

When the carriage came to a halt, she opened the door and clamored out without waiting for the step, nearly falling onto the cobbles in the front of the town house. Straightening, she looked over her shoulder at the startled marquess. In a flash she took in his rumpled appearance, his startled eyes.

He was so handsome. Her heart wrenched. Why did it have to be this way? Why couldn't he be different?

She said, "You are a contemptible pig, and I never want to see you again."

<hr />

RAPHAEL NEVER TRESPASSED on his grandmother's private retreat. The little parlor situated off the family withdrawing room was more of a solarium. She had hung the windows with heavy draperies and had a massive brazier—some medieval monstrosity she had dug out of the attics—brought in to ward off chills that crept through the loose panes of glass. The place was a mess, with clutter everywhere and no redeeming charm that some places have when they contain the treasures of an eccentric.

He had been summoned here today and now sat slumped in an old divan that sagged under his weight. Chewing on his nail, he stared at some faraway point, only half-listening to his grandmother speak.

"You have no choice," she was saying. "You have to marry the girl."

Marriage. Christ Almighty, the very word conjured up nightmare images that made his blood run cold.

"You know how I feel on that subject," he growled.

He had known for his whole life he would never marry. It wasn't Julia. *There* was an incentive if ever there was one—access to her luscious body whenever he wished, ownership over it, even. He'd be her husband, her master. She'd be his. No other man would know what he had sampled, and he could indulge himself in her lively spirit, her sensuality, her intoxicating presence anytime he wanted.

But his mother had defied her parents, given up all to move to a foreign country for supposed "love" of Marquay. He remembered the cesspool of pain and bitterness and petty revenge that love eventually became. It must have happened very quickly. Their fascination with each other hadn't lasted very long.

"I do not think it wise to refuse me, Fontvilliers."

He glanced up, aghast. "Are you threatening me?"

"We are all the family left to each other, and at my age that counts for something. But even that thin sentiment will not stand up to this latest debacle." Folding her thick fingers in front of her, she paused, eyes narrowing. Even wrinkled with age, she could still compose her face into an expression that would chill a demon. "Here are the terms, and they are nonnegotiable. Your part is simple. Marry the girl. In return, I am prepared to place one-third of my estates in your name. Surely you are not so wealthy on your own that you can do without the Wentword fortune. If you refuse, I will disinherit you. Completely. Cut you off, disown our relation. I cannot tolerate your destructive behavior any longer."

"You will injure yourself in the process. You have no one else, either." He sneered, although a flicker of disquiet passed through him. He didn't care so much about the money, but his grandmother knew well enough that his connection to the Wentword name meant a great deal to him. He wasn't sure if she knew about the question of his paternity. He had never told her. If her daughter had confided the matter, no one had ever given any hint of it. Nevertheless, she didn't err when she used that particular persuasion to push him into doing her will. The Wentwords were the only blood he could claim, his only grounding in heritage.

The woman's broad face didn't stir, not one bit. "I'll hand it to the beggars on the street if I please. The point is, Fontvilliers, you'll get nothing. You will lose claim to the Wentword estates forever." Her expression did change then, to a scathing look of scorn. "You would only have your connection to your father, and Marquay hates you. I never understood that, especially when you turned out so much like him."

There was absolute quiet. The steady tick of the mantel clock sounded huge. It seemed that she didn't know about Marquay possibly not being his father, after all. Yet all the same she sensed, somehow, the importance she represented to Raphael. Uncanny instincts, he groused silently, like a meat-eater could smell fear.

Very bloody well. He'd marry. Why the devil not? At least he'd enjoy his wife for a time, and when it began to sour, he'd move on.

Marriage. Christ! Bound for eternity, locked in an obscene trap forever . . .

It would be necessary to make clear to Julia from the start that there should be no expectation of happily-ever-after. He wasn't going to change for her and he wouldn't tolerate her thinking he would. *She* would be the one who would have to change. She would have to grow up and learn to live with a husband like himself—an unapologetic scoundrel who was not going to alter one whit, damn it all!

Poor Julia. It surprised him he could pity her fate. She hadn't bargained on this. But neither had he.

When Raphael spoke, his voice was rough. "You realize, of course, that you condemn the sweet child to a life of misery. I do not like her having been forced on me, and she will know it every minute of every day."

A thick hand waved at him. "I care nothing for your happiness or hers. I am old, and am weary of your antics. I want you to start breeding heirs, *legitimate* ones. That is all I care about."

"I want half, not one-third, of the money. And I want a contract drawn up to ensure I receive the other half upon your death." He only said that to bleed her, make her pay more than she was willing. It was punishment, plain and simple. He could have asked for more—and gotten it—but it didn't really matter apart from having the upper hand.

"You'll get it," she said. "You'll get every ha-penny, but you must do as I wish."

His voice was low, heavy with resentment, but a stirring of excitement as well. There were advantages here. He was not too embittered to see that. "Agreed."

I T WAS A strange limbo that overtook Julia as the scandal rode the tide of London gossip. Her family was stunned, and despite her deep remorse at the hurt she saw in their faces, she could not be moved to shame. Nor could she explain that although she knew it was wrong to have done what she did, she could not regret it. Raphael was the truest thing that had ever happened to her—true enough that the strength of this knowledge sustained her throughout a week of quiet, downcast faces and hand-wringing anxiety.

Besides her parents, she'd had to contend with Simon. She hadn't seen him since the night the scandal broke, but he had said all he needed to in the carriage ride home. She didn't see him again after that, nor did she expect to.

Her sister, Laura, was sympathetic, but she couldn't understand, not really, and she was quiet and subdued over something Julia knew had to do with the Marquess of Strathford. Her gentle prods at encouraging confidences brought only vague answers and shrugs. If Julia had the energy, she would have put her mind to breaking through Laura's uncharacteristic reserve, but her mind was taken up with the unfortunate situation in which she found herself, and what would happen next.

Her father had talked briefly of paying a call on the Viscount—a call of the kind any angry father might make to demand justice for their daughter, but Julia knew he wouldn't. She was glad, too, that her father was so sensible. Raphael was *ton*—nobility by blood, breeding, and right. Her father was in society upon the good graces of a business acquaintance. The Cravensmores had become friends when an investment tip Francis had given the duke had paid off outrageous dividends. Cravensmore credited Julia's father for his fortune, but Francis Brodie didn't forget that he was only a commoner in favor with the nobility. He could not, even under these circumstances, presume to demand anything from his "betters," even if that man was a rake of the first rank and had behaved abominably.

Yet through this week of tension and uncertainty, Julia had an odd serenity about it all, a conviction that Raphael would not abandon her. Why she believed this, she could not explain. He had made her no promises and his reputation spoke for itself. And yet, she did not despair as the family settled in to deal with the crisis.

And then one day, without a word of warning, Leah the spy rushed into the solarium and told her the Viscount de Fontvilliers had just been announced and was right at this moment being shown into the study to see Father. Julia was summoned after a tense hour, an hour she spent pacing until the soles of her feet ached. There could be little doubt as to the purpose of Raphael's visit, or for his asking to speak to her father first. He had come for her, just as she believed all along.

When she entered the room, neither man would look at her, and she felt her first twinge of apprehension. Her quick eye took in the situation. Raphael radiated tension. And anger. He was very angry. Her father was nervous.

Francis Brodie cleared his throat before saying, "The viscount has asked for your hand in marriage."

Frowning, she turned to Raphael. He still hadn't so much as glanced at her.

He was dressed to perfection in a snowy lawn shirt with an elegant waistcoat. Around his neck was an impeccably tied cravat. Trousers of soft wool matched his finely tailored tailcoat. His hair was tame, for once, his expression blank.

This wasn't what she had expected. She had supposed he would be brash and bold and devil-may-care, but this . . . this frigid snub was disconcerting. "Is it true you wish to marry me?" she asked softly.

He steepled his long fingers, studying them. "That is correct."

"Why will you not look at me?" she asked. The room

was deadly quite for a moment, then Raphael turned his head and gave her a glare.

It was she with whom he was angry, she realized. "You blame me?" she said.

He pulled his lips back to bare his teeth, a gesture that just barely passed for a smile. " 'Nothing is fortuitous or by chance.' Someone put the word out about us. There is only you and I who knew of what had transpired between us privately. I puzzled about it after a while, and I thought, 'What if the little minx did it herself?' How else to force my hand when you knew I would never marry you willingly?"

She gaped at him. "Why would I throw myself into disgrace? You think you are such a catch as that?"

His eyes widened, taken aback. Then she thought she saw amusement in them, just a flash, before they narrowed on her. "You didn't seem to think me such a bad prospect before."

"With all the wretched trouble you've brought with you, I cannot see how I missed the obvious liabilities!"

His face twitched, but he remained stern. "Will you marry me or not?"

"Certainly not!"

Her father stepped up, taking Julia's arm and pulling her aside. He was mortified, judging by the crimson that had crept into his face, but he looked her steady in the eye. "Think on the offer, Julia. It will settle much and put a swift end to . . . eh . . . the, ah . . . situation."

Julia felt betrayed. She couldn't believe he would endorse the viscount's suit, having heard the disdain in which he so obviously held her. "Is it what you advise?" she asked with incredulity.

His eyes saddened with uncertainty. Giving Raphael a dubious look, he merely shook his head. "It is up to you, Julia. I believe only you can make the right choice for yourself in this matter. If you once trusted this man enough to—" He frowned and broke off. "It is up to you."

Taking in a slow breath, she squared her shoulders. There

was no decision to be made, really. She'd thought it out thoroughly during these past days. "If the viscount is bitter at having his hand forced, then let it be known I am equally so for having to accept an unwilling husband. But there are my sisters to think of, especially Laura, whose season has been wasted on the frivolous marquess who seems to have flown, as all our other true 'friends' have done. A marriage will put things to right, rest the buzzing tongues, and clear the way for her next season. Leah, as well, is coming up soon. For that sake and that sake alone, I accept the offer."

"Then it's settled." Raphael all but leaped to his feet. "I'll obtain a special license so that we can have the deed accomplished as quickly as possible. I'll inform you when all is ready. In the meantime, I suggest you pack your things and be waiting. I shall not give you much notice."

Raphael took a few steps when suddenly Julia's father stepped in his path. Francis's face was alarmingly red, and not from embarrassment this time. "You will treat my daughter with respect. Now, you go and take proper leave of the woman who is to be your wife."

Looking more amused than intimidated, Raphael perused the older man slowly from head to toe. Then, to Julia's absolute surprise, he turned on his heel and came to take her hand. Lifting his mocking gaze to her as he bowed over it, he said in a tone that managed to be both caustic and pleasant, "Good day, future wife."

She had never seen him like this. Everything about him spoke of bone-chilling threat. A shiver of apprehension played along her spine like the dance of ice-cold fingers.

When he departed, her father came up and wrapped her up in his arms until she stopped shaking.

Chapter Fourteen

⟿

J ULIA FOUND HERSELF stunningly vindicated in the eyes of society on the simple fact that she was to become a viscountess. Her mother seemed to be in awe at the wealth and station of the man who was about to become her son-in-law. Those she had once called friend began to call again, eager to hear snippets of gossip on the plans and prod Julia on the delicious details. Preparations for the wedding took on a gay tone.

It was a small gathering of family and friends that came to bear witness to the demise of the most renowned rake-hell in London. The presence of the duke and duchess and some of their well-titled friends, as well as the preening Countess of Wentword and her circle, made certain that it was not a tawdry affair, despite it being rushed. However, it was as unorthodox a wedding ceremony as any of them were likely to see.

Raphael pulled out his pocket watch on two separate occasions as if he found the proceedings exceedingly boring. He stifled several yawns and recited his vows in a droll monotone that raised more than a few eyebrows.

When given permission to kiss the bride, he snatched Julia so hard that her head snapped. Almost bending her backward, he brought his mouth down over hers and opened her lips to allow his tongue to boldly stroke hers until she twisted free.

For a moment, neither one of them was aware of the sea of faces gaping, nor the wide-eyed clergyman peering over his spectacles at them. Raphael's nostrils flared and his mouth curled in a snide twist. "Well," he said softly as they gazed in shock at each other. "We still have that, at least."

As he marched her out of the church, she turned to him and said in a low voice so as not to be overheard, "I think you are quite enjoying yourself."

Raphael didn't have a quick retort for that. Enjoying himself? He was frightened out of his wits was what he was. He was married—*married!*—for Christ's sake, and he was trying his best to not let any of these eager-eyed spectators see a glimpse of the hot rush of panic flooding his limbs.

A bridal luncheon was held at the Cravensmores' town house. Raphael threw back several glasses of champagne as he circulated among his guests, making vaguely insulting comments. He made a tasteless joke of the Earl of Shifflan's bald head and stared in a manner that was anything but subtle at Dame Judith Rothchild's abundant bosom. When he announced that he and his bride were going to take their leave, Julia looked apprehensive about being alone with him, and that only made him feel meaner. He knew he was destroying everything, and he couldn't even help himself.

In the carriage his wild recklessness subsided. He reclined on the opposite seat and folded his arms over his chest.

Julia let loose with her pent-up fury. "Do you want me to hate you?"

"Why not?" He shrugged. "Everybody does. It is a talent of mine."

"You are drunk."

"Not nearly enough."

"Then you are an idiot."

He sighed. "Where are the epithets? Didn't I tell you, in order to be effective, you have to have those vile words flying about?"

"Go to hell."

"There." He pretended satisfaction. She turned away, refusing to talk to him. Silence reigned until they pulled up in front of his house.

Once inside the large foyer, Julia watched him warily, wondering what manner of humiliations he had planned for her now that they were alone. He merely headed toward a room and left her to her own devices without so much as summoning a servant to take her cloak.

She followed him, hands clenched at her sides, her heels clicking soundly on the bare marble floors. He had shut the doors behind him. She flung them open, startling him as he stood over an assortment of decanters clustered on a sideboard. He was in the midst of pouring himself another drink.

This room was the library, a very masculine retreat. There was nothing colorful or pretty to welcome a woman within its walls. But she had spent far too much time with the duke in his masculine domain to be intimidated by heavy paneling and leather upholstery. "Are you the injured one here, Raphael?" she asked, cocking a hand on her hip.

He looked amused, as if he found her ridiculous. "Impertinent today, aren't we?"

"A skill I learned from you."

He turned back to pouring his drink. "Yes, well, don't take it too far."

"I think you've had enough to drink," she said. "Or is it you need it for courage?"

A sharp bark of scorn was her reply, but he only filled the glass halfway. A small concession, she supposed.

"When you are settled, I have something to say to you." He took his drink and sprawled lazily on an armchair. "I am at your disposal. *Wife*."

She took a seat across from him. "You say it like it's a

foul word." He only gave her a suffering look before raising his glass to his lips. "And I wonder what I have done to deserve your hatred. I mean really done, not what you have dreamed up in your imagination."

Leaning on an elbow, he stroked his chin and stared at her.

She continued, "An imagination that conveniently has forgotten your own part in causing this marriage to come about."

His brows shot up. "Would you rather I'd have left you alone? You'd be bored silly, married to Blake, and working diligently to secure your place in the hearts of society mavens."

She shook her head. "I have no regrets about not marrying Simon. He was a good man, however. In some ways, I wish my heart had remained steadfast. It certainly would have been less trouble."

He chewed on the lining of his mouth, watching her.

She went on. "But I am wed to you. I didn't connive to produce that end as you have accused me of doing. You know it very well, too. You are just looking for someone to blame. In any event, we are married now. I don't understand why you are being so hateful. We didn't chafe in each other's company before. In fact, we got on quite splendidly. It seemed . . ." A thought occurred to her. Her gaze shot up to meet his. "Unless that was all for the sake of getting me to . . . to allow you to . . . If it was just about making love to me, and none of the rest of it were true."

Appearing disturbed, he couldn't meet her gaze.

She rose, her brow creased thoughtfully. She tried to speak, but the words caught in her throat, making it impossible. Turning quickly, she left.

That was it, then. That was why he despised her. He had desired her for a time, but he hadn't truly cared for her, not as he had pretended he had. Oh, God, he was actually appalled to have her as wife—it wasn't just his pride chafing.

The feelings she had felt from him had existed only in

her own mind. A dream born of her own love for him. She was nothing to him, truly nothing.

Pausing in the hallway, she looked about helplessly. Raphael had given her no indication of where she was to have her rooms. Not wanting to be caught out in the open, not with the storm of tears threatening, she dashed quickly through a parlor into a dark room. It was colder in here. The air felt wonderful on her scalding cheeks.

The place was overcrowded, cluttered with all manner of paraphernalia. Dolls with blank, staring china faces, skeins of wool rolled into balls and partially unwound, half-finished knitting, and yellowed paper fans. In startling contrast to the neoclassical gracefulness of the rest of the house, boldly printed fabrics hung with scarlet fringe were draped everywhere. Cushions abounded, as if this were not at all the middle of fashionable London, but a sheik's tent in the midst of the Arabian desert.

She flounced onto a huge pile of pillows in the corner and curled up.

Without meaning to, she dozed for a bit, roused awake when someone entered. She sat up, startled, causing the intruder to start as well.

The Countess of Wentword stopped in her tracks, staring aghast with her heavily bejeweled hand pressed against a large bosom. "Goodness, Julia, you gave me such a fright. Come out of there this instant."

Like a naughty eight-year-old, Julia rose on trembling legs. The countess seemed like such a hard, unsentimental woman. "I am sorry, my lady," she murmured, dashing away the humiliating tears that had sprung up suddenly. "I didn't know where to go. That is, which room."

"That rascal didn't take you to your room?" She sighed and moved slowly to her chair. "He's sulking. He's always been a bad sport when it came to losing."

The reference to her marriage as Raphael "losing" only brought on more tears. "If you'll excuse me, I'll go to my room if you would just summon someone to take me."

"Sit down, gel, and dry your eyes. Crying never solved anything."

Julia had had quite enough bullying for one day. She drew herself up and said, "It solves a great deal. If not the circumstances, then some of the ache in one's heart."

"What? Who told you that nonsense? Hmmm. I didn't suspect you had a tongue in your head. My grandson would have to choose a saucy bit, just to annoy me. I had heard you were docile." Chuckling, she shrugged. "But then, you wouldn't have been leaping into his bed if you'd have been all you were thought to be, now would you?"

Julia's anger blazed in a sudden white fury. "If you've a mind to taunt me, I warn you I've had my fill. I may forget my manners."

To her amazement, the countess looked pleased, pressing her lips together in a tight smile. "What have we here? A gel with spirit! Ha! It is what the young scamp deserves. Sit, sit, gel. I'll ring for tea."

"I am not hun—"

"Sit." She picked up a bell and tolled it loudly.

Julia sat, miserable as the obnoxious noise clanged, hurting her ears.

RAPHAEL WAS OF a mind to drink, but he kept lapsing into thoughtful stares and forgetting to attend to the level of whiskey in his glass. When he realized it had not been decreased in an hour, he abandoned it.

He had played with fire so often in his life, he had thought it his right to emerge unsinged. Why had that never before struck him as insufferably arrogant?

He hadn't really believed Julia had broken the scandal, but as she so aptly put it, it had suited him to have someone to blame. He could accept it wasn't her—but who? Who had even known of their secret assignations? His household staff were beyond reproach. It was a slight possibility his grandmother might have learned of it. It certainly suited her ends to see him wedded and breeding on a girl—any girl—as quickly as possible. Or could Blake have known somehow and taken his revenge in public censure?

Rubbing his temples, he squeezed his eyes shut. No answers seemed forthcoming. God, he was restless! The air seemed charged. The house was different, as if just her presence under this roof altered the very substance of everything within it.

He just now remembered that he never showed her to a room. In fact, he hadn't selected one for her, not being able to make up his mind between a guest apartment or the beautifully appointed chamber that adjoined his. He wasn't quite certain if he wished to accept their roles of husband and wife enough to allow her so close to his domain.

The idea of her taking her rightful place pleased him in some respects, and yet part of him rejected the domestic situation. *Too cozy, too intimate,* it cautioned, *she shall be privy to every move you make, give her wrong ideas about this arrangement.*

He would have to see to it, he supposed. Hauling himself to his feet, he went to search for her. With every step, his pulse jumped in anticipation. The fog of rage had cleared a bit, and underneath it was still the undeniable desire that had drawn them together from the first.

She was his wife, after all. Legally wed. *His.*

He found his grandmother coming down the hall from the direction of his room. She was probably looking for him, no doubt to have some say about his behavior today. As she was the last person he wished to speak to at the moment, he tried to push past her, but she closed her fingers around his arm. She said, "Leave her. She's resting."

Ah, so his grandmother had taken the matter in hand and put Julia in the room connected to his. He was surprised how much this suited him, for all his previous misgivings. However, he kept his tone sharp as he replied, "Is she your wife or mine?"

She sighed. "I know it may pose a seeming insur-
mountable challenge to you, Fontvilliers, but try not to act
like an ass. I swear, each and every day you remind me
more and more—"

"Yes, I know. My father." He rode the familiar surge of
unpleasantness whenever she said this. He wondered what
her reaction would be if he told her there was likely no
blood relation between the two of them. He wondered why
he never did.

Her eyes narrowed. "You two are a soulless pair. And
that one in there"—she darted her eyes to the closed door
to the chamber where Julia resided—"surprises me. Not at
all as foolish or useless as I imagined she'd be."

"Not like my mother, you mean." God, he was trotting
out all the demons now.

The age-worn features didn't blanch. "That girl is not
Violetta, and she doesn't deserve your misery."

"Your affection for my wife is touching." He sneered
cockily, trying to hide the effect of her words. Of course
Julia was not his mother—why should she state such an
obvious thing as that? And why should it pierce him? Drolly,
he added, "I fear I might weep."

"I wonder if you have anything inside of you but bile,
Fontvilliers." She shook her head and glanced at the door
to the mistress's suite. "As for your wife, I find myself unexpectedly fond of the girl. I don't know quite how it happened, and so quickly, but she surprised me in my lair and
we had tea. She has spirit, but genuine softness as well.
She is too good for you." Her gaze returned to him and
grew threatening. "I swear I will make you miserable if
you harm her."

"As opposed to deflowering her and forcing her into
marriage amid a public scandal? God, Grandmother, what
worse could I do?"

"What a strange comment," she said, peering closely at
him. "You could not possibly be suffering from such a thing
as a conscience, could you, Fontvilliers?"

Raphael closed his face to her. "Why, *Grandmère*, that would make me almost human. You should know better."

He did break away then. In defiance of her edict, he went straight to Julia's room. He entered without bothering to knock.

Julia stood directly in front of him. She was startled, poised in midstride with a folded garment in her hand. On the bed, her valise was opened.

That gorgeous mouth of hers was half-pursed in surprise, her eyes wide and wary. The light coming in through the opened window cast them pale, pale amber finely shot with gold. Minute shadows delineated her features—the narrow nose, the tender hollows underneath her lofty cheekbones.

The sight of her broke something inside him, and all of the rabid beasts he'd been wrestling suddenly subsided. He stared at her, dumbfounded for some reason, as if seeing her here in his house, unpacking her belongings, made something real he had feared he'd only imagined.

His throat was suddenly dry. "The servants will do that," he said, and it came out in a rough rasp.

"It is no trouble."

A cascade of feelings, both physical and emotional, swept over him, pooling in his gut, knotting with need and regret and desire all twisted in together. He took a step forward. His movements felt jerky, not at all the fluid, feline gracefulness he had cultivated as part of his charm. Another step.

"Julia," he said, and reached for her.

She shrank away. It horrified him so much, he said, "I'm sorry," before he even knew he would.

And then he said it again.

The garment she held fell from her numbed hands and floated to the floor, forgotten. Her eyes stayed locked with his. Raphael moved. This time she didn't retreat.

"I'm sorry." He had her in his arms. He buried his face in her neck, breathing in her scent in long, nourishing gulps scented with jasmine, or rose . . . no . . . undefinable and mysterious as the woman herself. Murmuring softly, he repeated those two words over and over, then her name again.

Then he kissed her.

She kissed him back, and his soul felt as if it would burst into a thousand pieces.

I T WAS WEEKS later when Raphael glided into the front parlor of his home, paused to take stock of his guest seated in one of the chairs, then proceeded without further acknowledgment to the fireplace. Hand on the mantel, he struck an arrogant pose. Dryly, he commented, "Isn't it a bit early for you, Atvers?"

"It's twelve noon, which is like the cock crow to me under normal circumstances. But my revels are not what they used to be since you've deserted us." He had the audacity to look chiding. Raphael chose to ignore it, hardly able to care.

"However, we have a bit of business left unfinished." Atvers opened his purse and drew out a wad of crisp banknotes. "Strathford sent me here, to finish this for him. Oh, and he sends a message." He laughed like a hyena, his slight shoulders shaking up and down. "He was quite taken with that sister of Julia's, I think. He wanted to make certain I told you—what were his words?—oh, yes! To keep her safe and make sure the man she winds up with deserves her. And, by God, I think he was serious!" He hooted, stomping his feet on the floor. Holding out the notes, he said, "And by the way, here is the five thousand."

Moving quickly, Raphael snatched the money out of Atvers's hands. With a quick glance at the open door, he stuffed it roughly into the inside pocket of his coat. Thank God no one had seen. "Where is Strathford?" Raphael demanded impatiently. "And Martinvale, for that matter?"

Atvers's face clouded. "They've flown, the cads. Strathford's gone off to the country. I heard a rumor his romancing of Lucy Glencoe has come to nothing and his

family is angry with him. Martinvale, he will not receive
me, but then he never was up for the game, not from the
very start. But what of them, anyway? We have a cele-
bration to see to, and the tables at Whites have been the
poorer for your absence. Quince and Tellingham are up in
their markers and bragging about it to everyone. Ah, but
it will make their fleecing all the more grand. So," he said,
clapping his hands loudly and rubbing them together, "when
will the pretty bridegroom be done with his duties"—he
rolled his eyes and leered—"and be ready to take up some
old sport?"

Raphael chewed on the lining of his cheek. "Flown,
have they?"

Atvers's face fell. "Come, Fontvilliers, this is your finest
hour. Now we can tell everyone of the wager and how you
won so cleverly—"

"Don't you dare!" Raphael thundered. Stalking the short
distance to come hover over the other man as he shrunk
down in the chair, he growled, "Leave the matter be, Atvers.
You've taken far too much upon yourself as it is."

The smaller man stared incredulously at the object of
his admiration. "What was it all for if to keep secret? You
put everything into this seduction, and now you want to
stuff the entire matter into a cupboard and ignore it? Is
that why you told no one after you'd had her?"

Raphael shot up straight as knowledge dawned, flooding through him until he was hot and throbbing. "My God!
You idiot, Atvers!" Pacing a few steps away, he stopped
in front of the fire, eyes clenched tight, jaw even tighter.
He pinched the bridge of his nose to counter some of the
tension. "It was you. You broke the scandal. Blast you,
Atvers, you fool!"

Atvers answered in a high-pitched whine filled with de-
fensiveness. "I heard voices when I was stuck in the parlor that night, when your man had me waiting all that time.
I watched through a crack in the door when you brought
her downstairs, and it was obvious what had happened. I
waited and waited for days for you to announce your vic-

tory. My God, you had done it and you said nothing—not a word! How could you cheat me of that?"

Raphael's eyes snapped open. Atvers gripped the arms of his chair as he explained further. "It was almost as if you didn't care about the wager anymore. You would have become a laughingstock, Fontvilliers—Strathford would have seen to it. I had to do something. Already, people were starting to say that you'd changed. You hadn't taken a mistress in months, you were socializing within the *beau monde* as if you were some dandy infatuated with its charms. Going to balls, to Almacks', for God's sake! I had to do it, to show them all that you were still *Fontvilliers*— the leader of the Bane of the Ton."

Raphael was on him in an instant, as quick as the strike of a snake, hauling him to his feet by his collar and shoving him toward the door. "You half-witted little ape. I could snap your worthless neck in my hands. Do you know what you have done?"

Stumbling, Atvers gaped incredulously. "I didn't know you would be forced to marry her! I hadn't thought it would go so far. I am sorry! But surely the fact of a silly ceremony having taken place makes little difference."

"Don't try my patience too far, worm. I warn you." Raphael gave him another shove. "Be off, before I throttle you."

Untangling his feet, Atvers rushed to the door. He stopped, pulling himself up in some semblance of dignity. "You'll cool down when you realize I was right."

Raphael lunged and Atvers scurried out.

He didn't pursue. He had only wanted to frighten him off, to have some peace from his grating boasts.

Taking a seat by the hearth, he stared into the empty grate. The visit from his old bosom bow had disturbed him deeply. He felt it was an intrusion, a violation. His life of late had so little to do with his past, and he found, to his surprise, that he wanted to keep it that way.

Since their first night together, the relationship between himself and Julia had become unexpectedly pleasant. No, *pleasant* was not a strong enough word, but more than that he was not ready to admit, even to himself. That first night he had held her and kissed her and somehow opened up something in himself.

It had led them to knock the half-emptied valise off the big four-poster bed in her room, a feminine creation hung with crepe and silk that was designed to look like something out of a faerie tale. There he had undressed her, kissed her, made love to her in a union that had been intense and sensual and magnificent. The next night they christened the large mahogany half-tester in his chamber. She hadn't slept again amid the feminine flounces of her own bedroom from then on, for they both preferred her to be curled up by his side, where he could touch her and pull her under him and make love to her whenever he wished.

With tentative steps, they had come together again, spending long hours together, talking about themselves, their lives, their pasts. He was hardly ready to fling open the portals of his seedy origins, but he did share with her his travels, at least the more civilized aspects of his journeys abroad. Needless to say, he didn't mention the whores, and his father figured into the tales only minimally. But when he described the sights he had seen, from the dramatic majesty of the Parthenon to the rugged splendor of the Salzburg Alps, she absorbed every detail. He loved to watch the look on her face as he made the places come alive, embellishing shamelessly just to increase her joy. He was still, after all, a superb liar.

The places became real for him, as well, even if his tales were only half-authentic. It certainly was better to imagine a grand tour filled with culture and art and architecture than the sordid truth.

When he was with her, he never thought about anything other than the moment. He never examined himself too closely, or his sudden disinterest in visiting his old haunts, carousing with friends, or the freedom he had once valued so much. Time was spent with Julia, and the past did not exist. He had nearly succeeded in forgetting it.

Atvers's visit had reminded him that it was not harm-lessly at rest. In fact, it left him with the distinct feeling of a threat. He experienced a deep conviction that his sins would return to tear him into shreds. That it was inevitable and it was coming fast.

Shaking off the cryptic thought, he admonished him-self. It would be a fine day in Hades when Raphael Gis-card had something to fear from the likes of Charles Atvers.

Withdrawing the packet of banknotes from his coat pocket, he thumbed through them absently. Thank good-ness Julia was out with her sister—she could have walked by just at that moment and witnessed the exchange. He rose and went to the desk, placing the money in a drawer, still pensive. It was foolish to be so riled up over that weasel's visit. It was over, the wager was settled. He did-n't want anything more to do with Atvers. Strathford, ei-ther, but Strathford was already gone. Martinvale was in a snit, gone, too, to nurse his bruised conscience. The Bane of the Ton was a thing of the past.

He felt a curious lack of emotion at the end of an era.

Chapter Fifteen

RAPHAEL TOOK HIS cravat apart and began again, arching his chin to give himself more room to maneuver. "Blast and bloody hell. I am having no luck tonight."

"Where is Thomas?" Julia asked lightly, gliding in through the connecting door. His hands stilled as he caught sight of his wife, draped artfully in champagne crepe de chine with clusters of silk rosettes and pearls swagged from shoulder to hemline. With her hair wound intricately and a touch of cosmetics to enhance her vivid coloring, she looked stunning.

"Still with his mother, damn him for the betraying sod that he is. How the devil am I to get along without my trusted valet?"

Julia laughed. "I hardly think visiting an ailing mother constitutes high treason."

Ripping out the elaborate knot, Raphael growled in disgust. "I cannot imagine how the man does this. This is the seventeenth try, I swear."

Julia brushed his hands aside. "Let me. Perhaps one has to be facing the person to get it right."

"You have no practice with such things."

"Well, I may be able to puzzle it out. We still have plenty of time."

He made no complaint, though it was unlike him to sit still for a woman's fussing. The advantages of the situation made themselves immediately evident, and he had always been a shameless opportunist. The daring décolletage furnished an irresistible sight of swelling flesh. The soft brush of her fingertips against his neck created a flood of sensations that darted into the pit of his belly and stirred his desire.

"You do not seem nervous," he commented, forcing his eyes upward and his thoughts to tamer topics. "In fact, you look the picture of calm."

"Do I? Good. This is our first appearance since that delightful performance you put on at our wedding ceremony. I still could lay you low for that, you know."

"Any luck with the cravat?" he asked. He smiled blatantly when her expression told him she wasn't fooled by his change of topic.

"Your tact serves you well," she muttered, crossing one end of the cloth over the other. She frowned. "It seems it should go thusly. Hmm. No, that is not it at all. Perhaps if we twist this just so . . ."

The way her teeth caught at her bottom lip as she studied his mangled cravat was nearly his undoing. Torn between laughter and lust, he stayed perfectly still and fully enjoyed the moment.

"I have come to an important decision, Raphael," she finally pronounced, throwing up her hands. "You must raise Thomas's salary immediately. The man is obviously a genius and we cannot do without him."

"Well and good, my dear, but what of tonight?" Taking the ends of the cloth, he wound them haphazardly about his neck, finishing with a fat knot with artless stubs sticking at odds ends. "This will do our efforts to achieve respectability no good. They will certainly stare until their eyes pop clear out of their head to see me thus."

"No," she agreed, biting her cheeks, "that will never do."

His arms went around her waist. "How much time did you say we had?"

"Not time enough for you to be having such thoughts."

"What thoughts?" he asked indignantly.

"Oh, stop acting the innocent. I've taken note of that look on your face."

His lips brushed along her temple as he said, "What look?"

She turned her face up to his and smiled a seductive smile that incinerated him. "The one that tells me you want to make love. It's this intense sort of expression you get. Like you are going to devour me."

"Then I must go about the day looking like a wolf, for I assure you, my dear, I always want to make love to you." Three steps backed her up against the wall. He pressed closer, touching every part of her body with the length of his own.

She laughed. "Before we were married, when you would look at me like that, it used to frighten me."

His hands grabbed her waist and pulled her up against his hips, pressing his arousal against the deep gathers of her skirts. "Does it frighten you now?" he murmured.

She slipped her arms about his shoulders. "On the contrary. I confess I find it quite exciting to see that gleam in your eyes." She tilted her head. "It makes them cloudy, like jade."

"Poetic," he commented before taking her earlobe gently between his teeth. His hands worked quickly to gather her skirts up around her thighs. Her slim legs, sheathed in white silk stockings with blue satin garters tied at the tops, were bared. His hands slid behind the exposed thighs, cupping her bottom.

Letting out a soft moan, her head fell back as he bent to the graceful column of her neck. He helped himself to the creamy flesh as his hands quickly worked the closure of his trousers to free himself. Lifting her against him, he murmured, "Wrap your legs around my waist."

She roused, somewhat bewildered. "What are you going to do?"

"I am going to finish what you started. You have no business coming into a man's dressing chamber looking that delicious. And since we don't have the time to summon your maid to finesse you out of all those buttons and I can't fling you on the bed for fear of the wrinkles it will put in your dress and most of all because I can wait not one moment longer, I am going to take you like this." He claimed her mouth and levered her in position. Although she was not a small woman in height, she was slender and he managed her weight easily.

Settling her over him, he thrust forward. Into her ear, he rasped, "When we return home tonight, I shall take my time with you. I shall touch you and taste you—all over. I want to linger at your breasts and taste the secrets enfolded within your thighs. Ah, most especially there. I will tease you until you beg me for release." He thrust again, tearing a cry of pleasure from her. "I shall make you come until you are too weak to move and then I shall fit myself inside you, like this." Another push and his excitement nearly crested. "And ride you until neither one of us can breathe."

Pleasure exploded, jerking him in its crushing fist as a flood of heat poured through him. He felt it pulse through his whole being, keeping the rhythm until every last tremor was spent and a golden lassitude suffused his body.

Letting her down gently, he stepped away to fasten his trousers, replace the studs in his shirt, smooth his hair back in place. She fluffed her skirts busily until he caught her to him, caressing her cheek and kissing her with a tenderness that was quite different from the raw passion of a moment ago.

"Julia," he said solemnly, "you must do something about this."

He held up his neckcloth helplessly.

E VERY EYE AT the Duke and Duchess of Shelbourne's
musicale evening was focused on the newly wedded
couple who made a rather spectacular entrance amid a swell
of hushed gossip. Some displayed faces alight with greedy
curiosity while more prudent onlookers hid their expressions behind fluttering fans or, in the case of the curious
male, a strategic cough.

Spots of color rode high on Julia's cheeks as she entered the room on the arm of her husband. She walked
with her head held high, her eyes straight ahead, her hand
locked fast in the crook of Raphael's arm. Her subdued
dignity dropped a few jaws and silenced the more sala-
cious of comments. None of her inner thoughts showed as
she presented herself as every inch the Viscountess de
Fontvilliers.

Raphael moved beside her with his usual careless
saunter, bending low to brush his lips against her ear. "They
sound like a hoard of locusts. Look like them, as well,
some of them, don't they?" This won the tiniest of smiles
from his bride. For once, she didn't mind his brash behavior. The warm glow of what had taken over in his dressing room still had her floating in a daze. His fingers closed
over hers reassuringly, and she felt a sudden surge of confidence. There was the strongest impression that the two
of them were united, and that they would see this through
together.

She had to blink rapidly to clear the sting from her eyes
as they neared the receiving line. The Duke of Shelbourne
welcomed them with genuine warmth, and for the first time,
Julia thought it was all going to be all right. The thought
amazed her, filled her with joy, and drove out the last of
her lingering fears.

Yes. Everything was going to be all right.

For the rest of that week and on into the next, Julia watched as calling cards were delivered every day, laid on a delicately etched salver and served up smartly by a gloved footman for consideration. She was very selective about whom she received, and which occasions she selected for her and Raphael to attend.

She was seeing to this new flood of social demand one morning when the head footman, Smith, entered the drawing room. "Sir Simon Blake," he said, coming to offer an embossed card on the much-used salver. "He instructed me to say it was quite urgent."

Instantly alert, Julia said, "Send him in." Pushing away from the ladies' desk, she stood with her hands folded in front of her.

Simon entered a moment later, that long, loose-limbed stride of his a bit tight with the awkwardness of this meeting. Otherwise, he was looking well, she thought.

A tall man, he appeared fashionably slender in his dark tailcoat and trousers. His face was handsome even set in stern lines as it was at this moment. The tension in him was evident, but she had expected him to be so. She would always regret the pain she had caused him. She knew she had no right to any expectations of friendship, so she surmised his reason for calling was not social. She braced herself.

Indicating a chair, she asked, "Please have a seat. Would you like tea?"

"I have come on some unpleasant business, Julia." He did not move to sit. Standing with legs apart, his hat held before him, he looked uneasy. "Just last night I learned of some distressing rumors. It concerns you and your new husband."

Julia had the ridiculous urge to flee before he could continue. "Simon," she admonished with a nervous little laugh, "you are positively cryptic today."

"Despite our past differences, it gives me no delight to tell you this." His expression remained grave. "Last night, at my club, a man introduced himself to me. He was a friend of Fontvilliers. A former friend, I'd say." He paused. His eyes mellowed. "Julia, I believe it would be best if you were to be seated."

As much as she would have liked to remain on her feet and squared off against him, she knew immediately that she should follow his advice. She could feel it coming. Something horrible, something disastrous. She sank weakly into a chair.

Simon drew in a long breath. "It seems there was a wager . . ."

RAPHAEL WAS NOT troubled by the coach and four pulled up outside his residence. His grandmother had many friends, and they frequently called. Upon entering his household, however, he was taken aback to see the countess pacing the center hall.

Her aged face was drawn into deep lines. "Simon Blake is here," she said quickly. "Why is your wife's former fiancé in our drawing room?"

He wasn't known for being an intuitive man. One had to be sensitive to other people in order to cultivate that gift, but the presence of Simon Blake was a rather obvious source of disquiet, and Raphael had an immediate and powerful premonition. Without a word, he went to the drawing room doors and flung them open.

Julia and Simon stood facing each other, only a few feet apart. Upon his entry, they turned in unison to stare at him. No one moved for a long moment.

Unbidden to his mind came the image of the two of them upon the grand staircase at the Brunley house just after they announced their engagement—together, united, belonging to each other. And he the outsider with his nose pressed up against the window, wanting. Why did he get the feeling that that was exactly where he was once again?

Julia frowned at him, blinking rapidly as if she had

never seen him before. As if she were seeing him for the first time. Simon reached out a hand to stop her, but she pushed it aside and came to stand before Raphael. She spoke in a quiet, steady voice. "Was there a wager to seduce me?"

There was one wild, dizzying moment as it all came crashing down around him. This was it. The end of everything.

Raphael answered. "Yes."

Her brows jerked down momentarily, but only for an instant and then her features returned to their expressionless state. "It was a lark among your friends, to prove love did not exist. If you could break the bond between Simon and myself, you would be declared the winner. Strathford staked the five thousand. You collected it not long ago. Is this correct?"

He ground his teeth together in frustration. "Yes," he answered.

She nodded. "There was no problem with Lady Catherine Drummond. That was a lie. She was in actuality your mistress."

"No. That part is not true. But the rest is accurate."

"Everything was a lie."

He darted his eyes to Simon nervously, wishing he would have the tactfulness to go away. When he remained planted where he was, eyes blazing, mouth set in a grim line, Raphael forced himself to answer. "Not everything."

She bowed her head. Raphael's hands fisted at his sides as he battled with his own impotence. He wished fervently that he could take away all of it. He wanted to explain, to deny it. Because although it *was* all true, it wasn't any longer. But he said nothing.

Simon came to stand beside Julia, laying his hand on her shoulder. "Come with me now. I'll take you home."

Raphael moved without thinking, overcome with a blast of rage. He grabbed Simon's wrist and bent it back until the man flinched. He'd give him credit, though. The pain had to be excruciating, but Simon bore it with white-lipped stoicism. "Take your hand off my wife," Raphael growled. "She *is* home."

"Stop it," Julia hissed.

Raphael released Blake.

The baronet rubbed his wrist. "Your nerve is boundless, Fontvilliers. I should call you out."

Raphael shrugged, finding his way easily to his old snide self. It seemed as good a tact as any. "If you have a wish for death, be my guest."

"I do, then. I call you out, Fontvilliers. To a duel."

Raphael bared his teeth in a smile. "I accept. Where?"

"Outside the city. Wimbledon Commons. Sunrise."

"Pistols or swords?"

"Your choice."

"I believe pistols. Far less work involved." Raphael was back in control of himself. "I'll bring mine. I have a fine set."

"For what you did to me, to Julia, to her whole family, I shall enjoy putting a ball in that black heart of yours."

He gazed at Simon drolly. "Why, Blake, you are frightening me."

Simon took a step forward. "No, I don't. You are too arrogant to be frightened. Men like you don't care about anything, not even yourselves."

"Simon, please leave." Julia stepped between the two men, her back to her husband. Raphael almost snarled in frustration at her gentle touch on Simon's arm. She said softly, "Let me talk to him, alone please."

Simon's eyes blazed, never leaving Raphael's face. "Yes. Have your talk. Get all your answers now, Julia. Tomorrow will be too late."

"There isn't going to be a duel," Julia said more firmly, "Go home, please. Leave me to deal with this."

Simon stormed out. There was a dull silence in his wake.

Julia moved to a settee and sank onto it. She seemed very composed. "I have a few questions."

Raphael remained where he was. "Of course," he answered with a slight incline of his head.

He wouldn't beg her to listen to him; he wouldn't fawn or explain. Something inside wanted to, but he fought it. If nothing else, he would keep his dignity. There existed inside him a sort of resignation to the whims of fate that seemed, from all indication, intent on bashing his brains out on the sharp edges of his own misspent cunning.

It made tragic sense, really. He hadn't ever deserved her in the first place. Losing her was simple justice, that was all. He had to look at it like that.

She spoke. "Please explain to me how this wager was made and why were Simon and I chosen?"

His resolve faltered. How could he stand here in front of her and put it into words? "Julia, I don't think this is wise—"

"I haven't asked you for advice. I've asked for facts."

He forced himself to speak. "We were at the ball. Someone made a comment about love. I said it didn't exist. That love was merely lust, that . . ." This was more difficult than he could have ever imagined. Each word cost him a piece of his soul until he couldn't speak. He drew in another breath, firming his resolve, and continued. "Strathford challenged me. We made a wager. You and Simon walked by. Someone said you were the romance of the season. The greatest challenge, therefore, and so I picked you."

"You were to make me fall in love with you?"

He looked at her. She remained without any expression. "I was to destroy your love for Simon and his for you. I chose to do it by diverting your attentions to myself."

"I see."

She rose, took two steps, and stopped. "What about Laura?"

Oh, yes. His sins spread far beyond her and Simon. He would be held accountable for it all. "I made Strathford pay court to her. It gave me a way to you. Information about you and what your plans were, and access when I wanted it. "

"It was certainly convenient to have him working for you, so to speak. He never cared for her, then? Poor Laura. I suppose it was my fault, in a way. She is so unhappy."

He didn't like how unruffled she was, how matter-of-factly she ingested all of the vile details he had supplied. She hadn't yet looked at him. Folding her hands in front of her hips, she moved slowly, pensively around the room. "Why did you marry me, then, if it was all just a test?"

This was the hardest of all. He didn't falter. "My grandmother insisted. She wanted me to settle down."

"Did she threaten you? Bribe you?"

"An incentive. Half her fortune. The other assured to me upon her death. Or else she'd cut me off."

She flinched, the first sign of pain. He wanted so badly to go to her. But he had nothing to say that would take any of it away.

"No wonder you were so angry," she said. Her breathing was growing shallow, a sign of her rising emotion. "I didn't understand that at first. Now I see just how far things got away from you."

One hand massaged her temple as she thought aloud. "How foolish of me to ignore all those coincidences—I was daft not to examine the improbability of you always happening to be wherever I was. But my mind was ensnared with the little intrigues you pretended. You were so clever. So clever."

He didn't feel very clever. Suddenly he didn't feel clever at all. "It began—"

"No, no." She covered her face with her hands and shook her head. "I can't hear anything else right now. Not now, not yet."

He was silent. He was numb, completely helpless.

"How vain I was," she mused. "When you pretended

friendship, when you singled me out, I believed you. I believed you *needed* me."

I do need you!

Raphael asked, "What will you do?"

"What will I do?" she repeated softly. She was clearly too dismayed to think clearly. "I don't quite know yet. I suppose I should go. I don't think I could live here with you any longer."

He controlled the denial that sprung to his throat. Carefully he suggested, "But that might prove disastrous to Laura. She is just now getting invitations again, so you said. Our own acceptance back into the *ton*'s favor has had a beneficial effect on her. A separation would ruin what progress has been made."

She looked up at him with dawning disgust. "You are still trying to manipulate me. Have you no shame?"

" 'Repentance is not a virtue, for it does not spring from reason.' I am merely being practical, Julia."

"Yes. I must be practical as well." Her eyes rounded and her head snapped up. "And you must not meet Simon on the morrow."

He stiffened. "That is a challenge already made and accepted, madam. I have no choice."

"Have you not done enough? You took everything from him, for no other reason than a whim, and now you will kill him? I won't allow it! I will send the authorities to arrest you for murder if I have to. I forbid it, Raphael. I mean it. Do not harm Simon."

He paused, watching her, thinking. Inclining his head, he said at last, "Very well. I swear no harm will come to Blake."

She relaxed. "Thank you." Looking about her absently, she set to rubbing her temple again. "I believe I have had enough of you, of all of this for the time being." Starting for the door, she blanched when he grabbed her arm. "Don't touch me!" she snapped, suddenly full of vigor.

He dropped her arm. A painful knot in his throat choked

him, preventing the words he would have liked to say. But what would they have been, anyway? More lies? Lies were all he had, after all.

He let her go.

Chapter Sixteen

THE FIRST THOUGHT Julia had when she opened her eyes was that the events of the precious day had been but a nightmare. Then she turned her head and saw she was in her own bed. And Raphael was not beside her. She knew then it had been no dream.

The pain rushed in on her at once, pushing her back down in the bed and weighting her limbs so that it was difficult to rise. She dragged herself from under the covers and went to unlock the door she had bolted in case Raphael had taken it into his head to try to speak to her again. The servants would be up with freshly warmed water and to assist her in her morning ablutions. She didn't want them to know anything was amiss, at least until she had decided what to do.

There was little to consider. She had to leave. Staying was unthinkable, unimaginable. Last night she had come up with a plan of sorts, in the wee hours before sheer exhaustion had claimed her. Raphael owned a number of estates. She would choose one and retire there. All that was left to decide was exactly what story they would put out, for she would do anything to divert any further scandal against her family. There was Laura to think of, as Raphael had reminded her, and next season would be Leah's debut. She had to be very careful.

She had thought perhaps some claim of illness might do. It wouldn't fool many, but it was a plausible excuse that would at least keep them guessing. That is, if word of the . . . the *filthy* wager had not already been put out. She was still pondering this possibility when her maid, Margerie, came in, looking wide-eyed and uncertain. "Madam," she said in a trembling voice.

Julia looked up at her absently. "The brown and tan muslin, please. And just a simple dressing of my hair today."

Margerie swallowed, not moving. "There is a man here. He says you must come with him immediately. There has been a—a duel."

"What duel? That cannot be." Julia came slowly to her feet. "He promised me!"

"The master . . . oh, madam." Her eyes glistened with tears and her chin trembled. "I am so sorry to tell you. He has been shot!"

THE PAIN WAS all-consuming. He could barely breathe. Raphael lay on his back as the surgeon, his white shirt-sleeves rolled up and forearms drenched in blood, went after the ball.

"More brandy," Raphael rasped. The surgeon's assistant pressed the flask to his lips, and he swallowed greedily, ignoring the burn. The smell of tallow and sweat nearly made him sick as he lay back. He heard the muttered curse of the surgeon and felt him probe the wound once again.

He hated himself for crying out, but he couldn't help it as the surgeon slipped his fingers into the narrow hole torn into his side, creating an agony that was scarce to be borne. He clenched his teeth together, panting wildly as the excruciating exploration went on for a century. To his dismay, Raphael felt wetness on his cheeks. It tasted of salt tears when he touched his tongue to it.

"I can't reach it," the surgeon said, then swore vilely. Raising his bloody hands to his forehead to swipe at the sweat, he left a smear of crimson on his temple.

"Do you need to cut?" The assistant's voice shook with panic. "Where did I put the knife?" To which the surgeon replied, "Too near the spine. It will further the injury. We must close up the wound before he bleeds to death. Bring the needle and thread."

Raphael fixed his gaze on the ceiling and forced himself not to think of what they were doing to him. Damn Simon. The man was inept. He could not even kill properly, not even when Raphael had made it so easy.

At dawn they had paced off the field, turned, raised their pistols—beauties fitted with mother-of-pearl handles and scrolled hammers already cocked and ready—took aim. And then Raphael had stopped.

He had waited for the wretch to go ahead and shoot. It wasn't something he had planned. It was just that when the time came, he had been unable to discharge his weapon. The weight of the promise Julia had extracted from him— which he had had no intention of keeping at the time— suddenly made itself felt.

He realized he could no sooner shoot Simon than he could Julia. Innocent lambs, both of them. They were not in his league. It would be murder, and he realized that his vices didn't extend to taking blameless lives.

Simon had fired and shouted out simultaneously, as if protesting what he was forced to do. Even as Raphael became aware of the first blossom of pain, he realized his error. The horror on Simon's face seemed to say, "Look. You have made me a murderer."

So even in being noble, Fontvilliers corrupts, Raphael had reflected wryly as he had laid there on the dew-soaked grass staring up at the lightening sky. Burgeoning dawn was changing everything, casting light on what had been darkness before. He marveled at his undaunted sense of irony for which he was so well known.

The surgeon poured some kind of liquid into the wound,

and his side, inside and out, felt as if it had been set afire.
He arched, biting down hard and gasping against the agony.
Getting himself under control, he settled himself in for the
sewing. With fatalistic resignation, he bore each stitch.

Then Raphael noticed the surgeon's assistant had rested
his hands on his thigh, perhaps anticipating a kick of protesta-
tion against the pain of the needle going in and out of
the aggravated flesh. He didn't feel those hands. He studied them, confused as his mind wrestled with the implica-
tions. The assistant was gripping quite tightly. By rights, it
should hurt like hell.

A tidal wave of horror flooded though him. *God. Oh,
God, no!*

His gaze went to his foot and he concentrated on moving it. He tried, thinking wildly that he must be delirious.
He had to be.

A cry tore out of him that sent the assistant halfway to
the ceiling and the surgeon jerking painfully on the thread.

TIME AND DISTANCE would make the events of the spring
season seem far away, Julia hoped.

Three months had passed. While she had remained in
London, all through the long, hot summer, she had been
fixed in numbing uncertainty. The decision to leave had
grown out of a need to start anew. As they clattered over
the pitted roads of the northern shires, she prayed it had
been a good one.

They were on their way to the Cumbrian lake district.
There, one of the small manor houses owned under the
auspices of the Wentword fortunes, Glenwood Park was
situated between Windemere and the pair of small lakes,
or tarns, knows together as Tarn Hows. There was a village nearby, called Hawkshead, which was proported to be
quaint and friendly. Julia had chosen the place of all of
Raphael's properties because of its remote location. It had
seemed an excellent place to lose the world.

Her companion in the post chaise would no doubt scoff at her, had he known her thoughts. Not that she would ever tell him. They were not apt to converse. In fact, Raphael had spoken very little to her since the days of his recuperation when he had lain stoic and silent in the large half-tester she had once shared with him.

This suited Julia just fine. She had nothing to say to her husband.

He looked wretched. Paler, thinner, with thick pockets of sallow skin under his eyes and lips that were bloodless with constant tension, he managed to appear always to be smoldering like a bed of hot coals. His morose presence grated on her nerves, more so for the flask he kept tippling from. At each and every of their frequent stops, he been insistent about having it refilled. It was the only time he demonstrated an interest in any detail of the journey.

The direction of their travel added an unfamiliar chill to the air, and she welcomed it as a harbinger of change. She thought of a time when the air had been sweet and warm. In the spring, she had believed in pretty things. That season seemed to belong to another lifetime. It was fitting the bite of winter should erase those sultry memories.

The carriage slowed, then jerked to a halt. The driver called out to someone and that one answered with a greeting. Pulling back the brocade curtain, Julia peered out to find they had arrived at a house. She supposed it was Glenwood Park. All she could see was a pair of stone staircases winding up the front façade in matched semicircles to a second-floor entranceway. The stone was white, or gray, rather, with signs of weathering that indicated it was a rather old residence.

Raphael said, "Home at last." His tone dripped with derision.

The footman arrived with the step and she alighted. Thomas, Raphael's valet, was waiting. He and two footmen whom they had brought with them from London went inside for his master.

Julia turned away, drawing her pelisse more tightly about her body and moving quickly up the steps where she waited by the door. She fervently wished she could escape what came next. The chore of extracting Raphael from the carriage was horrible to watch.

The burly servants, Gregory and Franklin, struggled to wrest Raphael from the seat. It was a Herculean task to take their master through the narrow door without dropping him ignominiously onto the paving stones. Of course, a special carriage could have been ordered for easier transportation, but Raphael had balked at the suggestion.

His only concession to his condition was a sedan chair, which another servant now held beside Julia as she waited for her husband to be brought out.

Raphael emerged, his muscles straining as he held fast to the door frame, supporting his weight while Gregory maneuvered the lifeless limbs into position. Thomas squeezed by him, followed by Franklin who under the valet's instruction, caught Raphael's weight. They all three carefully lowered their master out of the carriage.

Julia swallowed, not wanting to watch and not able to look away. Raphael looked murderous as the larger footman took his full weight in his arms and carried him, legs dragging behind, up the stone steps and to the chair.

Raphael had said nothing, not one word of protest or exclamation of pain during the entire proceedings. Once seated, he jammed his fist into his coat pocket and drew out his silver flask while his legs were tucked into position. Julia saw how his hand trembled as he tipped it back for a long, long draught.

Replacing it, he stared straight ahead. He didn't look at her as the servant took the chair by the handles and wheeled him around and through the door which had been opened for their entrance into their new home. She waited until he had cleared the doorway, then followed him inside. He waved to his handler, and they veered off in one direction. Julia headed in the other.

An hour later Julia was in a drafty study giving instruction to the housekeeper and butler.

"The condition of the house is appalling," she stated at the portly couple. They were neither brother and sister nor husband and wife. Similar only in their stature, Mrs. Anson was fair-haired and pleasant-miened, with the air of a woman anxious to win her new mistress's approval. Mr. Conrad on the other hand was—or rather had been—quite dark. Nearly bald now, his countenance was one reminiscent of a sullen schoolboy called to task for handing his tutor a sloppy assignment.

"This room, for example," Julia went on. "The window dressings are nearly threadbare, quite inadequate to keep out the chill. I want heavier draperies brought in and new rugs to replace these—look at the stains on them. The fireplace looks like it has not been swept out in months."

They all three cast baleful glances at the skinny log burning in the grate. No other wood waited in the hearth basket to be thrown on.

Mrs. Anson cleared her throat. "We didn't have much notice you were coming."

"We live on a fixed stipend, you know," Mr. Conrad said more stridently. "We've had to cut some corners. The house hasn't been visited in years. What's the sense in keeping it up if it's for nobody but us, and we never come in these rooms?"

Julia took a moment to decide on her tact. She couldn't afford to alienate them. She needed as much support in the upcoming endeavor as possible. "I appreciate your constraints, Mr. Conrad. It is not my intention to admonish you." She turned and walked to the sideboard set up with dusty decanters. They were empty, their contents long since evaporated, or siphoned off by the help. Tiny cobwebs laced the innards of the vessels. "However, I am anxious to see my husband's comforts. This room especially must be made livable as soon as possible, as it will, no doubt, prove his favorite haunt."

"Touching," Raphael said from the doorway. Seated in his sedan chair, he grasped a cut-glass tumbler filled with amber liquid in his fist. Behind him, a servant waited. "Over by the fire," he ordered curtly as he was wheeled into the room. Addressing himself again to Julia, he said in a tone dripping with derision, "How thoughtful of you to be mindful of my needs. A wife is a handy thing, it seems."

She felt the hairs on the back of her neck prickle. His eyes blazed with malice. An equally intense determination burned inside of her. He was not going to undermine her with the servants.

Ignoring him, she turned back to the housekeeper and head footman with a lift of her chin. "Mrs. Anson, please send word when the parlor I ordered converted to a bedroom is ready."

"If it is, shall I go ahead and unpack the master's things, madam?"

"Yes, do. Are the stables in better shape than the house, Mr. Conrad?"

"If you mean are they dusted and aired, I'd say no." A corner of his mouth hiked up in appreciation of his own jest. "But they do have horses in them."

She ignored his quip. "And the carriage house is well-equipped?"

"A phaeton, an old one and a few carts and such." He shrugged. "There's a carriage, of course, but I can't vouch for its condition. It hasn't been used in a while."

"No doubt the horses are hungry for exercise. Send word to the groomsman to have a tame one ready in the morning. I believe a jaunt in the phaeton shall be invigorating. That will be all."

He cast her an insolent look before following Mrs. Anson out.

"Very impressive." Raphael's tone was scathing. "Why, it was as good a 'Mistress of the Manor' performance as my grandmother is likely to give." With a few jerks on his wheels, he maneuvered himself closer to the meager heat. "Who knew a mouse like you had it in her?"

The insult stung, more for it being true. Indeed, she had been a mouse. A silly, easily fooled mouse without a thought in her head other than love.

"I see you have decided to speak," she replied. "I might have guessed the first thing out of your mouth would be unpleasant." Coming to stand in front of him, she crossed her arms over her chest and studied him for a moment. "Allow me to tell you something about mice. I once tried to catch a mouse and it bit me. It sank its teeth into my finger clear down into the bone. It was one of the most painful injuries I ever received, and that includes being kicked in the leg by a horse when I was five. So don't dismiss us mice so easily."

His eyebrows shot up, his smile was pure mockery. "Ho! I didn't imagine you had any fight left in you. I mean, look at you. Your overdeveloped conscience brings you all the way out to this wretched country with a husband who is no longer useful, in bed or anywhere else. Why? Is it not to scurry after approval? Loving wife and martyr—society will love you!"

The bitterness in him was potent, and for a proud man like Raphael to be brought so low, she could understand it. But why it was directed at her, she couldn't fathom. She had not done him any ill, far from it. *She* was the injured one.

Quietly she countered, "I'm not here for them, and I'm not here for you. I have a very specific purpose in coming, and it is my own."

"And you haven't seen fit to tell me this mysterious purpose." His eyes glittered. "Need I tell you how little I appreciate that oversight?"

She had her reasons for not telling him. Mostly because she knew how vehemently he would protest. "I will explain it all to you when we can speak calmly."

"Don't tease my temper, Julia. You will find yourself outclassed. My mind is as keen as it ever was, and just as

devilish, despite this broken body . . . and . . . the loss of
my . . ." His words stumbled to a halt. Drinking deeply
from the flask, he turned his head to frown darkly into the
weak fire.

"The true loss is that of your character," she said very
softly.

"It was twisted into its grotesque shape years ago. It is
fitting that my body should follow suit." His nostrils flared
and he was glaring at her again. "How you must despise
me."

To her horror, her eyes misted. It would be so easy to
let pity erode her resolve. But to show weakness in front
of any predator was a deadly mistake. She pulled herself
up and said with an aloofness she didn't feel, "No more
than you have despised me."

He scowled. No, he wouldn't like being reminded he
was not the one being put upon. He was the author of his
own demise, though it gave her no pleasure to remind him
of it. Whenever she thought of the demeaning circumstances of her marriage, it brought a swift, sharp pain into
her breast.

What an utter fool she'd been.

"All right, you brought me here," he said, "and it was
probably a good idea. I'll give you credit. I couldn't stay
in London. But now that you have seen me safe to this retreat, go on. I have no more need of you."

"No. I suppose you do not. You've won your wager.
You've collected your money. But I shan't leave, Raphael.
I am here for my own reasons, and I will stay until they
are satisfied." The pressure in her chest had grown to an
ache, and she knew she had to get away from him. "I am
going to my room now. I will trust the servants to see you
to yours when it is ready."

She retired to the apartments she had selected earlier. It
wasn't the traditional mistress's suite, situated as their London rooms had been to adjoin the master's bedroom, but
a smaller one which Mrs. Anson had called the dowager
suite. Julia had liked its soft rose hues accented with mint

and butter-yellow. The furnishings were fine and unpainted, giving the room a simple elegance that suited her.

Undressing, she bathed quickly and donned a comfortable dressing gown of cotton. Stretching out in front of a nicely built fire, she wrapped a shawl about her shoulders and felt the fatigue settle on her bones.

She didn't check on Raphael's bedroom to see if he was comfortable. She had a premonition his foul mood would only get worse in the oncoming days. Tonight, before she would implement her plan, she treated herself to an evening of relaxing in her new private retreat.

Tomorrow she would begin, and so she would need her rest. Then Raphael would learn what she was about. She was taking charge, and she was going to be free. Free of him and his betrayal and his lies and his self-pity.

In time, she would begin another life, a quiet life apart from him. But for now, she was holed up in a drafty, ill-kept manor house with a vile-tempered convalescent, away from every family member and friend that she ever held dear.

Was it any wonder she felt so tired?

───────

"WAKE UP," JULIA commanded.

Raphael groaned and turned his head away, burrowing deeper into the covers.

Julia swallowed, forcing herself to move past the soft flutters of emotion billowing in her chest. It was difficult to see him like this, groggy from sleep and looking pleasantly mussed. She had always loved the mornings, with the both of them sleepy and languid after a night of making love. It had been a time of casual caresses and whispering and laughter that sometimes, but not always, led to a lazy mating that had never failed to get their day off to an agreeable start.

Two things spared her from being overwhelmed by these recollections. One was the presence of the two footman, and the other was the bleary-eyed look of her husband being roused against his will. He was furious.

"Wha . . . ?" He lifted his head up, his hair sticking every which way. "What the devil are you doing in here?" He clamped a hand down on the top of his head, mashing down the wild hair. "Jesus Christ, my head is splitting."

"From too much drink. You should be more moderate to avoid the headache."

"Thomas, who let her in here? Good God, man, close those drapes. The light is burning my eyes out of my head."

Thomas stayed where he was and rolled a wide-eyed glance at Julia. She stepped closer. "Thomas is under my orders to see you out of bed. Come now. Don't make this more difficult than it already is."

"What are you talking about? I am staying right here in this bed and going back to sleep."

"We are to have a drive in the phaeton," she explained patiently. To the two footman, she said, "Please remove your master from his bed."

Raphael leveled a blistering look at the men. "You do and you'll regret it."

"Madam," Thomas said, sidling nervously up to her. "The doctor said he is not to be moved, that rest was important. Surely this outing you plan is not—"

"What could be more healthy than fresh air and exercise, Thomas? The doctor's orders were that the Viscount be kept quiet. I intend for our drive to be peaceful. Surely, it will be more so than the master drinking his weight in whiskey and throwing tantrums." More brightly, she turned to the footmen. "Now, go ahead."

"Julia, I swear—umph! Get your hands off me, you idiots. I swear—damn you!"

She forced a smile. "Try putting in a few choice words, Raphael. I am told a solid epithet or two does wonders for emphasis. I'll wait outside while you enjoy your toilette. I'll see you in the dining room."

"I am not going to the dining room! Leave me be, you conniving little—"

She closed the door just in time. The slamming of the portal and the word he had been about to say—no doubt very uncomplimentary—coincided, the former drowning out the latter. All she could hear as she went down the hall was his howling attempts to get his men out of his room.

It took an hour and a half, but he did arrive, wheeling himself in with long strokes. He was silent, however, as the servant he had outraced came behind him to push the chair into place at the table. When the youth grabbed the cloth napkin and shook it out, Raphael snatched it from his hands and plopped it on his own lap. "Get out," he growled. The youth bowed and stepped away. Glaring at the servant who came up with a plate of porridge, he snarled, "You, too."

Julia took a steadying breath against the rising of temper. "You are grumpy this morning. Perhaps you need food to improve your mood. And less whiskey."

"Do you find it amusing all of the sudden to bully helpless men?"

"Probably less amusing than you did in corrupting helpless women," she countered.

"Ah, so this is your revenge, is it?"

"Not at all." She took great care to keep any emotion from her voice. "It gives me no pleasure to see you this way. Unlike you, I do not have a wish to punish others just because I am hurting. You see, I want nothing from you, not even your suffering." She was appalled to see her fork was shaking as she lifted a bite of whipped eggs to her lips. She put it down and reached for her tea. "I amend that statement. There is something I want from you, and I will have it. In time."

"What is that, dear wife? My money? I can be generous in that regard. A house? Take the London town house. You can entertain your lovers, if it's that sort of freedom you are after. Go ahead, flaunt them if you have the need.

I seem to recall you quite enjoy the rewards of bed sport. I shouldn't dream of denying you your pleasures, as I am rendered inadequate in that capacity."

She half rose out of her seat. "My God, Raphael, even you can't be this base!"

"Oh, I doubt you can even imagine the full blossom of my baseness. A malady I will indulge until you finally realize that you have no choice but to leave this place. I don't care where you go—to London, to the Continent, to the Americas if you wish. Go to bloody hell for all I care, just *leave me alone!*"

Those last words, shouted as they were, nearly blasted her out of her chair.

She gripped the arms until her fingers hurt. Her breath was coming fast—shallow and full of the rage trying desperately to tear out of her. It took a full minute of struggling with her self-control, but she was finally able to speak. "Raphael, please do not shout. It hurts my ears."

Her refusal to be baited incensed him more. He pounded his fists on the table. "Damn your ears, and damn you!"

She wanted to let loose the wild torrent of emotion locked inside her. It would be the easiest thing imaginable to rise this very moment and walk through the door, take him up on his offer, and leave, forget he ever existed.

Drawing forth his flask, he tipped it back. His Adam's apple bobbed from the long gulps. When he was finished, he wiped his mouth with the back of his hand. For effect, she guessed, as a linen napkin was right by his left hand.

When she had herself under control, she stood. "I am going nowhere. Now I suggest you eat something to keep up your strength. You shall need more than that whiskey you've been nursing. In either case, we are going for a ride in the phaeton in exactly one half hour. If you wish to keep any of your dignity about you, I suggest you do not force me to have you carried out like a babe in the arms of Gregory or Franklin."

"You've become quite a bitch, Julia," he said as she headed for the door.

She didn't let him see her reaction to those words. "I am what you've made me."

When she was gone, Raphael fumbled at his flask, drinking deeply once, and then again after he had caught his breath. God, the stuff burned like a fire in his gut, but he savored the pain like one would an exotic scent.

The prissy, emotionless prig—standing there in that . . . wisp of a dress looking tall and straight and proud and holding her head up as if she were the Queen Charlotte herself, having the audacity to command him. . . .

His rage sputtered out. Feeling suddenly drained, he went for his flask.

Damn her. Damn her. After this summer, seeing her every day and knowing she hated him, knowing that even if he wasn't reduced to this weak excuse for a man, he'd never touch her again, or hear her laugh, or tell her stories of his travels—it was unbearable. It kept him crazy, tense, like a bull constantly taunted by glimpses of a scarlett cape. He had to get her away from him, where he couldn't feel her presence in every bone. He'd drive her away by fair means or foul.

"Thomas!" he bellowed. "Thomas! Get the bloody hell in here!"

His valet raced in, his features full of alarm. "My lord!"

Dangling the silver flask, he stared darkly at Thomas until he understood his wishes. "Right away, my lord," Thomas said, and took the flask to be refilled.

Chapter Seventeen

⌒

JUST BEFORE NOON Julia entered her apartments and collapsed on the divan. Her whole body trembled. The outing with Raphael had been a disaster.

He had gotten impossibly drunk, although how he had
managed this so early in the morning, she hadn't the vaguest
idea. The sour smell of whiskey was nearly enough to set
her stomach heaving, but she had managed to persevere
enough to drive them a short distance. The phaeton, a small,
light vehicle precisely designed to be easily handled, was
still a bit of a challenge for someone without any driving
experience. Her lack of practice was telling, and she was
soon physically drained.

Disgusted as well. Raphael took to shouting bawdy songs
at the top of his lungs. Knowing that he would only get
louder and more vulgar if they were to come across anyone along the road, she quickly saw the wisdom in heading home.

He had bested her, curse the man! She felt a failure, utterly deflated, wondering what could she do when her presence seemed only to goad his rage? How could she ever
persuade him to cooperate with the program of restoration
she planned to begin soon?

The surgeons at hospital had all agreed that Raphael's

condition was permanent, that the lead ball had lodged in his spine and he would never recover. They had cautioned her to guard against the ill humors that beset the bedridden. In order to extend his life, it was recommended he have regular bleedings and herbal tonics to purge the body. No sunlight—it saps strength. No loud noises—it disturbs the body's equilibrium. And in no manner was he to become excited or distressed.

She had received this news with the countess by her side. The old woman, for all her forbidding bluster, had crumpled, her wrinkled face quivering. Julia remembered grabbing her hand, and they had looked at each other, two women who understood that what these men were describing was unthinkable. It was worse than death for a man like Raphael; it was living entombment. The countess had pulled herself together and ordered the men out of her house, peppering her speech with such choice invectives as "charlatan" and "ghouls."

After long hours spent together, trying to decide what was best, she had finally pronounced, "He is my grandson, for all else that he is. He cannot be made to live the life they describe. If he is to die, then let him do so, but at least he will die a man."

If Julia had believed that the measures the surgeons had dictated would extend his existence one half day, she would have done every last one and fought whoever would try to stop her. Call it instinct, however, but she knew the countess was right. Raphael must have life, not just existence.

But Raphael seemed to *want* to absorb the slow death the doctors had predicted, resisting every effort to bring him out of the foul humors in which he submerged himself. In his room with only the steady supply of alcohol to keep him in a semi-stupor, he languished in bitter silence. Julia knew he craved death.

Julia could not—*would not* accept Raphael's wasting away like that. It was then she told the countess a story she had heard of a Lincolnshire man who had recovered after a fall from a horse left him unable to walk. She had no idea if the tale was at all true, and it had been a while since she'd heard it so she was sketchy on many of the details, but she recalled the paralysis had proven only to be temporary.

The countess and Julia traveled to Lincolnshire.

William Douglas received them gladly, sharing his extraordinary tale. After his injury, which had left his entire body lifeless from midchest down, he had felt very similar to the way Julia and the countess did—that a mere existence as a cripple was not to be accepted. He had worked at moving his body every day, he said, convinced that his legs would "wake up." He had employed two burly men to drag him about, one working his legs as if it could retrain the muscle and nerve to reanimate.

It had worked. Although his recovery had been painful and agonizingly long, he now walked, albeit with the help of a cane and even then not so well, but he walked. Right there before them, he rose proudly and showed them his rather awkward stride. The countess had turned away, overcome with emotion. Julia felt a cold, hard resolve form in her breast. Raphael would walk again. She would make him.

And when he did, she would leave him. She would go and none could ever denounce her for abandoning a cripple. Her conscience would be clear.

Julia took over from there, surprising the countess and herself. She had requested the matter be hers alone. The countess had agreed, reluctant at first. She was not a woman who easily relinquished control. But she must have seen the determination in her granddaughter-in-law's eyes. Arrangements were made for Julia to take Raphael away. Glenwood Park was selected. Franklin and Gregory were sent to Lincolnshire to be shown how the rehabilitative procedures were done, all in secret as Raphael lay moldering in his bed.

They had acted quickly, perhaps before they had really thought it through fully. Now that she had him here, she didn't know how to handle his vicious outbursts, his relentless determination to destroy himself and everything in his path. She had tried to be calm and authoritative, but it had no effect on him.

She wished the countess had come. She wished she had someone else, anyone else whom she could talk to in order to shore up her flagging courage.

She wished she didn't feel so alone. She feared she was no match for the infamous Bane of the Ton.

Julia didn't approach Raphael the following day. She made some excuse to herself as to why she wasn't going to brave the hazards of his inner sanctum, reasoning that it was important for her, as mistress, to learn the layout of the house, become familiar with the servants and the daily routine of her new home. In actuality, she spent the day in the library, lost in a book.

Ashamed of herself for her cowardice, she resolved the next day to do better. But that day, too, was whiled away. She discovered, upon venturing into the kitchens, that the cooking staff were a lively group of women with ready laughter and merry smiles. It was such a warm, inviting place to be, she lingered, defying propriety by taking her lunch on the scrubbed oak table and chatting merrily all the way until tea.

She was tired, then, and napped until supper, which she had in her room. The day was already spent. Tomorrow, she promised herself, and knew she could not put it off any longer.

Early the next morning, she intercepted Thomas outside the parlor that had been converted to Raphael's bedchamber. He carried a tray of porridge, toast, and a steaming carafe of coffee.

Reaching for the tray, she said, "I'll take that. I wish to speak to my husband alone."

The servant sputtered. Thomas was firmly in Raphael's camp. She hadn't even tried to include him in her plans, knowing he would never go along with it.

"The master wishes a bath this morning," he informed her.

"I can take care of that for him as well."

Thomas looked apoplectic. "Madam, you must be joking."

"No," Julia corrected sweetly. "I am threatening. Now, please see that we are not disturbed."

She whisked into Raphael's room with his breakfast, a forced smile firmly in place, and firm resolve to be pleasant.

He was awake and sitting up. Upon her entry, his brows shot down to hover low over his eyes. Saying nothing, Julia brought the tray to his bedside table. "I've brought your breakfast," she said as brightly as she could manage.

"I didn't realize your absence these past few days meant you had been working as a servant."

She ignored the jibe as well as the sneering tone with which it was spoken. "I am flattered you took note."

He leaned his head back into the pillows behind him. "Your charity is done. You've cheered me up tremendously. Now send Thomas in."

"Thomas has been instructed to leave us alone. There is much we need to do."

His head snapped back up. "What the devil are you talking about? Get me my man—now!"

She regarded him levelly. "Or you'll what?"

"My arms are not useless." He smiled thinly. "Nor are my hands. I could happily throttle you."

She shrugged, pretending his dark promise didn't send a jolt of apprehension through her. "If you can reach me."

He started.

She swallowed hard, wondering if she'd gone too far. More pleasantly, she said, "We are going to begin our exercises today."

"Oh, really. And what exercises are those? Shall I leap out of this bed and begin a vigorous routine? Perhaps show you what Jackson taught me of the feint and jab."

She'd had it. "Oh, do shut up, Raphael. Your puerile squabbling is tiresome."

His jaw fell open and she felt a moment of complete

satisfaction. She gave him her shoulder as she turned to his feet and drew back the covers.

He yelled at her to put that back, demanded to know what the bloody hell she was doing. She ignored him, picking up a strongly boned foot and rotating it in the manner Douglas had told her. Raphael exploded in a storm of expletives, many of which Julia had never heard before. She supposed it was a good thing she didn't know what they meant. He tried to grab at her, but it was easy to evade him.

"Stop this at once. I won't have it. Julia! Damn you. Stop treating me like a helpless child!"

"When you cease this childish tantrum, I will." Her words were controlled, but inside she quaked. She had no idea what she was doing and his violent reaction unnerved her. But she wouldn't show him. Picking up the other foot, she inquired, "Is this helpful?"

"It would be helpful if you would permit me to kill you."

She turned back to her task. To her surprise, he ceased berating her. A sullen silence descended. Done with the second foot, she slid her hands up each leg, starting from the ankle and proceeding all the way to the thigh.

She found herself shivering. Tiny tremors of reaction shot through her at this way she was forced to touch him. Although he had lost a good deal of weight, his legs were still firm and hard with muscle. As she ran her hands higher, she became acutely embarrassed. Even during their lovemaking, she had been somewhat shy about exploring his body. What it cost her to slide her hands so freely over his flesh like this was incalculable.

Somewhere in the region of his upper thigh, as her hands moved to the outside of his hips, he reacted. She looked at him, astonished. "Do you feel that?"

He appeared to be frozen but for the rapid rise and fall of his chest. His forehead was creased in concentration. "I can feel it," he said in a rusty voice. They were the first noncaustic words she had heard from him.

Excitement sharpened her voice. "That means the numbness begins much lower than the injury."

His eyes locked with hers, intense, searching, trapping her. He didn't seem angry with her anymore. His gaze dropped to her lips and his lids grew heavy. She felt a familiar heat from long ago and had to look away, fearful that her rising color would betray her.

Steeling herself to attend to the business for which she was here, she moved her fingers back down his legs, massaging the skin. She was more self-conscious now. It made her movements stiff, less fluid. But he didn't balk.

Taking up his foot again, this time bracing a hand under his thigh, she began bending the knee as Douglas had told her to do. It was heavy work, and she concentrated so intently that it wasn't until after she had skirted around the other side of the bed to get at Raphael's right leg that she noticed the beads of sweat on his brow. "Does this hurt?"

His skin was tinged gray and his face once again reflected his fury. "What a stupid question. I can't feel a damn thing down there, so how could it hurt?"

Working the other leg, she finished with the massage. Covering up his motionless limbs, she pronounced. "Later, Franklin and Gregory will work with you privately in a series of exercises which they have been specially trained to do. We will do this every day."

"The hell you will. While I am still man enough to find this little performance interesting, you will keep your hands from my person in the future."

An incongruous explosion of laughter burst out of her. "Raphael, you sound like a prig!"

He looked shocked and unbelievably insulted. Jerking his head away, his face like a thundercloud, he groused, "My porridge is cold."

RAPHAEL SHOWED UP with his flask at the supper table that evening in a mood to dole out punishment for the

morning's intrusion. He made lewd comments about everything, culminating in his picking at his stuffed game hen
and wondering at its sex. Spreading the small legs, he pronounced it female and launched into a bawdy assessment
of its merits as a bed partner for a man whose love life
was not up to snuff.

"You are not amusing," Julia told him as she sliced a
bit of meat. She kept her tone casual, having decided in
the long hours since this morning, that it was best if she
resisted any reaction to his rudeness. As much as she could
help it, that was. He did have a dubious gift of pushing
one far beyond limits of endurance.

Tonight, however, he merely glared at her.

Heartened, she went on. "There were signs of progress
today. So soon, too. I am quite encouraged. I fail to see
why you are so wretched."

"Really? Then you must be profoundly stupid. How
about this for a reason—*I am a cripple!*"

She drew in a breath, slowly let it out, then tried again.
"Then why do you resist me when I try to help you?"

"Because I want no help from you. Or for anyone else
for that matter."

"So you shall just rot away? That indeed is a brilliant
plan, Raphael."

"What does it matter to you?" He tossed his fork on his
plate. The jarring clatter made Julia start. "Goddamn it,
why don't you hate me? You should, God knows."

She stopped, stared at him. "Sometimes I think I do."

He threw his hands out, almost in an appeal. "Then go
on your way. Leave me alone—"

"You are repeating yourself," she said testily, jabbing at
the morsels on her plate. "I've heard this too many times
before for it to be effective."

"—Because I promise you the only thing you will find
in my company is more of the same as you've been getting. I'll make you miserable, I promise that."

She paused, leaning on her elbows to stare at him. "When
I leave you, Raphael, it will be a clean cutting of all of

our ties. I shall owe you nothing and want nothing from you. And there will be no bindings on my conscience."

"What do you owe me? I betrayed you, I humiliated you—set a price on your innocence and took it without a qualm."

"Yes, you did." She looked closely at him. "Why, I believe you actually feel guilty."

"Oh, madam, you are a piece!" He threw back his head and dug his fingers into his hair as if searching out the thoughts tangled within. "God, you are such a cursed innocent. You should have married Simon. A pair of babes, you could have existed in your own pretty world and never known monsters such as myself existed."

"How can you say that with pride?" she challenged.

"Not pride, my dear." He shook his head. "You misunderstand."

"It seems a malady of mine. I never know how to take you."

He dropped his hands. His eyelids lowered to half mast. "Oh, you always knew. You didn't realize it, did you? You are really too ingenuous." He laughed scornfully. "I would think it rather funny if it weren't so damnably irritating."

"So I irritate you?" Julia pulled herself up and said with dignity, "You, who are detestable to me when I've done nothing to deserve it, find fault with me? Oh, Lord, at times I could . . ." Catching herself, she once again stopped her rising temper in its tracks and redirected herself. "See here, Raphael, we are tied together for better or worse, just as we vowed. Would it be out of order for us to behave civilly toward each other?"

He blinked, turned his head to look for his flask. After taking a draught, he replied, "But you are forgetting that I am a monster." He flashed a ferocious smile. "We are a carefully nurtured breed, we monsters. Rather like a hothouse flower. Meticulously tended with scathing insults, our good intentions pruned religiously. We are fed only the exotic brews of hate that our monster-maker knows will infuse our veins with evil and turn our hearts to blackest pitch."

She was silent. A look came in his eye as if he realized he'd revealed too much. He snapped his head away.

Julia's nerves hummed. The roots of her hair tingled with the tension rising between them. Quietly she asked, "Who was your monster-maker, Raphael?"

He wouldn't answer. He wouldn't look at her. His face was inscrutable.

"Coward," she said with soft vehemence. "You cannot face me, not when there is truth to be said. You are afraid of the truth, aren't you? That is why you always hide in your nasty lies. Making crude jests, ridiculing everyone else, that is how you prefer it so no one will see how helpless you really are."

He shifted, tucking his chin into his chest. She watched his hands, restlessly picking at the linen tablecloth. They were large hands, with blunt-tipped fingers and squared-off nails. Gentle hands, at times, they now flexed with power.

Finally he replied, "I never realized how much you suffer from delusion. First you mistake yourself for a nurse-maid, and now you want to be my confessor."

She shook her head, giving up. "There was a time when I was the one you spoke to about everything."

He threw up his head and thundered, "Don't you dare speak of that! I never want to hear of those times, do you understand? Christ, can't you understand the only thing I want is for you to leave me in peace?"

She rose. "I will give you your wish. For now. I will see you in the morning."

"I do not want you to come," he called as she headed for the door.

"Perhaps one day when you walk again, you can do something about it."

ONE AFTERNOON JULIA sat at the escritoire desk in her apartments to write overdue correspondence to her family. First, a letter to her mother, speaking chiefly about the house, it's faded grandeur, the lax servants, and then one to Father to talk chattily about the agreeableness of the roads she had experienced on their journey. Those out of the way, she set about writing Laura.

I find myself in a situation largely unchanged from the one this past summer in the town house. Oh, Raphael speaks to me now, but all he has to say is vile and hateful. He blames me, I think, for his misfortune. I fear he may be right in some respects. I should have prevailed upon Simon not to duel, as I did Raphael, but never did I think Simon would prove such an expert marksman. In any event, I am still committed to my present course. I look forward to the day when I can retire to a house of my own, but cannot act on this wish until Raphael is on the mend. To leave him in this state is not acceptable, as we have talked about so often. As to his recovery, I have great doubts that my efforts will prove successful. I believe the Lincolnshire man wanted to be well, and this had to have a salutary effect on his progress. If my fears are founded and Raphael makes no improvement, I dread to think of what my future will hold.

Enough of my woes. I hope you are enjoying the seaside. Please send my love to Hope and Marie. And Leah as well. I was distressed to hear in your letter of her latest escapades. I know Mother will deal with her harshly and although she no doubt deserves it, I cannot help but pity her. Like myself, she is a wayward spirit. As I have landed in an unenviable situation, perhaps she will take a lesson from my folly.

I think of you all and miss you terribly. Kiss Father

for me and tell Mother none of my troubles. If she asks, say I am well and that Raphael . . .

She paused, then ended with, *remains unchanged.* Not that it would reassure anyone, but at least it wasn't a lie. Folding the vellum, she melted crimson wax and set the Fontvilliers seal to it. It was strange to think of it being her family crest now. Nothing about being Raphael's wife seemed real anymore.

She took out a fresh sheet of paper to begin a short note to the duchess. She had barely written the address when Mrs. Anson knocked on her door. The housekeeper informed her that visitors were waiting in the formal reception room known as the crystal parlor. Smoothing her hair, Julia placed her pen back in the pot and followed the woman downstairs, wondering who could be calling.

A pair of ladies stood in the middle of a rather bare room. Julia was instantly embarrassed to note the shabby curtains and faded furnishings.

"Hello, madam le viscountess," the one woman said, dropping into a quick curtsy. She was a thin creature with brown, rather coarse hair pulled back into a loose bun and a sharp little nose jutting out over a smiling mouth. Her companion, who was both more stout and more serious, inclined her head slightly.

The tiny woman spoke again. "I'm Mrs. Cecile Wren and this is my sister, Mrs. Eulalia Peavenstover. We are so pleased that you agreed to see us."

"A pleasure. Have a seat, ladies. May I offer you tea?"

Mrs. Wren twittered. "Oh, no—"

"That would be lovely," pronounced Mrs. Peavenstover in a booming voice.

"Let me call Mrs. Anson, then." Julia summoned the housekeeper. Given the sorry state of the house, she had great trepidation about the kind of tea Mrs. Anson would place before guests.

Mrs. Anson answered the summons so quickly she could only have been hovering just outside the door. Julia instructed, "Tea, please, Mrs. Anson, and tell Janet to make those special little sandwiches we enjoyed the other day. I am certain our guests would like them. And cake, too, if she has it. And jam. And biscuits. I believe we still have some in the tin." Mrs. Anson only nodded and left, giving no indication that she had taken Julia's hint to put out a decent show.

"Tea shall arrive presently," Julia stated, coming back into the room. She was mortified to note the furniture was a tad dusty. Mrs. Peavenstover wrinkled her nose slightly as she lowered herself onto a chair and a cloud of the stuff wafted into the air.

Mrs. Wren, taking a seat with nary a twitch, gushed, "It is so very good of you to receive us."

"You said that, Cecile." Mrs. Peavenstover's voice was deep. It seemed to resonate off the faded silk-covered walls.

Julia raised her eyes to the chandelier. It was a magnificent piece, supposedly what had given the room its name. Although dulled by dirt, the crystal prisms caught the light coming in from the filmy windows and sent it off in a shower of refracted light. Julia was overcome by a curious sense of sadness at seeing that grand piece brought so low by its humble surroundings. It seemed such a waste, a sentiment that caught her up in pensive thoughts for a moment before she snapped out of her reflective mood and attended her guests.

Mrs. Peavenstover folded her chubby hands on her lap. "We have come to pay a social call, madam le viscountess. As the wife of the churchwarden—that is myself, you understand—and the constable's misses—that would be my sister, Cecile here—we felt it our duty to welcome you to our neighborhood."

Mrs. Wren squeaked and broke out into one of her smiles. Julia found it infectious. "It is a rather *large* neighborhood, I am sure, when one thinks of what you are used to in London!"

"I am originally from Hampstead," Julia said. "I have fond memories of the country."

Mrs. Peavenstover's thick eyebrows jerked upward and she seemed to approve of this. "Do you know the Kelmers?"

"I am afraid I do not. Hampstead is rather a large place."

"Hmph." Clearly, Mrs. Peavenstover thought very little of a person who would not be acquainted with the presumably illustrious Kelmers.

Tea arrived shortly. To her surprise, Janet, the parlor maid, wheeled in a well-appointed cart.

"Look at this, Eulalia!" Mrs. Wren exclaimed.

The telltale eyebrows jerked upward. Julia could have guessed Mrs. Peavenstover would appreciate the generous assortment. The woman had the look of one who enjoyed food.

Despite her earlier trepidation, Julia felt herself relax. Her two guests made for pleasant company—even Eulalia (Julia had insisted after the second cup of tea that they dispense with needless formality) warmed upon acquaintance. In any event, it was as good companionship as any she'd had these past weeks.

In no time, they were conversing easily. Julia was careful what she told them about herself, but was able to speak freely of her family. They were astonished at the tale of how she and her sisters had been invited to stay at the Cravensmores' and the noble couple's sponsorship of her debut into society.

"Oh, dear," Cecile exclaimed, clutching her sparse breast, "such a wonderful story. I suppose that was where you met the viscount?"

"Yes," Julia answered, and changed the subject in the quickest way she knew—she asked Eulalia a question about herself. As the woman launched into an enthusiastic explanation of her interests, a movement drew Julia's gaze to the door.

Poised just outside the room was Raphael. His chair was off to the side, blocked by one of the double doors which was still closed so that their guests were unaware of his presence. Julia stared, her heart slowly sinking into the pit of her stomach.

He would make a scene. Oh, God, he'd come in and start with some outrageous comments, maybe even sing one of his depraved songs.

His green eyes were dark. He held her gaze—eye to eye in perfect understanding of his threat and her dread— for a moment before she snapped her head away. The ladies, having engaged in a mild disagreement over on what street exactly their one nephew lived these days, were unaware of her lapse.

Julia braced herself, sipping her tea to wet her dry throat. Raphael would be merciless. He'd make her pay for all the exercises she put him through that morning, every morning, over his repeated protests, orders to get out, and all manner of insults.

And he would enjoy every moment of it.

Cecile Wren asked her, "Were you aware that we have a parish school?"

"No, indeed I was not," Julia said, trying desperately to overcome her tension and attend their conversation. At any moment Raphael would be coming in to ruin everything, but until that time she was determined to retain her dignity. "I have, or course, heard about Hannah More's experiment."

"Oh, we are very progressive here in the Lake District," Eulalia said importantly. "We take pride in bringing new ideas to our little corner of England. Education is so very important in helping people better their lives."

"We're very active in charity work, as well," Cecile chimed in. "We have an orphanage we support as well as the Quaker home for . . . well . . . unfortunate girls."

That, Julia supposed, meant unwed mothers. It was absurd, of course, that mention of a woman's pregnant condition was not done in polite society, but there it was.

She smiled and said, "I should like very much to hear

more about all these projects." *How much longer did she have before Raphael came bursting in?*

A surreptitious glance at the door shocked her to the core. He had gone. He had left her in peace, all without making the slightest sound.

Chapter Eighteen

HAWKSHEAD WAS A lovely village with narrow stone-paved streets and Elizabethan houses clustered in quaint profusion. Timbered façades over wattle and dab brought to mind another era, and Julia soaked up the charming ambiance. The phaeton was in the inn's carriage house, the horses being watered and given a helping of oats, while she walked the picturesque streets and entered shop after shop. It was glorious to spend the day away from the gloomy confines of Glenwood Park.

Her welcome among the villagers was heartening. The people of the area had been curious about her, there was no mistaking that. Everyone came at her with smiles and offerings, as if she were Prinny himself come to stroll along their lanes.

The ladies at the dress shop fussed over her, dragging out gloves and reticules and garters and stuff for dresses, all for her admiration. The cobbler tipped his hat to her shyly before going inside his shop to send his wife after Julia with a basket of biscuits for which, she modestly imparted, she was famous.

The milliner proved a garrulous fellow who gossiped freely despite Julia's gentle hints that she disliked such talk. She moved on to a shop boasting the impressive name of "Repository of the Arts," which housed an intriguing collection of paintings, statues and other pieces one would use for interior decoration. Taking her time, she browsed before departing for luncheon at the inn under the exuberant supervision of the cheerful innkeeper.

On the way home, her head was filled with the lingering pleasantness of the day. The Repository had given her some ideas about how to spruce up the house. She hadn't thought to involve herself in tackling a job like redecorating Glenwood Park. After all, she had always intended her stay to be only temporary. Yet for the duration of their visit, they deserved to be comfortable in the drafty old place. She would speak to Mr. Conrad about it. Before she began making purchases, she would want to see what, if anything, was stored in the attics.

She left the carriage in the forecourt and told the head footman to send a groom to bring it round to the carriage house. When they had been short of staff, she would have seen to it herself. However, several new servants had been brought in, and Julia was pleased with the increased efficiency in the house.

She untied her bonnet and turned toward the stairs, then froze when she saw the familiar face of the woman standing in the hall.

The Countess of Wentword smiled. "I see I have surprised you. Didn't you get my post?"

"No. I am afraid the delivery system out here is much inferior to London. Oh, but it is good to see you." To her surprise, Julia found herself rushing forward. She held her arms out for the older woman, and the countess, without missing a beat, took her up in a motherly embrace. Julia whispered, "I'm glad you've come."

The countess's voice sounded choked. "You may not be when you learn what I've done." Pulling back, she slipped her arm about her granddaughter-in-law and lead Julia into the crystal parlor. "Perhaps we should talk. I know you must be tired, but I think we must speak right away."

"What is it? Is something wrong." Julia stopped in her

tracks as hot panic came over her. "Is it Raphael? Is something wrong—has something happened to him?"

The countess was stunned. "No, child. He's fine. He's in the library, with . . . oh, dear. Can we not sit down and I'll explain all of it to you?"

Julia complied, sitting stiffly as the other woman arranged herself on a freshly cleaned divan. "I must say, Julia, you have done wonders here in such a short time. I inquired into the place right after you selected it and was doubtful it could be made a suitable residence."

Too anxious to bother with the compliment, Julia uttered a quick thanks and said, "Now please tell me what is going on. I am afraid you've peaked my curiosity."

The woman folded her hands, studying them for a moment. "Julia, dear, I've brought someone with me." He bosom heaved as she sighed. "I don't know if Raphael has told you of his family. Of his mother, my daughter."

"I know of her, of course, although Raphael mentioned her little. She lives in France and he sees her infrequently."

"Indeed. They are estranged. Polite strangers, nothing more. I am afraid there were events that occurred, ones I am not quite certain of myself, which drove an irreparable wedge between them. I believe it is this situation which feeds much of my grandson's ill moods. I am not making excuses for his behavior, mind you, but I must allow that something wretched had a most unfortunate effect on him as a youth." A sad look came into her eyes and she shook her head slowly. "He came to me like a lost pup, all proud and cold on the outside, but like a pup, I tell you, when one looked in those eyes. He learned to cover that, too, in time, but I gave him a home and tolerated him all of these years because of that look."

"Yes. I've glimpsed it myself."

The countess seemed surprised. "Have you? Then you have seen more than most, for he has grown into a hard man. The duel . . . it made it worse, didn't it? I could tell by your letters, although you tried very hard to be cheerful."

"He is having trouble accepting his new circumstance—"

Julia was cut off by a dismissive wave of the countess's

hand. "I know my grandson well, and I know he's been deviling you most unpleasantly. Now, listen to me, child, for I
fear it is about to get worse. My daughter has been writing
to me through the summer after she learned of what happened and has been insisting on coming to see her son. I put
her off with excuses and lies, knowing it would be a disaster if she did so. She is still afraid of me, it seems, and so
I was successful for a while, but maternal instinct won out
in the end. She came to London last week and demanded
I bring her here. She would have come without me if I
hadn't agreed."

"His mother is here?" Julia didn't know why this settled
like a weight of dread upon her chest.

The countess nodded gravely. "She is. In the library, right
at this moment. She wanted to speak to him alone."

They shared a look of apprehension, then Julia asked,
"Have you heard anything from them?"

"No. It has been quiet in there." The countess looked to
the door. "I half expected a row to wake the dead."

Julia followed her gaze and swallowed. Raphael's mother
here . . . it felt frightening. He had always been decidedly
closemouthed about his parentage, mentioning both his
mother and father only rarely and in the most curt of tones.
She remembered once she had even misinterpreted him to
have said that she was dead, and then understood that what
he had meant was that she was, in essence, dead to him. She
had certainly been curious but it wasn't something she ever
dared broach.

From this little amount of information and the warning
tone of the countess, Julia knew there was a potentially ex-
plosive situation brewing. Yet she couldn't be sorry. The mo-
notony and immobility of the last weeks were wearing her
nerves raw, for she was certainly not making any headway
with her husband on her own.

The countess offered, "Why don't we order tea. It will re-
fresh us and pass the time while we're waiting."

Julia rang the bell, but doubted she would eat a thing.

RAPHAEL SAT IN the aftermath of his mother's performance feeling not at all the way he would have expected. When she'd arrived, he'd nearly taken her head off, ordering her out of the house and calling for his servants to take him back to his bedroom. His instinct had been to hide away—he wasn't too proud to flee from her cloying theatrics, nor did he see any shame in it. Good God, Violetta Giscard, of all people to walk through that door—had he not enough to bear? But, of course, there was little he could do to stop her. His physical limitations put him rather at a disadvantage. Sullenly, he relented, seething all the while in anticipation of his mother's performance.

She'd started out very calm, telling him the usual mother things one might expect. This wasn't unusual. He could have guessed that she'd been worried when she'd heard of the duel, that she had feared for him and his health, prayed he would recover, but it didn't particularly move him.

Then she changed. Subtly at first. She told him when she'd first received word of his injury, it was at a time when they'd been uncertain whether he would survive and it had brought upon her an epiphany of sorts. Then she began to talk in a way he had never heard her before, and . . . she had started to weep. Not the delicate, sympathy-garnering sobs he had always associated with her emotional outbursts. This was far more uncontrolled. Her eyes swelled and her cheeks were blotched and patchy. Her nose went red and began to run. He had to give her his handkerchief because she hadn't been able to locate one of her own. Although he wanted to deride her show, he'd been fascinated against his will, listening as she talked about her weakness, her mistakes and regrets. She was sorry, she had said, that she'd taken his father from him with her impulsive confession in one hot, misspent moment. In all probability, he was Marquay's son. If she had kept her secret to herself, she would not have destroyed their bond.

She said it just like that—*she* would not have destroyed their bond. It was the first time he had ever heard his mother take responsibility for anything. She even seemed to mean it. This Raphael noted with a degree of bewilderment. He didn't like the knot that formed in his chest.

He'd never thought of his mother as suffering for what was his own loss.

The old demons stirred, restless as they considered his mother's pandering must serve her somehow. Cynicism burned low, sputtered, and died out. Somehow, the beasts within didn't rise.

She had nothing to gain from coming here. He wanted nothing from her, so she could not use him in any way, and he could not see how she benefited from gaining his pardon.

He could understand being imperfect. He found himself thinking of how he had done things he wasn't proud of, things he'd felt driven to. Hell, he still did them. It gave him no pleasure to see the hurt on Julia's face every time he shut her out. No. It was not from choice that he drove her away.

Her emotions spent, Violetta sniffled as she tried to bring herself under control. Raphael said at last, "I'll pour you some Madeira," and heard his voice much gentler than he'd intended.

Violetta looked up at him, blinked, and gave him a wavering smile. "Thank you."

JULIA WAS IN the village tea shop one day when she happened upon Mrs. Peavenstover—*Eulalia,* she was corrected with a mild scold. The woman was excited about a neighborhood dance which was coming up soon. She was keen on Julia attending and making the acquaintance of the other prominent members of the area.

"I'm afraid that is impossible," Julia replied with a weak smile. "You know my husband is not well. But thank you for the invitation."

"Of course, dear, but in the country we are much more accepting than in town. You need not stay home. And surely he will not mind. La, I'm sure he can spare you for a few hours."

Julia thought miserably that Raphael could no doubt spare her for much longer than that. "I suppose."

"You could do with a bit of getting out, I daresay. That house . . . well, dear, it's not exactly cheerful. I don't mean to insult you."

"It is terribly dreary."

"Just so. You are young yet, and a bit of socializing couldn't hurt you. If I can tell everyone that you *might* be there, it will mean more tickets sold. Didn't I tell you? The Quaker home is the beneficiary of our evening. Everyone donates their services, from the musicians to the food, and we charge admission. The proceeds will go to the young women at the home."

Intrigued, Julia leaned forward. "You didn't tell me it was a charity event. I would like to help."

"We would love to have you. We need all the help we can get."

The new project buoyed Julia's spirits. On the ride home, she made some plans. Raphael had made a generous offer for funds to be available for her. He kept a good deal of banknotes on hand in the safe in the library. He'd told her before she had merely to take what she needed, just leave a receipt for his accounting. So far, she'd barely made a dent in what he made available to her, even with all her refurbishing expenses for the house. Her mind churned with possibilities. She'd love to make donations, see her efforts go to beneficial causes.

At supper that evening, she spoke about her ideas to the countess and Raphael's mother.

"I think that's rather exciting," the marquese said. Her voice was flat. She didn't sound excited at all.

Julia had discovered early in their acquaintance that she and her mother-in-law had little affinity for each other. It was nothing hostile, just a lack of things in common to serve as the basis for mutual understanding.

"Is Raphael eating?" the countess boomed, slapping down

her utensils. "If he doesn't see fit to take his meals with us, then I at least wish to be reassured that he is getting some sustenance other than from a bottle."

"He takes tea. He eats." The marquese kept her eyes lowered as she cut up her meat into tiny morsels. On most days, Violetta Giscard took her tea in the library with her son. It was something of a surprise to Julia that he tolerated it. And she was a bit jealous, too. She herself only saw her husband on those mornings she forced herself to see to his massage. They didn't talk at all anymore while she performed the exercises on his legs.

"Well, see to it that he has more than confections and jam and bread, will you Violetta? If you are the only one he lets near him, then it is up to you." The countess's tone was imperious, but as thin as an eggshell over the thwarted concern she tried not to show. She kept her distance from Raphael, but when they chanced to pass there was always a certain expression on her face that was akin to longing. Julia always turned away when she saw it. She understood the emotion very well.

To divert the conversation, Julia told them about the dance planned for after the new year.

"Oh, I expect I shall have returned home by then," Violetta said breezily. "But I do think you should go, dear. Will you accompany her, Mother?"

"I am to travel up to Inverness with the Kendricks, Violetta. You know we always spend February in Scotland, a respite of blissful peace before heading back to town for another season."

There was nothing objectionable about the marquese, yet Julia was relieved at the news that she would be departing soon. But she wasn't happy to be hearing of the countess's leaving. She needed something to do to keep herself from going mad once they had gone and she was once again alone with Raphael. She mused, "I think I shall involve myself with this Quaker house they've taken me to see. I think it fitting Fontvilliers's money should go to help the unfortunate."

She didn't mean any offense. But once the words were

said, she looked alarmed. The countess had a smile on her face, the marquese did not.

Violetta inclined her head and said loftily, "Just so, my dear. Just so."

Julia had no idea what in the world she meant, but kept quiet and begged off directly after the meal was concluded. In her room she took up some correspondence she had been neglecting. Her family was back in London, for the Christmas social whirl before going off again to the country in the nomadic way of the *haute ton*.

After her letters were written, she was still restless. She supposed she might go to the library for a book.

The room was quiet, with the low-burning fire throwing lazy shadows up onto the walls. No other light burned. Raphael was in his chair pulled up to the hearth. He seemed to be asleep. When the floorboards creaked under her feet, he snapped his head up.

She said, "Oh, you startled me."

"You are the one sneaking about." His voice was soft, with no rancor. He settled back into position, dismissing her, it seemed.

She would have expected him to roar her out of the room. His lack of ire surprised her. "I was looking for you, actually," she said.

Heavy-lidded eyes regarded her, then slid away. He seemed distracted, as if he'd been pondering things of substantive weight when she'd come upon him.

"I'm sorry, Raphael. I seem to be interrupting."

"No," he replied, waving a hand at her. "You are not disturbing me."

Julia stood awkwardly as she tried to fathom this mood, to decide if she should stay or run. She wanted to remain, though she didn't know why.

He roused somewhat and looked around him. "The lamps haven't been lit yet."

"You just noticed?" Julia pulled on the bell. Anxiousness made her movements clipped and efficient. What a strange mood it was between them tonight. Strange and interesting. "I'll have Doris come in and do it."

He inclined his head, then asked, "What did you want to see me about?"

"Oh." Julia came to take a seat near him. "I was just wondering where you had gotten to." Her smile felt forced. "When you weren't at supper last night, and then I missed you at breakfast, I just wondered . . ."

Giving her a shrewd look, he said, "And you didn't come to do the exercises."

"I thought maybe you'd prefer not to."

"I always preferred not to."

Yes, but this was different. She was losing her confidence, her sense of purpose. She had neglected the exercises because it was getting harder to face him every day; to face the feelings she still harbored for him. So much easier to entrust him to his mother and hide in her own world that was rapidly filling with activities and new friends. Distractions, they were. Desperately needed distractions.

"Here's Doris!" she exclaimed, and rose to give instruction to the maid to light the lamps.

"This room is quite cozy in the evening." Raphael's voice was low as Doris performed her duty. "You may join me if you like."

"Thank you," she said.

She had expected to find him at his worst, all bluster and spleen. But this . . . she'd not thought he would be pensive, soft, brimming with something so alarmingly close to gentleness, it alarmed her.

"Is this the post?" she said, going over to the desk. Was she being as transparently jittery as she felt?

He had fallen into contemplation again. "Hmmm?" He flickered his gaze to her, touched her, then slid away. She shivered, intrigued. What *was* going on with him tonight?

She sorted through the pile. There were letters from her sister, mother, and the duke. Seeing those familiar scripts had the power to make her forget Raphael for the moment. She rushed to the chair, now bathed in light from the glowing lamp next to it, and opened the seal on one.

She had selected the duke's first by mistake, having meant to grab Laura's. But she read the short missive and found herself smiling wistfully, caught up in fond memories of the man.

. . . miss you most in my library. No one puts the books back for me, or frightens me monstrously when I come in and find an unexpected person in that old leather chair.

She laughed out loud, thinking that was exactly what had happened tonight when Raphael had startled her. Must be a thing with libraries.

"Something amusing?"

She looked up. "Oh, the Duke of Cravensmore wrote to me." She was not of a mind to entrust any of her thoughts to him, not tonight when this unreal mood hung over them. She folded up the letter. "He used to share his library with me. He misses that, he says."

Raphael found himself pulled clear of his thoughts, a sensation not unlike being dragged out from under a huge rock. It was that smile of hers that did it. It had been a long time since he'd seen Julia smile like that. Or laugh.

He didn't press her to tell him whatever it was that had brought it on. He just watched it, appreciated it, like one would a painting. And that made him remember the museum in London, looking at art together, discussing it. A pang of loss twinged him, so slight he almost didn't notice it because here she was again, sitting easily by his side, and for some reason she didn't feel so far away tonight.

As she read, he caught the way her eyes widened, and her free hand, the one that wasn't holding the letter, came over her gaping mouth.

Curiosity got the better of him. "What is it?" Was that his own voice, so mild?

She shook her head, read a bit more, then smiled. "My sister Leah is far too clever for her own good. It seems she has found some fresh trouble for herself."

He noticed the way the pointed corners of her mouth curled upward and observed, "You seem to be amused."

"She took the two daughters of the Earl of Messing off to investigate some rather . . . eh . . . unconventional behavior of the servants in the stables." Her eyes sparkled—yes, he'd forgotten just how they did that when she was delighted with something. "It might be the sort of thing I can imagine *you* doing as a child. However, Leah is not so adventuresome. She and Mother share this kind of natural understanding of each other I never had. I wonder what has caused her to become so rebellious."

Himself as a child—following his father to the servant's wing and finding all sorts of "unconventional behavior." Why didn't that memory sting? Rather, he was caught by her admission about a distance between herself and her mother. He remembered watching her at the theater. "You favor your father."

She nodded, "He became much busier once he was successful than when he worked at the bank. He invests now, privately, for some of his old bank customers, you see, but it takes all his time and I never see him. We used to play chess and he'd sometimes take me traveling with him."

"Was he the one who encouraged you to read?"

"Mmm. He hardly ever goes against Mother, but he did take up for me in that. I received books for Christmas three years in a row. Mother frowned, but as long as I didn't actually *discuss* my love of books, then it was allowed." She flashed a smile again and began to chuckle. "Leah, the sister that's in trouble, was always the worst tattletale. I'd go to the library and sneak out books on lend, and she'd snoop about my room to find them, then march in triumph into the family withdrawing room. Oh, she was a wretch, but I always got the sense she thought me a rival and was rather desperate to win over Mother's approval. And Marie would get so angry with her! Oh, she'd scold her and stomp her little feet and Mother, who has a soft place for her baby as all mothers must, conceded and admonished Leah. Poor Leah. She would be far less disagreeable if she didn't try so hard to prove herself." That was when she realized what she was doing. She pulled herself up with a straightening of her spine and blushed. "You must think me rather silly going on so. My family is rather eccentric in our blend of personalities."

With some effort he found his voice. "It all sounds so . . . normal." And his own background was anything but, wasn't it? What would she think to know of his childhood? His parents—their charming ways of slicing off bits of each other with stilleto insults and bleeding all over their son. God, she'd be revolted, and rightly so. Next to her quaint family quirks and small-scale strife all underlaid with the affection he saw brimming in her amber eyes, the mess of his home would seem like a nightmare.

His was filled with a scalding sense of shame. It was ironic how in the past he had derided family, laughed at the entanglements, and exalted his freedom. But right now, he couldn't have mustered so much as a curl of his lip to dismiss this intimate glimpse Julia had supplied.

He had better say something, he thought, and found his newfound masochistic streak wasn't done with the subject. He wanted to hear more. "You must miss them."

That beautiful smile disappeared and she nodded, not meeting his gaze. "Yes. Terribly."

"You must go visit them soon."

Her eyes flashed and leveled a blazing glare on him. "Is all this part of your design to get me to leave?"

Taken aback, he replied, "No, I didn't think of it like that. Only that it would be natural that you would want to see them again. Surely, you don't think to hole away here for the rest of your life, never seeing anyone else or venturing out into the world?"

She was mollified. "I suppose I could plan something."

"Maybe for the start of the season. I recall this Leah must be of an age to come out this year. She would probably like to have you about to help her along. She sounds like she could use some advice."

She looked suspicious but said nothing. He shared her mystification at his comments. He himself didn't know where they came from. It felt good, however, not to be fighting with her. But it mustn't feel too good.

He was dancing with the devil, here, and finally lost his nerve. He sought to change the subject. "Have you had a chance to look at the books in here? Did you see anything of value?"

She glanced up at the shelves. "I've had them dusted, that's about it. There are no novels. I am partial to novels, although I have been reading a volume of Shelley's I brought with me."

"Hmm. See if there's anything on philosophy. Or history."

She rose, taking a lamp to light her way. He liked the way she moved, in a sort of feminine glide. Peering closely at one of the shelves, she wrinkled her nose. "A biography of the fifth Earl of Wentword." She laughed as she took the book off the shelf. "An Elizabethan. Are you interested in your ancestors?" She thrust the book at him for consideration.

He took it from her, thinking these were the only ancestors he could be sure of, the ones on the Wentword side. A wave of self-pity soured him. "I was thinking less personal history. Too many ghosts." He placed the book on the table without even looking at it.

"All right. Umm. Oh, here is an account of the War of the Roses." She pulled the book out, began to flip through it. "Were the Wentwards Yorkists or Lancastrians?"

"Why must everything be about my family's history? I don't know."

She gave him an impatient look but didn't take offense. "It was merely a question. By the way you prickle, I'd think you were still frightened of Richard III coming to take your head."

He couldn't help it—it simply struck him funny, and the pert tone she used just made him have to laugh. He shook his head, realizing, not for the first time, that this woman could be quite exasperating. She was deviling him—he, the master of deviling.

Yes, he saw that smile of hers, a soft little twist to her full mouth. He'd missed her wry sense of humor.

"Such a clever wit," he muttered, trying to sound droll. "You are absolutely incorrigible."

"I learned it from you," she countered, throwing her chin up. But the smile was still in place.

"Then you should know not to tempt the master."

She sauntered toward him, merely a few steps, but he detected a definite sauciness in the sway of her hips. "Have you never heard of the student becoming more proficient than the master?"

My God, they were flirting!

His chest burned. He wanted so badly to reach out for her just then, saw himself in his mind's eye grabbing her wrist and pulling her onto his lap. And kissing her. God, how he wanted to kiss her.

She seemed to sense the danger and turned away, still pleasant but losing some of that crackling tension between them. He was grateful to her. She was wiser than he.

She took her seat and resumed reading her letters. They were silent for a while. He pretended not to notice the surreptitious glances she kept throwing at him. Finally she said, "Raphael, what did your mother come here for?"

He was taken aback, marvelling she would dare to ask such a question. Didn't she know he was likely to flay her with his tongue? Had she no sense, no fear?

Of course she knew, perhaps better than anyone. And it wasn't that she didn't care. That canny look in her eye told him she was braced for his reaction, but she'd asked anyway. She was very brave, he thought suddenly. Why didn't it annoy him?

Because he'd had something to do with that brave girl standing before him. She'd not always been so. He remembered she'd nearly walked into marriage with a man who'd bury her alive in a world of formalities and gossip and petty thinking, and smile all the while. He'd had something to do with her escaping that, and the knowledge lay silken smooth on his heart.

But she was expecting him to answer. "We had things to

settle, a misunderstanding from long ago that still separates us." Christ! Why had he said so much.

She frowned. He wanted to take his fingertip and run it along the adorable crease in her forehead. "It must have been a rewarding visit," she mused. "You seem much different. At peace, maybe."

"Believe me, nothing about my mother would bring me peace." *Except to give me back my father.*

But then . . . would he want Marquay?

What a thought. He'd always been so single-minded on the subject, craving the man's affection in those years before he'd learned of his mother's affair, mourning his loss after he knew. Thinking about Marquay now that he was an adult, was it so bad to think of himself as different, if not by actual heritage, then certainly in heart, than a man like that?

"I suppose I shouldn't ask. It's none of my business." She turned her head to the side. He felt his pulse respond. He loved that gesture. "It's just that I'm curious. You've told me so little about yourself."

Claws. Ripping. He gritted his teeth, hit by a tide of stale pain. He wanted to be rid of it. "There are things about my family," he admitted slowly, "that would shock you. I don't think you could ever understand them."

She frowned. "I won't speak ill of my family, but we are not without our problems. Perhaps I'd understand better than you would think, Raphael."

A bust of damning hope caught him and, damn it, he was seized by those golden eyes for one fatal moment. He said, "My mother needs devotion. It's like air to her. She married a philanderer. She took his affairs as the ultimate rejection." Rubbing his thumb along his chin, his voice ground down to a whisper. "What they did to each other was unspeakable."

"What did they do to you?" she asked faintly.

He hiked up the corner of his mouth. "Monster-makers. Remember?"

"Raphael." Those magnificent orbs grew sad. "You aren't a monster."

"I have been. Look what I did to you. Can you pardon that?"

She blinked. "I've never pardoned it."

"No? Good girl."

"I am glad you told me. I wish . . ." She paused, and he could see her deciding if she should say what was on her mind.

"Tell me," he urged, wanting to know it all.

"Why . . . why was it important to prove love didn't exist?"

Oh, that was not a fair question! He riled a bit. There was nothing to say that wouldn't be self-pitying. Which should tell him something.

He closed down, looking away. The night's confidences were at an end. No more. He could do no more.

"It amused me," he said. But his voice was so flat, he didn't expect her to believe him.

With the instinctive sensitivity women were purported to possess—but which he had never seen any evidence of in the other females in his life—she lowered her lashes and said, "I think I should say good night."

"Good night." Too quick, too eager, he sounded desperate.

"I'll see you in the morning."

And because he always said it, he told her, "Don't come."

She smiled, as if she recognized this as ritual only. As if she knew—God forbid it!—that he would wait for her. And be disappointed if she obeyed him.

It was a pleasant parting, but within moments he regretted having allowed himself to be vulnerable. He felt the sting of humiliation, prickles at first, then growing into an agony as he replayed in his mind what he had said.

Bloody hell! He had all but cracked himself open. Well, he wouldn't beg her to understand him. He refused to plead for her pardon, for her . . .

For her?

For her love?

Jesus Christ!

Chapter Nineteen

❦

IN RETROSPECT, JULIA could only blame herself. She walked into Raphael's room the following morning still caught in the spell of the previous night and without a shred of defense to keep her safe. She knew as soon as she saw him what a mistake this was.

He was still in bed. At her approach, he lifted his eyelids slowly, unveiling dangerous eyes. His mouth curled—contemptuous, derisive—then he spoke. Flat, hard syllables fell cold on her cheerful mood. "I told you not to come."

It brought her up short and infused her with an immediate flush of burning disappointment. She quelled it, and quickly. Raphael would show no mercy if he caught the scent of her hurt. "And I told you I would."

"God, you are pathetic."

How true, she thought, drawing down the coverlet. He still had his clothes on. When he slept still half-clothed like this, rumpled trousers, shirt open, no stockings, she knew he'd been drinking.

It was harder to take, his biting attitude. This morning, above all the others before, it was much too hard to take.

She forced cheer into her voice. "I have missed too many days of doing our exercises."

She took away the breakfast tray that lay across his lap.

He hadn't eaten much, she saw. It had always made her smile that his favorite food for breakfast was porridge. It was such a childlike choice, almost endearing if it weren't so opposed in virtually every other aspect of his personality.

Touching him was never ordinary. She would like to pretend she had gotten used to the massage, but it thrilled her every time to run her hands up his muscled calves, all the way up to his hips. Flexing his knee, she cupped his calf muscle. It felt like steel under smooth, male skin that was hairy, rougher than hers. *Concentrate,* she told herself, working it back out to a straight position.

She did the other leg, then each ankle in turn. She realized with a sense of disconcert that she was sweating. Wiping her brow with the back of her hand, she darted her tongue over lips that had gone dry.

Maybe she'd cut it short today. Just another skim of her fingers, stimulating the skin the way the Lincolnshire man had told her, all the way from waist to toe. She darted a look to her subject. Raphael had closed his eyes and laid his head back. He seemed very still. Sometimes he cursed her, sometimes he ridiculed her. Sometimes, like today, he stewed. The latter was by far the easiest to deal with.

When she touched his upper thigh, his eyes flew open and he took in a quick, sharp breath.

She drew her hands back sharply. "Oh, my God. Raphael."

His eyes immediately narrowed, swiveled to her, and he said, "I think we're finished."

"What? What had just happened? You felt something, didn't you?" She was trembling, her entire body.

"I don't feel anything."

"You are a liar. You felt that, I can tell. Tell me, I demand you tell me!" The stubborn set of his chin, the way his arms were crossed in front of his chest told her he wasn't going to give her a thing, she could demand all she wanted. She stepped close to him and crossed her own arms. She was stubborn, too. "Go ahead and sulk all you want. I know why, too. You're mad at yourself because you were actually nice to me last night. You showed your human side and—that sin of all sins—the fact that you actually have emotions." Oh-ho, look at that glare he shot! She'd hit home on that one. "Now, let's not let that interfere with this. It's too important, Raphael. You *are* getting feeling in your legs, I know it."

"Forget about last night. It was an aberration. There is no feeling in me. Not in my legs or the whole rest of me. Your florid imagination is working much too hard to conjure up what you wish were true."

Oh, no, he couldn't do this! Not now, not with this—he was recovering feeling, for goodness' sake! She wanted to scream at him. At her sides her fingers curled and she felt her breath coming so fast she thought it might make her dizzy.

She was furious. She couldn't stop herself. Picking up his bowl from the side table upon which she had placed his food tray, she dumped the entire contents of boiled oats upside down over his head.

He gasped, arms outflung in shock as the cooled cereal oozed in thick white globs all over his hair. The entire side of his face was covered, and large plops were landing on his shoulders and chest.

"Do you feel that?" she inquired sweetly, and spun on her heel to stalk out of the room.

She slammed the door behind her and stood in the hallway until she was calm enough to think. A rush of repentence hit her.

My God, what had she done? How could she have left him like that?

Guilt washed away the last traces of her outrage. She spun around and went back inside.

The bowl came sailing past her head, hitting the wall and shattering into pieces. A string of expletives followed. She considered immediate retreat. Instead she went to the commode and fetched the bowl of water that was still warm from his morning ritual. When he swiped at her, she stepped back.

"You have my apology for what I did. There is no excuse. Will you sit in cooked oats all day or will you allow me to clean up the mess?"

He ignored her. Since he would be hurling insults at her if he were absolutely not going to allow it, she took that as a yes.

"Here, put that in this towel," she said, holding out a cloth for the handfuls of cereal he had scraped off his hair. He complied wordlessly, shaking off his fingers so that droplets of the stuff went all over the front of her dress. A tiny speck landed in her lashes. Another in her hair.

She made no protest. It was the least of what she deserved. Dashing the offenses away with the back of her hand, she set to work.

She helped him off with his shirt. His movement, jerking and angry, didn't make it easy. She wound up with much more porridge on her. Then she undid the ties of his trousers. Draping the sheet over his lap for modesty—hers more than his—she grabbed the cuffs and yanked them off.

The sight of all that flesh exposed made her mouth go dry. His well-sculpted breast was touched with a sprinkling of short, soft hair, and his wide shoulders were beautiful. The hard muscles of his arms had developed greater bulk from heavy use in the sedan chair.

God, oh, God, why did her heart feel as if it were shattering anew every time she looked at him?

She forced herself to concentrate on her task. Preparing to wash his neck and shoulders, she soaped up the cloth. He throbbed with restrained violence. His mouth was set, his eyes clenched closed. The way his nostrils curled with pent-up frustration didn't escape her notice

Placing the washcloth on his forehead, she began by stroking it around his face. She hadn't meant to be so tender as she caressed his high brow and square chin. Catching herself, she concentrated on washing his hair. Her fingers worked the sudsy water lightly in and rinsed it out by wringing out the cloth. The bedclothes became soaked. She fetched a fresh pillow and blanket from the cupboard and had it at the ready as she peeled away the soiled linens and replaced them with the new ones.

He was naked, a fact of which she was acutely aware. She took great care to keep as much of him covered as she could, but the oats had oozed everywhere. It was important to keep her mind on her work, and she managed to get most of it off of him without giving away the tide of sexual awareness that was creeping over her—until her gaze fell on the shocking swell of arousal under the linens she had laid on his lap.

Her hand, which had been absently wiping ineffectual circles around his ridged abdomen, stilled. Looking up, she saw he was watching her very closely.

Raphael's brows went up in a mocking gesture. "What do you know?" he drawled. "I believe I feel something after all."

His eyes blazed, belying the casual tone. Her body felt singed. It tingled from the roots of her hair all the way down to her toes. She half expected to look down and find the charred remains of her clothes curled in a heap of black ash at her feet. How did he do that—make her feel such heat with just the touch of his eyes?

His hand snaked out and grabbed her wrist, jerking her hard so that she fell forward to lay across his torso.

She tried to push up, but her hands were caught behind her and her face ended up inches from his. Nose to nose, she stared deep into those green pools of his before he tilted his head and slanted his mouth to take her in a savage kiss.

The impact felt like a punch. She arched, her entire body shocked. There was a mewling sound coming from somewhere. It took a moment to realize it was she who made it, a feeble token of resistance that was all she could muster. It changed in a heartbeat into a sound of pleasure, and welcome.

Her nerves jumped to life—panic blended with the scald

of passion. She felt helpless. Hungry and hot, but frightened, too. He was no longer holding her hands. They had been freed—when?—and now gripped him desperately as if clutching a lifeline.

His tongue parted her lips and invaded, turning her insides into molten fire and making her aware of an ache in her, a need between her legs for him to fill her and take away all of the emptiness she had lived with for months.

His hand closed over her breast. She moaned, her breath catching in ragged gasps against his lips as his fingers pulled at the neckline of her dress. There was this crazy, intense need to help him free her breasts, but he managed the fasteners himself.

It surprised her that he was so gentle when he cupped her flesh. His hands were warm, making little circles with his flattened palm against the peaks until she writhed. She felt her flesh tighten, strain against his hand as if yearning for more.

Stopping, he pulled away and glanced downward. She followed his gaze. The aroused peaks were small and pink. Her breasts, never particularly large, looked taut and swollen. He molded his hands against each one and squeezed gently. Then he flicked his thumbs over her nipples, watching the way it made her sort of crumple as a delicious melting sensation shot through her body.

He kissed her shoulder, then moved lower and she held her breath. Her mind reeled with the knowledge that she held him in her arms again. It was drugging her, pulling her under like an undertow of passion and she slipped into it willingly. *Raphael.* In her mind, she said his name over and over. It was like a song. The anticipation of his erotic kiss held her motionless, spellbound.

She clasped him tighter, fingers threaded in that wild mane of streaked brown hair and brought his mouth to where she needed it to be.

So good. Her bones liquefied as his tongue darted wickedly over the sensitive flesh. He caught her in his teeth, pulled. Sucked. Slow, then hard.

She felt it building, the feelings she craved, gathering around her, tightening in her belly and her thighs, forming a wave, cresting it, reaching. She felt his hands on her legs. Up, along her thigh, slipping inside. She opened her legs, letting him . . . She felt his fingers stroke. Once. Oh, again—yes.

"Yes."

She heard her own voice and realized she had spoken aloud. She didn't care. Tilting her hips, she took the next stroke into her. Her head fell back. He suckled harder, and she dropped forward, convulsing in a long, sharp spasm. Over and over she came, aware of so many things at once. His touch between her legs, the press of his other hand on her back to hold her. His ragged breathing—or was it hers?—and the sweet heat of his mouth on her, easing her down from the peak as her body rode each tremor.

He withdrew his hand, tilted his head up, and claimed her slack mouth, rousing her from the draining lassitude sweeping her under after that incredible release. Firmly he grasped her hips, gathered her skirts about her waist, lifted her over him, brought her down.

She felt him, every inch of him as he filled her. She cried out, arching, aching, wanting again. She'd forgotten. No, she hadn't, not really. She simply hadn't allowed herself to think of this, of how good it felt. Her whole being thrilled as he pressed her down on his lap, impaling her, driving home. His shaft felt thick and hot, abrading the tender insides of her thighs and stretching her until her body felt like live flame.

His large hands cupped her bottom, showing her the motion. She moved her hips, sliding over him the way he wanted. It was such a gorgeous feeling. After only a moment, her body moved without her having to think.

He said something else, pressing his forehead into the curve of her neck, and she clasped him. She was going to climax again. The scent of him filled her nostrils, mingled with the musk of sex, made her dizzy. She rose up, knowing now exactly how to please them both, sheathed him again. He moaned, his powerful hands digging into her shoulders. His hips jutted up to meet her on the next thrust.

"Julia." It was muffled, but she heard him say her name, and it spilled her over into fulfillment once again. He bucked under her, drove up sharply as he peaked hard. He made a sound that sounded like a sob.

Gliding her hands over his shoulders, she felt them flex and shift as he strained, caught in pleasure so intense his hands gripped her hard enough to hurt. She didn't mind. She reveled in the feel of him. He was touching her. He was loving her. And she was loving him.

She held him tight as he relaxed. His head still rested under her chin, face pressed to her throat. The sound of his breathing seemed loud even when it slowed.

When she pulled back, he turned his face away. She felt something cold on her collarbone, something wet. Then she saw his hand cover his eyes, shield his face.

Had he wept?

She looked down to see where her flesh glistened. When she looked at him again, she didn't see any evidence of excessive emotion. He just looked guarded.

Reaching for him she brought him back to rest on her breast.

And he let her. He wrapped his arms around her and settled them close together, bringing her down so that they could lay back upon the rumpled bed.

For no reason she knew, she played with a waving lock of hair, letting it twine around her fingers, and whispered, "It's all right."

She meant it for him, but it did her good to hear it as well.

───────⌒

JULIA ROSE OUT of the bed and adjusted her clothes. Her hands still trembled and her insides buzzed. She felt soft and glowing, like the white ash from a dying coal.

In a polite tone, and without looking at her, Raphael

asked her to send in Thomas. The dismissal hurt, but she was too bewildered to realize what he was doing. The dazed feeling kept her from thinking clearly.

Euphoria faded as the day wore on and she knew his coldness had been deliberate. She understood she had done the unforgivable, broached a bastion he never wanted to allow, and could never, never accept.

I have no feeling in me. It was what he wanted, what he hoped for—oblivion, numbness, safety from the wild, out-of-control emotion that had started to flow when she had held him against her breast. How he would hate her for that.

Why? What was so wrong inside him that he felt he had to hide it all away?

Self-pity was part of it, but it went beyond his present infirmity to the past, deep and secret and festering like an infection. It had been there when she met him. Sensing it like the faint scent of musk, she had felt its pull, it's inexorable intrigue. Whatever had happened, there existed inside Raphael a fatalistic resignation to his baseness. It was why he was debauched. It was why he couldn't accept tenderness from anyone.

Why? What had his monster-makers done?

So many questions, and never answers. Raphael wouldn't allow them. He'd block her, push her, fight her to keep her away from what she ached to know.

After lunch she saw Thomas in the hallway. He was carrying a full bottle of whiskey into Raphael's lair. Rage inflamed her, and Julia stepped into his path. The valet paused for a moment.

Julia looked at the bottle he carried and then at Thomas, who stared back at her with concern. He would have to give her the bottle if she demanded it, but it would fetch him hell from his master.

She wanted to break the damned thing over her husband's hard, thick skull.

The flash of anger simmered as she decided what to do. And then an inspiration hit her. She daren't. Oh, she would.

It was for Raphael's own good, she reasoned, liking the plan more and more as she thought it over. Oh, but was she wicked if she enjoyed the revenge aspect a tiny bit? After all, if anyone had a comeuppance due, it was the disreputable Viscount de Fontvilliers.

———◦———

THE FOLLOWING MORNING Raphael finished his coffee and looked at the clock on the mantel. Nearly eleven o'clock. He wheeled himself into his bedroom.

The two footmen came in. Franklin touched his forelock quickly, a worried look upon his bullish face. "The mistress has ordered you taken into the phaeton, my lord."

This news shocked him. "She what?"

The other man, Gregory, shifted nervously from foot to foot, staring at the carpet in order to avoid making eye contact. Franklin said, "She says there is to be an outing."

The little—! What the devil was she doing? He would have thought he had made it perfectly clear that she was to stay clear of him. He had even entertained hope that the unexpected events of yesterday, and mainly his subsequent snub, had proven the last straw, and she was going to leave at last.

It was absolutely essential that he get her out. He'd convinced himself his humiliating display of emotion in the bedroom was an aberration, a weak moment—understandable when one considered the impact of claiming his masculinity again. But he wasn't going to give her another chance to wheedle under his skin and stoke alive those demons.

He reached for his flask, taking a long draught and wincing as it burned its way down to his stomach. Even dulling himself with drink wasn't helping much anymore. To tell the truth, he'd never been very good at losing himself in his cups. His mind just churned all the harder, making the morning after a lesson in hell.

He tapped his fingers on the armrest. She wanted him to go on an *outing?* It was unlikely he could do a damned thing about it. Yet, the thought of spending the entire day with her, when he felt like his defenses were coming apart at the seams, it was impossible.

Well, he would show Her Stubbornness once again just whom she was dealing with. He was not known as the leader of the Bane of the Ton for nothing! "Call Thomas," he said.

Gregory's head snapped up, his features showing his shock.

"My lord?" Franklin, too, was astonished. "You are going to cooperate?"

"Of course." And he did. He dressed, humming the whole while, ate a quick breakfast, and fairly flew out of his room on his chair, eager to get under way.

No doubt, his enthusiasm made him early. He had to wait for her, but only a short while. When she came outside at last, she was dressed in fawn muslin trimmed with sable-colored piping, a matching spencer trimmed with fox to ward off the chill. She looked smart and stylish and completely unattainable. The sight of her nearly took the wind out of Raphael's sails.

He experienced his first, but not last, misgiving. "Where the devil are we going?"

Her smile was pert. "It's a surprise."

"I hate surprises."

"I know." She settled back and looked out the window. He was annoyed with her, and so began to sing softly one of the filthy songs he had shocked her with that first day after they arrived. She merely kept staring outside.

The carriage pulled away from the house.

He didn't like this. She was too calm, too self-possessed. His mind raced over a hundred ideas of what he could do next as he reached for his flask. Contemplatively he unscrewed the cap and touched it to his lips.

She moved quickly, sitting forward and taking the silver container right out of his hands. He barely had time to register what she had done before he saw her draw aside the curtain and fling the flask outside.

"Christ! Are you mad?"

She didn't answer. Settling back, she looked back out the window.

"You arrogant little chit, stop this carriage!" He began to pound on the side of the coach. The driver, alerted by the sound, called down a question as to what was the matter.

Julia shouted back, "It's all right, Charlie. Keep on."

He was speechless. For the first time in his life he was absolutely speechless. Confounded by her unflappability, he lapsed into smoldering silence, and considered his options.

By the time the carriage pulled to a halt, he felt like he was going to come out of his skin. It was important, however, to remain in control. Or at least appear to be. He donned his most insulting manner and drawled, "Oh, goody. We're here."

Julia alighted, and Raphael's sedan chair was brought up. Brushing aside his footmen, Raphael dragged himself to the open portal by grasping the top of the doorway and used his arms and hips to slide his legs out, thereby avoiding the awful chore of having to have someone hoist him out. Gregory took his weight and settled him easily into the chair. Looking up, he froze, not believing what he saw.

She wouldn't dare.

Julia was being greeted by a man and a woman. The man wore the dark clothing and wide Dutch collar of a Quaker. The woman next to him wore similar somber attire.

The presumptuous little vixen had brought him to the Quaker home for unwed mothers!

Julia presented the couple as Daniel and his wife, Elizabeth. Raphael responded absently, too stunned to do any damage just yet. Julia had gotten the upper hand and he had no idea how to recover. As Julia, Elizabeth and Daniel started in toward the large wooden house, Franklin came to take up Raphael's chair.

They entered by way of a small, makeshift ramp that

had been set up. This led Raphael to understand that this visit had been thoroughly planned. For some reason, this disturbed him even more.

The door opened into a long inner chamber bustling with activity. Perhaps twenty or so young women and girls were performing various chores, some scrubbing floors, some dusting, others carrying stacks of clean linens to tables while others painstakingly polished the wooden surfaces with—by the smell of it—lemon oil. So intent were they on their tasks that they hardly took note of their visitors.

But Raphael took note of them. They were, each and every one, pregnant.

Raphael struggled to find some way to assert his outrage, but his attention kept being drawn by the girls. Or rather their protruding stomachs. It was a disconcerting happenstance, to be sure, to find one's self surrounded by so much fertility. Especially when one had lived the kind of life he had. This *condition* was to be avoided at all costs—feared even. For a rake such as himself, this represented one of the most dreaded aspects of a hedonistic lifestyle. Consequences.

He found it difficult to breathe properly. About to start roaring demands, he stopped when one came rushing up to greet Julia. He watched her as his wife hugged the girl with a smile and a warm welcome, before turning to present her to him. "Suzanne, this is my husband, the Viscount de Fontvilliers."

The girl dipped into a curtsy. "How do you do, my lord?"

Raphael stared.

Julia ignored his rudeness. To Suzanne she said, "You are looking so much better. How are you feeling now?"

"Oh, very well, now that the medicine's done its job. Thank you so much, viscountess." She pronounced it hard, with no French inflection, so that it was "viss-count-iss," and it made Raphael want to sneer at her. He didn't, for some reason. She and Julia wandered off to greet other girls who had noticed the arrival of their benefactress.

He blew out a breath, trying to appear impatient. Hoping no one would see, he wiped a line of sweat from his brow. Julia returned with another girl in tow. "I want you to meet Greta," she said.

The awe on the child's face—and he did mean child; surely she could be no more than thirteen!—was uncomfortable to view. Raphael muttered a hello, forcing his voice to work so that the girl wouldn't think him annoyed. Something about Greta's wide eyes inspired the need to be solicitous of her. She looked very fragile. She appeared to be unable to say anything in reply. Julia led her away after an awkward silence.

It went like this until each girl had been presented. He lost track of their names. That was all Julia told him, their names. He found himself wondering about some of them, for although most had the hard look of veterans of the street life, there were some with polite voices and soft eyes and winsome smiles that demanded an explanation as to how they had landed themselves in such a place.

After a while Julia came to his side, pulling up a crude straight-backed chair. She was silent.

"What is she doing here?" he said gruffly, waving his hand to indicate a very tall woman. She moved with slow, deliberate movements. From this and the large size of her belly, he assumed her pregnancy was far advanced.

"Diana. She has no husband to care for her or her child. She thought she did. You see, her lover took her to a quiet little church after she refused to give him her innocence outside of the blessing of wedlock, and they spoke vows before a vicar. Only it wasn't a vicar, but the scoundrel's best friend pretending to be one. She found out about the ruse when she told him the happy news that she was with child. Only, he wasn't so happy about it."

A strange feeling curled in his gut. He reached inside his coat for his flask, feeling around for it before he realized it wasn't there.

He had heard of this ploy before. God help him, he had laughed over it when one of his university chums had done it to a local girl. His eyes watched Diana's cumbersome form, taking in the serene beauty of her face. He looked away, hating himself for his curiosity, but he had to know. "And Greta?"

"She was raped. Her parents are servants at Henleigh Grange. Lord Henliegh's son took her."

He felt his throat tighten, making his tone sharper. "How old is she?"

"Fourteen."

"Good God. Was he punished?"

"He denied it even happened. Now, what do you think would happen to the son of aristocracy when a poor maid's daughter cries foul?"

"What happens to them after their children come?"

"It depends. Some take their children and try to find work. Others give the baby up. The Quakers help in finding a good home if they are able. If not, the child goes to the orphanage. Your money has gone to that facility, as well. The children there are well taken care of."

"You gave them money?" he asked, as if seeking reassurance.

"Yes. And my time. But I cannot change their situation."

He nodded. He wanted to say things he was too proud to allow. Instead, he demanded, "Are we through?"

"Yes. I'll call Franklin."

Chapter Twenty

M R. HARCOURT RAWLINGS was a barrister. A rather successful and famous one whose typical honorarium put his expert services within reach of only the most wealthy. He was much sought after for his legal advice because he was considered brilliant, and his companionship, considered equally as desirable, was welcomed by the same aristocracy that vied for his services.

His eldest son, Nicholas Rawlings, was a handsome man of twenty-five who had traveled extensively on the Continent. It was rumored he had gone all the way to Africa and India. Some wild speculation added that he had kept a harem in the east, but anyone knowing the sandy-haired gentleman with his infectious smile and indomitable good nature never believed it. Upon his recent return to England, he had been in as much demand as his father among the social events of the *bon ton*. Everyone was curious about him, and there wasn't a single woman or girl who didn't thrill when introduced.

Therefore, it caused quite a stir when during a soiree he requested to be presented to a pretty blond standing just off the dance floor. He asked his friend, Richard Evans, Lord Martinvale, to do it. For some reason, Nicholas's interest seemed to please Martinvale.

Laura saw Martinvale approaching and broke from the

group with whom she was talking to come and greet him. He took both his hands in hers, and she smiled warmly up at him. She had long since realized the great favor Martinvale had done for her. It wasn't difficult to understand, looking back in retrospect, that his having come upon her and Colin Strathford "accidentally" was actually a well-planned rescue. Although she didn't understand why he should put himself out to do such a kindness, Laura had grown convinced that Martinvale had acted as a sort of guardian angel.

Martinvale and Laura had become frequent companions whenever they chanced to meet at a social affair. She never spoke of her gratitude, for it would break their silent understanding that the past was not to be mentioned.

Seeing him brought on the usual rush of sisterly affection. "Hello, Richard."

"Laura." He bowed low over her hand, his azure blue eyes twinkling. "You look especially lovely tonight. I would like to present a friend, Mr. Nicholas Rawlings."

Laura turned to the man behind him and felt the entire room melt away.

Nicholas smiled and gave a short bow. She remembered—thank goodness—to drop into a curtsy, but their eyes never left each other.

He was tall and rather thin, with light-colored hair and dark eyes that formed crescents from the pleasure of making her acquaintance. His face appeared weathered, as if he were a seaman or a laborer and had spent time out of doors. While this was completely out of fashion in general, it suited him, as did the premature brackets around his mouth, carved from frequent smiling.

"A pleasure," he murmured. It sounded incredibly intimate, the way he said it in his low, soft voice. A strange, weakening warmth seeped through her and for the life of her, she could not remember how to frame a suitable reply.

Then he asked her to dance and she accepted even though she had promised this quadrille to a friend. Telling herself the other man would understand, she stifled a delicious tremor of anticipation as he took her onto the dance floor.

He moved well enough through the complex steps, although he got tangled up once or twice. She did not mind. Every time his white-gloved hands slipped over hers, she felt an extraordinary rush of pleasure.

Afterward, when they were sipping punch after Laura sent her next two dance partners away with pleas of fatigue, he apologized for his clumsiness. Lack of practice, he explained, for he had been away from society for a long time. This led to a discussion of his travels, which in turn led them into various points of conversation that took them through the night until the orchestra stopped playing.

They laughed often, for he seemed to find her comments delightful. She thought him especially clever and some of his insights quite poignant.

When the guests began to disperse, they took their leave of each other. Nicholas asked if he may call on her, and Laura pretended to consider this before she agreed to allow it. They laughed together, because they knew already in these first few hours of meeting that their future was with each other.

<hr>

CHRISTMAS CAME AND went with a modicum of observance. Certainly not a surfeit of joy in the house, but passable. Julia missed her family, that was evident. Raphael noted it, felt a twinge of sorrow for her.

He'd been reflective of late. Which was good. It was refreshing; new. He hadn't done a great deal of reasoning, just walking—nay, *rolling*—about under a cloud of self-pity since the summer. Objectively, he considered that he was certainly entitled to be morose for a time. He was a cripple, for God's sake. Hope was a frightening thing. He was afraid of it. It was much more comfortable to brood. The trouble with it, though, was that it got boring. And so he grew pensive as anger eased its grip.

Life settled into a pattern as the winter wore on. Julia was busy, out of the house often, sometimes for the entire day.

It left him free to his business, and he was glad to have her gone. He didn't want to take any chances she'd find out what he was about.

In the afternoons, his mother came to sit with him. They took tea. These times were civil, even occasionally comfortable. They never spoke of anything further than her telling him the neighborhood gossip or the plans she had made with Julia for the refurbishing of the house. She made no complaint, but he understood that she was bored here. He could appreciate that, although, surprisingly, he himself wasn't. Imagine the Bane of the Ton settled in nicely as a country recluse.

A time or two they laughed, sharing some memory that wasn't all too bad. He was surprised there were a few. More than a few, perhaps. Like the time Raphael discovered the village bully in the stream behind the mill. The older boy had a particular liking for venting his contempt of the local nobility on its smallest member whenever he caught Raphael alone and unguarded. Grabbing his chance, Raphael had stolen his clothes. Violetta had found the homespun garments, obviously not her son's, stuffed in one of his wardrobes. She had laughed when he fessed up to his prank, something Raphael had not expected, and that night at supper they had had a special feast to celebrate his little victory. It had been one of their gayest times, and the boy never bothered Raphael again.

Most days, though, they sat in silence. His mother would sew or knit or tat or whatever. He would read. At times he would catch her eyes on him, sometimes misty, other times clear and fond-looking, and he'd pretend not to be aware that she was thinking about the past.

He didn't know it then, but it was a time of great healing. And when his mother told him she was going to return to her home, he felt a passing flash of regret. He didn't show it, of course, but it gripped him hard for a brief moment before he pushed it away.

Julia was leaving, too, but for a short while only. She was finally visiting her family in London where they were celebrating Laura's engagement with a party before the season started in force. She must be looking forward to it, he observed, taking note of the cheerfulness in her, her quick smile and light step.

They didn't discuss it. They were merely cordial to each other, distant and brief when their paths crossed. Strangers. She still came in for the exercises. He looked forward to it, even though he groused from time to time. He supposed her going would give him time to think, really think, without the distraction of wanting her every time he saw her.

When his mother was ready to depart with the countess, she came to take her leave. Leaning down close, she kissed his forehead and told him, "I love you, Raphael. I've always loved you. If I wasn't any good at it, the blame was mine entirely."

He felt as if she'd hit him with a board. His grandmother, who had overheard this, looked at her daughter disapprovingly. The countess was never one for sentiment. But when she bent down to give him her goodbye kiss, the old woman stroked his cheek and swallowed, as if there were tears caught in her throat. He nodded to her and she did the same. "You eat. You can't get thin, you'll lose your strength," she insisted, and her voice was strong and hard.

He smiled about that when they were gone. Practicality was a potent antidote for mawkishness.

His thoughts turned to Julia. He found, to his astonishment, that he was able to do so without the old bitterness. These days he could almost feel his insides unknotting from time to time. Tentatively he began to think differently, to indulge a fantasy he had not let himself entertain before. A philosopher had once said that fantasy was the first step in forming a vision. A vision for his life, if he had the courage.

He thought he just might. Julia was set to leave for London in a few days. A break they needed, he told himself. Yet a sense of urgency took him over, as if there was something he needed to do before she was gone. He thought he might talk to her, explain some things. Tell her of what he himself was only now discovering. He braced himself to do it.

Then he saw her leaving one evening dressed in a gorgeous confection of pale green. He asked a servant where she was going.

And that was how he learned about the dance.

———————

JULIA WATCHED THE festivities from the edge of the dance floor. The country dance was so different from a London gathering, so much more vigorous, less formal, and definitely a great deal of fun. The large hall, which boasted the presumptuous name of the Cotillion Room, was filled to bursting. The music and laughter and the sound of cutlery clinking were as loud a din as Julia ever heard.

Looking around, she felt a swell of accomplishment. Her suggestions on how to make the evening as grand as possible had been greeted with enthusiasm from the other members of the committee. Emboldened by this reception, she had taken a leading role in organizing the fete. She hadn't had to defer or pretend meekness, and if some thought her bold, they made no complaint of it. Having a brain and using it didn't seem at all a serious liability to these people. They were remarkably accepting, and in no time she had felt comfortable with them.

The countess had once told her that only commoners were considered odd. The rich, the titled—no matter how outrageous or appalling their behavior—were tolerantly dubbed "eccentric." She should be thankful to Raphael for that, at least. Quite incidental to everything else, he had given her the freedom, by way of her elevated social position, to be able to speak and act as she liked.

Cecile came through the crowd at a frantic clip. "Here she is, Paul. I told you we would find her with no trouble. Julia, Paul has asked to be presented." She stopped, a bit out of breath. "He is my older brother's son."

Paul Bently stepped forward and bowed. He was very tall,

dwarfing the small woman, with broad shoulders that filled out his tailcoat quite nicely. His hair was a rich brown with a wave to it even a generous portion of pomade hadn't been successful in taming. His eyes were a very bright blue, and they stared at her with undisguised pleasure. "My aunts have told me so much about you. I was quite looking forward to making your acquaintance."

Julia smiled and inclined her head. "Your name is familiar to me, as well. Your aunts mention you with great fondness."

"Would you care to dance?" he inquired.

"No, thank you." It had been her answer to every request that evening.

"Oh, Julia," Cecile scolded. Despite the difference in their social class, Cecile had a tendency to mother. Julia found it endearing. Cecile continued, "You can't think to stand here by yourself all night."

"May I remind you I am married?"

"So am I and I am still recovering from the reel I danced with George Wells."

Julia smiled, unable to say what she was thinking. It wasn't the same thing. Two old friends taking a whirl together was quite a bit different than a nice-looking man taking an unescorted married woman onto the dance floor for a stately turn.

But she would like to dance. Reconsidering, she said at last, "Well, then, I suppose we younger folk have to keep up."

"There you go, then. Off with you!"

Paul led her onto the floor. The two of them together drew some stares. She remembered the night her affair with Raphael had been discovered. People had stared then. Insread of the narrowed eyes and nervously fluttering fans, she now saw smiles and nods. These were her friends, and that knowledge filled her with warmth as Paul took his position for the quadrille.

"Are you feeling well?" Paul asked, stepping forward for the bow.

She lowered to a curtsy. "Yes. Just memories, for a moment."

"Of your husband?" They came together, palm to palm, and circled.

She started, amazed at his acuity.

"I only ask because he is not here. Surely you must miss him."

She studied his face to see if he were mocking her. Then she realized what she was doing and silently chided herself. This was not Raphael, bent on slicing her pride with every syllable he uttered.

"You are far too lovely a woman to be sad," he observed. His blue eyes drifted down her face, lowering briefly to the scooped décolletage. Although it was a modestly cut dress, she suddenly felt bared.

Disconcerted as they separated and joined separate circles, she rather belatedly registered the shocking realization that Paul was flirting with her. It was a flattering thought, as well as a frightening one.

"Your husband is extraordinarily generous to let you attend tonight's festivities without being here to keep a watchful eye."

She passed close, her back brushing against his front. She smelled his soap and closed her eyes against the reflexive jolt of memory of Raphael's distinctive scent that had never failed to make her lose her senses. "He is ill," she choked out.

Twirling her, his breath fanned across her forehead as they promenaded down the twin columns of dancers. "How dreadful. It must be serious, for I know I would have to be quite laid low to neglect a woman such as you."

But he doesn't care what I do.

"I feel rather light-headed," she said quickly to cover the rise of emotion that came over her.

"I am sorry. Here." He took her hand and tucked it in the crook of his arm. With rapid strides, he had her by the open door, where a cooling breeze was blowing in. "Better?"

"Yes, thank you." The swell of panic hadn't subsided,

however. She didn't belong here. She had no business dancing, or flirting with a strange man, even if all it did was remind her of something that was long gone.

"I think I would like to leave," she managed, looking desperately about for one of her friends to help her. "Do you see your aunt Cecile or aunt Eulalia?"

"I'll fetch your carriage. Stay here."

He returned with her wrap. Her gratitude was boundless as he managed to extricate her quite gracefully from the gathering. Outside, he handed her directly up into the waiting carriage.

Standing at the door with his foot on the step, he said, "I hope nothing I said distressed you."

"It is not you. You were very gallant. You have my appreciation."

"May I speak plainly, madam le viscountess?"

She hesitated. She was not certain she wanted to hear what plain speech he had to say, but she nodded anyway. He gave her a sympathetic look. "I was in London this past winter."

Her voice trembled when she spoke. "Did we meet?"

"No. But I had some dealings with your husband. He had quite a reputation. There were many at Whites and at Gentleman Jackson's who considered his . . . illness to be a just comeuppance."

"Please," she protested, turning away to the darkness of the carriage.

"No, let me finish. And if they were angry about the wrongs he was known for before your marriage, there was a positive outcry to his having interfered with your happiness as he did." He meant breaking up her and Simon's engagement. Everyone thought Raphael was to blame. Well, he was—wasn't he?

"If this distresses you, madam le viscountess, I am deeply, deeply sorry. I only intend for you to know that you have a friend, a sympathetic ear, if you will. I will be staying with my aunt Eulalia through the fall."

"Thank you."

He closed the door and called up to the driver. The carriage lurched into motion.

It was a mere half hour's drive to Glenwood Park. She alighted from the carriage and went inside, where the hall was lit with candelabra and several sconces. She had left instructions that she was not to return home to darkness. Things were going better now with the servants. Really, it had only been Mr. Conrad who had been unwilling to work harder. A calm reassurance from her that she would not hesitate to serve him notice if he failed to meet her expectations did the trick to win his cooperation, if it was grudging.

Looking about, she took in her surroundings, wishing it could give her more of a sense of accomplishment. The place was meticulously clean. Matching pedestals flanked the portal to the left, and busts she had had special ordered from Milan adorned them. A cluster of potted plants livened up a corner, next to a table set with a large urn and miniature Florentine statuary. With the help of the countess and marquese, she had made the entire house as fine as this.

And yet the place felt no more like a home than it ever had. Walking toward the stairs, the crisp click of her heeled slippers on the marble echoed around her. Passing the open doors of the study, she saw to her surprise that Raphael was inside. He looked up at her. "Come in," he called. His voice was tight.

He'd probably been drinking. She'd be a fool to go. "I'm tired," she called.

He wheeled himself to the threshold. "From all that dancing? Have you worn holes in your shoes, like the seven sisters?"

"It's late." She turned on her heel and headed for the stairs.

"Yes. You are very busy these days."

She whirled. "What is it, Raphael? Why do you suddenly care about what I do?"

The false joviality fell from his face. "Because. You are my wife." Each word fell hard.

"Wife?" Oh, God, she could feel it all coming now, everything she'd been holding back these last weeks. "You treat your footmen with more deference."

"Perhaps because they don't go off to parties until the wee hours of the morning. Did you dance with anyone?"

"What?" She blinked, taken aback, then admitted, "Once."

His jaw worked furiously. "Who did you dance with?" She saw his fists clutch the arms of his chair.

"No one in particular." She felt a wave of guilt. Whatever he thought, he was right. She'd danced with another man. She'd *flirted* with Paul Bently.

But she had only missed Raphael all the more.

Look at him now—he was as enraged as she'd ever seen him. It hit her then that she'd been mistaken. She didn't see how it was possible, not in view of how he treated her, but it mattered a great deal to him that she had gone tonight without him.

Why . . . he even seemed jealous.

How selfish I am! she thought suddenly. "Oh, Raphael, I'm sorry. I didn't mean to be thoughtless. It simply hadn't occurred to me that you would mind." She went closer to him, arms folded in front of her, head down, and murmured, "All you seem to want from me is that I stay away from you."

There was a long pause. He shrugged, seeming to have been mollified. "It is merely the talk. I mean, people will *talk*, Julia."

That was her undoing. A sharp bark of laughter escaped her before she could catch it. "Oh, I am quite sure. I know how careful you always are of gossip."

Even he couldn't keep a straight face. His lips twitched. Pretending to rub his chin as if in thought, he covered his mouth. "So." He gazed up at her, his green eyes sparkling. "What did you dance?"

"Oh, a waltz of course," she lied, saying it with a wide smile and so much flourish that he would know she was teasing him. "With a stooped old gentleman who trod all over my feet."

"That so?" He stroked his chin, but she saw it quiver.

"He tried to drag me out onto the terrace. Mrs. Peavenstover had to intervene. She hauled off and swiped him with her reticule, and the poor man was laid low. She carries a great deal in her reticule, you see."

"Serves him right."

"Well." She sighed, all round-eyed innocence. "That was my evening. How was yours?"

"I," he said darkly, but with that glint still lighting his eye, "had no one to dance with."

"Which is just as well. You might have gotten the same treatment the old gentleman who made bold with me received."

"No doubt."

"And you would have deserved it."

He grinned now, not bothering to hide it. "Indeed. I most certainly would have."

Ah, God, the thrill that went through her was like the crisp crackle that came into the air when lightning was about to strike. Impulsively she held out her hand. "I'll brave it. I think I know how to handle a scoundrel."

"You've had practice," he conceded, considering her hand. Slowly he placed his in it. She curtsied. He bowed his head. "I believe my waltzing days are behind me," he warned.

There was a queer, crazy sensation in her head. She *knew* this was as dangerous as putting her hand in a lion's jaw, but she couldn't seem to help herself. There was nothing, nothing quite as exhilarating as Raphael.

There never would be.

She stopped and said, "I wish that weren't true. I missed you tonight, Raphael."

He sobered. "I . . ." He frowned, looked away. His hand tightened on hers.

She went down on her knees, gazing up at him as he gathered her face in his hands. "I . . ." He couldn't say it. What was he trying to say?

In a giddy moment she thought he was going to say he had missed her, too. Just the idea, the hope of it was her undoing. She surged forward and pressed her lips to his. He reacted with shock. Twining her hands around his shoulders, she held him and opened her mouth, touching her tongue to his, asking the most terrifying question.

His answer was all she hoped for. With a strangled sound, he angled his head and ravished her mouth. Long strokes of his tongue whipped her into the euphoria she could always find in his arms. Their breaths mingled as he held her face in strong fingers and ran his tongue over her lips. She did the same to him and it made him ravenous again. He kissed her deeply, his arms holding her so close that she could feel his racing heartbeat thunder all throughout her body.

They broke apart, looking at each other with guarded amazement. Julia smiled. Raphael tried to, but his lips wavered. Before she could think, or try to stop herself, she said, "I love you."

His reaction was not what she might have wished. He seemed startled, disconcerted. She saw him, felt him, retreat. "Raphael?"

He said only one word. "Don't." And then he pushed her away. Taking the wheels in his hands, he whirled his chair about to present his back to her.

Squaring her shoulders, she said, "I'm not going to hide. I know you don't love me." He raised his hand, slicing an abrupt cutting motion into the air. It meant he wanted her to stop speaking. She walked around his chair to confront him. "I don't care. I'm not ashamed. I used to be. I thought it would hurt worse if you knew, but there isn't anything worse than keeping what you feel inside a secret. I'm done with secrets. I've done nothing wrong and I've nothing to be ashamed of. I love you, Raphael, and if that doesn't please you, then . . . the devil take it!"

"Don't do this," he growled. "You can't know what you're saying. I'm not . . ."

In love with you. That was what he was going to say, wasn't it?

"I don't care." No. That was a lie. She cared. She wanted his love.

Raphael raked both his hands through his hair. "What the

devil do you want from me, Julia?" he cried. It shocked her, the way his voice sounded. "I'm not— Damn you, you don't love me. You *pity* me, you feel *responsible* for me."

She was confused. "You don't want me?" She sank onto a chair. "You never did, did you? It was only for the wager. Why do I always forget that?"

"It's not that! Christ, Julia, don't say that! Why can't you see that the wager . . . it was a farce in so many ways. An excuse, perhaps. I would have never approached a woman like you. I went and made this ridiculous boast, and I was trapped in it, even when things got away from me. What a half-wit I was, caught in my lies and my pride, and all I wanted was you." Her head lifted. His voice lowered to a whisper. "I wanted you more than anything else. I still do. Do you think that"—he waved his hand to where they had kissed—"happens between just anyone? I don't *want* you to go, I never did. But, Julia, what would happen if you stayed? Desire dies, and when it does, it rots everything around it."

She couldn't breathe. Movement was impossible, speech beyond imagining. She listened carefully, wondering what exactly he was telling her.

"Ill-fated, that's what we are. 'Lust easily passes into hatred. It becomes a species of delirium and thereby discord is cherished.' You see what Spinoza tells us—if you stay, we'll destroy each other, it's inevitable. And you don't love me. You don't even know me. I pretended everything. Trust me. You've got to trust me, Julia. This is the most unselfish, most honest thing I've ever done in my life." He looked pale, awful. "I'm not the man you think I am. You don't even know what I've done."

"But I do know, Raphael, I—"

"Not the wager, not even this hell we've been caught in since we've been here. I'm still doing it, don't you understand? I haven't changed."

She went suddenly, absolutely cold. "What?" What could he have done? *Oh, God.* He's been with someone else. Who? Who could she be? A servant? A woman who lived in the neighborhood—how could she have known nothing about it?

He was very still. "How despicable do you think I am?"

"I don't believe you are." Ah, but even she wasn't sure what he was capable of.

His look was bitter, regretful even. He pulled his sedan chair up to a large, sturdy Elizabethan settee and grasped it firmly. And then he struggled to his feet.

Shakily, straining with every muscle, he transferred his grip and twisted his torso. And then he moved his feet—first one, then the other—until he was facing her.

Julia stared, shock spreading through like a thick, hot liquid, robbing her limbs of strength. Clutching for a handhold, she braced herself. He took a step, then another. He walked.

He walked.

She hissed in a breath. "Oh, my God."

"I've continued to work with Franklin and Gregory," he explained sotto voce. "Every day, while you went visiting, we'd work on our own. Progress was slow at first, but now I—"

"You kept it secret," she whispered. She felt horrified and elated all at the same time.

"I didn't want you to know if I failed."

"How could you?" She shook her head, trying to clear it. "I gave up everything—my whole life, my family and friends, and came here and you did this. You slunk off by yourself, like a coward, to do it on your own because you could not allow anyone inside your precious self-sufficient world. I suppose all my good intentions were a joke to you."

"Julia, I didn't do it to hurt you." He stopped, then bowed his head for a moment. "But I knew it would."

"Yes. Yes you did. You wanted to show me . . ." She swallowed back the thickness in her throat, determined not to let him see her tears. "To show me you didn't need me. Well, bravo, Raphael. You have done beautifully without me. As I should have known all along."

"I couldn't let you be part of it, Julia. I could never have borne for you to witness how it was. It was punishing, grueling. How could I let you see me like that? I may be a cripple, but I still have pride, damn it all."

"Too much pride. And not enough of anything else." She felt her teeth begin to chatter. Had he not known the guilt she had felt from the duel, a duel fought for *her* honor? It was *her* promise that had kept him from firing. He had sealed her out of his life, and done it so neatly, so thoroughly, it was crushing.

This was the final betrayal.

"Now you are free," he pronounced solemnly.

That caught her off guard. "What?"

"It's what you told me. You came to heal me, and now I am healed. You are free."

Free? Free to do what, go where? To London, briefly, but after that . . . what would she do with this freedom?

"Yes. I suppose I am. I am free."

⌒

RAPHAEL DREAMT THE drowning dream. He could breathe again, and he and Julia the mermaid swam with gregarious abandon in the undersea paradise until he pulled her to him and then she wasn't a mermaid at all. She was a real woman, winding her thighs about his hips and crying under him as he drove into her. She said she loved him, and in his dream, he was joyful and unfettered.

He awakened to find himself stiff as a pike and alone in the bed.

Thomas came in. "Your bathwater will be sent in presently, my lord," he said.

"Has my wife left?"

"The mistress departed at sunrise. I suppose it was earlier than planned. Did she not tell you?"

He was quiet at first, then he laughed. He was alone, finally rid of her. Isn't that what he had wanted all along?

Chapter Twenty-one

LAURA WORE HER betrothal ring proudly. That is what she called it, with the flare for the dramatic that only she could make charming—her betrothal ring, like some medieval lady in flowing robes. She gazed at it now, as she sat with Julia out in the folly for a private chat, the kind sisters and best friends don't want to be overheard.

"Nicholas is wonderful," Laura gushed. Sighing, she held up her hand and surveyed her "betrothal ring." The three diamonds, alternating with emeralds and lined in a row, sparkled brilliantly. "He went down on one knee and vowed to care for me, shelter me, and love me for always. Then he gave me this and asked me to be his wife—no, he said, 'Will you do me the *honor* of becoming my wife.' So I said yes and started blubbering like a fool. I was so embarrassed, but he just told me it was one of the things he loved about me."

Julia touched her own plain wedding band, but continued to smile. "Oh, Laura. He sounds wonderful. I am so happy for you. I cannot wait to meet him tonight."

"His father is coming to dine, also. You mustn't dislike him, Julia. He is stern and serious, but he loves Nicholas a great deal and has settled a generous allowance on him for our marriage."

Acting on impulse, Julia embraced her. "Oh, it *is* good to be with you again."

Laura drew back, her expression concerned. "We are all so worried about you. Mother had to stop Father at least a half dozen times from going to Cumbria. He had his valise packed and the carriage waiting the one time before he was dissuaded."

Julia's vision blurred. "None of my worries tonight. This is a time for joy."

"Do you think I am that selfish? I've been going on and on trying to cheer you up, but it's not working. It's like the light's gone out in you, Julia. I heard Mother say it and it's true. He doesn't mistreat you, does he? Oh, Julia, he—"

Julia quickly assured her sister. "Nothing like that. Raphael has never harmed me. He gives me great freedom to spend his money, to see my friends. I've made so many, Laura, and become deeply involved with some important work with an orphanage and home for women. I've written you about that. When I'm with them, working on the charities, I feel like I'm exactly where I belong." Her sister's look told her that more of an explanation than that was expected. "If I am unhappy, it is because . . . Raphael is very troubled. At times I think he might care for me. But it doesn't last. Oh, I'm just very confused." She smiled at her sister, trying to brighten the mood. "Don't worry about us, really. I'm certain we'll find a solution." What trite words they sounded, for she believed no such thing.

Laura touched her arm and squeezed affectionately. "I understand a little bit, maybe. Colin was always so mysterious. I never knew if he liked me or hated me. But when I was with him, I couldn't help myself. I knew my pride and dignity were being insulted, and yet . . ." She paused, then ventured, "Does Raphael ever mention him? Did . . . did he wed Lucy?"

"You do not still think of him *fondly*, do you?"

"Indeed not." She pulled herself into a stiff posture. "I was merely curious. I love Nicholas now, and am absolutely delighted that it all turned out as it did. It is simply . . . I suppose Colin was my first love. I cannot help but wonder about him."

Julia allowed the matter to drop, although she wondered if her sister could still have an interest in the wretched man. She of all people knew it simply didn't matter what the brain said—the heart never followed the dictates of reason. Good Lord, she was thinking like one of Raphael's philosophers.

She wished everything she said or thought wouldn't constantly remind her of that exasperating man.

THE PARTY THAT night was delightful. Julia was favorably impressed with Nicholas Rawlings. Everything about him was pleasing—his lean good looks, his frequent smile, his solicitousness of Laura. Laura shined, her happiness filling the room. And her parents were so happy.

Her father came up to her after the men had joined the ladies again after dinner. "What do you think of our Mr. Rawlings?"

"The elder or the younger?" she asked, and they shared a knowing smile. The paunchy, dour Mr. Harcourt Rawlings had droned boringly over dinner. Nicholas's expert managing of his father's seriousness endeared him all the more to Julia, as if Laura's delirious happiness weren't enough.

"Your letters have been cheerful," Francis said. It was her father's indirect way of telling her he hadn't been fooled by the missives she had composed. She hooked her arm through his and said, "And yours have been a great delight to me."

"Your husband's health is well?"

"Quite improved. He is walking, or at least beginning to." It still hurt, to think of his deception.

"How marvelous. I trust there have been equal improvements in his character."

Julia gave him a startled glance. At the knowing look

in her father's eyes, her own fell away. "He is . . ." Troubled? It is what she told Laura. It was beginning to sound like a refrain.

She felt the tension as her father decided whether or not to pursue the conversation. To preempt him, she tossed her head back and donned her brightest smile. "But we are to be happy tonight."

"Rightly so." Francis's agreement held a tone that meant she had merely postponed their talk. Julia swallowed her nervousness and directed her attention to their company.

Her family indulged in their usual hilarity, even under the austere eye of the preeminent barrister. Leah was outrageous, as she usually was when she feared the center of attention would be focused elsewhere, but there was a certain delight in her antics Julia had not seen before. Her absence from home had increased her tolerance for each of their foibles, made them endearing. Mother didn't seem so intimidating, her sister so grating. Marie was just as charming, though, and Hope was so very quiet. So easily overlooked, Julia noted, and so made a special effort to include her, to which the pretty little blond girl responded with shy gratitude.

She remembered telling Raphael about her family, a bit embarrassed by them at the time. He had sounded wistful when he commented on how normal it seemed. Yes, it did feel wonderfully normal. Comforting, splendidly ordinary to be here among them.

Later, when she climbed into her old bed, she felt almost herself, as if the evening had revived her, reminded her of her origins. Inevitably she thought of Raphael and wondered if he had felt similarly in those secluded hours spent with his mother this winter. She hoped so. And she hoped it was as pleasant.

The following weeks were spent shopping and visiting. Julia hadn't missed London, but with the season coming on fast, it held a certain excitement that the country couldn't match. She indulged herself in some new gowns, although she thought the Hawkshead dressmaker could have done as well, and went completely giddy at the haberdashers. Old acquaintances were renewed, familiar faces whom she had known last season treated her with a strange deference she found amusing. She was no longer "Julia," but "Madam le Viscountess." Her mother beamed, and Julia felt a bittersweet sense of irony that she had managed to please her, after all.

The Countess of Wentword arrived back in town toward the beginning of March, and the season began in earnest. Julia spent a good deal of time with her grandmother-in-law, whose wisdom and friendship she appreciated deeply.

The haunting emptiness existed as it had when she first arrived, fresh out of the wars with Raphael, but it seemed more and more remote as the months of her absence increased to two.

It was one morning in early April, at breakfast with the duke and duchess, that her peace came to an end. The rest of the family was sleeping in, an indulgence they loved, but Julia liked to rise early and spend these early hours with the Cravensmores.

The duke was saying, "I told Kenwood to stay away from that crowd. The Prince Regent is a scoundrel, for all of his airs, and nothing better. To be born to privilege is, well, a privilege, what!"

The duchess puckered her forehead. "I don't believe I want to play cribbage, no, Charles."

Julia smiled, filled with her affection for these two. How kind they had been to all of her family. They had never flinched in their staunch support during the worst of the fiasco with Raphael.

That thought was prophetic, for it wasn't more than ten minutes later when a servant came in and said that the Viscount de Fontvilliers was here to see the viscountess. Julia looked up sharply, thinking there might be a misunderstanding. How could that be—Raphael, here?

She looked to the duke, who regarded her with a speculative raising of his eyebrows and a half smile. The duchess said, "Who ordered more chairs?"

"No, Eleanor," the duke said loudly and patted the frail hand. "Font-ve-ay. The servant mispronounced it. You know, Julia's husband. He is here." His smile deepened, crinkling his old face. "For our Julia."

"Oh!" Turning to Julia, the duchess said, "Well, child. I think you best greet him properly."

Still fighting disbelief, Julia rose on trembling legs and walked out of the dining room. She gave one backward glance, and the duke shooed her, like a child he expected to scamper on out of the room.

She went into the foyer and found that her husband was indeed here.

His valet, Thomas, was with him, helping Raphael doff his redingote. He leaned heavily on a sleek black cane with a silver knob, smoothing the lines of his frock coat. Then he straightened and looked directly at Julia and broke out in a melting smile.

"That is all, Thomas," he said over his shoulder, his eyes never leaving hers.

He looked wonderful. Standing tall, dressed impeccably with a smartly tied cravat and snowy lawn shirt, his tidy, gentlemanly appearance and broad, generous grin with just that hint of mischief—it was enough to knock the wind from her. He took her hand, bowed over it, and said, "Your servant, madam."

When she couldn't find her voice, he inclined his head, as if he understood perfectly. "May I come in?"

"Yes. Yes, goodness!" She tried to pull her hand from his, but he kept his grip. He had already removed his gloves. The feel of his skin, the callused palms, roughened from working to build back his strength, was startlingly sensual.

"You look lovely, Julia." His voice was hoarse, his eyes staring into hers as if he'd not seen her for ten years rather than merely a pair of months. "You look very, very lovely." His thumb moved over the ridges of her knuckles, and a knot of pressure formed in her chest.

She pulled her hand from his with a bit too much force, placing the trembling fingers to her forehead, as if she could clear her confusions with a bit of pressure. "Come in. Here. In the . . . ah . . . in the withdrawing room." Her mind was slowly recovering. Some distance helped. She made certain there was as least enough space between them so that he couldn't reach her. "Oh. Where are my manners? Have you breakfasted?"

"I did. With my grandmother. I arrived at the town house late last night."

"Oh." He walked behind her as she led the way, slowly but with longer steps than she would have thought him capable of. He had improved greatly.

Once in the room, she felt his presence even more keenly. The furniture, carved and fine and perfect for a gathering place mostly frequented by ladies, seemed too delicate to support his broad-framed body. He selected a sturdy-looking settee and lowered himself into it, relying heavily on his cane. Perhaps he was still unsure of his strength. Julia took a step toward him, then stopped herself, knowing he would not appreciate her solicitousness.

His eyes caught hers, however, and they were warm. He settled back. "Are you not curious?"

What was wrong with her, she demanded of herself impatiently. "Of course. Yes. Um, tea?" She was acting like a ninny—he had already breakfasted and it was not the hour for tea.

What was wrong with her was that Raphael was here, as if conjured out of a dream she dared not admit, looking wonderful and acting like a perfect gentleman. Without waiting for him to respond, she turned and found a seat for herself, far enough away from him that it raised his brows.

His next words shocked her out of inanity. He said, in the softest, sincerest of voices, "You left without a word."

She sputtered for a moment, then managed, "I thought we had said everything."

"Not goodbye. You didn't even wait to tell me goodbye."

"I apologize." She said it churlishly. Her defenses were rising to full mast now.

He inclined his head as if accepting. She forced herself to relax, realizing her back was as stiff as a board. "Why have you come here?"

"I've come for you. I want you back."

She blinked, then tried to laugh, making only a dry, rough sound. "As I recall our last meeting, you directed me to *leave* you, as you'd done on many occasions before."

A sardonic twist appeared on his beautiful mouth, but he didn't seem to be directing it at her. "Yes, about that . . . It's sort of a long story, not something I can go into at the moment. But allow me to say I wasn't in my right mind."

"I never knew which of your minds was the correct one. You have so many."

He nodded, as if in complete agreement. "I shall explain all that, but not today. Too many surprises are bad for the humors, I'm told." He said it mockingly, as if they were sharing some intimate joke between them. "Perhaps we could start with dining together tonight, then perhaps the theater. My grandmother has offered the use of her box, suggesting that it would be good to be out together. To stem the gossips, you understand."

"Yes." Her lips twitched involuntarily. "I recall how concerned you are with what the wags should say."

"That is, if you've nothing else planned."

Her memory keyed onto the time when he'd waited for her in his room. Bold, outrageous Raphael—no feat was too daring. And here he was sitting like some suitor calling on a lady and acting so incredibly tame—it should have been funny, but instead she felt a brush of tenderness because she sensed he was treading softly, taking great care. Whatever he was up to, it mattered a great deal to him.

And she was intrigued. "Yes. I shall be ready. You may fetch me at seven."

He rubbed his chin and frowned. "Yes, well, about that. It has been brought to my attention that your continued

residence here at the Cravensmores'' would raise some speculation since I've arrived and am staying at the town house.
Would you consider staying with me?"

He was being so charming. Was it on purpose, to dis-
arm her? Just look at the way he angled his glance up at
her. Goodness knew she should be thoroughly familiar with
the tact. He was very adept at this particular approach, the
self-deprecation blended with a hint of naughtiness. It was
irresistible and he knew it; after all, it had worked so well
before. She fought the allure of it now. "Raphael, I refuse
to believe you are suddenly such a slave to public opinion."

He seemed startled. "I'm not. I was thinking of your
family. Your sisters."

Yes, of course. Scandal was such an insidious thing, it
could stain an entire family. He had struck on a truism, but
whether he really felt a concern for such things or was
merely using the fact to his advantage, she couldn't tell.
"Not to mention that it suits your ends, no doubt," she
commented.

He bowed his head. "Madam, I am a self-confessed and
unapologetically shameless opportunist come to London to
dare the fates one last, glorious time. I will either succeed
in my quest or go down in a blaze of abject humiliation.
I am prepared for failure, but hoping for success."

This was the Raphael of last season—so devilishly attractive it melted her very bones. When his eyes danced
like green sparks and he held his head just so she believed
every single word. After all these weeks without him, feeling strong, thinking herself independent, he simply walked
in and reduced her to a quivering mess with his beguiling
smile.

Ah, but there were times when he'd been far less poised,
when he'd laid himself open for her and she'd seen such
a different man. Even now, she sensed an urgency in him,
a kind of desperation behind his facile words that wasn't
completely repressed.

She was a madwoman, and she knew it. Like holding

fire in your hand because it was beautiful, ignoring the inevitability of pain. "Yes. Of course, I should come to the town house. I'll have my things packed."

His reaction stunned her. He tilted back his head and breathed in deeply, his eyes closing for a moment, such as the devout might do when mentally deferring to God. Then he let out the breath and gazed back at her, the moment of transparency gone. "I'll have one of my footmen come to fetch them. What hour?"

"I should say four."

"Very good. Shall I tell my grandmother to expect you for tea?"

"Yes."

"She'll be glad you are coming home."

The word hung in the air. *Home.*

He rose, which seemed to be a laborious undertaking, possibly even painful. She clenched her hands to keep from reaching one out to aid him.

He said, "I hope you will pardon the early hour. It is important for me to keep the afternoons dedicated to my recovery. As I am in Town for a spell, I shall be continuing my lessons at Jackson's boxing school. It is an excellent expulsion of pent-up tensions." His eyes slid to her and there was no mistaking the fire in them. "When a man has no other means to release them. I am not one well-suited to celibacy."

Her mouth dropped open in shock.

He scowled at her and said, "Please try not to look so delicious, will you, Julia? It is downright cruel."

<hr />

RAPHAEL SUFFERED FROM the most frustrating infusion of tension. It had been with him that afternoon as he had bathed, donned his formal evening clothes, reverberated through him now as he stood as still as a statue while Thomas tied the cravat. He made the man undo it and retie it three separate times until he was satisfied. Thomas left in a snit, but Raphael hummed lightly and hardly noticed.

The air was charged, alive with *her*. He could even imagine he could smell her particular scent, as if she had just passed this way and a whiff of it still lingered in the air. It was pure fancy, of course. Yes, she was back in his town house, but not in his chamber.

Oh, not yet.

He chastised himself, then grinned and shook his head, caught in a battle between caution and excitement. Another seduction was in order, and with him now on his feet, in his home with his wife in residence, and in London—*his* Town—he was feeling very eager to begin. And yet, the stakes were higher than they'd ever been before. It wasn't just pride any longer, or some unimportant amount of money, but something else more precious, more profoundly essential. It was Julia—forever in his life. A bedmate, yes, but a partner in so many other ways.

To say he had missed her would be an absurdity in understatement. He'd burned for her, every moment, an agony fired by the uncertainty of whether or not she would return to him.

And then he had thought—what am I doing, waiting in a cavernous old house stuck out in the Lake District like a helpless old woman? He was Raphael Giscard, Viscount de Fontvilliers, lately the Bane of the Ton, and that still meant something. Surely, he could do better than this! And so he'd worked himself, days filled with exertions to increase strength, restore function, and compensate for what could not be achieved. With *her* face before him always, he'd pushed himself past limits he couldn't be bothered to observe.

How often he'd laugh at himself, fighting now to get back what he'd had up until a short time ago worked so hard to discard. But he wasn't one who took to lessons easily. He supposed he was doomed to learn things the hardest way. Once he had thought himself to indeed be that very thing—doomed. He refused to entertain that any longer. *He* was in control of his life.

He was indeed a stupid man. But he was no fool, after all.

Checking his reflection in the mirror, he felt a most preposterous surge of uncertainty. He kept smoothing the line of his jacket, as if it displeased him, but it was perfect. He was just delaying, he realized. Lord, he was nervous.

The realization was such an insult to his pride, it spurred him out of his chamber and down the hall to Julia's. He didn't use the connecting door through their dressing rooms, guessing she had locked it.

His soft rap on the hallway entrance was answered by her maid. "May I see the viscountess?" he asked humbly.

Julia came up, then, and opened the door wider. "It's all right, Jean. You may go."

In the absence of the other woman, Julia regarded him much like a lamb eyeing a slavering wolf. She kept her grip on the door. "I am almost ready, Raphael. Would you wait for me downstairs?"

Removing from his pocket a small locket, he presented it her. "I just wanted to give you this."

"Oh," she replied in a faint voice, taking the sparkling gold object from him. "How lovely." She held it close and examined the surface, notched with facets that caught the light. Raising her eyes to him, she smiled slightly. "Thank you, Raphael. But what is this for?"

"For the fact that I've never given a thing to you in all the time I've known you. But that is going to change, beginning tonight."

He trusted she would understand what he meant, that he wasn't speaking about material things at all—although he hadn't so much as handed her a trinket on this Christmas past—but a generosity of much greater depth.

"There's an inscription," he said. He almost laughed at himself. He felt like a boy giving some grubby wildflowers to the object of his heart. Except that he'd never been a boy, not even when he'd been young, but he supposed this is what that felt like, awkward, impossibly eager, and thrilling as hell.

She turned the locket over and read. "It's Spinoza."

"Do you remember?"

"Yes, of course. The book you gave me in the park that day. *Foundations of a Moral Life.*" She read the quote: " 'He who strives to drive out hatred with love fights joyfully.' " She looked at him, puzzled.

He bowed and said, "I will await you downstairs."

It was a nerve-racking fifteen minutes until she appeared. She wore the locket, touching it self-consciously when she saw him take note. A ludicrous surge of joy buoyed him, causing him to offer his arm with a flourish that was quite unlike him.

They dined at an inn famous for its prestigious patronage, in one of the private parlors. It was very intimate, which served to provide him with almost too much temptation. He kept having to wipe sweat off his brow and told the servers to lower the fire. It was only after seeing their startled faces he realized his feeling overheated had nothing to do with the external temperature.

Julia's golden eyes held him as they conversed. He kept getting distracted by her lips, taking notice of how full they were and how they appeared so temptingly soft. He decided he liked her hair styled that way, with much of it left to fall in a tumble of loosely wrought curls down her back. He wanted to sink his fingers in that artful mass and pull it out of its pins.

Julia was not ignorant of the predatory way Raphael was looking at her, although she had to admit he was behaving the gentleman through and through despite it all. It surprised her that Raphael wished to dine before the theater. Most people preferred late suppers. It was the way of Town life. The early diners were from the country. It seemed like such a provincial quirk—a word certainly one never expected to apply to the Viscount de Fontvilliers.

She kept touching the locket, wondering what it meant, afraid to think what she *thought* it meant was what it *really* meant. And she recalled how in their last conversation at Glenwood Park, he had taunted her with words from this same philosopher. Was this his way of apologizing, or did she misunderstand?

Sighing, she mused on how she had nearly forgotten how exhausting her husband could be.

He was charming, however, throughout dinner, delighting her with discourse that allayed her reserve. Raphael had a way of drawing her into conversation and stimulating her thoughts so that she was unself-consciously debating him by the time the second course arrived.

"I disagree with Kant. I cannot believe in his *a priori* claim. How can you account for differences in siblings, for example? They are raised by the same parents, in the same home, the same community, and so forth, and yet they can be, as my sisters and I are, completely different."

His eyes danced and he leaned forward, enjoying the debate as much as she. "Madam, you would argue predeterminism?"

"Neither extreme. I say it is both influences—our inborn natures and how they are singularly affected by experience—that shapes character."

And so on until they concluded their meal and it was time for the theater. They continued their discussion in the carriage, and it was not until they were in front of Covent Gardens that Julia realized she didn't know what play they were seeing.

"*Romeo and Juliet*," Raphael answered in reply to her inquiry. She stopped in her tracks, and he laughed. "I am teasing. It is *Hamlet* this night. A study in madness. Fitting?"

She tried to sniff, as if she disapproved, but she was too disturbed by the leap of emotion that had arisen to her breast. She had come to think of *Romeo and Juliet* as *their* play. Did he?

How absurd. The Viscount de Fontvilliers had no such sentimentality in him. No sooner had she decided this than they arrived at their seats and she found a single perfect white rose on her seat to prove her wrong. A glance at her husband only won her a wiggle of his eyebrows and a lopsided grin, masterfully apologetic and suggestive at the same time.

It was her turn to laugh. She even had to stop herself from touching his arm in a manner that would be . . . playful. Really, she should not encourage him. He was far too delighted with his wickedness.

But then again, she had always loved that in him, hadn't she? Oh, Lord, what was happening to her? How could she even allow herself to consider this was at all real? She had been here before, enthralled in his appeal, that singularly intoxicated sensation he could weave about her in an instant. She knew its deadly risks, and here she was, dancing on the precipice again with all the abandon of a woman . . .

Oh, Lord. A woman in love. There lay the crux of it. She loved this man so much.

But Raphael didn't love. He could be as delightfully alluring as a rake of his repute should be, but it wasn't the same. It wasn't what she wanted from him. He didn't even allow that love could exist. A man such as that . . . a man without any love in him . . .

A man such as that would break her heart all over again.

They settled down to watch the play, and she touched the rose to the tip of her nose, inhaling its fragrance and telling herself not to fall to pieces. It was only a flower, after all.

Chapter Twenty-two

INTERMISSION WAS ALWAYS a crush, and always filled with familiar faces. When Richard Evans, Lord Martinvale, approached him after Julia went into the ladies' retiring room, Raphael couldn't believe the swell of pleasure as his old friend offered him his hand. Since he held his cane in the hand delegated to this masculine greeting, there was a moment of awkwardness before Raphael grabbed the offered hand with his left and the two men laughed.

Martinvale bowed. "Fontvilliers, by the devil himself, it is good to see you. And walking. By God, you are walking!"

There was more than hearty good cheer behind his words, but men didn't acknowledge such things. "Thought I'd been done in, did you?"

Martinvale laughed louder, drawing some looks. "I should have known better. Walking, breathing, showing up at the theater—you continue to surprise me."

Raphael flexed his leg and said, "Julia will be rejoining me momentarily. Come with me to walk a bit. I've grown stiff in those bloody uncomfortable chairs." Martinvale fell into step beside him, and they headed toward where the crowd was thinnest.

Chewing the inside of his cheek, Raphael said, "I heard

you introduced Laura to Nicholas Rawlings. I thought that was well done. I rather regretted the way I encouraged her infatuation with Strathford. Although you did not do it on my behalf, your intervention removed a certain burden."

"It is rather a shock to me that it should matter to you."

Shrugging, Raphael said, "No less than I. What has become of him?" They drew up to a pillar and Raphael paused to rest.

"Strathford? Laying low, I should think. He had a bit of worry about being connected to the scandal. He retreated to the country this winter. He could be back in Town, but I haven't seen him. Of course, I haven't been to any of our old haunts. I've reformed my ways a bit." He smiled. "I'm to be married, Fontvilliers."

"Then congratulations are in order, my old friend. Who is she?"

"The Honorable Judith Danvers. I don't believe you know her. She, well, she was hardly in our circle of acquaintance."

Raphael chuckled. "Thank goodness for that. I can't say I think much of our female companionship of old. Well, I do wish you well on your marriage. I trust you will do a better job of it than I."

"Thank you for your good wishes. You also may not have heard about Atvers. I heard he'd been utterly ruined at the tables. He is going to have to leave the city for fear of the creditors on his tail."

"Does it not bring you satisfaction to see me brought low as well?"

Martinvale shook his head. "It should. But it does not. Pain can be a dreadful but effective tutor. And there is something different about you, Fontvilliers. Less mischief, less bite. I believe you have changed."

Almost drolly, Raphael crooned, "Now, wouldn't that be something?"

"I've known you a long time, Raphael, and I've known you well. Chillingly well, and at times I've wished I didn't. I've seen that arrogance of yours slip. That business with the wager was your lowest point. I think you even choked on it after a while."

"Indeed." Raphael was sober. "I am still gasping for breath."

"How is your wife?"

"Beautiful," Raphael answered without inflection. "Completely fascinating, absolutely delightful, and, unfortunately, abjectly mistrustful of me. Not that I blame her. But it does leave me with a rather formidable task. God, man. I'm done in." He shrugged and gave a snort of mirthless laughter. "Why the devil didn't I listen to you while there was still time?"

"Raphael," Martinvale said, his voice low and confidential. "I can hardly believe . . . Are you in love with her?"

The word fell soft and right, and even as old dying demons flared in reaction, Raphael smiled and coughed out a flat chuckle. "You have no idea."

"Now you truly have me amazed. When I think of the four of us, just last year this time and now look—look at you! It is divine intervention, I swear it."

"Martinvale—you are a genius!"

"Pardon?"

"The four of us—last season. The wager, man. I just realized . . ." He trailed off, his mind working swiftly on the possibilities. A slow smile crept across his face, and he rubbed his chin.

Martinvale said, "Oh, no. I never liked that look. It means you have another wretched idea."

"Oh, on the contrary, friend. I believe you will like this one. In fact, I must enlist your aid."

⁓

JULIA WAS ANNOYED. So much for Raphael playing the attentive husband. She came out of the ladies' retiring room, and he was nowhere to be found. Probably off with some old acquaintance, making plans to go out gambling later after he'd deposited her at home. Then a dreadful thought occurred to her, and she peered about, searching for a bright head of blond hair. She had never gotten any clarification, after all, on precisely the nature of his relationship with the Lady Catherine person he had dragged about.

That was when she saw another face. As she locked eyes with Paul Bentley, she lifted her hand in response to his. The person next to him began waving and Julia saw it was Eulalia Peavenstover, who immediately rushed toward her.

"Julia, I mean, Viscountess!" Eulalia cried happily.

"Oh, Eulalia, please, no formality, even here," Julia said, returning the woman's embrace. "It is wonderful to see you. Hello, Paul. It is good to see you again."

He bowed stiffly and said, "And you, madam le viscountess. If you will excuse me, I see an old friend I would be remiss to ignore. Aunt Eulalia, I'll return for you."

"Oh, my dear," Eulalia said, grasping Julia's hand in hers, "Paul pointed out the viscount over at the other end of the hall. It's the first time I've ever seen him." Eulalia moved closer and linked her arm through Julia's. "It is odd, isn't it, after my coming to your house all those times? But then he was so ill." She giggled. "I must say, he looks quite recovered. He *is* a handsome one. My, yes. And so very generous. He's made quite a name for himself in the neighborhood. You must be so proud."

Julia said, "Pardon?"

"What he did, silly! I know he wanted to be anonymous, but I couldn't help but notice the improvements at the Quaker house, and when I asked about it, Daniel confided how the viscount's generosity has made such a wonderful difference. It is marvelous, what he's given them. Why, it's a small fortune, yes, indeed."

Julia stared at her and Eulalia laughed shrilly. "Goodness, did he neglect to tell you? Oh, how modest of him." Her eyes rounded. "Oh, dear. Then you don't know about Greta, do you?"

Julia remembered the shy young girl who had been so horribly treated. "Oh, no, did something happen to her?"

"Nothing bad, dear, thanks to the viscount. She is working at Glenwood Park now. Her child was fostered to a nearby family, a childless couple who were so pleased with that little boy, I'll tell you. Then your husband fixed her with a position so she could stay close and still see him from time to time. Oh, and *then* there was the business with that footman. Nasty man, he tried . . . Oh, dear, no, don't be alarmed. Greta screamed like a demon, and the viscount got to her before any harm was done. As for that dreadful, horrible manservant, he was let go without a reference, and you know what a curse that is! Anyway, I heard poor Greta was so frightened after that, your husband had her moved out of the servants' quarters and into a regular bedroom. Imagine!"

Julia was weak with shock. "Yes. Imagine."

"And there's Diana, of course. You remember her—tall girl, beautiful girl, thought she'd been married but it had all been a sham? Well, she's secured a position as a governess. That was your husband's doing as well. He vouched for her—fibbed outright, but all for a good cause, of course—saying she was a widow of a friend of his. Now she and her baby daughter are at Holmstead Grange."

"Raphael did that?" It seemed impossible.

Paul appeared, bowing low before speaking to his aunt. "It is time to take our seats again."

Julia grabbed her friend before she could go. "Please call on me soon. I want desperately to speak to you."

"I will, my dear," she assured her.

"A moment, please, Aunt," Paul said, and Eulalia moved away to leave them alone. "I just want to say it is good to see you," Paul muttered. "You look so much happier tonight than when last we met. I wanted to wish you well."

Happy? Was she? She pressed her hands to her cheeks and felt the heat under her palms.

Paul bowed and said good evening. It was only a moment after that when Raphael arrived with another man. "There you are." He took her hand and folded it in the crook of his arm. "Do you remember my friend, Lord Martinvale?"

With a flourish Martinvale bowed. "Your servant, madam le viscountess. I am afraid I am to blame for your husband's absence. When I saw the viscount, I had to speak to him. He wanted to walk, to work away the stiffness, and we fell into conversation. I trust you did not feel neglected."

"No," she answered. "It does not signify." She was only relieved it was Martinvale who had been with Raphael. What a jolt to realize that she hardly trusted her husband, for all his flattering attentions, when he was out of her sight.

But . . . he had given money to the Quakers. He had taken those women into his home, found positions for them. Raphael, the Bane of the Ton, had done that?

Raphael offered his free arm and she took it. "Intermission is nearly over. Let us take our seats. Good evening, Martinvale," he said over his shoulder. "Do see to that piece of business we discussed, will you?"

Martinvale broke out in a broad smile and bowed low with an uncharacteristic flourish. "It will be my pleasure."

~~~~~

THE CARRIAGE RIDE home was enjoyable and easy. Raphael and Julia talked a little bit about the theater, but mostly sat in comfortable silence, swaying gently, listening to the muffled sound of late-night traffic beyond the drawn curtains. In the quiet moments Julia wondered about what Eulalia had told her, and marveled she would have never suspected Raphael had been moved in the least by the visit to the home she had forced upon him.

So much of himself he kept closed off from her. It made her sad, in a way, but happy, too. There was good in him, tremendous good. Perhaps in time he would not avoid its demonstration. It was simply Raphael's nature to be secretive. As much as it pained her, she would just have to accept it.

A glance over caught him staring at her, a smoldering look that caught her unawares. Hot and cold flashed throughout her body. Turning away, she loosened the ties of her pelisse. Warm fingers came up to help her, drawing the overgarment down off her shoulders. She shivered. Raphael chuckled. "I thought you were warm."

The prickle of her skin had nothing to do with a chill, and it was very likely he knew it. A night spent under the unrelenting charms of Raphael was a potent bewitchment. He probably knew that as well.

Draping his arm over the back of the chair, he let his hand hang loosely so that it brushed her bared shoulder. Lifting a soft lock of hair, he quirked the side of his mouth up in a half smile. "Do you know what drove me to near madness when you were gone?" Those soft, rough tones in the dark increased the tremors coursing through her. For some reason—although she wasn't tired—her eyelids grew heavy. "I couldn't recall the texture of your hair. It is very soft. But it is thick, so one doesn't imagine it would be. I suppose that was what confounded my memory."

"I . . ." His knuckle brushed her cheek, stealing the thought.

"Do you know something else?"

"Mmm?" His fingers were on her neck now, stroking lightly.

"I missed you terribly. Every day, over and over, I'd think where you were and when you'd be back, and then I'd remember that you'd gone. I was afraid it was for good. And it was like a punch to my solar plexus every time."

"Solar plexus?"

He placed his free hand over his chest. Right about where his heart would be. "Here."

She swallowed. "I hardly believe you suffered so acutely." With admirable effort, she pulled herself back into the realm of reason. "You seemed to do quite well without me. You even seemed to prefer it."

"No. Oh, Julia. Will you allow me to explain something?"

"I would never deny you the privilege of explaining yourself."

"All right." He ducked his head, and angled a look up at her from under drawn brows. "Maybe I can help you understand something about me. You once asked if I was a lonely child. I was. Deeply lonely. It's not self-pity to admit it, is it? It was true in any event. My parents were absorbed in their private wars, they barely noticed me. When I was a young man, I found that there was some question of my parentage." She felt his hand still, his body grow tight beside her. "My mother had had an affair and was not certain who my father was. I still do not know, not for certain. It was the final blow, sealing me in the idea that I had no one. Do you see?"

"Yes," she admitted softly. "I can see how it must have been." She could—vividly. Here was the boy she had always sensed in him. Alone, frightened even. And angry. Very angry.

"I looked at families like yours, at couples, those who had found happiness with each other and felt as if . . . God, I can't tell you what it was like. I was the beggar at the feast. So I told myself it wasn't real. Lust, or pretense for appearances' sake, or greed for money—anything else but what it was because I couldn't tolerate that it was something beautiful and I had never experienced a day of it."

She was stunned. Just a moment ago she had told herself to accept his reticence. And now, here he was telling her everything. She managed to say, "You must have been so lost."

"Lost? That, certainly. And damned. I felt damned." His voice held emotion unchecked, and she reached up and took his face in her hands. Despite her resolve to remain immune, she couldn't help herself.

He grasped her wrists and pressed a long kiss into her palm. "I pushed you away because *that is what I always did.* I was so used to pushing everyone away, and that's how I lost what tenderness did exist for me. I couldn't see it, or maybe I couldn't bear it. I learned about that lately, that I had caring all along but didn't know it. So I kept myself removed from everyone. And then I met you and you scared the hell out of me. From the first day I saw you, I wanted you—physically, yes, but even more, and I didn't understand that, not then. It was so new, so damned disconcerting. I didn't like it. Julia, am I making any sort of sense?"

She drew in a ragged breath over the gathering tears in her throat. "Perfect sense."

He let out a rough laugh. "Do you know the moment I knew I was absolutely gone? When I saw you on the street with Marie. Good God, my heart nearly tore a hole in my chest, and I was scrambling like a madman, trying to come up with anything to engage you, keep you with me awhile." He shook his head. "And then I grabbed you and tasted you, and I think I was more shocked than you."

"But you never showed a bit of it," she said, amazed. "You seemed as if you knew exactly what you were doing."

He ran his finger along the line of her nose. "Of course. We scoundrels keep such things very close to our hearts."

He kept speaking of his heart. But he hadn't said he loved her. She was waiting for it, wanting to hear it. She needed to hear it. It was a magical word. Because she sensed for him it was the hardest word in the world to utter, and if he said it, it would mean he had conquered something within himself.

The carriage came to a stop, and it broke something of the mood. The footman came up with the box, and they alighted, walking in silence up to the town house. The lights were down low, although it wasn't very late. The silence stretched between them. They entered and he murmured something about a drink together, but she replied that it was late and she wanted to go directly upstairs.

What was the matter with her? As they walked along, she wanted to scream a thousand things, yet the words seemed to clot in her throat.

In front of her boudoir she managed. "Raphael . . . thank you for your explanation, but I—"

"It is all right," he said. "I've given you too much at once."

"No. Yes. It's just that there is a great deal left to say."

He smiled, moving closer. "Maybe we shall leave things as they are tonight." He didn't seem at all as if he'd like to let things alone. He was moving closer, lowering his head even as he spoke. She took hold of his shoulders, at first thinking to hold him off. But once her body came in contact with his, she curled her fingers into the soft give of his coat.

Raphael sensed the moment her mood shifted. Brushing her nose with his, he kept his mouth just out of reach. For a second or two their breaths mingled. Then, with his hands doing what they'd wanted to do all night long— twining in her hair, spilling pins everywhere, yanking it free to sift silkily through his fingers—he murmured, "Julia," and slanted his mouth over hers.

His body reacted instantly, becoming aroused with stunning swiftness. She made a soft, kittenish sound, and her hands grasped his neck, dug into his shoulders, and he reveled in her passion, a passion for him. After all he'd done, she was still here, in his arms, giving him all of herself. She was more precious to him than anything he'd ever held dear, ever imagined. God, how stupid he had been to have once laughed about the myth of this emotion. Nothing in his life had been truer than this.

She was pressing her body up against his, and he knew what she offered as his mouth moved over hers, his tongue delving inside to taste her, to feel her textures, to boldly stoke the fires of passion. He held her tightly, so as to best feel the soft feminine curves he had itched to roam these last lonely months.

Reason tapped him on the shoulder, and because he was so terribly afraid to make a mistake, he stopped and listened to the cool, steady voice for once in his life.

Would she think this was mere seduction, all for carnal pleasure? Didn't she know that he burned for her not only in his body, but in his soul?

Hadn't he told her? Damnation—he had. Hadn't he?

There was much he had revealed, but not that she owned his heart. Not as plain as she deserved to hear it. Ah, what a coward he was.

But no, it was not mere cowardice that kept him from confessing. There was one last thing undone, a final act, so to speak, and he wanted that in place before he moved any further. He was suddenly afraid if he got ahead of himself, he would lose more than he would gain.

With tremendous effort, he pulled away. She looked up at him, utterly stunned, and he chuckled. He wasn't above liking the passion-dazed look of her. Very much. Enough almost to make him falter. "I want it all, Julia. All of you to all of myself. And I will have it, I am quite determined. I haven't come this far to settle for anything less. Leave it to a scoundrel and scamp to find a way. So until then, good night."

"Raphael?"

"Oh," he said, turning back to her. "Do not misunderstand. I am not pushing you away this time." He gave her his most wicked grin. "Quite the contrary, but I will prove that in time."

"Raphael!" Why, she actually looked miffed.

"Madam le viscountess," he said, and bowed. "Your servant."

"You are playing games again!"

"Indeed, madam, you are, as always, amazingly astute. I play now for the highest stakes imaginable. Love." And then he left her.

Julia stared after him in stunned disbelief. Had he really said . . . *love*?

THE GAME BEGAN with a note delivered to Julia's bedroom the following morning, along with a box of chocolates. She wasn't particularly fond of sweets and was puzzled by the gift until she noticed the bright magenta bow. The distinctive flourish marked the box from the elite confectioners' on Bond Street.

Where he had . . . licked her lips. She shivered, then smiled giddily. Raphael was indeed a master, and he was not going to disappoint.

She ripped open the seal of the note. It read: *Tonight.*

Rushing down to breakfast, she found her husband had already gone out on several errands. She was left to ruminate on what exactly would happen *tonight.*

Thinking of how he had left her the previous evening, with that glint in his eye and cryptic promise, made her gleefully impatient. She was surprised she was enjoying this so much. Always a practical girl, she was usually not the sort to entertain these sorts of follies. But with Raphael, no rules ever held true.

The day was the longest on record, Julia was absolutely sure of it. Just as certain was that she must be making a horrid fool of herself with the countess, who actually grew concerned. Once she started so violently when the countess spoke to her, she dropped her china cup and spilled tea all over the carpet. Julia excused herself to walk off some of the excitement building inside her.

When she came in, she went up to bathe and dress, even though it was early. Her hair she insisted be styled as it had been last night, and her dress she chose with care. She donned the pale yellow crepe she had worn to Covent Garden to see *Romeo and Juliet.* Raphael had seemed to admire her in it. If Raphael could invoke seductive memories, then so could she.

Dawdling to waste some time in her room, she dabbed perfume behind her ears, touched up the tendrils of hair left to frame her face, examined her nails for cleanliness, and sighed, then puzzled over what to do next to pass the time. Although she was not much of a drinker, she considered a glass of sherry might steady her nerves, so she grabbed her gold reticule and swept out of the room and down the stairs. She felt as if she was floating, her entire body dancing with thrilling tremors of anticipation.

As she descended the stairs, however, she heard male voices coming from the library. Her steps slowed, then stopped.

Who was here to spoil their evening? Curiosity spurred her closer. The door was ajar, and she could see Raphael's back. Beyond him, she spied that unpleasant fellow—Atvers was his name. Colin Strathford was also inside.

Stunned, she stood frozen in a moment of uncertainty. Why would Raphael bring men here on the night he had promised to her?

What were they doing here? What should *she* do?

Martinvale passed the open doorway and saw her before she could make up her mind. "Madam le viscountess," he said loudly, and everyone looked out the doorway at her standing there, her heart on the floor.

Raphael came and opened the door. "You are early. I was about to come up and get you. Come in, Julia."

She moved, every inch of her reluctant. She didn't like this. And yet Martinvale's smile was kind, and there was a sort of excitement buzzing between the looks he exchanged with Raphael. Her husband held his hand out to her, and his face, too, was soft and eager.

She looked about her again. Strathford's mouth drew up in a smirk, and he gave her a quick nod by way of greeting. Atvers just glared.

"Come, Julia," Raphael said. His tone pulsed with an undercurrent of tension. "Stand with me."

She obeyed, still unsure. Then he took her hand and squeezed it. She looked up at him, and he gave her a bracing smile. "I have asked them here for a very specific purpose. There is something we must settle between the five of us."

Letting go of her hand, he sauntered forward to stand among his former bows. He swept out his arms. "Here you have before you the four gentlemen who were once known far and wide as the Bane of the Ton. We deserved a good portion of the foul rumors circulated about us, for indeed we sowed much mischief. But the most reprehensible act we committed was a little-known wager. I boasted once that I could prove love was but a delusion, a pretty dressing for lust. I believed it so fervently that I wagered five thousand pounds against the strongest love the *beau monde* had to offer. There crossed our path a young woman of excellent character and her suitor. Their devotion, which had charmed the jaded *ton*, was deemed the most excellent test of my theory. If I could turn their love cold, it was assumed I would have proved my point."

He extracted a banded packet of notes from the inside pocket of his coat. "As you all know I was successful in turning the beautiful woman's affections from her supposed true love to myself. I was given this as a reward."

Holding the money as if he were weighing it, he stared down at his boon. "Five thousand pounds. But I received something else in the bargain. That was a wife, with whom, for a short time, I knew more happiness with than I had ever imagined existed. That did not please everyone, however, and the truth of the wager came out. Charles Atvers, I believe, did us that favor. I did not behave in the most admirable of ways when this happened. This I regret. You see, I thought her lost to me. As for my subsequent actions . . . I can only plead to weakness of character."

He gave a slight bow to her, as if in apology.

Julia's gaze shifted to the other men. Despite his efforts to look bored before, Strathford was watching Raphael closely. Martinvale, too, listened with rapt attention. Atvers was visibly alarmed as Raphael fanned the notes with his thumb. The room tensed with hushed expectation.

Raphael continued, "But you see, there is one very salient fact that has not yet been revealed. And it changes everything." Raphael walked to Strathford and tossed the five thousand onto his lap.

There was a moment of surprised silence.

"I concede, Strathford," Raphael said, tossing another packet of notes to match the first. "There is your five thousand returned, and mine as forfeit. I admit before all assembled that I was wrong. I lost the wager."

Strathford stiffened. "What is this, some trick?"

Atvers exploded. "The devil take you! I saw you—"

Over the swell of voices, Raphael's voice carried strong and sure. "The wager was, if you recall the precise wording, that *love did not exist.*" He turned and came to stand before Julia, and though his words were for his companions, his eyes never left hers. "Breaking the love affair between Julia and Simon was only the means to show that my point had prevailed. But make no mistake, it was not the demise of their relationship that was up for debate."

"Raphael?" Julia asked tremulously. Her heart pounded forcefully against her chest, threatening to burst. She was beginning to understand. At least she thought she did. Or was it just wild hope?

He took her hands in his. With eyes as bright as green fire, he said, "I lost the wager, Julia, because I fell in love."

"Blast her—!" Atvers's ejaculation was cut short by Martinvale's intervention.

Strathford began to laugh.

Julia didn't even blink. She didn't breathe. She dismissed them all, keeping her attention trained on her husband. There was a tiny twitch in his jaw as he spoke. And his fingers, when they touched her cheek, trembled.

"I love you," Raphael said softly. "God, Julia, I love you completely." Having said that, his face split into an enormous grin. He laughed. "Did you hear that, you sods? Fontvilliers is head over heels in love with his wife!"

"No!" Atvers shrieked. "No—humph!"

Martinvale pulled the smaller man up short. With an apologetic smile, he said, "Perhaps if our presence is no longer needed, I'll take care of this little problem for you." His bow was as courtly as if he were at a Carleton House fete. "Good evening." With a jerk, he snapped Atvers around and marched him out the library and out of the house.

Strathford hauled himself to his feet. "I shall take my leave as well. I thank you both for a most gratifying encounter." On his way out, he winked at Julia and saluted Raphael with the packet of banknotes.

Alone with Raphael, Julia found herself gathered tightly into his arms. She could feel him all along her body, close and hot. She lay her head on his chest, inhaling that scent and remembering that first night on the terrace at the Suffolk ball. She had started here, in his arms. Since that night, no other place had done half as well.

He kissed her forehead and murmured into her hair. "Ah, Julia, nothing was any good after you left. I've never been so terrified in all my life." Tipping her chin up, he said, "I love you. I said it before those fools. I'll say it before anyone you wish, as many times as you wish."

He loved her. *He loved her.* She closed her eyes and smiled.

"I vow to give you the best of myself," he continued. "Indeed, if there is any good in me, it is because of you. If you could forgive me for all I've done . . . Oh, no, please, don't cry. God, I hate it when you cry."

"No," she sniffed, opening her eyes. They glistened, pale and golden, with spiked lashes like stars. "I'm not crying, really. I'm just happy."

"Well, it's damned peculiar," he scolded, wiping away her tears. "I won't have it."

She laughed at his stricken look. "Oh, Raphael, it's only a bit of tears."

"I *won't* have you unhappy."

"But I *am* happy. I just told you."

"My mother wept so often. I hated her tears."

"Darling, women cry. I suppose men do, too, but they don't like to show it. It's natural, in happy times and sad. But we shall never have the tears in our life that you were used to seeing in the past. Those are spent."

He bowed his head, taking her hands by the wrist and peeling off her gloves, each one in turn. Then he twined his fingers in hers, pressing his palm against hers. "What a wise girl you are. How did you ever end up with a rogue like myself?"

She gulped a shaky laugh. "I believe I had little choice. Your seductive powers were quite potent. As the saying goes, I never had a chance."

"You don't regret it, do you? I mean, married to a reprobate?"

"Raphael, how absurd. Don't you know what you've given me? You saved me from something I never wanted. You gave me everything that I am, and it's so much more than I ever thought I could have in my life."

His smile crept slowly over his mouth. "Then, you do love me."

"Of course, Raphael." She tilted her head and looked at him curiously. "I thought you already knew that."

"Well, you told me once, and it was a while ago," he observed with a petulant shrug, "and here I am professing my heart to a nauseating degree, and you haven't said one word in return. I mean, a man starts to wonder."

Taking his face in her hands, she said, "Listen to me, you stubborn rake. I adore you. There. I shouldn't tell you that, for it will swell your head, but I suppose I shall simply have to live with it. I love you with all my heart, and I fear I always will."

"Ah, that was well done. You have cured me of all doubt." Brushing his lips over her temple, he sighed. "It is the strangest thing, this feeling. I would never have thought it would be this . . . intense. It's almost frightening. I need you to breathe, to think, to eat. God save me, woman, I am utterly gone with loving you."

"Mmm," she murmured, grazing her cheek along his. Her arms came around his neck, and she let her eyelids drift to half closed. "You are surprisingly adept at it for a man who resisted it so fiercely."

He pretended to boast. "Well, it must be a natural talent. I do have a few."

"A most fortuitous one for my sake."

"Perhaps we should explore this newfound aptitude of mine."

She giggled. "I have a fair idea of what type of exploration you have in mind."

He laughed, too, a low sensual sound. "I fear you know my propensities too well." Sobering, he stroked her cheek gently. "I am serious, though. My most precious love, let me show you. Every day, every night, I'll prove that I am true."

Releasing her, he held out his hand. She slipped hers into

it. As they headed out of the library and up toward the stairs, Julia asked, "Raphael, did you plan all of this as an elaborate seduction?"

"Madam," he drawled, pausing a moment to touch his lips to the back of her hand, "it is the very thing I've been planning from the first moment I set eyes on you."

"Yesterday?"

"A year ago. And every moment since."

"Not really."

"Really."

They arrived at his room and he brought her inside. He kissed her until her senses were blunted and the only awareness was of him. Removing each other's clothing, they touched, reacquainting themselves with each other's bodies.

"I love this birthmark," he said, kissing her shoulder blade.

"I love the way you feel," she told him, sliding her hand over his chest.

And when they joined, it was with a rapturous exhilaration that went beyond the physical pleasures they shared. They murmured in low tones of love, gasped it out loud as the sensations took them up and over into ecstasy, and whispered it against each other's lips when they had settled quietly in the aftermath.

For Raphael, this felt like the impossible had come to pass. Everything had happened just as he dared hope. He wasn't doomed. No longer.

He was Raphael Giscard. And for the first time in his life, he knew who that was. It didn't matter where he had come from, who had sired him. What mattered was this, here and now with Julia. The past was gone, but she was his future, and what mattered . . . well, what mattered was love.

He believed in love, and in Julia, and in himself. And it was worth far more than five thousand pounds to have found such faith.

"Why are you smiling?" Julia asked, looking up at him.

"I am deliriously happy. I love you, you know."

"And I love you."

His smile deepened. "I know."

Epilogue

TWO FIGURES EMERGED into the darkened garden of Glenwood Park. Moonlight spilled over everything, lighting the trees in a silvery glow and dappling the leaf-strewn ground.

The woman was dressed in a sheer negligée of softest lawn. The man wore tight-fitting trousers and his dress shirt open, billowing in the gently scented breeze that hinted of autumn. She pulled him along as the deep resonance of his laughter floated on the air.

"Come back here," he called. "You shall cut your feet."

"I will not. I cannot possibly sleep tonight, so I want to enjoy what's left of the mild weather."

"Do not be daft. There is a chill."

"There is no such thing. It is a glorious night."

"You have to think of the child."

"The child will not chill. He's inside me, nice and warm." She placed her hand over her still flat stomach. "You sound like an old woman, Raphael."

"Madam! You cut me to the quick."

"Come sit with me." She ran to the covered swing, its sheltering columns wound with ivy. It was a mythical picture worthy of Botticelli himself.

He took it in, drinking every nuance of color, every brilliantly drawn detail as if he were taking in the glory of a masterpiece. "You look like a nymph," he said hoarsely. "You make me want to ravish you all over again."

As he slipped beside her, she giggled playfully. "How dreadful." The moonlight slanted across her face just then, casting her in an ethereal light and catching fire in the golden hue of her eyes. "Are you happy, Raphael?"

He smiled as he put his arm on the back of the bench seat. He toyed with a thick lock of her hair, feeling the silkiness of it, studying the way it gleamed. "Let me take an accounting of my present circumstances. I am a man desperately in love. As fate would have it, the woman who holds my heart is my wife."

"How unfashionable," she scolded. "What would the *ton* think?"

"I fear it might cause a scandal, so we must keep it to ourselves."

"Since I know how you dread gossip, I swear it shall never escape my lips."

"And we live together in a rambling mess of a house, which you love for some reason."

"Because we are changing it into a lovely home. Come now, you must admit the progress is excellent. Your grandmother was duly impressed on her last visit. The lawns are finished, the gardens put in. Most of the interior work has been completed, and I love the collection your mother brought us from France."

"All a bother," he grumped, even while his eyes gleamed.

"Oh, you don't mind it so much. Why, I even have you choosing the window dressings."

"For my library only," he clarified sternly. "And God help me, it is true that it is not so onerous. I admit I like making this home with you. Together. It seems more *ours* and not just some relic belonging to my ancestors. These two things—wife and home—would be enough to make this man content. But now . . ." He paused, and a silken sense of wonder came into his voice. "I am to be a father. It doesn't seem real."

"It will seem real enough in five months," she said with a laugh. "I trust you will learn to change nappies."

He laid his head back and looked up through the latticed canopy at the brilliant array of stars. "You ask me if I am happy, madam, and I must admit that I am. Blissful, even. Delirious—is that the word? What would be adequate to describe my present state?" Turning back to her, he mused, "Perhaps, if I simply say that there has not been another man more fortunate than I, that might do some justice to what I feel. I am surely more favored than any rogue like myself has a right to imagine himself ever being."

"But now you are my rogue," she said, curling her hand along his cheek and smiling up into his face. "And I must advise you that I find your scandalous propensities quite enjoyable in certain circumstances."

He readily slipped his hand down to her waist, pulling her up close. She made a small sound, a sound of desire. For him. That hadn't ceased to thrill him in these last two years of marriage, and he suspected it would never fade. "Which of the scandalous . . . uh, *propensities* I just demonstrated upstairs did you find particularly enjoyable? Was it when I—?"

She pressed a single finger against his lips to silence him with a sultry laugh. Holding the finger captive, he slid it into his mouth and stroked the underside provocatively with his tongue.

"God, Raphael," she gasped as her head lolled weakly onto his shoulder. "You are truly wicked."

"Oh, madam," he drawled, moving to claim her luscious mouth. "I promise you, I am just getting started."